THE LONDON SATYR

Robert Edric

BLACK SWAN

TRANSWORLD PUBLISHERS
61–63 Uxbridge Road, London W5 5SA
A Random House Group Company
www.rbooks.co.uk

**THE LONDON SATYR
A BLACK SWAN BOOK: 9780552777087**

First published in Great Britain
in 2011 by Doubleday
an imprint of Transworld Publishers
Black Swan edition published 2012

A CIP catalogue record for this book
is available from the British Library.

Addresses for Random House Group Ltd companies outside the UK
can be found at: www.randomhouse.co.uk
The Random House Group Ltd Reg. No. 954009

The Random House Group Limited supports the Forest Stewardship
Council (FSC®), the leading international forest-certification organization.
Our books carrying the FSC label are printed on FSC®-certified paper.
FSC is the only forest-certification scheme endorsed by the leading
environmental organizations, including Greenpeace. Our paper-procurement
policy can be found at www.randomhouse.co.uk/environment.

Typeset in 12/15pt Granjon by
Kestrel Data, Exeter, Devon.
Printed and bound by
CPI Group (UK) Ltd, Croydon, CR0 4YY.

2 4 6 8 10 9 7 5 3 1

For Bill Scott-Kerr

The only way to get rid of temptation is to yield to it. Resist it, and your soul grows sick with longing for the thing it has forbidden to itself.

Oscar Wilde, *The Picture of Dorian Gray*, 1891

London, Summer, 1891

Part I

Part 1

1

Careful to avoid being seen, I left the theatre and followed my usual circuitous route to Marlow's studio. By 'usual' I do not mean that it was a single route, always taken, but rather that it was as convoluted and as seemingly directionless as all the other paths I had ever followed to that place.

Upon first being given these instructions by Marlow – his hand resting loosely on my collar in the lobby of the French Hotel – I had doubted and then silently wondered at the need for such secrecy, believing it to be merely another instance of the man's desire to exert control over all those who fell within his orbit. But as the months and years had passed, I had come to share in this craving for secrecy, even if only for the undeniable 'edge' it afforded our otherwise perfunctory transactions.

Leaving the Lyceum, I turned away from the Strand towards Long Acre and into the Market. From there, a narrow cut through the rear of New Row brought me to St Martin's Lane. Emerging on the Charing Cross Road, I paused, walked briefly north, and then equally briefly and swiftly south, losing myself amid the converging cabs and buses there. The usual jam of traffic filled the entrance to Trafalgar Square and I moved amid this river of trapped vehicles towards Haymarket.

At first, early in my dealings with Marlow, I was never truly able to convince myself that I was being followed as I made my way to him, or even that I would be able to identify anyone who *was* attempting to follow me. Needless to say, I have grown considerably more capable and confident in respect of this.

Reaching Haymarket, I turned towards the Prince of Wales and stood there for several minutes reading the advertisements and endorsements. It seemed somehow appropriate and propitious to me to observe these theatrical points along my route. And as I read, I glanced around me, searching for a familiar face, for someone behaving as aimlessly as I behaved, someone who might avert their eyes from my own wandering gaze, and who might then feign a similar, unwarranted interest in the notices.

But there was no one. There had never been anyone. I had been acting out these small subterfuges and dramas for almost three years. And each time I remarked on this to Marlow, he dismissed my concerns and complaints with the amused remark that I knew nothing of what was happening in the world around me; that I was blind and deaf, ignorant of the wider scheme of things, oblivious to all those putative, secretive followers, all those others who sought only to expose and undermine and destroy him. And every time he told me this, of course – every exaggerated word and dramatic flourish – what he did not say, what he did not *need* to say, was that if he was destroyed and punished, then the same thing, in its lesser way, would surely befall me too.

On one occasion he had grown angry and said that a single error – the two words shouted an inch from my eyes – would undo us all, and he had asked me if I imagined my own fall would be any less precipitous or calamitous than his own. Because it wouldn't be. Because he, Marlow – and this time he had hissed his name into my face – would make certain of that. No one would escape. We were inextricably bound, he said, inseparably connected. If anything, he went on, growing calm and releasing his grip on me, I might even have *more* to lose – have more to be taken from me – than any of them, himself, Pearl and Bliss included, because of the *nature* of my involvement with him, because of my own specific part in our *enterprise*. He emphasized each word like a threat and I flinched at them all, however softly spoken or wreathed in cruel amusement they now were. Both Pearl and Bliss had been beside him when he'd impressed all this upon me, the pair of them watching him with their own eyes wide, their lips pursed, and their heads nodding in accord with the force of his argument. To conclude this humiliating dressing-down, Marlow had said that he hoped we better understood each other, he and I, and that we never again had to have this same unhappy conversation – as though I had contributed anything to the exchange except my doubts, concerns, fears and silence.

'Show me what you have for me,' he'd said the instant his fingertips withdrew from my chest. He smiled at me and rubbed a thumb across my chin, our transaction and the complicity of our understanding once again established and strong in this so-called bond between us.

Beside him, Bliss had turned quickly away, as though to hide any suspicions or uncertainties he himself still harboured, and Pearl alone had held my gaze, gentle confirmation of all Marlow had just said. I remember she'd smiled at me, her lips parted, possible suggestion in her searching eyes, all of which had registered upon me in less than a second.

'Show me,' Marlow had repeated.

Pearl had closed her eyes briefly, and when she opened them again, she was looking at him.

I'd immediately slid my hand into my inside pocket and felt the slender package there.

'You see?' Marlow said, first to me, and then to both Pearl and the departing Bliss. 'You see, Bliss? You see what a perfect understanding we all now possess?'

But Bliss had not answered him. Instead, he had continued walking away to the side of the studio, beyond the screens and the women already gathered and waiting there.

I left the Circus via Glasshouse Street, passing the fruit- and flower-sellers, deaf to their entreaties. A woman pushed a bunch of lavender in my chest, brushing it back and forth as I tried to avoid her. The scent stayed with me as I continued walking.

At Brewer Street I repeated my manoeuvre of turning both left and right. A man stood at a corner ahead of me and watched me closely as I approached. When I reached him, he asked me bluntly if I was lost.

I told him I wasn't.

'You *look* lost,' he said. 'Where you looking for?'

I smelled the drink on his breath and saw the Bridle Lane public house a short distance away, its doors already open to the warm street.

'I'm not lost,' I repeated, moving to pass him and continue towards the Apollo. But instead of letting me go, he put out his arm and asked me why I was in such a hurry. First I seemed scarcely to know which way to walk, and now all this urgency.

I pushed his arm down and stepped from the pavement on to the road, conscious of his drunkenness and the need to avoid whatever confrontation he now seemed determined to provoke. A horse made a noise immediately behind me and the man grabbed my arm and pulled me clear of the passing animal. And when it had gone, he released me.

'Careful,' he said, winking at me, and before I could respond to this, he took several paces backwards towards the open door of the ale house.

Rather than demand the meaning of this brief and hostile interruption, I resumed walking, unwilling even to glance back at him as he took up his position in the doorway.

A narrow alleyway, no wider than a man, passed from opposite the theatre to Ingestre Place, and it was only as I emerged from this, coming from the cool darkness back out into the summer warmth and light, that it occurred to me that the man might have been one of Marlow's look-outs, sentinels at the border of his small domain, unlikely gate-keepers to that inner realm to which so few of us were afforded the privilege of access.

The streets here were filled with such alleyways, perfect diversions for the cautious traveller. Look out for breathless men awaiting your reappearance, Marlow had told me. Men exhausted from running the long way round to await your own arrival rather than reveal themselves as followers in the narrow space behind you.

There was no one breathless and waiting in Ingestre Place, and from there I went swiftly to Golden Square, performing my usual full circuit of its railings before turning into the entrance behind the church wall which would lead me to Marlow.

But even here, so close to my destination, the subterfuge was not over.

I waited for a moment beneath the archway, watching the few other walkers in the Square, the two or three carriages waiting at the rank approaching Beak Street, the few shoppers crossing west towards the broad, flowing river of Regent Street.

By comparison with these busy thoroughfares, Golden Square always seemed a lost and abandoned place, calmer, darker, and considerably quieter than its surroundings, a place perpetually overcast – either by cloud or by the circling shadows of its buildings; a place in which it was forever late autumn and seldom summer; always later rather than earlier in the day, whatever time one entered it.

The church bell tolled the hour. The hour of my appointment with Marlow. Not that he was punctilious in his own time-keeping; quite the opposite, in fact. There had been many occasions when he had been genuinely surprised by my appearance and when he had then told me it was impossible for him to see me. Sometimes he had snatched what I had taken to him; at other times he had told me to return the following day, occasionally the following week. And when this happened, I surprised myself by the submissive nature of my acquiescence. But I had returned, of course, either the next day or the following week. I had always returned.

On yet other occasions, I had arrived to be greeted by Marlow as though I were his closest friend in the entire world, someone upon whom he depended completely, someone without whom his whole enterprise might cease to function, someone without whose presence he himself would see little point in continuing. I soon understood what acts these various greetings were, but nonetheless I allowed myself to be convinced by them. Convinced, encouraged, persuaded, flattered.

I was always aware, of course, of all those others Marlow drew into orbit around him, not least of whom were Pearl and Bliss; and those who worked more closely with him in his studio – our circling paths held by the magnetic lode at our centre, each of us spinning on our own predictable course. And this comparison is not entirely fanciful or exaggerated: within only weeks of my having made his acquaintance, Marlow referred to me in the company of Bliss as his 'rogue star'. Even today I still cannot explain the pride I felt at hearing him say this – announce it almost, to his closest confidant – his arm around my shoulders, a drink lifted from a tray and held to my mouth. Rogue star. Either word would have felt like a recommendation from the man, but together they acquired a potency and a potential that made the blood race in my veins.

Again ensuring I was unobserved, I turned from the archway into the small yard, crossed this and entered the doorway there. The door was unlocked, and the narrow passageway beyond unlighted. I closed the door behind me and waited again in the near-darkness. The space was filled with the noise and faint echo of my breathing. Nothing of the few outdoor noises penetrated the corridor. A follower, Marlow explained to me, would have seen the unlocked door and come quickly to it, imagining me, once inside, to have gone on swiftly to somewhere more secure. And anyone opening this door to nowhere obvious could not then but fail to reveal both themselves and their purpose in appearing there while I waited in the darkness within.

In almost three years of following these instructions and these routes, no one had ever approached the door behind me. Had they been so bold or so stupid to reveal themselves in this way, it would have been a simple enough matter to have either knocked them down in the dark passageway or to have pushed them back outside and then to have departed myself, revealing nothing of my purpose there, or of what lay beyond the passage.

A carriage crossed the Square, and I waited until the clatter of hooves had faded before continuing.

At the end of the corridor an equally narrow flight of stairs – all this narrowness, these pinch-points, these one-man-at-a-time places – led to a first-floor landing, along which were two further doors. I approached the first, paused, prepared myself, and then knocked loudly. Six steady raps, evenly paced, each one distinct from the last, cleanly started and finished. There had been no sound beyond the door at my arrival, no change within as I'd knocked, and no apparent response to my summons upon finishing. I remained carefully silent, conscious too of making no noise with my boots on the bare boards.

Waiting a moment for the note of my final rap to fade completely, I then moved to the second door, ten or twelve feet distant. Here again I composed myself, counted silently to twenty and then gave the same six clear raps.

This time I heard the distorted murmur of voices within. Again I waited. A man who did not know of this arrangement, Marlow said, would be unable to resist knocking again, perhaps calling out, uncertain of what he might have imagined he'd heard beyond this second door. All a man who understood and followed this arrangement needed was patience.

A further full minute passed. The whispering voices no longer sounded, and again all I could hear was the sound of my own breathing. It had long since occurred to me that entering that silent building was like entering an echo-chamber, regardless of its constricted, twisting spaces.

After a further minute, a small panel slid open and an eye looked out at me. This panel was equally swiftly slid shut again and a bolt immediately drawn. This was followed by a second and then a third.

An instant later the door was pulled wide open and the dark corridor behind me was bathed in light. And along with this light – yellow, merging to orange and red across the dull canvas of the opposite wall – there also spilled from the room both warmth and noise, the latter a low cacophony of voices and laughter and music.

And in the doorway, framed by all this unexpected change, was Marlow himself, a dark and sudden outline against the blossoming light. My eyes adjusted quickly to this glare, but I knew even before he spoke to me that the figure in the doorway was definitely him. Knew it was Marlow before he spoke my name or held out his hand to me, before he drew me to him and embraced me, perhaps already feeling for the stiffness of the card in my jacket pocket, and then as he held me at arm's length and grinned at me.

'Your heart,' he said to me. 'I can feel the beating of your heart.'

I struggled for something to say in reply to this, but before I could frame my answer, conscious of the others in the room now watching us, he said, 'Which tells me what? That you enjoy all this? That you *indulge* yourself as much as any of them? Or merely that you know what lies within, beyond that final door, and that – again like the rest of them – you cannot help yourself?' He laughed at the melodrama of it all, at this small and flamboyant flourish. And then he drew me into the room, ensuring that I faced Pearl, who stood close behind him, as he slid back the bolts on the door and as the silence and the dark was shut out and made to vanish.

Pearl came to me and kissed me on the cheek, but close enough to the side of my mouth for me to feel her lips there.

'It's Webster,' Marlow announced to the others in the room. His close friend and associate Webster. Charles James Alexander Webster. Rogue Star.

Few among these other men paid me any real attention. Pearl stayed close to me, a glass of drink held to her chest.

'Are you thirsty?' she asked me.

I ran my tongue along my lower lip, watching as Marlow returned to the centre of his waiting audience.

'Here,' she said, and she gave me the glass she held. 'You're always so punctual.' The words were more mouthed than spoken, not even whispered, another motion of her lips.

2

I woke to the sound of Alice's shouting. I heard her footsteps on the stairs. At first, I imagined she was calling to Cora, perhaps to wake her, or to remind her of an appointment she might be late in keeping. But as she came closer, arriving at the second floor and pausing at the stairs to my room, I heard more clearly what she was saying, and realized that her words and her anger were directed at the new maid she had recently employed. The girl had come to us at the end of the previous week and I had yet to meet her.

A short silence was followed by my door being pushed open.

Alice came into the room and looked around her. My cases and other pieces of photographic equipment lay scattered on the floor beyond my bed. The door into the room beyond – my own grandly titled developing room – lay open. Prints hung from lines across the low, sloping ceiling.

I feigned sleep, sensing my wife's gaze. She pretended to cough and I, playing my own predictable part in another of our small, common dramas, pretended to wake.

I rubbed my eyes and waited for her to speak.

'You were late home,' she said. She looked around her, crossing to the window set into the roof and drawing the curtain. It was another bright morning and a block of vivid light filled half the room. The cramped space beyond was windowless and cast perpetually in gloom. Alice sniffed the air and stepped over-cautiously over the clothes and the clutter on the floor.

'Midnight,' I said. I pushed myself up in the bed. 'I didn't want to disturb you.' It had been nearer two.

'Disturb me?'

I had spent my first occasional night in the attic room five years ago, when I was working late, or when I returned from the theatre in the early hours. In the past month, I had spent perhaps fewer than a dozen nights in the bed in the room directly beneath me.

'You were sleeping,' I said, as though I'd been sufficiently concerned to look in on her. 'You and Cora both. Is that who you were shouting at?' The remark was intended as a diversion away from the previous evening, though in truth she seldom any longer concerned herself with my unexplained or prolonged absences from the house.

'Calling,' she said. 'Not shouting. And certainly not shouting *at*. The new girl. As for Cora . . .' She left whatever she might have wanted to say about our daughter unspoken. Where Cora, nineteen years old, was concerned, little needed to be said. 'She's still sleeping. She needs her sleep.' Cora seldom rose before midday. 'I told the girl to bring your tea,' Alice said.

'What's her name?'

'Her name?'

'The girl.'

She considered the simple question for a moment. 'She *calls* herself Isobel,' she said. It was too fanciful a name for the girl to possess. She was the third Alice had employed in the past six months, or perhaps even the fourth. 'It's not something I shall feel comfortable calling her. Something plainer would suit her better. Something less . . . less . . .'

I told her I understood. She came closer to the bed, and for a moment I thought she was going to sit beside me where I lay. But, as usual, she kept a careful distance, and instead she pulled straight the crumpled sheet beneath my arm, which I raised to allow her to fold the counterpane. I'm sure that, in her own mind, these small gestures still passed for acts of kindness between us, intimacies almost.

'They keep you too late,' she said. 'I hope—'

'It's a busy time,' I said. 'They're rehearsing two new plays. Irving wants a record of every costume and set. Sixty extras. Most of the outfits are in the depot at Southall. You know him – everything has to be an improvement, everything brand spanking new. There might be twenty near-identical outfits, but he still wants a record of each and every one of them, and with the actors and actresses in full make-up. It all takes time.' I spoke quickly, this time feigning an eagerness I no longer possessed. Some days – or so it sometimes now seemed to me – my whole life was a contrivance of dramas and performances purely for the benefit of others.

'*Your* time,' she said, interrupting my thoughts 'Not his, not Irving's. *His* time is spent praising himself to the skies and swanning round with his Lord and Lady friends. You're the one whose time is being burned away.' She made it sound like a chronic illness over which I had no control.

There was nothing I could say in reply to this. Some lies, I knew, blossomed like crystal salts dropped into water – ever more complicated and yet ever more fragile as they grew and multiplied, always ready to shatter and to disappear, to turn from breathtaking miracle to powdery disappointment at the first solitary careless word or blow.

I laid my arms across the folded sheets, spreading my fingers, putting the tips together. The skin of my hands and forearms was blotched and marked with splashed chemicals.

Seeing this, Alice said, 'You should take more care.' And again it seemed like the furthest she could allow herself to move towards me.

I wondered why she had come up to me. It was more usual for her to wait downstairs. I was a light sleeper. She knew I seldom overslept. My days at the Lyceum rarely began before noon, and even then I would be at work before most of the others arrived. At work, unnoticed, uninterrupted.

'You did remember, I suppose?' she said. She looked at me directly for the first time, waiting. It was clear to her that whatever I was supposed to have remembered, I had forgotten. 'Tonight,' she prompted me. 'I'm having a meeting.' She half turned away from me as she said it.

'A séance?'

'A gathering. Of the faithful. All old friends.' They were customers, not friends.

'Of course,' I said, relieved that I had forgotten nothing of consequence. 'I didn't forget,' I told her.

'Like I said, old friends and true believers. Nothing too strenuous. All seekers after a greater understanding.' Five years ago, there might have been a faint note of irony or even self-deprecation in her voice, but not now. Five years ago, I might have challenged or provoked her with the same note of my own, but not now.

She looked up at the window, turning her face from side to side, warmed by the sun. She closed her eyes.

'Do you want me to stay out?' I asked her. It was what usually happened, another of our compromises.

'I can't command you to do any such thing.'

'Still . . .'

'Mrs Ellsworth has recently lost her mother. Ten days ago. She hopes the poor soul might still be wandering close enough to return and speak to her. Much longer and she will be beyond all our reach.' She smiled as she spoke, unsettling me further. I should not have been discomfited by hearing her say these things – not now, after all this time – but I still was. A boundary had long since been crossed by her, and now only I hung back on this near side.

'What time will you begin?' I asked her.

She flicked the question away. 'The usual – around eight. You know how better suited even the summer dusk is to these arrangements.'

It was late summer, light until nine. Any dusk in the house would be one of quartered blinds and drawn curtains, of dim, flickering, shadow-throwing candles and mantles.

'*Are* you working tonight?' She opened her eyes and again looked directly at me. And for the instant that our eyes met, I imagined she understood perfectly everything I was hiding there.

'Very likely,' I said. 'Irving said something about photographing the moments of heightened drama at rehearsal. He'll want the results before the paper's dry. I daresay he'll want us all . . .'

But she was no longer listening to me, her face tilted firmly away from me, her chin down, her eyes again closed, and with another thin smile on her lips, as though listening to other voices entirely. I had seen her sitting like this, distracted, calm, devoid of all other expression, all too often. To begin with, it had been something she had practised and perfected, something for her customers; but more recently I had seen her like this when she was alone – when I had passed a room and glanced in through the open door, or when I had come upon her in the kitchen, sitting in perfect silence by the range, her closed eyes towards the wall. With some of her private, more profitable sittings, she professed to put her 'believers' into a trance using a small glass disc set into ebony which she wore around her neck on a cord, letting it dangle and spin before them as she started one of her hushed routines.

And just as swiftly as she had taken herself into this small trance – unassailable beyond its own vague and shifting boundaries – so she returned from it.

'How did she die?' I said. 'Mrs . . .' I had forgotten the woman's name.

'Ellsworth,' she said. 'After a long illness.'

That's good, I wanted to say. *Good for you.* She would already know a great deal about the woman, most of it from the dutiful and desperate daughter anxious now to draw in the reins on her own uncontainable grief. And what the daughter hadn't already revealed, then the undertaker or doctor might have sold to her.

'Are you hopeful?' I said.

'You know how far beyond my own control these things are,' she said. 'If I was able to exercise even the smallest power over the wandering, unhappy dead, then—'

'Of course,' I said, unwilling to hear whatever she might have been about to add.

She smiled at me. 'Cora has another interview for a post.'

'Oh?' I was happy to be back on this safer ground, however uncertain and unmapped it too remained.

'Scott's the milliners. I'm certain she has a facility.'

Facility? 'For selling hats?'

She looked at me sharply. 'For selling whatever she puts her mind to selling.'

'Of course.'

Since leaving school four years earlier, having achieved and gained little there, Cora had moved from one post to another every few weeks. Service was beneath her — beneath the pair of them — and not even to be considered.

'Who knows,' Alice said, 'she may one day wish to have a shop of her own.' It seemed an impossible leap to make, but I said nothing.

'Of course.' It was the least I could contribute to this hopeless ambition.

'You should have more faith in the child. You're hardly—' She stopped abruptly. I knew better than to confront her on these points, to insist on her telling me what it was that I was 'hardly'.

'I only meant . . .' she said. It was an apology of sorts, and I accepted it as such.

Neither of us spoke for a moment.

'She just seems so . . . unsettled,' I said. Since leaving school, Cora had spent most of her time in the house and had gained a great deal of weight. She spent considerably more than she ever earned, and she and Alice had grown closer. The girl followed her mother, clinging to her, their arms locked when they walked, even inside the house. And when they were on good terms — when Cora wasn't sulking or throwing another of her tantrums – she was also becoming more involved in this other world of her mother's, supporting and encouraging her, helping in small, practical ways whenever Alice's infrequent gatherings took place.

A month ago, I returned late on the night of Alice's previous séance to find Cora wiping her mother's face with a cloth, Alice stretched flat upon the sofa. The girl was making soothing noises, as though appeasing a baby. And Alice had laid there, the same calm smile on her lips, her eyes closed, allowing her daughter to do this. I had gone from the doorway without either of them seeing me.

Alice rose from my bed and returned to the door. She paused at the mantel above the small fireplace. Three photographs stood there, each in its silver gilt frame. A picture of Alice, the first I ever took of her, two years before our marriage; a picture of Cora when she was still a child of six or seven; and a picture of our second, lost daughter, Caroline, aged seven, less than a year before she was struck by illness and taken from us. There were other pictures of her elsewhere in the house, but this one – these three – remained special to me, each of them a weight of loss that I once thought I should be wholly unable to bear.

'Do you still think of her?' Alice said, meaning Caroline.

'Often,' I said, the word drying in my throat. Of the two of us, I had been the closest to our second daughter, and even at her young age she had showed a genuine interest in what I did. It was a bond I had never felt between Cora and myself. This was something I had once regretted, considering it a failing on my part, but not any longer.

'Me, too,' Alice said. She rested her hand on the mantel. 'Did you ever imagine . . .'

Did I ever imagine that such an unbearable loss could be borne for so long? Never. Did I ever imagine that the years since my small daughter's death would pass with so little ease to be gained? Never.

She was about to say more when the sound of crockery being dropped rose up the staircase and we both remained silent for a moment, content to savour whatever memories we had so suddenly and unexpectedly summoned between us.

'I ought to go,' Alice said eventually, distracted, caught between emotion and duty.

'Will you be strong enough?' I asked her.

'For tonight? I shall have to be.'

There had been other occasions recently when a particularly vigorous séance had kept her in her bed for the whole of the following day.

'How can I refuse someone when time may be so short?'

I nodded in agreement. 'Are you going with Cora to her interview?'

'Her appointment. Of course I'm going with her. There are perhaps a few things I shall be able to impress upon Scott's.'

'Of course,' I said.

'Are you getting up?'

I imagined my breakfast tray spilled in the passageway. The noise of someone clearing up whatever had been dropped could still be heard.

'They'll be expecting me,' I said.

'At the theatre?'

I had once suggested asking either Stoker or Loveday about a position for Cora at the Lyceum, convinced that something would have been found for her, and Alice had simply stared at me, careful to betray no obvious emotion – and certainly not the utter disbelief she so clearly felt – before contriving another of her particular smiles.

I drew the bedclothes from my legs and swung myself up-right. I rubbed my face, feeling the rough skin of my palms. When I looked at the door, Alice had gone.

3

I arrived at the theatre shortly before noon. My usual side entrance from Burleigh Street was blocked by a group of stage-hands and flymen removing scenery and props. Burleigh Street itself was filled with the horses and open-sided carts on to which all this was being loaded.

I made my way back to Wellington Street, climbed the steps and went in the main entrance. Men were polishing the doors. A man up a ladder threw down dirt and clutter from the bowl of one of the torches. A man below him quickly swept this into the street.

Inside, the day cleaners were still at work on the stairs, pausing in their scrubbing to watch me pass. I walked up the centre of the carpet. I recognized some of the women, and they me.

I made my way across the rear of the auditorium towards the side exits.

Others were already at work on the stage. The seating too was filled with women beating out the padded backs and sending up small explosions of dust into the few beams of natural light which fell into the space, and which, like all day-light in all theatres, was otherwise carefully excluded.

As I arrived at the curtained exit which led up to my

workroom, my name was called from somewhere beyond the stage. Bright lights moved back and forth there and I shielded my eyes to see who had shouted.

It was Stoker, his voice muffled by the drapes hanging around him, and drowned further by the voices of the scene-shifters. He came to the edge of the stage and beckoned me to him. I called to him that I was busy, that I had things to attend to. He said nothing in reply to this, merely took out his watch and looked at it pointedly. He turned his back on me and I went to him.

By the time I reached the stage, he had gone back into the wings, where I found him sitting with Jimmy Allen, our chief prompt. The two of them were talking excitedly, and Stoker was laughing. Jimmy held something which I couldn't see, passing whatever it was to Stoker.

'Jimmy was showing me his pictures,' Stoker said, still without turning to me. 'Something in your line, I imagine. I thought you might be interested to see.'

Whatever the extent of my interest in the old man's old photographs, they had hardly been Stoker's purpose in summoning me.

Jimmy Allen passed a few of the brittle prints to me. Sepia gum prints, forty years old, and from poorly processed plates.

'From Jimmy's time in India,' Stoker said. 'Where he served.'

Where Jimmy Allen was concerned, *everything* was about his time in India. His Army service was mother and father, history and geography, anchor and sail to him.

I feigned interest in the pictures. Native tribesmen posing with soldiers. Perhaps even a youthful Jimmy Allen himself.

'See the detail,' Stoker said. 'The grouping and composition.' He knew nothing. Everything was another prod in my chest.

I handed the pictures back to Jimmy Allen.

'Have you been working elsewhere?' Stoker said to me, still not facing me directly.

I hesitated, considered my answer.

'This morning, I mean. You are somewhat late in arriving.'

'I was in Southall late yesterday evening,' I said.

'Ah, Southall. Of course. Henry's catalogue and pictures.' He handed me another of Jimmy Allen's photographs. 'Look at this one. A rare treat.' Half a dozen native girls, Cora's age, naked except for their headdresses and beads and the strips of embroidered cloth at their loins.

'I bought that one,' Jimmy Allen said. 'Not one I took myself.'

'Another excellent composition,' Stoker said. 'Such innocence, naturalness. So unselfconscious.' He glanced up at me.

'Heathens, mostly,' Jimmy Allen said. 'In their habits, I mean.'

'But pretty as . . . a picture.' Stoker smiled coldly at me. 'And is everything in Southall proceeding smoothly?'

It was four days since I'd last been there.

'I should say so.'

'You should say so. Then I suppose we must depend upon your word, Mr Webster. I was asking Jimmy here how much more is being removed there, and what repairs might need to be made. For the accounts, you understand – my reckoning.' He gave the word an ominous edge.

'Oh,' I said, wondering if I was being asked to contribute to these calculations.

'And, like you, he assures me that everything is proceeding

35

smoothly and, as always, that the work is in capable hands.'
Everything he said was shaded by suspicious disbelief.

Jimmy Allen glanced at me as Stoker said this. 'I didn't . . .
I mean . . .' he said.

'No worry,' Stoker reassured him. 'I'm sure the last thing
Mr Webster concerns himself with is what people might say
about him behind his back.'

It seemed an overtly provocative remark to make and I
sensed that Stoker was carefully noting my response.

'Of course not,' I said.

'Are there more like this?' Stoker then said to Jimmy, who
did not immediately understand him. Stoker turned the
picture to him.

'Some,' Jimmy said.

'Many?'

'A few, perhaps a dozen.'

'Then I should very much like to see them. Native scenes,
wild excesses, cannibal islands, all grist to the theatrical mill.'
Stoker smiled again. 'Of course, I doubt if even Henry could
get away with presenting anything quite so − so risqué or
titillating, anything quite so close to the bounds of common
decency, however innocent or guileless in intent, however
nobly nature might be dressed.'

It was all still being said to another purpose, and I was
certain that Stoker was aware of my own understanding of
this.

'No,' Jimmy Allen said. He held out his hand to retrieve
the photograph.

But Stoker drew it back from him. 'May I keep it? Borrow
it. This one. Briefly. Just to show the missus?' He exaggerated
the word.

Jimmy Allen looked concerned at the suggestion.

'Jimmy and Florence are great friends,' Stoker said to me. 'Besides, she has not a solitary prurient bone in her body.' His confidence faltered slightly.

'Oh?' I said, my first prod back. It wasn't the tale told behind *his* back.

'Great friends. She asks me endlessly when Jimmy Allen is returning to visit us. The boy, too, is beside himself with excitement. Your Indian swords, scimitars and sabres hold him spellbound. Almost as much as your tales.'

'Tales of India?' I said to Jimmy Allen. Whatever next?

'Tales of derring-do and great adventure,' Stoker said.

'My ordinary life,' Jimmy Allen said flatly.

'Ordinary life?' Stoker said, but then he too could think of nothing to add.

'Keep it,' Jimmy Allen said, meaning the picture.

Stoker tucked the naked girls into his pocket.

When I'd arrived at the Lyceum five years earlier, the Burleigh Street exit had been for the sole use of Irving and Stoker. The tale is that Irving used it to avoid his crowds of admirers and well-wishers front of house, and that Stoker came and went via the near-hidden door so that he would be neither noticed nor commented on as he embarked on his so-called 'nocturnal travels'. The dressing on the tale was always that he had a great deal of theatre business to think about and that these long, solitary night-time walks gave him the time, the freedom and the uninterrupted peace to work things out and to make his calculations.

'Thank you, Jimmy. I'm sure Florence will be delighted.'

I wanted to laugh and to shake my head.

Stoker looked again at his watch.

All around us the men dismantling and removing the sets and flats continued with their work. Dropcloths rose and fell above us, their straining ropes and pulleys squeaking in the wings.

In all the years I had known him, Stoker had only ever called me by my surname, making every single mention of it either a peremptory summons, a dismissal or a correction. I cannot explain this more fully; it was simply how I felt. And yet I had seldom ever heard him call Jimmy Allen anything but Jimmy. Never James. Another part of what Stoker considered to be his common touch, I suppose.

'What do you want from me?' I asked him.

'Want?' He seemed genuinely surprised by the blunt remark.

'Other than to remark on my time-keeping.'

'Oh, please, I had no intention of . . . We're all professional people here, Mr Webster. If you imagine I impugned . . . please.' He turned to Jimmy Allen, still seated between us. 'Jimmy, tell Mr Webster.'

Jimmy Allen looked up at me, the rest of his prints held like a deck of cards in his hand.

Before he could speak, Stoker held my shoulder. 'Please, I meant nothing. I forget myself. How is your own charming wife? In good health, I hope.'

I wondered if he was struggling to remember Alice's name. Five years.

'Alice,' Jimmy Allen said. I heard the dull note of sympathy in his voice.

'Of course,' Stoker said. 'And your daughters?'

Jimmy Allen held my gaze. He had been at Caroline's burial and funeral ceremony. 'We're keeping you from your work,' he said to me. To Stoker, he said, 'Was there anything you needed from Mr Webster?'

Stoker shook his head, confused by this sudden switch of allegiance.

Waiting until I had climbed down from the stage, he called after me, 'Please, remember my book-keeping, my stacking-up, my balances, Mr Webster.'

I raised my hand to him without turning.

A year after my appointment at the theatre, I'd arrived at the far end of Burleigh Street, approaching from the direction of the Opera House, when I'd seen a man and a woman standing close together in the doorway. There was some kind of argument, the woman raising her voice, the man trying unsuccessfully to calm her. I'd stopped where I was, slipping into the shadow of Palmer's warehouse. The woman came away from the doorway into the dim overhead light. Her hair was loose and her hands empty. She pressed her palms to the man's chest, lowering and sweetening her voice, and then something passed between them which caused the woman to laugh and then to applaud herself. She walked a further few paces from the door and stood opposite it, her back to the wall. She leaned forward slightly and then spread her legs, as though to prevent herself from falling. All this time, the man merely stood and watched her, careful to remain hidden in the shadow of the doorway. Eventually, he spoke to her, quietly, and the woman shouted back at him that he wasn't to worry, that she was going, that she'd got what she wanted. It was a simple enough transaction to decipher, and it was only then, as I moved further along the wall of the warehouse to avoid being seen by the woman as she passed me, that I recognized Stoker. He stood for a moment watching the woman go, waiting until she had turned the corner into Exeter Street before unlocking the theatre door and letting himself inside. I wondered if the woman had even been aware of the connection between the man and the place, and if this hadn't been the thing he had been most anxious to keep from her. I knew better than to reveal myself to him. Besides, it was by then too late. The door was locked behind him, and hidden again in the darkness of the wall.

Now, reaching the auditorium side-exit, I passed through into the corridor beyond and waited there for a moment. I was alone, unobserved, and better able to attempt to understand what Stoker had intended by this contrived encounter with Jimmy Allen between us.

I climbed the stairs into the labyrinth of small upper rooms towards the rear of the theatre, arriving at my own locked door. Other men and women came and went all around me, above and below me, left and right of me, ahead and behind me, but mostly unseen, and all of them busy with their own work, their own small roles in the endless drama of the place.

I took off my jacket and began to sort through the pictures and catalogues on my desk when there was a solitary knock at my door.

I jumped at the sound. Whoever had come had arrived silently, not an easy feat along those boards.

'Hello,' I called.

The door opened and Charles Howson came quickly in, opening the door only wide enough to admit himself, and then immediately closing it once he was inside.

I waited for him to speak.

'Busy?' he said.

'I try to give the impression.'

He laughed. 'Especially to Mother, eh?'

Ellen Terry called Stoker 'Ma', so dependent did she profess herself to be on him. It was the least of her affections for the man. Elsewhere, whispered among those – myself and Howson included – who did not share that affection, the word had changed and curdled. It was Howson's way now of making himself clear to me.

'*Especially* to Mother,' I said.

Howson sat down. He was the Lyceum's true accountant and he resented Stoker's involvement in this side of things. He had been appointed by Irving directly, after which Irving had publicly expressed to Stoker his desire for his *manager* not to become so deeply involved in this side of the trade, thus offending both Howson and Stoker equally when he had intended precisely the opposite. It had not been in Stoker's nature to withdraw his fingers completely from the accounts, and it had similarly been beyond the limits of Howson's bravery to slam the heavy and meticulously kept ledgers shut on those fingers.

Irving, Stoker and Loveday were often referred to in the press as the Lyceum's 'Unholy Trinity', and I was never entirely certain if this was a mark of respect or otherwise. I was similarly unsure how the three of *them* regarded the title. Henry, I imagined, would appreciate it and laugh it off, whatever its implications; I could not imagine either Loveday or Stoker dismissing it quite so easily.

'What did he want?' Howson asked me.

'Just to point out to me what great friends he and Jimmy Allen are, that his man-with-the-common-touch act is still serving him well.'

'Allen should have gone years ago,' Howson said. He took a small pewter flask from his pocket and offered it to me.

'They were looking at photographs of naked women,' I said. 'Girls.'

He shrugged. 'Indian, no doubt.' He looked slowly around at the pictures scattered over all my own surfaces and pinned to the boards beside him. Costumes of the current production – *The Merchant* – and of the next two – *Becket* and *Romeo* – to be staged.

To have asked him what he wanted would have resulted in no quick or honest answer. It was how Howson operated. He considered himself to be as unappreciated and, occasionally, as maligned as I was, and it was all the reason he needed to approach me.

'He's a compiler,' he said. 'Stoker. All he does is *compile*. Pounds, shillings and pence. Halfpennies and farthings. Everything in its place in its neat little column somewhere. It's me who does all the real calculation, all the necessary credit and debit stuff, all the cashing up and paying out. We've got sixty permanent employees here. Sixty. Not including the theatricals. And every one of them taking something different. And look at today – a further twenty piece-work staff for the removals. Who does Henry think takes care of all *that*?'

It was a familiar grievance worn smooth by repetition and resignation.

'I know,' I said. I might have been looking in a mirror.

'All Stoker wants is charts and tables to show to the Guv'nor. And all Irving wants to do is to look at them, pretend to understand them, and then for the pair of them to pat each other on the back.' He stopped talking, suddenly deflated, as though even he had finally come to accept the ballast of defeat he carried with him. He sipped again from the flask.

'Jimmy Allen's a good prompt,' I said. 'He's been with Irving a long time.' I wondered why I'd said this, except as a gentle warning to him.

'I know. And Irving trusts him.'

Like he trusts neither of us, not truly?

The thought hung unspoken between us.

'How old were the girls, the Indians?'

I made a guess.

'And they were . . . you know . . . ?'

'Just enough to make it safe enough for Jimmy Allen to show them to Stoker.'

'And for Ma to lick his lips at and pretend his buttons weren't tight?'

'He told Jimmy he wanted to take one of the pictures to show his wife.'

He laughed. 'That stick? It's the last thing he'd show her.' He grinned even wider at the buried joke.

Someone ran along the corridor outside, briefly silencing us.

'I need expenses, figures for all the recent Southall work. Is it finished?' He seemed little concerned.

'Almost,' I said. 'Irving keeps changing his mind. More and more costumes keep turning up. He puts in new orders without telling anyone.'

'He tells Mother,' he said. He rose from where he sat, hesitated, and then said, 'You must see that kind of thing all the time.'

At first, I didn't understand him.

'Jimmy's pictures, I mean. Your line of work, all your . . . sidelines.'

'Sidelines?'

'Your private photographs. Your portraits, wedding parties, pictures for the cabinet.'

'They mostly keep their clothes on,' I said, and we both laughed again.

'I imagine so,' he said. 'No offence meant.' He put his hand on the door. 'You'll let me have all the paperwork, the figures?'

I promised him I would, and he was gone before I'd finished speaking, and long before I began to consider how all this 'paperwork' – all these 'figures' – might now be sought or compiled or conjured up out of the thin air into which they had all long since vanished.

4

Two days later, and with little accomplished in the meanwhile, I was on top of a bus crossing Haymarket when I looked down and saw Pearl standing at the entrance to Her Majesty's.

Pearl, in her way, was as mysterious and as unreachable a figure to me as Marlow himself remained, and it had taken me many months to even begin to understand the smallest part of the true nature of their relationship. Even now, these three years later, I was still not entirely certain of what I knew or believed I knew of what bound them so closely together.

On instinct, I left my seat and went downstairs, appearing on the platform at the same moment as she turned from the road and looked into the theatre entrance. My first impulse had been to call out to her, to leap from the bus and stand immediately in front of her as though I had arrived there by magic. Our encounter would thus appear entirely fortuitous, something governed wholly by chance in this tide of strangers.

But I did not do this; instead I remained where I stood, watching her until the bus reached the end of Jermyn Street, where I stepped down as it slowed to negotiate a turn.

I was on my way to Somers Town, to see Solomon, taking

with me a case of plates for multiple printing. He was expecting me at some point during the afternoon; our arrangements were seldom any more precise than this. I might appear at Solomon's in the early hours of the morning – in fact, I frequently had done – and he would show no more surprise, concern or suspicion than if I had arrived to the minute of a midday appointment.

Walking back, I saw that Pearl remained standing at the kerb. The doors to the theatre were open and people were emerging. She searched among these, and I saw by the way she moved from foot to foot, shifting and raising her head to look above and through the passing crowd, that she was anxious not to miss whoever she was waiting for.

I held back, uncertain of why I had sought to contrive this encounter in the first place, and why I was now reluctant to show myself. Perhaps it had something to do with the fact that, even after all that time, I had only ever seen her either in the presence of Marlow or in direct connection with my dealings with the man.

I approached slowly, crossing to the far side of the road, where I looked into a shop window and saw her reflection in the glass.

Eventually I saw her raise her hand to someone. She left the kerb and went to the theatre entrance, holding out her arms to a young woman who had just then emerged, and who stood fastening her jacket and looking around her. Seeing Pearl coming towards her, the woman – little more than a girl – ran the few paces to her with a grin on her face. She called Pearl's name, and the two of them met, embraced, and then held each other tightly for several moments, their faces pressed close, each looking over the other's shoulder.

Eventually, they disengaged, and Pearl stepped back. She held the girl at arm's length and examined her more closely.

Others emerged around the pair, and I saw that the girl was acquainted with these. They struck me as a small chorus, chorines, leaving the theatre after a morning's rehearsal. The girl introduced Pearl to several of these others, and a small, excited group clustered around the two of them.

I turned from the window to watch them more closely. They seemed like close friends, too long absent from each other. My further racing thoughts imagined the girl to be Pearl's sister – I knew Pearl had a background in the theatre – or her grown daughter, even. Pearl was in her mid-thirties; the girl might be as young as fifteen or sixteen. Or both might be a few years older.

It was a short leap to imagine that because Pearl was there, then Marlow himself was involved in the encounter, and that Pearl was acting on his behalf in some way. Perhaps here, recruited by Pearl, was another of his models, his actresses, his 'odalisques' or 'sylphs', another girl seeking to rise above whatever position she was then starting out at. I had frequently seen Pearl with all these others, their numbers forever growing and changing as they came and went, as they either took to Marlow and his work, or became disgusted and disillusioned by it. But something about the way she behaved with this one caused me to believe that there was something apart from all that.

I watched as Pearl straightened the girl's hat, fastening its ribbon tight beneath her chin, like a mother might her child. Her hand stayed close to the girl's cheek and neck. They spoke to each other and laughed again. Pearl brushed creases from the girl's coat, running her hands down the front to the belt, which she pulled tighter. It was all affection, great affection, and considerably more than the attention I'd seen her pay to others among Marlow's models.

When the two of them were alone – the others having swiftly lost themselves in the crowd moving towards Shaftesbury Avenue – they came back to the kerb and looked left and right as though undecided about which direction to take. Pearl pointed towards Piccadilly, and the girl nodded her assent. She held Pearl's arm, clasping her hands together and holding herself close to the older woman as the two of them started walking.

They quickly gained a rhythm and were able to walk like this in tandem, a single figure, swerving through all oncomers, and stepping up and down from the kerb as though they were playing a kind of game – a game where a great deal might be irretrievably lost were they to become separated for even a moment.

I followed them, keeping my distance, certain that neither had seen me amid so many others, until they entered Piccadilly Circus, where the flowing crowd seemed to slow a little, running in a circle as though it were water, and leaving the centre of the road to the even slower-moving buses and carriages. The whole of that part of town, like Shaftesbury Avenue and Trafalgar Square behind me, was still under-going reconstruction, and high platforms of scaffolding and mounds of sand and stone filled much of the street. Fires burned in braziers, adding to the day's heat, and causing the warm air to ripple and distort with their fumes and smoke. The smell of burning pitch filled the air.

My first thought was that, having come in this direction,

they were headed for Golden Square, but as I prepared to pass through the crowd and follow them in this direction, the two of them turned the opposite way, along Regent Street, where they walked more slowly, and paused more often to look in the windows there.

I knew now that I would not approach them, that I would in fact avoid being seen by Pearl at all costs. I saw that whatever pleasure she was deriving from being with this girl, it had no connection whatsoever with Marlow and their work together. Had she seen me – for however brief a time, or however accidental or coincidental our encounter might have seemed – then that connection with Marlow would have been instantly established and her pleasure spoiled. She would not have believed my protestations of innocence. I would have said too much, insisted too much, and she would have despised me for it. Perhaps she would have introduced me to the girl, perhaps not. But whatever she said, she would have said it unwillingly, and it would have been an act of severance rather than connection.

The two of them paused to examine a window of clothes on display, and both pointed from one dummy to another. Pearl's hand, I saw, closed around the girl's, and the girl responded by locking their fingers. It still appeared as though they were pointing to the dummies and their clothes, but in truth they were merely standing there, surrounded by all these passing others, clasping their hands tight together for the simple pleasure of being like that. I felt a sudden envy at their easy affection, a pain made even sharper as I grew increasingly convinced that the girl was indeed Pearl's daughter, and that this was a rare excursion for the pair of them.

As I watched, anticipating that they might retrace their steps to the shop entrance and go inside, they turned without warning and faced directly where I stood. I turned away immediately, and in the glass in front of me I saw the reflection of the two of them coming towards me through the traffic.

I held myself closer to the glass, my hand to my face, feigning interest in the display of hardware I found myself looking at, half my attention on this, half still on the confusion of reflections behind me. I lost sight of them briefly, and then saw them again as they reappeared to my right. At first they seemed to be moving away from me, forced to release their close hold on each other because of the thickening crowd, but then they paused again and turned back to where I stood. Knowing that if they continued walking they would pass immediately behind me, I turned and walked ahead of them, conscious of the people between us, hoping that Pearl was not looking too closely ahead of her, and that some opportunity would soon present itself for me to remove myself completely from their path. If I attempted to cross the road I would only reveal myself to them.

It was difficult to know how close they might already have come to me, and so I carried on walking, increasing my speed through the oncomers, hoping that the two women would be moving even more slowly through this gathering mass of shoppers.

After several minutes, and as Regent Street neared its junction with the Mall, I turned into an entrance and ventured a glance backwards through the curving glass of yet another window display, confident now that the two women would be far enough behind me not to see me.

There was no sign of them. I looked harder through the

distorting curve of the glass. There was still nothing. Either they had entered a shop, or they had turned back, or they had taken a hidden turn from the main thoroughfare. And despite my earlier fear of being seen, I now felt inexplicably disappointed at finding myself so suddenly alone in the crowd.

Perhaps they had been unable to resist returning to the shop that had earlier attracted them. Perhaps Pearl had insisted on buying whatever had caught the girl's eye. Perhaps she was dressing her for an appointment with Marlow. Perhaps she was buying the clothes at Marlow's suggestion. Perhaps that had been the whole purpose of their outing. Perhaps even now they were following another of those convoluted routes that led only to Golden Square. Perhaps Pearl's arm was firmer than ever across the girl's shoulders. Perhaps she was whispering into her ear, feeding the girl's excitement. All this ran in a confused and unstoppable torrent through my mind as I searched for them.

I waited a few minutes longer, planning my route back to Somers Town and looking at the buses passing in both directions. I felt a guilty pleasure at having followed them like this, and simply guilt for having allowed my thoughts to have spun so rapidly and to have become so tangled. But however great my inquisitiveness, I knew that it would forever be beyond me to approach Pearl directly and to ask her about what I had seen. My own bravery knew its bounds. And I knew, too, where she stood with Marlow, and where I stood with him.

I was distracted from these thoughts by the jolt of a cab which drew away from me where I stood. The driver swore at me, waving his furled whip, then flicking it at the horse when he would rather have struck me. I stepped backwards, colliding with a man standing behind me. As he passed, the cabman laughed at this, and looked down at me with an exaggerated sneer on his face.

5

Solomon's wife spoke little English. A 'Good day' as I came into the shop; the occasional 'Sorry' and 'Please wait,' perhaps, as she went into the room behind to find her husband. Usually, she pointed to the clock to indicate that I should wait until Solomon was free to see me, and then to the solitary chair where I might sit while I waited. And usually while I waited, she sat behind the counter watching the passers-by, occasionally glancing at the sparsely stocked shelves around her, at the dust-covered frames and photographs arranged there, and paying me as little attention as possible.

A man entered a few moments after me, looked at me where I sat, and then hesitated before approaching Solomon's wife at the counter. She greeted him, stepping to one side as the man scanned the shelves around her. In addition to Solomon's photographic supplies and services, the shop served as a small, equally poorly stocked pharmacy for the neighbourhood. I saw by the woman's reaction to this customer that she knew him. I pretended to look at the street through the frosted glass of the window, glancing at her and catching her grin as she waited for the man to indicate what he wanted to buy. She spoke to him in Polish, pushing him to make his decision. He looked back at me – though whether wishing I was not there to witness this embarrassing charade, or in the hope that I might be able to communicate with the woman and help him, I was uncertain.

Eventually, he tapped his forehead and pulled a pained expression. She spoke to him again, several sentences, the same few repeated words. She took down a box of tablets and indicated the price to him. He paid her in coins and she made a drama of dropping each of these into the cumbersome till and then of pressing the requisite keys to register the sale. Only when this was completed did she hand the pills over to him. He looked hard at the small white box. Turning to me, he said, 'Terrible headache. You'll understand.'

I shrugged, as though I too might have been Polish.

'Headache,' he repeated.

I caught the woman's quick look, another of her fleeting, knowing grins.

'Foreigners,' the man said.

This time, Solomon's wife shrugged with me.

The man left.

'"Bloody foreigners",' she said to me. '"Bloody foreigners. Go home. Go home and never come back here. Stay where you belong."'

As she said all this, the curtain beside her was pulled aside and Solomon appeared.

'Another satisfied customer, my love?' he said to his wife.

She answered him in Polish and he kissed her cheek.

'*Two* bloody foreigners,' he said, coming from her to me.

'I think you lost a sale,' I told him. At first he didn't understand, but then his wife explained about the aborted transaction. She came to me and held out her hand.

'She asks after your wife,' Solomon said to me.

'Very well,' I told her.

'And thank you for asking?' she said.

'Yes, thank you.'

'And your daughter?' Solomon said.

'Very well also. Thank you for asking.'

'You answer my greeting wishes to them?' his wife said.

'I shall answer your greeting wishes.'

The woman smiled at me, as though fully aware of her small mistake, and of my complicity in compounding it.

Her name was Marta, which I imagined was an anglicization – though not to its fullest 'Martha' – but I seldom thought of her as anything except Solomon's wife, the small ante-chamber to the room of the man himself.

The name above the shop door said 'Salomon', though he assured me there was no 'a', and when upon meeting him for the first time I asked him if this was a first or a second name, he merely smiled at me and said it might be both, but that for professional purposes he preferred simply to be called Solomon.

On many occasions since, I had heard his wife address him as 'Moyshe', and when I had asked him if this was Moses, he had laughed and asked me if he looked like a Moses. 'So is this the promised land?' he had said, laughing. 'Have the waters parted, have we passed safely across, and is this the far, safe shore?' I had heard the sadness in his voice as he'd said all this, and had not persisted. Afterwards, he had confirmed that his name was indeed Moses, but that he still preferred to be called Solomon.

Marta left us briefly, and then returned. I smelled cooking meat from somewhere beyond. Cooking meat and the usual mix of ether and alcohol, nitrates, sulphates, rinses, fixers and varnishes.

When Marta was back at the counter, Solomon indicated that we should leave and he drew the curtain from the door.

He said something to his wife and she pretended to slap his arm before resting her fingers on his chin for a moment. I saw the affection between them in every small transaction.

I followed him along a corridor, past their cramped living quarters, to his developing room. The door was locked and he opened it using a heavy bunch of keys.

Once inside, he told me to wait, and then he bolted the door before turning up the dim light.

I gave him the case I carried and he put this on the already crowded table.

If the shop along the short corridor was empty of everything it might have possessed, then Solomon's room was full to overflowing, every shelf and surface covered and piled with the tools and products of his trade as a developer.

'More work for our friend in Holywell Street?' he asked me.

I shook my head. He meant Marlow. The lie about Holywell Street – well enough known as a centre of pornographic photography – was my own: something both to keep Solomon at one remove from Marlow, and also to clumsily sever my own uneasy connection between the two of them. There was little doubt in my mind, however, that Solomon now colluded in this deception, and that he knew exactly where Marlow's current studio was situated.

'Not his line,' I said, meaning that the plates did not come from Marlow. 'Lyceum work. Costumes. Theatrical stuff.' Something, perhaps, for Marlow to pick and choose from. Something special in which to dress his girls upon demand.

'I worked for him when we were both still in Whitechapel,' Solomon said.

I knew this, too. It was why I had gone to him in the first place.

'Montaigne Street. He was able to leave long before my own . . . Exodus.'

We both laughed at the small joke.

'Was he in the same line then?' I asked him.

He shrugged. 'I think it was something he was developing a taste for. It was certainly . . .' He rubbed his thumb and fingers together to suggest money.

I looked around me. Even in that disorganized and over-crowded state, it was a room I would have been happy to have called my own, somewhere I would have worked longer and harder at what I did. A room apart, familiar in all its dim, warm and pungent details.

'You're busy?' I said.

'Some days. You know this work. Some days too much, others too little.'

I knew that this was not a complaint.

He took down a bottle and searched for two small, heavy glasses. It was what he always did. One drink of the clear, raw spirit swallowed quickly, another sitting in our hands for the rest of our hour together.

He sat opposite me, our knees almost touching, and gave me a glass, the liquid filled to its brim and spilling over my fingers. He proposed the usual unintelligible toast – the one I always endeavoured to repeat – and we drank. As usual, I braced myself against the bite of the spirit, and as usual I was unable to prevent myself from coughing and then holding a hand over my mouth. I occasionally exaggerated this, knowing how much it amused Solomon. I had seen Marta drink the same spirit without flinching.

He picked up and opened the case of plates I had taken to him. He took several of these out and held them to the dim bulb.

'And you want the usual copies?'

'I imagine so,' I said. Illicit, unmissed copies.

'He uses you, you know that?' he said, taking out other plates and giving them the same cursory examination.

'I imagine he uses everyone,' I said.

'Oh, absolutely. Everyone and always.'

'Even—'

'Even his closest associates, those who imagine themselves to be his friends and confidants.' He added a cold edge to the two words. It seemed an unnecessary warning after so long a time.

'You've known him for much longer than I have,' I said.

He considered this. 'Perhaps too long.'

I knew better than to insist on an explanation.

He had come to Somers Town from Whitechapel two years earlier, largely at the insistence of his wife, who no longer felt settled or comfortable or safe there.

'We live and advance by degrees,' Solomon had told me upon my first visit to these new premises. 'By degrees and shading; by small pieces discarded and others taken on.' He was talking about assimilation. He had told me about his names – *all* their names, I realized later – and all I had done was resist telling him that Alice was then insisting on being called 'Alicia' by her sitters.

Within weeks of the move, the room was as filled and as cluttered as though he had been there a lifetime.

I had never asked him if his wife had known of Marlow and his enterprise, or of my own role in their connection now. Likewise, Solomon himself had made nothing clear to me. Our true understanding, I suppose, existed in our asides and silences, our hints and evasions.

'Your wife is still communicating with the dead?' he said unexpectedly, distracting me from these thoughts.

At first I imagined he was going to make another joke, anticipating that I might laugh with him.

'It gives her a kind of . . . purpose,' I said, uncertain why I had chosen the word or what it implied.

But instead of laughing, Solomon said, 'You still don't take these things seriously enough.'

'I suppose she fulfils a need.'

'But still not one that you yourself recognize or accept?' He went on looking at the plates as he said all this.

'Things have changed,' I told him. 'From when she started. *She*'s changed.'

'And because you do not accept this change, then you fear you are growing apart, that something is forcing its way between the pair of you?'

I said nothing for a moment, uncertain how or why we had come so swiftly on to this other path.

'Forgive me,' he said eventually, returning the plates to the case. 'Marta, she too believes in all this . . . this . . .'

'Does she—'

'Indulge herself? There is a woman close by. Hampden Close. She occasionally visits. Nothing formal, but she goes all the same. Wednesdays. The woman calls it an "Open House".'

It was how Alice had started out ten years earlier.

'Is it because of your son?' I asked him.

Three years earlier, Solomon and Marta had lost their only child at sea. He was a Master on a cargo vessel and had drowned during a wreck in the Bay of Biscay. His body had never been recovered, and none of his possessions had been returned to them. There had not even been a public service, merely a formal and unfeeling letter of condolence from the shipping company and a cheque for his back pay.

'Tomasz, yes,' Solomon said. 'But I fear the woman here is a charlatan and I wish Marta were not so eager or so desperate to believe her. Perhaps . . .' He stopped speaking and looked at me, lifting the second glass of spirit to his lips.

It was a moment before I understood what he was asking me.

He waited. 'Tomasz spoke perfect English,' he said. 'If that were to be a barrier . . . I mean, to communication. Or perhaps your wife would simply repeat the *sound* of what might be said to her.'

I was again alarmed by how far we had suddenly come. I was also surprised to learn of his wife's belief – however rooted in desperation it might have been. I had always imagined the pair of them to share a strong understanding of the necessary practicalities of life, with little time for – what? Diversions? Indulgences? – such as this. The death of their only child was another reason why they had left Whitechapel behind and come here.

'Do you encourage Marta?' I asked him.

'What else can I do? He was our only son.'

'I mean do you encourage her belief?'

'Or merely her need to have her hand held in reassurance? I am not sure. How can the two things be separated?'

'I'll ask Alice,' I said. 'About Marta visiting her.'

'If it gives Marta some peace . . .'

When Alice, Cora, Caroline and I had first moved to Holloway from Pimlico, Solomon had been one of our first visitors, bringing with him a gift of bread, coal and salt, and explaining that it was the custom in his homeland to bring such gifts to ensure prosperity, good health and fair fortune for whoever lived in the house. After he'd gone, the first thing Alice had done was to throw out all three items. 'Mumbo-jumbo,' she'd said, but even then I'd known that it was more than this that had caused her to respond so harshly.

I understood what he was sacrificing in making this plea now on behalf of his wife. I had felt something similar every time I was confronted by one of Alice's sitters, forced to listen to her praises being sung, agreeing with everything that was said, often in the presence of Alice herself.

'I'm sure anything would be better than the woman on Hampden Close,' Solomon said. 'She is like a fairground gypsy.' He held out his free hand and rippled his fingers over an imaginary crystal ball. 'Whoo.'

Alice had once used the balls, though seldom these days. They still sat in a cupboard in our bedroom.

'That man,' Solomon said unexpectedly.

'The man in the shop?'

'She plays with them. You know what he was there to buy, what he hoped *I* would be present to serve him with?'

'I imagine so,' I said.

'We profit from propriety and embarrassment. I shall go into the shop later in the afternoon and they'll all return.'

'Do they ever . . . ?' I indicated the pictures around us.

He smiled. 'Sometimes. They imagine all sorts, make all their veiled inquiries. But I finished with all that when I left Whitechapel. I was never truly suited to it.'

'Not like—'

'No – not like Marlow is suited to it.'

I could not deny that it was what I'd been about to say.

'You should be more careful,' he said.

'Of Marlow?'

'Of what you are doing. Stealing these costumes and props.'

'Borrowing,' I said. 'Lending. I only lend him the stuff.' I knew it was a poor rebuttal.

'And is that how Irving would see it? *You* lending *his* sacred costumes to a pornographer to profit by them?'

'I doubt if anyone has the faintest idea of what's happening, or if' – I had a sudden memory of Howson referring to my 'sidelines' – 'it would truly concern them.'

He smiled at this faltering denial.

'Just be careful,' he said. 'You surely know enough of Marlow by now to know that he is capable of anything, that there is nothing and no one he would not sacrifice to protect himself.' He had suggested the same to me often enough before.

'I'll keep a watchful eye,' I said. Another of his sayings.

He touched a finger beneath his eye. 'It's good advice.' He finally drained his second glass of spirit, indicating for me to do the same.

6

I met the new maid for the first time the following morning.

Three days had passed since Alice's séance and I had spoken to her on only two occasions in the meantime. When I'd asked her about the sitting, she'd insisted that she was unable to talk about it. As usual, and little concerned about these abrupt dismissals, I didn't persevere. She understood my feelings on the matter, and I daresay that, as ever, she did not relish the prospect of my scepticism contaminating her own belief.

I had been awake only a few moments when the girl knocked. I called for her to enter, but there was no response.

I called again and the door opened. She came into the room carrying a tray and looking around her. The door swung shut behind her.

'I called when you knocked,' I said.

But she paid me little attention; instead, she continued looking slowly around at the dimly lit and untidy room. It was clear that nothing she saw there appealed to her in the slightest, and she did nothing to disguise this.

'Your wife said to come up.' She raised and lowered the tray she held, and I indicated the cabinet beside the bed, pushing its residue of clutter to one side.

I guessed her to be in her early twenties. She wore the usual plain apron, and the elasticated band in her hair that Alice called a cap. She had light-brown hair, long and fastened up. She was not unattractive, in a plain and photogenic way. There was a smear of soot on her cheek, another on her neck where her collar touched her skin. A further stain ran the length of one forearm.

She saw me looking at this.

'From the fires,' she said.

Having put down the tray, she drew aside the curtain and looked again at the room around her.

I apologized for not having made the effort to greet her earlier. She had been there for almost a week. I asked her where she lived.

'My mother was in service to Lord Derby,' she said, leaving me wondering whether or not she'd deliberately avoided answering me. She said the name as though I might know the man.

'Lord Derby?'

'A proper High Court judge. House in the country, another in Knightsbridge. My mother practically ran the Knightsbridge house.'

I guessed it was an exaggeration.

'I imagine we must seem . . .' I wondered what to say. 'By comparison, I mean.'

She looked at me for the first time. I pushed myself upright in the bed. The sheets, as usual, lay in crumpled disarray, half on the floor. I poured myself a cup of tea. In the summer, the rooms high in the house seldom cooled; in the winter they never warmed.

'Your wife said you were a photographer.' There was a first

note of interest in her voice. 'At the theatre.' The note lasted.

'The Lyceum,' I said. No less.

'She said it was the best. She said you photographed all the actors and actresses there.'

'I do. But mostly for a record of their costumes. For the dressers and seamstresses.'

'Famous people?'

'Most of—'

'Who have you photographed?'

I recited a list of names, few of which she recognized, and most of which – the true actors and actresses, those beyond the flaring light of passing celebrity – meant nothing to her. I added a few music-hall turns, and she recognized these. She knew Ellen, of course, and had heard of Irving.

'*I* had my picture taken,' she said. She sat on the chair beside the cabinet and smoothed her skirt over her knees. She looked at the mark on her arm, licked her thumb and rubbed it.

I told her she had other marks on her face and neck and she wiped these with the edge of her apron. She leaned closer to me, asking me to tell her when they'd gone.

'Photographer up Holborn way. Brett, he was called. You probably know him.' She waited while I pretended to think.

'There are hundreds of studios,' I said. 'More every year.'

'He's supposed to be one of the best. At least, that's what he told me.'

I lied and told her that I'd heard of the man, that he had a good reputation.

She pulled up her sleeve, revealing her pale upper arm. 'I didn't realize she'd want the fires doing. I thought you'd have a scullery maid for that. And especially not now, in all this heat.' She fanned herself to emphasize the remark.

'We're not very grand,' I said.

'Meaning you don't see the need for even me?' She smiled at me to disarm the remark.

'My wife's a very busy woman,' I said.

'So she keeps telling me, and what—' She stopped abruptly, aware of having said too much.

'It's all right,' I told her.

She nodded to the closed door at the far side of the room. 'That your – what is it? – studio?'

'Not really. More of a simple developing room, and then only for emergencies.'

'Perhaps you could take a photograph of me. Your wife said you work up here most nights, that it's why you sleep up here.'

I knew by her tone that she understood the arrangement perfectly.

'Only recently,' I said, wondering why I'd felt the need for even that vague excuse.

She said nothing for a moment. Then she poured milk into my cup and spooned in sugar. 'Two,' she said. 'She told me. She said you had a sweet tooth.'

'My wife and I—'

'Said the pair of you had a taste for the finer things, and that I was to watch whatever the delivery boys dropped off. So, are you interested?'

I didn't understand her.

'In taking my photograph. Seems a pity not to take advantage, so to speak, you being in the trade. The man up Holborn said I was a natural, that I had an . . . an . . .'

'Aptitude?'

'That's it. Said I had an aptitude.' It was clearly a lie. 'You

66

should have heard all the other things he was suggesting to me. Besides, perhaps one day I might actually belong with all those other famous people you've had sit for you.'

She made it sound as though they came to me at my command. I was the Lyceum photographer because five years ago Stoker had looked at the accounts of all the farmed-out private photographic commissions and realized how much he might save by employing someone as part of the theatre's permanent staff.

'Of course,' I said.

'I could come to the theatre, or wherever it is you take them. Last thing I'm going to do is have my picture taken looking like this. Mind you, the Holborn man said there was a market for all sorts.' She looked at me until I understood her. And then she struck a pose, her head tilted back, her fingers at her chin. 'Like this, perhaps,' she said.

'Possibly.'

'Or perhaps you could fit all of me in the picture.' She straightened and pulled back her shoulders so that her chest appeared in sudden outline beneath her blouse. 'Lord Derby's house is full of pictures, everybody he ever knew, hundreds of them. What do you think – face or head to toe?'

'Either,' I said. 'Both.'

The answer pleased her. She wiped dust from her shoulder.

'You just let me know where and when,' she said. She glanced at the photographs on the mantel. 'You take them?'

'I did,' I said.

'Your wife told me.' She bowed her head briefly.

A strip of dried laurel lay behind the pictures. We'd filled Caroline's small grave with the branches, a kind of nest in which her coffin was then laid.

'My mother died two years ago,' she said. 'Year after Lord Derby. His family were meant to see her all right, but nothing happened. She was close to him, see.'

I wondered what she was suggesting, how much more of this loosely spun tale I was expected to believe.

'She always used to say that she had "expectations". She was forty when she died. She went and I was left to my own resources.'

'You seem capable enough,' I said.

She laughed at the word. 'That the same as having an aptitude, being capable?'

'Similar,' I said.

She came from where she sat, scooping up a blanket from the floor and laying it across the bottom of the bed.

'I ought to get going,' she said, and before I could answer her, Alice called up the stairs to her, demanding to know both where she was and what was taking her so long.

She would be in the house until midday, perhaps returning for an hour or two later in the afternoon.

I heard the reluctance in Alice's voice as she called out, 'Isobel.'

The girl also heard this and said, 'That sound too *ex-ot-ic* to you? It's my name and I've probably got a certificate somewhere to prove it. She tried "Belle" for a few days, but said it sounded too French. I told her it was the French for "beautiful", so that put the mockers on that one and we went back to Isobel. What do *you* want to call me?'

The question, implying as it did so much more, caught me unawares and I hesitated in answering her.

'I wouldn't object to Belle,' she said. 'And certainly not if it made things easy between us.'

I was having difficulty gauging her true intent with these remarks – in knowing whether she was continuing with this openly flirtatious behaviour merely as a means of getting her portrait taken for free by the man who had photographed all those other famous people, or if she already understood more of the tensions between Alice and myself than had so far been made clear to her.

Alice called again, and this time Isobel answered her, going to the door and shouting down that she was on her way. She held her ear to the wall, waiting to hear the door slamming shut behind Alice as she left the stairs.

'Are you going to the theatre today?' she asked me.

'You ought to go down,' I told her.

'I'm on my way. You get a feel for these things.'

'What things?'

'When to jump, when to wait. Sometimes people just like to shout. You get lords who whisper and ask politely, and tarts who shout the odds over every little thing.'

This last remark surprised me, and she saw this and said quickly, 'I mean women who could just as easily be doing all this for themselves. I didn't mean women who—' But this time she knew she'd said too much, and she waved away whatever she might have been about to add. 'I didn't mean Mrs Webster. Nor your other daughter.'

'Cora,' I said.

'That's right.'

'She and her mother are very close,' I said. It was another gentle warning to her.

'I can see that they're much alike,' she said. 'You want some hot water bringing up?' She picked up the basin from its stand, careful not to spill what it contained.

69

'Please,' I said.

'You won't get a peep out of me when you do my picture. I'd sit as quiet and as still as a corpse for however long you told me.' She held a hand over her mouth and froze where she stood. It was still a popular misconception. 'I can keep my mouth shut for hours at a time as and when required and needed,' she added. It seemed another strange and suggestive remark to make.

'I'm sure you can.'

She laughed again at this, looked one last time at the room around her and then left me.

I heard her singing to herself as she descended the stairs.

A few minutes later, as I considered all that had just happened, I heard someone coming back up to me. My first thought was that she was returning with the water, but I knew as I listened that the footsteps were not hers, that they were slower and more measured, that Alice was coming up to me.

She knocked once. 'Are you decent?'

You're my wife, I wanted to shout to her, but instead I called out that I was.

She came in and closed the door behind her.

'Well?' she said.

'She seems . . . efficient.'

'I doubt she could even spell the word.' She looked at the sheets which remained draped on the floor. And then she looked at me, at my face, my chest, my shoulders.

'I heard you talking.'

'I asked her about herself.'

'*You* asked *her*?'

'She was telling me about her mother, about Lord Derby.'

'And you believed her?'

'I had no reason not to,' I said.

'She likes the sound of her own voice, that's all. What else did she say?'

'Not much. She was asking about my work.'

'I hope you told her to mind her own business, not to disturb you. It's important to impress things on these kind of people from the very start.'

'Of course,' I said. I sipped at my cool tea.

Alice sat on the end of the bed, looking at the mantel for a moment. She cleared her throat, a hand to her lips. 'Cora and I have been talking,' she said, her eyes still averted.

'Oh? Is there anything on the horizon? The milliners?'

'What horizon?'

I wondered which of her common excuses for our daughter was about to be repeated.

'I take it the position wasn't suitable for her,' I said. I knew by then how to gauge and frame my own disappointment.

'That's what we were talking about,' she said. 'She's expressed an interest.'

I waited for her to explain these cryptic remarks. It was clear the two of them had already discussed and decided upon whatever was about to be revealed to me.

'A genuine interest,' she said.

'In what?'

'In those matters of consequence . . . to myself.'

I began to understand her.

'I don't follow,' I said.

'You don't "understand". Say "understand".'

I refused to comply. I understood perfectly the small advantage I momentarily held.

'She has expressed a wish – a desire – to assist me in my own work.' She was relieved at having said it, the worst over.

'In your séances? How? How can she assist? You've never needed an assistant – assistance – so far.' I sounded twice as incredulous as I felt.

'Thus far, no. But I am feeling the—'

'You're not suggesting to me that Cora has expressed an interest in – a talent – I mean, a *capability*—'

She understood what I was struggling to say – or, rather, avoid saying.

'In a gift such as my own? No, no, no, nothing of that nature.' She feigned laughter. 'No, no, nothing so – so—'

'What, then?'

'Precisely what I said: she has expressed a desire to assist me. To be my *assistant*. To help me prepare myself and then to recover from my exertions.'

'Your exertions?'

She grew exasperated. 'You surely cannot have failed to notice how exhausted I am of late each time I make contact. I'm no longer a young woman.' She was thirty-eight, three years younger than myself. 'Surely, you cannot have grown so blind or so – so insensitive?'

'It never—'

'So unfeeling.'

'No, of course not. I merely—'

'You merely anticipated that I would take upon myself a greater and greater burden until I collapsed beneath that burden.' Even she seemed unhappy with the overblown and unconvincing remark. But it was the precise point at which my argument was lost. Every small detail of this 'arrangement' had already been calculated and agreed by the pair of them.

'I *give* everything,' she said, again pitching the balance of conviction and melodrama too far in favour of the latter. 'Everything of myself. Each time. I need to recover. I need to allow myself all the incidentals, all the peripheral necessities of my calling to be undertaken by someone else.' She already sounded as though she were reading from a contract.

'"Peripheral necessities"?' I said, trying to make the phrase seem even more ridiculous.

'Greeting people at the door. Making small talk, fetching drinks, getting people seated, setting up the room, making the necessary arrangements prior to all this, putting things back afterwards, seeing people out, taking further bookings. Can't you see what a great help all that would be to me?'

'I suppose . . .' I paused, anticipating another interruption.

'Go on,' she said.

'I suppose I can see that it might make things easier for you.'

She brightened. 'Easier *and* more professional. Think of it. I need not appear until Cora has made everything ready. Imagine the drama of my entrance. Imagine how much better my performance might be were it not to be squandered on all these worthless incidentals.'

'Your performance?' I said.

But now she refused to be drawn.

'My visitations, my conversations, wanderings. Imagine how I would appear to my sitters if all *they* saw and experienced of me was *that*, doing *that*, fulfilling my one true part in the whole enterprise.'

I saw some sense in what she was suggesting. The theatres and halls all had their warm-up shows and performers; the mechanics of the stage were well hidden; everything was sacrificed to the illusion of the drama itself; the lights were never shone upon these small players and backstage operators, myself included.

'I take it you've already spoken to Cora?' I said.

'I told her it would be your decision completely.' Not only was my argument lost, but I was now also complicit in my own defeat. 'I told her I would abide absolutely with whatever you said.'

'I suppose that if she doesn't need to look for work elsewhere, then—'

'In addition to which, I shall be able to charge more. I might even be able to work more frequently. With Cora's help I shall recover more swiftly, be ready sooner to perform again.'

Again, there was no irony in the word.

'But will people *come* more frequently?' I said.

'Some. Many. Cora said I might advertise. Advertise properly, find new customers. I could undertake to give more private sittings. Perhaps find a better class of sitter, people willing to pay more for a higher degree of personal attention. Cora believes the bounds are endless.' She paused. 'She even imagines I am being selfish in restricting myself the way I do.'

I saw how swiftly the argument had leaped my own bounds, how it now fed upon and grew ever stronger with each excited suggestion.

In the few jobs Cora had so far held, she had shown neither the enthusiasm nor the willingness to learn even the basics of whatever she had briefly and reluctantly attached herself to.

Alice smoothed the blankets along my legs. 'You need some time to consider all the benefits and advantages,' she told me.

'And the pitfalls. You know Cora better than anyone.'

'And that's why I believe her when she tells me it's what she wants to do,' she said. It was a simple and an obvious trap, but I had walked blindly into it.

After a moment of silence, she said, 'Did you hear me calling?'

'Calling?'

'*I-so-bel*. Did you hear me calling her? She had the nerve to tell me – *me* – that Belle was the French for beautiful.'

'No,' I said.

'And *I* told *her* that I could well imagine the kind of people – the kind of *men* – who might take some salacious pleasure in calling her by it.'

'Perhaps "Bella",' I suggested.

She considered this before deciding that it, too, sounded too exotic – too foreign – for the girl.

'Bella sounds English,' I said. In fact, it sounded exactly like a housemaid.

'She said her mother called her it because Lord Whoever had a daughter of his own with the name. I'm beginning to regret not having insisted on a written character from whoever employed her last.' Girls without characters were always cheaper to hire than those who came with them. 'And then she had the nerve to tell me that there were plenty of people who already called her by the name.'

'Belle?'

'Precisely.'

Including, presumably, the photographer in Holborn.

She rose at the word and walked quickly out of the room before I could say anything more. I had only been awake half an hour, and already I felt exhausted by my small defeats.

7

I'd been at work for most of the afternoon, and most of it spent waiting for costumes to be delivered to me from the theatre storerooms, when Jimmy Allen appeared. He came along the narrow corridor, exchanging greetings with the few others at work up there, and then he sat on the chair immediately outside my door and waited. The door was ajar and I saw him soon after his arrival.

'Won't disturb you,' he called in to me, breathless after his exertions. He seldom left the ground floor, and stuck mostly to the edges of the stage, which had always seemed to me to be his natural habitat. He suffered from rheumatism and arthritis, and a journey that high, up such steep staircases, was a rare thing for him, and his presence there unsettled me.

I called out to him that I would be free in a few minutes. Smoke from my cigarettes filled the low ceiling. Drying prints hung amid this, faces and figures moving through a fog. I had been cleaning glass plates while I waited, and in addition to the smoke, the faint odour of gun cotton filled the warm air.

'No urgency,' he called in to me. 'No hurry. Take your time.' He took a rolled newspaper from his pocket, unfurled and straightened and then folded it. Everything he did spoke of his military background. He might dismiss this in the company of Stoker or Irving, but it was always something he wanted clearly understood about himself.

I heard the rustle of the paper as he turned the pages. He coughed dryly, and this too followed a pattern. A single uncontrollable cough, followed by a fist to his mouth and a succession of lesser clearings. He was not a silent man.

I took a number of prints from their trays, shook the liquid from them and clipped them to a waiting string, watching them drip for a moment.

I finally went to Jimmy Allen and invited him in.

He rose stiffly, easing the ache from his thighs. Standing, he tucked the rolled newspaper beneath his arm as though it were a baton.

'We don't usually see you up here,' I said to him. 'Let me help you.'

I held out my hand to him, but he avoided this.

'Been a lot higher than this in my time,' he said. He meant the foothills of the Himalayas – a joke which had once been genuinely funny.

He followed me into my room and looked around him.

I considered who might have sent him, and to what purpose.

'You on an errand from the Guv'nor?' I tried to appear unconcerned, distracted, still working.

'After a fashion,' he said.

I offered him another chair and he took it. He looked at the pictures hanging above him.

'*Love's Labours,*' I said. 'Everything's struck. Stoker was considering a provincial run with half the players.' Which meant half the costumes; which meant the remainder would soon be sent to Southall; which meant that I would be able to pick and choose among them. Ellen's seconds and thirds, perhaps something worn by Mayberry or one of the Susans.

'I know – Stoker said. Northern Circuit. No repair. Renovation only.'

'And some pictures for publicity,' I said.

'He'll want a Christmas start. Push the pantomimes for the money. Seasonal spend. You know what the Guv'nor thinks of pantomimes taking the bread from our bellies.' He coughed again, this time cupping both hands over his mouth and leaning forward slightly to ease whatever pain this caused him.

When the spasm was over, he tapped his chest and licked his lips. 'Do you have a drink?'

I indicated my sink, and then understood him better.

I took the brandy from the shelf beneath the developing table and poured us both a glass. It was a cheap brand, but he sniffed it as though it were the finest, before draining it in a single swallow and then holding his glass just close enough to the bottle to make his intention clear to me.

'You're on an errand,' I prompted him, pouring the drink.

Before responding, he kicked the door shut behind him.

'Is it private business?' I said. I tried now to sound serious, concerned.

'It might be,' he said. He spun the glass in his hand, raising and then lowering it. 'A number of costumes are unaccounted for.'

I sipped from my own glass, screwing up my face, supposedly at the taste, and thereby, I hoped, disguising my alarm.

'How do you mean? You mean pictures?' I gestured at the sheets above us.

Jimmy Allen kept his face down and I wanted him to look at me, for my own concern and uncertainty to register.

'From the depot, Stoker thinks.'

'You know what they're like at that place. Everything's confusion. They thrive on it. Everything last minute and lost until it's found. Mother never stops going on about it.' It was Stoker's aim – his *project* – to reorganize the stores and warehousing, both at Southall and in the Lyceum itself. He wanted to 'systemize' everything, to complete making a full record and then to make everything accessible and accountable for. A place for everything and everything in its place. To begin with, this craving for order and organization had been alien to Irving, and unwanted by him, but as his own commitments grew he had come to see the sense of Stoker's plan. It was why so much of the unused scenery, the props and costumes were now regularly removed from the theatre. It was why I was able to do what I did.

I waited for Jimmy Allen to say more, but he seemed reluctant. Perhaps he was unwilling to sound that first accusatory note.

'Do they have any idea what's missing?' I asked him.

He shrugged. 'Stoker thinks some of the *Faust* costumes.'

'*Faust*? There were hundreds of outfits, extras.'

'December '85. Seven hundred and ninety-two performances at the Lyceum alone. Smaller circuit runs. Three years, best part of. The scenery here was finally struck four years ago last February.'

'And Stoker's waited until *now* to decide something might have gone astray? He expects miracles. It was years ago.

You know better than anyone how many costumes were involved, how many repairs and replacements Irving kept sending for.'

'I certainly know what it cost him,' Jimmy Allen said.

'And how much it made. A small fortune.'

The critics still spoke of it as Irving's finest performance, his crowning glory, the peak of his acting career, his dramatic Parnassus.

'Stoker will have it all down in one of his ledgers,' Jimmy Allen said.

'Perhaps. But nothing regarding which costumes were replaced, which were repaired, which went back and forth from Southall, which stayed there, and which were beyond repair and never came back from the seamstress.'

'Seamstresses,' Jimmy Allen said, unable as always to resist these small corrections.

'Precisely,' I said. 'Do we even employ the same women?' I'd heard Stoker publicly accusing the women of being thieves; we all had. 'So who is Stoker pointing the finger at this time? The day labourers at Southall, the carters, the packers? Is he pointing it there, or here?' Or was this just Stoker firing another of his shots across *all* our bows?

Jimmy Allen sipped his drink.

'I hope he's not suggesting that *you* might not have been keeping a close enough eye on things,' I said.

He remained undisturbed by this clumsy deflection.

'Sorry,' I said.

'He wanted to know what pictures you still had of the stuff. It's mostly women's costumes. The Devil's assistants, nymphs, the female demons. Some of the chorus changes.'

'It's still not very specific,' I said. 'I thought *he* was the one keeping records. I only do what he tells me to do. I thought *he* was the one dotting all the i's and crossing all the t's.'

We shared a laugh at this, and we both grew easier about what he had been sent to disclose to me.

'Where else have you looked?' I asked him.

'Looked?'

'Who else have you asked?' I almost said 'accused'.

'I had a word with Joe Harker and the painters. Stoker can't place his inventory of all the dismantled flats and drops.' Joe Harker was the theatre's chief painter of backcloths and standing screens.

'Is scenery missing, too?' Another diversion. Marlow had his own backdrops and props.

'Stoker thinks so.' He seemed less certain of this.

'And what did Joe say?'

'He told me in no uncertain terms—'

'What to say to Stoker?'

'I won't repeat any of that language. I heard enough of that kind of thing in the lower ranks' barracks.'

'I bet you did.' I touched his glass with my own. The finger held out to push into my chest was now back close to his own. I wanted to ask him if Stoker had sent him to see me – me, specifically – or whether this bow shot was in fact more of a scatter shot, fired in the hope of seeing who might be flushed from cover. I smiled at the thought: it was Irving's theatre; metaphors like this were always scrambled and then either endlessly unravelled or wrung dry.

'Called me his eyes and ears,' Jimmy said absently. He looked again at the pictures hanging all around him.

'Anything you want a copy of . . .' I said, and then,

remembering my work of a few days earlier, I slid open a drawer and took out a pile of card-mounted pictures of Ellen Terry dressed as Gertrude. Irving had ordered several gross of the pose, ready to distribute to his select circle upon *Hamlet*'s forthcoming first night in Bristol. I handed one of these to Jimmy Allen now.

'A sneak preview,' I said conspiratorially. 'Big secret. I'm supposed to keep them hidden away until Henry decides to hand them out. Me, him, and now you – we're the only three who've seen them.'

'And Stoker?'

'Not even him. Me, you and the Guv'nor.'

He looked hard at the picture. 'She gets more and more beautiful,' he said. 'I doubt there's a woman more loved in the whole country.'

'Europe, even,' I said.

'More loved than Bernhardt, Modjeska and Duse put together.'

'No argument there,' I said.

Every Christmas, Ellen Terry gave Jimmy Allen a tie pin. Bought from her personal jeweller. And once or twice a year, she invited him, along with a few dozen of the theatre 'regulars', out to a meal. And if there was no woman more loved than Ellen, I doubted if any man – Irving and Stoker excepted – loved that woman more than Jimmy Allen. He was almost old enough to be her grandfather, but this didn't matter. It was love – none of its weaker, shifting adjuncts – and it bound them together. I knew all this. It was why I had put the picture in his hand.

He reached out to give it me back, but I raised my palm to him.

'Stoker won't like me having it,' he said.

'Having what?'

'The picture.'

'What picture?'

He finally understood me and drew the photo back a few inches.

I looked above and around me, everywhere except at the picture in his hand.

'I appreciate this,' he said.

'A trifle between friends,' I said.

'Will you make up the numbers?'

'Will I make them back up to the number Mother wants to record in his ledgers, you mean? Have no fear – no one's going to come pointing the finger at you.' I'd already taken a dozen of the pictures to Marlow, a small extra, something he always appreciated, something to confirm the provenance of the outfits. In truth, Terry and what she wore interested him less than the costumes of the chorus girls and other, lesser actresses, but he had let me know early in our dealings that there was always a market for such prestigious or 'elevated' pieces.

I gave Jimmy Allen a small sheet of tissue and a card slip-case in which to secure, secrete and protect his precious gift. He knew as well as I did what confusion and disorder the Southall store operated under; and he knew, too, that in the world of the theatre – especially *this* theatre – order was always somehow shaped out of chaos, and that most of what was ever lost or misplaced was eventually either found or retrieved or created anew.

My arrangement with Marlow was that he would view everything I was able to make available to him via my pictures – usually extra copies easily printed in the course of my everyday work – and then I would arrange for whatever he chose to be collected at a time when I was working at Southall. The place was used twenty-four hours a day, often busiest in the small hours and through whole nights when one stage was being struck and removed and another getting under construction. Carters came and went repeatedly between the theatre and its store. Invoices were compiled, checked, lost, forgotten, changed, left incomplete, checked again by Stoker, discarded in frustration, miraculously found and compiled again. As Marlow had been quick to point out to me, there was always plenty of room for error. For error, doubt and uncertainty, and all of it to be turned into a profit. And because no small part of that profit was my own, then I could only agree with him.

I arranged for collection and return, and then responded to whatever additional demands he might make. Sometimes he asked to see pictures of costumes I had not suggested to him; occasionally, an actress made such an unexpected hit that the costume she wore acquired an unexpected value; and sometimes, Marlow told me, he wanted a very specific costume as a favour for a valued – and, presumably, wealthy – client.

I worked with men and women at the Lyceum who had never once visited Southall, and vice versa; I worked with men and women at Southall who had no idea of what was coming and going between the two places. Costumes came and costumes went, starting points and finishing points. And in between there was always that profitable, unguessable, untraceable void.

'She bought me these,' Jimmy Allen said, distracting me.

'Sorry.'

'Ellen. She bought me them.' He held out both his arms so that his shirt cuffs slid from beneath his sleeves. 'The cufflinks. Amber. Amber and silver.'

I admired them, holding one of the studs for a moment. The cuffs were starched and rigid. More of the old soldier – standards and appearance above all else and at any price.

Jimmy lowered his arms and pulled down his sleeves.

'She thinks a great deal of you,' I said. 'We all do.' I began to wonder how long he intended staying.

'You can hear the sun warming the roof,' he said absently, turning his face to the occasional creak of the roof, the tick of expanding lead flashing.

He looked as though he might be about to fall asleep where he sat, but as I watched him, he sat suddenly upright and said, 'And I saw this. This. Look.' He pulled out his rolled paper again and gave it to me. 'Page five or six. A piece about Stoker's friend.'

I searched the paper as he spoke. It wasn't easy in the dim light.

'There,' he said, reaching out and rapping the top of the page I was searching. He took the paper back and folded it to a more manageable size. 'The Manxman,' he said.

At first, I didn't understand him. I took the paper back and read the short article. I saw the words 'Gross Indecency' in the headline. I started reading. It was about an American doctor working in London who, upon being charged with acts of gross indecency against several of his women patients – the accusation was made no more explicit than this – had fled bail and returned to America, where he would likely remain beyond the reach of the law.

'Man called Tumblety,' Jimmy Allen said. 'He's a great friend of the Manxman.'

The Manxman being Hall Caine, who, in his turn, was a great friend of Stoker's. A writer himself – mostly of women's melodramas and edifying fairy tales for children – Stoker occasionally bragged of the editing work he had done on several of Caine's novels, as though this in some way accounted for their success.

'It says he indecently assaulted his women patients while they were under chloroform,' I said. 'It says "heinous".'

'You're missing my point,' Jimmy Allen said.

'Oh?' I finished reading.

'He was once held and questioned by the police during all that Whitechapel business.'

'The murders?'

'They thought at one time that he might even have been the killer. And now this. Makes you think. Innocent men don't usually feel the need to run away across an ocean before shouting their innocence back at you.'

'And you think Stoker might also have known the man?'

'They're all very close, that little set.'

I'd met Caine only once, in Stoker's company at the theatre, and he had behaved dismissively and insultingly to everyone else present. His appearance was repulsive. His forehead bulged, his eyes wandered divergently and his tongue forever wetted his lips and tight beard. In this latter respect – colour aside – he and Stoker bore a remarkable resemblance to each other.

'Seriously?' I said to Jimmy Allen.

He shrugged. 'Just something worth knowing,' he said.

'And remembering?'

'And that.'

He laid a hand on the pocket in which the picture of his queen and goddess lay, rose from his chair and put down his empty glass. I could almost hear him counting out the slow and creaking rhythm of all this as he did it.

8

My first encounter with Marlow was engineered by Bliss. It was a little over three years ago, another midsummer evening, shortly after Alice, Cora and I had settled in our new home.

I say 'engineered' advisedly. I was with Howson, front of house, an hour after curtain-down on the opening night of a re-run of *Forget Me Not*, and almost everyone else – and certainly the inner circle – had gone from the Lyceum to Kellner's for a celebratory dinner. Irving's performance in the revival, though far from his best, had been cheered by the audience and acclaimed by the critics. In those days, everything he did was cheered and acclaimed by someone.

Stoker had come upstairs to me a few minutes before the final curtain to ask me if I'd stay on at the theatre with Howson to bring the new accounts up to date. A new play, a new ledger. I had started to protest that Howson and I had intended joining the party at Kellner's, but he had dismissed this, saying that they would be there for hours yet and that we might easily finish the accounts in time to join them later. Besides, he said, Howson had already agreed to the work and had asked if I might be approached to assist him. I acceded and he immediately clasped my shoulders and told me I should be well rewarded. I was always about to be well rewarded.

A month later, Stoker thrust four tickets into my hand for a half-empty midweek performance of the faltering play.

When I went to find Howson, the first-night applause already rumbling through the entire building like a breaking storm, he told me that he had said nothing of the kind to Stoker, and he, too, was angry at his exclusion from the dinner party.

'Gone to pay homage at the court of King Henry,' he said. He asked me if I'd ever eaten at Kellner's, and I confessed that I hadn't. I'd only started at the Lyceum on a regular basis two months previously. He told me he'd been invited to one of Irving's celebrations upon his own appointment a year earlier, and that both Irving and Stoker had treated him then as though he'd owned the theatre. Afterwards, he said, they had behaved as though they'd forgotten his name. 'It's how they operate,' he said sourly. 'All hail-fellow-well-met one minute, and then crossing the street to avoid you the next.' We both knew it was an exaggeration, but that its seed of truth remained intact.

I went with him to the theatre entrance to watch the people gather to await Irving and then applaud him again when he finally arrived, his entrance carefully orchestrated by Stoker – a short, expectant silence, people searching, a tremor of rumour through the crowd, and then, above them, out of the darkness and into the light, illuminated by a single, piercing lamp, Irving himself, his arms raised, his fingers conducting the rising murmur of adoration. Pausing, perfectly still, surprised, gratified, appreciative. The applause growing loud and prolonged, and Irving descending the steps slowly, one measured pace at a time, his hand barely touching the golden rail. And then he was down amid his adoring audience and they closed gently and completely around him like a warm sea around a wader.

Howson and I watched all this from a balcony. I too had started to applaud, but had known by Howson's quick glance to stop. A further five minutes passed before Irving was finally able to leave the theatre, pulling the crowd with him, a flurry of bodies descending the steps in a single mass, like swarming bees, all independent and yet all pressed together in their single form around their queen.

When they had finally gone, others appeared from the dimly lit side corridors. Cleaners and sweepers – the people Howson referred to as the 'toilers of the false dawn'. The outside torches were extinguished, torn posters replaced. Litter was piled into mounds and then swept away. Buckets of warm water were cast over the stone steps. Voices echoed in the suddenly empty space.

Howson announced that it was turned eleven, and that the work Stoker had insisted on being done would take at least three hours. He had already glanced at the accounts and said they were in disarray. He told me what he needed me to do. I was to visit each of the 'trades' – the theatre's other workers – and collect as many of their own reckonings and receipts as possible. This included all those still unrecorded and uncalculated by my predecessor. It would be a good thing to do, Howson said, to clear my own particular slate, to start anew and then to keep in step with Stoker, to give him no further cause to come poking and probing where he wasn't wanted. I understood him completely.

My predecessor – an independent photographer called Coates – had been notoriously unreliable in his record-keeping, and he and Stoker had had many angry confrontations before his eventual dismissal at Stoker's insistence. Irving had known Coates for twenty years and had been reluctant to bow to Stoker's wishes and replace him. Stoker's opportunity had come a few months earlier when he was able to convince Irving that Coates had been stealing from the theatre, using its suppliers to provide for himself and his work elsewhere at Irving's expense. Coates had pleaded to Irving that this was not what Stoker was making it seem, that these so-called 'thefts' were no more than customary 'borrowings' or traditional perquisites, but by then Irving was so in thrall to Stoker, so dependent upon him and his methods of organization, that he had had little choice but to accede to him and replace Coates. I had arrived with the necessary recommendations and a sufficiently impressive portfolio of work less than a fortnight later.

For a while, I suffered some resentment – Coates had had many friends in the theatre, not least of whom was Jimmy Allen – but I had slowly proved myself and found my own feet in the place.

I waited with Howson as the supporting actors and actresses came from the dressing rooms into the foyer. Usually, they came and went from the side entrances, but tonight they wanted to share in something of the sense of occasion that all first nights created. They came out into the high space and stood in the same warm air in which Irving had stood. They heard the same praise-filled voices, turned their faces to the same flattering lights. Howson shouted down to a group of girls, who shielded their eyes to look up at us. They called back to him, asking him what he was doing. He told them we were about to leave for Kellner's. Some believed him, some didn't. They shouted again and then left us.

All around us, the lights mounted high on the walls were extinguished. Irving had spent the last year replacing most of the gas mantles with electric lighting, rewiring the stage, the auditorium and the foyer. There seemed always to be builders in the place during the empty days, ladders and scaffolding somewhere in the theatre, piles of workmen's tools, mounds of freshly sawn timber, strangers in paint- and plaster-covered overalls wandering the corridors.

In those days, so soon after our own move and with the death of Caroline so close behind us, it sometimes seemed as though the whole of my life was in a similar state of flux, of uncertainty, the ground always unsettled beneath me, the way ahead never yet properly revealed.

It was then, as the last of these new lights were extinguished, that a man came into the theatre against the tide of others. He wore a heavy coat and a top hat, and carried a cane. I thought at first that it was a member of the audience come back in search of something he had lost.

Beside me, Howson slipped through a curtain, telling me to gather up whatever remained of Coates's old ledgers for him to run his eraser over. He again made it clear to me what an opportunity had been presented to both of us. If Stoker wanted his perfectly upright and balanced columns of figures to worship, then he would have them. He was gone before I could answer him.

I looked down at the man below. He came into the centre of the foyer and stood there, unhurried, unconcerned, looking around him, but searching for nothing, clearly familiar with everything he saw. He spoke softly to several of the men and women moving around him. My next thought was that he had returned to keep a rendezvous with one of the supporting actresses. It was a common enough thing, despite both Irving's and Stoker's warnings. Usually, these men waited outside, along the Strand, where these assignations might be made to appear less obvious, accidental almost, away from the theatre.

One of the costume girls passed him by and he held out his cane to detain her. He spoke to her and she laughed. She was carrying a bundle of clothing, and at a further remark from the man, she laid this bundle on the floor and then picked up a single costume and held it against herself for him to see. He gave her something – money, presumably – and she could hardly contain her surprise. He spoke to her again and she searched around them. Eventually, she looked up to where I still stood in the high shadow and pointed me out to him. She called for me to step forward and confirm my identity.

'Mr Webster?' the man said, his voice barely audible even in the echo of that empty space. He spoke again to the girl and she picked up the rest of the outfits and left him. He then came to the bottom of the main staircase, his eyes fixed on me. 'I wonder if I might have a quick word with you, a moment of your time.' He took off his hat, revealing the short silver hair beneath. 'On a matter of business.'

No one else paid him any attention.

'Might it be possible to join you, or for you to perhaps join me? Elsewhere, perhaps? Nearby?'

I told him to wait where he was, that I would make my way down to him, which I did via a steep, unlit staircase leading directly from the balcony to the rear of the ticket office.

He turned at my appearance there. He drew off one of his gloves and held out his hand to me.

'Forgive this ridiculous hour,' he said. 'I know how things

are. I stood across the road and watched your illustrious employer and his entourage make their grand procession to . . .'

'Kellner's,' I said.

'Perhaps you and I might also . . .'

I told him of the work I had yet to do, of Howson, who was waiting for me.

He took a case from his pocket and slid a card from it.

Its edges felt sharp between my fingers.

'My name is Thomas Bliss,' he said. 'More often than not, people simply call me Bliss.'

I read the card. It contained nothing except the initial and name, followed by a train of further initials, his professional achievements and memberships, none of which meant anything to me.

'I'm a photographer,' I said bluntly.

'I know.' He smiled. 'I was made aware of your appointment here by Victor Coates. Mr Coates is not a happy man. The world has turned against him and he cannot understand why. Mr Coates and I conducted business for quite some considerable time before his . . .' He pursed his lips.

'Stoker accused him of theft,' I said.

'Mr Stoker accuses a great many people of a great many things. He and I are also long acquainted.'

His dismissive tone made me wary.

He caught the flicker of doubt which crossed my face and said, 'Please, it was not my intention to speak out of turn.' He paused. 'Merely to approach you with a business proposition — an opportunity commensurate with your talents, capabilities and opportunities on behalf of a client of mine.'

'Client?'

'I act as a kind of agent and advisor.' He drew circles with his finger as he said this.

'In what way?' I said.

'My clients are mostly engaged in one or other artistic endeavour, like yourself, and I advise them on their markets, their potential for business profit.'

'Are you a dealer?'

He smiled, unperturbed. 'I suppose I am. Of sorts. Yes, a dealer. Or perhaps, shall we say, more of a middle-man, someone with the ability to keep his feet on the ground while all around him his associates, these artistic others, are standing with their heads in the clouds and gazing at the stars above.' He smiled at the phrase. 'Forgive me. Perhaps these things rub off.' He gestured at the room around us.

'And what use might *I* be to you?' I said. 'As a photographer, I mean.'

'A very talented photographer, we are led to believe.'

I might have said *We?* but didn't.

'My client would simply appreciate the opportunity to meet and discuss a proposition with you.'

'On Coates's recommendation?'

He considered this. 'Among others.'

'To take photographs?'

'There are always opportunities in that direction.'

It was my ambition to own my own studio one day.

'I wish you'd say more directly what it is you want,' I told him. A sweeper came close to us, a cascade of litter and dust settling at the bottom of the stairs, and we stepped aside to avoid this.

'My apologies,' Bliss said to the man. He tapped the dirt from his polished shoes and looked down at his feet. 'I daresay there are those who might revere this and call it magic,' he said.

At first I didn't understand him.

'Stardust,' he said, and then laughed, releasing the small tension between us.

'If Stoker could sell it, he would,' I said.

'I'm sure.'

'You know him well?'

'Well enough. I believe I once half-read a few of his half-readable books.' Again he was testing the water. 'You?'

I admitted that I'd read nothing Stoker had so far written.

'Childish stories, mostly,' Bliss said. 'Ghostly goings-on, ghouls, spectres. Stuff to titillate the weak-minded and faint-hearted. Though I imagine he thinks very highly of himself and his talents. I believe he has a brother, a surgeon, destined for equally great things.'

I knew nothing of this and so remained silent.

Bliss indicated for me to hand back the card he'd given me. He took out a pen and wrote on it, 'The French Hotel. Noon.'

'Is that acceptable?' he said. 'I'm sure my client will be happy to reimburse any expense you might incur. And if the appointment interferes with your work here . . .'

'Will you be there?' I asked him.

'Unlikely. Though I am certain that everything I am not currently at liberty to reveal to you will be explained by Marlow himself, should you choose to accept the invitation.'

It was the first time I'd heard the name.

'Is this Marlow your client?' I asked him.

'Perhaps my most valued and long-standing.' There was something close to pride in his voice. 'I've known Marlow for many years now. Believe me, I would not be approaching you – and certainly not with all this . . . all this seeming subterfuge and mystery – if I did not consider you more than capable of fulfilling his needs.'

I slid the card into my pocket. The connection was made.

'I've detained you for too long,' Bliss said. 'Are you expected at Kellner's later?'

'It's been a long day,' I said.

'Of course it has. I imagine first nights are always exhausting. I'll let Marlow know that you are at least willing to meet him and hear what he has to propose. No obligation, of course, as they say.' He smiled again at the phrase.

Above us, his voice muted and distorted by the walls through which it came, I heard Howson calling for me.

'Your colleague,' Bliss said.

'We're making the world a clean, tidy and well-ordered place for Stoker to walk through,' I said. It seemed at once a confidence and a betrayal.

'I'm sure it's what he prefers,' Bliss said.

Howson went on shouting.

Then Bliss said a strange, unprompted thing to me. He said, 'I pride myself on many things, Mr Webster. Chief among which is that I take a great satisfaction in knowing that on only a very few occasions have I actually reduced the value of a thing or of a person with whom I have been professionally involved.'

It was a peculiar thing to say, and to hear, especially so unexpectedly and at such a moment, but I believed that he was sincere when he said it. I also believed that I knew enough of the man in the short time I had been with him to know that he was better served by all these vague and indirect answers and revelations than by any greater directness or precision.

It struck me later, looking back, that I had learned as much about Bliss during that first unexpected encounter as I was ever to truly learn of him afterwards through all the years of our dealings. And I knew then, watching him leave the darkened theatre and listening to Howson's increasingly frustrated shouting above me, that I should also consider myself well-served to be called a 'client' by him.

9

I went into the scullery to find Isobel sitting propped in a chair with her feet resting on the oven door. She dropped them as I entered, but then, having clearly expected the arrival of Alice or Cora, she raised them again, holding them higher and letting her long skirt fall back to reveal her calves and knees. She pushed herself back in her chair until it was resting against the table. She tugged at the collar of her blouse to cool herself.

'It's too warm,' she said. She indicated the glowing coals in the small grate. Another fire, despite the continuing heat.

'Is my wife about?'

'Not so far.'

'Cora?' I knew what a ridiculous question this was at half past seven in the morning.

'Have a guess,' she said. She dropped back to the floor. 'You looking for something to eat?'

I crossed the room to the open doorway. The small rear yard still lay in the cool shadow of the house.

'I seldom see anybody before nine,' she said. 'Suits me.' And in case I might misunderstand this, she added, 'Means I can get on with my work uninterrupted.'

But I understood her perfectly.

'I'll get you something.' She searched the cupboards, putting bread and butter on the table. There was some cold potato mash from the previous evening.

'Just tea,' I told her.

She filled the kettle from a pan on the drainer.

Spilled water made the gas flame waver and change colour.

'You need a proper boiler, not a fire,' she said. 'Last house I was in . . .' She trailed off. 'You going somewhere?' She meant the early start.

'Only the Lyceum,' I said. 'A lot to do.'

She brightened at this mention of the theatre. I'd already heard her stories of how she'd always wanted to become something 'in that line'. 'You could put a word in for me,' she'd suggested, and I'd promised her I would. I waited now for her to ask me if anything had turned up yet. But it was an illusion buoyed by over-expectation and false hope, and we both understood this. It was why she didn't ask, and why I said nothing on the subject myself.

I was going to see Marlow before appearing at the theatre. Summoned by his usual method – a business note informing me that the supplies I'd ordered were ready for collection and 'suggesting' a convenient time. Everything was still drama and subterfuge, but unlike at the start, it was increasingly now also a matter of self-protection.

An engine sounded outside, followed by another, then another.

'The diggers,' I said.

A railway company was cutting a new embankment between the Holloway and Crouch Hill stations. The work had started earlier, in the spring, and the most that anyone could discover from the workmen was that it would last throughout the summer and into the coming autumn and winter. A wall had collapsed, or a tunnel, close by, somewhere; or the line was being re-laid, reconfigured, joined to another. The engines were stoked at six, and then the drills, buckets and steam-hammers started at seven. A watchman stayed with the machinery through the night. I could sometimes see him from my high window, attending to one of the braziers or wandering around the small cabin where he slept.

Isobel put my tea on the table. 'It's a racket,' she said. 'I was talking to some of the labourers. They're pulling down Saint George's, moving the cemetery, to put the new line through.'

It was the first I'd heard of this. My mother was buried in the graveyard. I'd been raised in that part of Holloway – the part Alice now insisted on calling Upper Holloway, having seen the name on a house agent's board. My mother's mother had been buried in a Wednesday grave in the Saint Giles Poor graveyard.

But most of what Isobel repeated was gossip and hearsay, leavened with her own excited speculation, and so I said nothing.

'Sugar?' she said. She spooned it into my cup. 'I'd have brought it up to you if you'd shouted,' she said.

It had been my intention to leave the house without disturbing either Alice or Cora.

The engines settled to their usual, coughing rhythm, their volume lowered. Men called to each other from the embankment at the end of the garden. A month earlier, they'd felled all the trees there in a single afternoon. Fifty mature elms and beeches, perhaps a hundred trees in total, all gone in a prolonged frenzy of sawing and burning.

'You should show them my picture.'

I hadn't been listening to her. She was talking again about her prospects at the theatre.

'Take one and then show it to them.'

'They mostly employ seamstresses,' I said.

'Anybody can sew.'

And anybody can stand in a one-piece tunic holding up a wreath or flit back and forth across the stage in a shoal of silent, silver fish for two hours without even blinking, let alone uttering a single word.

'I'll see,' I told her.

'About what — taking the picture or showing it to them?'

'Both.' It was where the predictable conversation usually petered out.

'The first would be easy enough.'

I heard heavy footsteps above us. Cora.

We both looked at the ceiling, and then Isobel rose from where she sat and started working at the sink.

I drank my tea, guessing that even if Cora had risen, she would soon return to her bed.

Instead, the footsteps resumed and then descended the stairs.

Cora was calling to Isobel before she entered the room. She fell silent upon seeing me there, looking back and forth from where I sat with my tea to Isobel at the sink. I felt even more like a stranger in my own home. I wanted to ask her why she was up so early.

She surprised me by grinning at me. She wore a housecoat over her nightclothes.

'Something to drink,' she said brusquely to Isobel.

Isobel, having caught my eye, curtsied slightly and said, 'Right away, ma'am.'

Cora, missing her tone, looked again at me, and then, deciding something, said, 'Stay where you are.' She pointed at me, pinning me where I sat.

Then she left us and ran back upstairs.

'What now?' Isobel said.

I guessed it would be something connected to the new arrangement between Cora and her mother, but said nothing.

'Probably something she's bought,' Isobel said. 'Something for you to coo over.'

Cora returned breathless. She carried nothing but a newspaper, which she laid on the table before me, pushing my cup to one side. *The Christian Herald*. She sat beside me and made room for herself. She opened the paper to its personal columns and pages of advertisements.

'There,' she said excitedly. 'Read it, read it.' She jabbed her finger at a black-bordered advertisement, two inches square.

Professional Medium. Lady. Available For Personal
Consultations or Small Groups. Guaranteed. Highly Regarded
and Recommended. References to View.

Followed by Alice's name, except now it was actually spelled 'Alicia'.

I read the advert twice. It seemed little different – a little longer, more ostentatious, perhaps – from a hundred others.

'I did it,' Cora said proudly.

'You wrote it?'

'Placed. I *placed* it. The man in the *Herald* offices showed me what they usually put. We sorted the words out together, but *I* placed it and gave him the money.'

She made it sound like a great achievement, something she had worked at long and hard to achieve.

'I even had to decide on the size of the thing. Look, it's the biggest on that half of the page. You tell me if you can see one that looks more impressive. And that border, it draws the eye. You just glance at the whole sheet and see if it doesn't do exactly that.'

Behind her, I saw Isobel cover her mouth with her hand.

'At extra cost, I imagine,' I said.

'That's what Mother said you'd say.'

Mother. The word sounded strange on her lips. Until then, it had only ever been 'Mum', and seldom even that. I saw what changes were taking place, how even this muted pattern was now slowly shifting.

'No, you're right,' I told her. 'It *does* draw the eye. The border works.' It made the advert look like a funeral announcement.

She grinned at this and then went on to explain in detail what subtle messages the various other not-so-subtly capitalized words were intended to suggest.

I could imagine the man selling her all this. A new arrival on his page of hopeful ensnarers, a few more pound and shilling signs filling in the blanks.

Cora cleared her throat and sat upright.

'He said that as a first-time advertiser I needed to make my mark. Make *my* mark. He said that if I was acting as this Alicia's advertising agent, then I needed to do the job properly. He asked me if that was what I was, or if I was just another amateur. He said he assumed I wasn't just a dogsbody. Said he could tell that just by my appearance, by my –' she paused briefly, 'my demeanour. Demeanour. That was the word he used. You can see what he was talking about.' It was why she'd sat upright.

And I could also hear the clerk's laughter and remarks to the roomful of other clerks sitting behind him the instant she had left the counter and gone back out into the street.

'He told me about their *sister* papers, about all the discounts I could take advantage of if I advertised in those, too. Then he apologized to me and said I'd already know about all that side of things. I told him I did. But then I got clever and I told *him* that I was only placing the advertisement with the *Herald* as a kind of trial. I told him Alicia didn't really need to advertise, but that a few vacancies had recently become available. He told me I was doing exactly the right thing.'

And next week, when she went to renew the advertisement, she'd swallow everything deeper. The only reason she hadn't bought more space this time was because Alice wouldn't have trusted her with any more money than she considered absolutely necessary.

I hadn't heard her this excited or enthusiastic since she was a small girl, and I saw then how involved she considered herself to be in this reinvigorated enterprise.

I'd once been with Solomon when a customer arriving to collect a single print had been persuaded by him into buying a dozen others – the original, of course, now being offered free of charge – because, as Solomon insisted, once friends and relatives saw that single print, then they would want one, too. A dozen prints now would represent an investment – half the price of a dozen prints bought individually in the future. The cost to Solomon was almost nothing.

Cora took back the newspaper.

Isobel put a cup in front of her.

'Careful,' Cora said. 'Watch where you're splashing.'

There was no splashing.

Cora folded the precious advert back into its protective shield.

I started to rise, but she put out her hand to me, both of us startled by the gesture.

'That's not all,' she said, but hesitantly this time.

Something occurred to me. 'How will all these new customers contact you?' I said, wondering if I would ever feel comfortable saying 'Alicia'.

'The corner of the advert. A box number. People seal their responses and deposit them in the *Herald* post room. As part of the cost, I – we – get a box. All I need to do then is to keep checking it. The man at the desk – well, boy, really – said twice a day was advisable. Especially if I got the *volume* of response I deserved.'

The *Herald*'s offices were in Copenhagen Street, which I passed most days on my way to the Lyceum.

'I could call in for you,' I suggested.

'You?'

'On my way to the theatre. It makes sense.'

She looked at me as though I'd said something critical of her, something to deliberately undermine her enthusiasm.

'And then read everything all those poor desperate people wrote?' she said.

It hadn't been my intention in making the offer. 'Of course not. All I—'

'Because you don't think me responsible enough to make my own collections?'

I said nothing, unhappy at being accused like this in front of Isobel.

'He only offered,' Isobel said to her.

'No one's talking to you,' Cora said without looking at her. 'Besides, it's none of your business, none whatsoever. Unless, of course, I find myself otherwise engaged and I'm forced to send someone in my place.' She smiled at the thought of exercising this new power.

'So, what's the boy at the desk like?' I asked her, already well aware of the profitable flattery he had employed on my gullible daughter.

The smile fell from Cora's face.

'You said there was more,' I said quickly.

'There is. But I'm not sure now.'

'Not sure of what?'

'Of showing you.'

'More advertising?'

She took a small package from her pocket and put it on the newspaper.

Business cards.

'There's five hundred of them,' she said, her voice lower. 'There was a printer's next door to the *Herald*'s offices.'

'And the clerk at the desk recommended them?'

'Clerk? Advertising manager. You could take some in to the theatre.'

I leaned over her shoulder to look more closely at the cards.

She shielded them briefly with her cupped palms and then withdrew. She picked one up and gave it to Isobel. 'Here – you won't get one any other way. I suppose you can read that much.'

'You want *me* to tout for business for you?' Isobel said.

I almost laughed at the barely veiled insult.

'You? Who could *you* possibly know who could afford Moth— Alicia's talents?' She turned back to me and pursed her lips. 'Will you take some? To the theatre?'

I almost said, 'But she's my *wife*.'

My second of hesitation was too long, and Cora said, 'What, you think you'll look – what? – ridiculous in front of all your high and mighty employers? These are professional calling cards. Best quality. Embossed. Run your finger over the printing if you don't believe me. You can feel it. It's all a question of presenting the right impression to the world, setting the right tone from the very beginning.'

I wondered who she was repeating now.

'What, you'd rather I just put a grubby postcard in a seedy shop window somewhere and then sat back and waited, grateful for the few pounds that *that* might bring in?'

'Of course not,' I said. 'You've shown great – ' I struggled for the right word, 'resourcefulness.' It was high praise; none of those others had so far used the word. Another jewel in her flimsy crown.

'You're right,' she said She counted out twenty of the cards and put them in my hand.

'Mostly everybody I know has their palm read regular,' Isobel said. 'Down Camden and round the stations.' She ran her finger over the printing on the card Cora had given her.

'Exactly,' Cora said. 'And this is a different thing entirely.'

I saw in her self-satisfied smile how swiftly and how far this strange partnership had already moved beyond even my smallest intervention. I wondered if Alice shared her daughter's new-found confidence; and I wondered, too, at the strange and exact nature of Cora's new self-belief. It was something I had never before seen in her. Excepting, of course, her belief that everything she wanted, she deserved to be given; or her belief that the world moved around her, and that she was under no real obligation to make her own hard-earned place or way within it.

She put the rest of the cards back in their box and then slid this into her pocket. Again, everything safely hidden away and unassailable.

Isobel, I noticed, took almost as much care in pocketing the card she held.

I had also been with Solomon when a woman had arrived to collect the single print he had made of her six-month-old daughter, her first child, and when, instead of the extra prints, he had sold her an elaborate frame in which to mount the photograph. The price he quoted was a small fortune to the woman, but she was persuaded by him and accepted his offer of mounting the picture there and then, promising to return weekly with payments.

When she'd gone, clutching the frame as though it were the child itself, I'd teased him, asking him why he hadn't pushed for an even easier profit by offering the woman the usual multiple prints. I had been unprepared for the solemnity of his answer.

'Because she shouldn't be having pictures taken of a child so young,' he'd said. 'It's not a good thing, not a good omen. Perhaps because soon it's all she'll have of the child.' He stared at the door through which the woman had gone, as though he might see the future into which she and her precious photograph were already walking.

I'd wanted to tell him he was wrong, but knew that he

wasn't, and that even if I'd attempted it, the words would have dried in my mouth.

Alice still had in her dresser the small box of soil from Caroline's grave, presented to her by the rector who attended the burial, and given, he said, to ward off evil, as though such a thing were possible, as though that evil had yet to come, as though it had not already flung the pair of us to the ground and kept our tear-soaked faces pushed firmly into the dirt there.

10

'I thought I saw you a few days ago,' I said to Pearl.

She paused briefly in unfastening her jacket. 'Oh?'

'On Regent Street. I was passing on a bus. I looked down and there you were.'

'It's perfectly possible,' she said. She concentrated on tucking loose hairs behind her ears.

'There were two of you.'

'Two?'

'You and another woman.'

'I imagine there were hundreds of other women.'

'I mean you appeared to be together.'

'Perhaps it wasn't even me.' She smiled at me.

Marlow came and stood beside her, holding the shoulders of the jacket as she slid her arms free. 'Perhaps what wasn't you?' he said. I knew then both that he'd overheard our conversation and that it was the reason for this casual intervention.

Pearl leaned closer to one of the full-length pier mirrors, straightening her collar. 'Mr Webster imagines he saw me,' she said to Marlow, and I again heard how perfectly attuned the two of them were.

'In one of his dreams, perhaps?' Marlow said, and laughed.

He turned to me, the laughter stopping on a beat. 'You saw her in your dreams? Were you in a long queue of others?' More laughter. He knew precisely how highly I regarded her, and I resented this mockery. I resisted the urge to remark on how he himself used this regard and the respect of others for Pearl in his own dealings with them. She, too, I also well understood by then, cultivated carefully her role as his intermediary. If, as the saying went, Marlow was the iron fist, then she was certainly his velvet glove. Her attributes may have been her own — her favours, her kindnesses, her small encouragements — but her shape was always that of the man standing immediately behind her.

She slapped his arm. 'On Regent Street,' she said. And again it was a signal flashed between them.

Marlow feigned disappointment. 'Hardly worth remarking on, I wouldn't have thought,' he said to me.

'No,' I conceded, and I knew not to persist.

He kissed Pearl on both cheeks and then tilted her face to one of the dim lights, first one way, then the other. She was perfectly happy to acquiesce in this; in fact she took pleasure in it. Marlow turned her face and then raised and lowered her chin, as though searching for the perfect position from which to look at her so closely. Pearl waited unblinking as he did this. When he was finished, he kissed her again, this time fully on the lips. It was another signal to me.

Released by him, Pearl came closer to me. 'You should have called out to me,' she said. 'Or perhaps you did. And whoever you'd mistaken for me didn't answer you.'

'I didn't call,' I said.

This uncomfortable conversation was ended by Marlow putting his arm firmly round my shoulders, turning me away from her, and saying, 'I understand from Bliss that you may be entertaining certain doubts.'

My first response was to deny what he'd suggested. I'd said little to Bliss, and I'd certainly given him no true indication of Stoker's veiled threats concerning the missing costumes. I wasn't even clear in my own mind what Stoker had intended by his remarks, so how on earth could Bliss have known about what might or might not have been said without having some other connection to the man, perhaps even directly to Stoker himself?

'Would "reservations" be more accurate?' Marlow said. He was again laughing at me. His grip on my shoulders loosened, but only slightly. He was plucking the words like petals from a flower, each one discarded on the breath that gave it life.

'About what?' I said. It was a clumsy, revealing answer, and he countered it by shaking his head slightly and saying nothing.

'I'm merely repeating what Bliss himself said, suggested, implied,' he said eventually.

'What *did* he say?'

'Please, don't concern yourself. We all harbour doubts or uncertainties of one kind or another at times. We're all men of the world – you, Bliss, myself . . .'

I tensed against hearing him add Stoker's name.

'We understand how these things work.'

What things? I wanted to say.

He led me a couple of paces away from Pearl, who watched us go.

We now faced the working part of his studio, where a man and a woman were being positioned in front of his array of fixed cameras.

He watched them for a moment before leading me closer.

'Is Bliss here?' I asked him. 'Perhaps he could explain more fully.'

'Not even in the country,' he said. 'Paris. It's one of our better markets. They pretend to be so brave, so liberated and advanced, but they are still so obsessed with protocol, propriety, decency, with their — ' he paused, 'with their boundaries.' He turned from me to call to the woman, who was now half kneeling on a chaise-longue. He told her that she was looking beautiful, that her skin was shining beneath the lights then being positioned above her. The woman, clearly one of his regular models, responded to this easy flattery with little more than a glance and a dismissive flick of her hand.

Marlow laughed at this. He worked best with these equals, all these others who better understood the controlling balance of things and the true nature of the power he held and exercised over them.

He directed me towards a fire, recently lit and burning high, casting its flickering shapes over the boards in front of it. Gusts of smoke occasionally billowed over the tiled mantel, rising and thinning before being sucked back down by the growing heat of the blaze itself. It was seldom warm in the studio, and Marlow was forever conscious, he said, of the effect of the cold air on his gold and gelatine plates.

He indicated the larger of two chairs beside the hearth and then sat opposite me.

'I value your contribution,' he said to me. He sounded sincere, conciliatory almost. 'But you, too, must surely be aware of the unique nature of your position. Just as Coates was before you. It's simply that if there *was* anything troubling you, then I would appreciate knowing. Perhaps I might be in a position to help.' He shrugged and held up his palms. '*Has* something been said – at the theatre, for instance?' He was backtracking, hoping for an honest answer, something to perhaps confirm Bliss's own suspicions or assumptions.

'Not to me,' I said. 'Nothing directly.'

'But you believe someone may be – shall we say "aware" – of what you might, on my behalf – on both our behalves – be doing there?' It seemed a threat and consolation, warning and reassurance all in one. And whatever it was, it was another prompt to me to consider all the possible consequences of everything I was engaged in. My half lie of a moment earlier had been to a much lesser and considerably less specific charge.

'Stoker is always prodding and poking,' I finally conceded. 'Wanting to know everything that's happening.'

He seemed relieved by my answer. 'Stoker's a man apart,' he said, gesturing. 'His sails are always full, his ropes always taut. You leave Stoker to me. Perfectionists see only imperfection.'

'I don't understand you,' I told him.

'Yes, you do. Perhaps what I'm really saying is that some men are much easier to understand than others.'

And once again, I knew by the way he said this not to persist in the matter.

'Believe me, you are ever a valuable commodity to me, Charles. If there *were* any genuine concerns on your part, then I should do my utmost to lay them to rest.'

This formality was as unsettling to me as everything that lay beneath it.

He then called to a man standing beside the cameras to fetch us a drink. The man left the room and returned with a silver tray, a bottle and two glasses. He put this beside Marlow. Marlow picked up the bottle and held it to his cheek, flinching at its coldness.

'Alsace,' he said to me, 'Sylvaner,' and then poured me a glass, waiting until I'd tasted it and nodded my approval before filling a glass for himself. He slid the tray away from the heat of the fire.

'I understand Henry has another great success on his hands,' he said.

'Everything he touches . . .' I said, and he laughed.

'I once took a series of photographs entitled "The Daughters of Midas" for which Pearl and I devised a golden sheath – you get my meaning. Hard to suggest completely, of course, but the attempt was much appreciated. A golden prick. All positions. She made it of painted paste, twice life-size. Even then the poor man had difficulty keeping it and himself upright. Midas and his maidens. A dozen *poses plastiques*, a further selection for the aficionados. Pearl even suggested painting one of the women. "Everything touched" and all that. We tried, but it didn't work. She merely looked as though she'd been fished out of the Thames. Every orifice. We sold five hundred sets. All on a subscription basis. I could have sold twice the number. I remember the women complained of the painted paste chafing them. Is it money?'

I was caught off guard by this sudden turn, still struggling to understand why he had just told me all this, and especially Pearl's part in it.

'What?'

'Money. Your concern.' He looked across the rim of his glass at me.

'No. You're more than generous,' I said. It was the truth,

but perhaps not what he wanted to hear. Perhaps a greedy man was another of those easily understood men. He had given me more each year I'd known him, and with a bonus as each New Year approached, and Bliss, presumably, tallied up his client's columns of profit and greater profit.

'I appreciate your honesty,' he said, though it was hardly that, just another small part of whatever was being played out between us. 'As you can see . . .' He motioned to a nearby table, upon which photographs were arranged in lines, and I rose slightly in my seat to look at these. I recognized some of the costumes, some of the women displaying them. Others I did not recognize. Perhaps this was his purpose in pointing them out to me. I knew he employed men similar to myself in other theatres and music halls, but I had little true idea of the number of these. The last thing he would allow, I imagined, would be for each of us to learn of the others' existence.

'You're a reliable associate,' he said. He said it the way he'd commented on the woman's skin. 'Will you keep me informed?'

'About . . . ?'

'Stoker. Anything that concerns you at the theatre. Anything that might . . .'

'Of course,' I said, more convinced than ever that either Marlow himself, or, more likely, Bliss on his behalf, had some other, direct association with Stoker.

He looked away from me back to the man and the woman beneath the lights. Pearl was now applying colour to the woman's lips and nipples. The man waited with only a towel around his waist. He was athletic and muscular, with no spare flesh on him. I imagined how he would photograph.

'More,' Marlow called to Pearl, and she complied.

The woman leaned back where she now lay, her large breasts falling beneath her arms. Pearl handled them, reshaping them, positioning them together as she applied more colour.

'Nature by unnatural means,' Marlow said to me. He refilled my empty glass.

It was even rumoured that he had his contacts in Buckingham Palace and other royal residences, from which clothing and other pieces were occasionally borrowed.

'I hope you don't mind my suggesting all this to you,' he said. 'I don't mean to place any further doubt in your mind.' He paused. 'It's just that when Bliss mentioned the matter to me, I couldn't help but concur with him. If you *ever* feared you were in danger of being exposed, then arrangements can easily be made. Everything can stop – temporarily, permanently – and everything can be back in its right and proper place in readiness for one of Stoker's tally-making rounds. I promise you, it can be done. Twelve hours' notice, less.'

Whereupon I would be discarded and replaced, after which I would be discredited and disgraced.

'Enough,' he called to Pearl.

The woman rose from where she lay and posed for Marlow. It was a routine and she was well rehearsed in it. She turned her back to him and leaned over, spreading her legs and then contorting herself until her face appeared.

'Yes, very good,' he called to her.

The woman laughed.

'She used to work in a circus,' Marlow said. 'I found her in Astley's Amphitheatre. Know it?'

I shook my head.

'Lambeth. A gaudy hall. Full of working girls and inverts.

Amphitheatre — what a name. It sounds barbaric. The management employed a dozen midgets, all of whom earned more from me than their full-time employers. "Midget Marvels", "Snow White?", "Delights In Miniature".' He laughed at the memory.

Then it was the turn of the man to reveal himself to Marlow. He drew off the towel he wore and turned to face us, standing with his legs apart. He moved his hips slightly to make his member swing back and forth.

'Completely loose?' Marlow called to him. There was no embarrassment in his voice.

The man put up his thumb.

'Maltese,' Marlow said to me. 'The dark skin works well. Look at him against the woman. Never any guessing where one ends and the other begins. Even darker when his blood's up.'

'I can imagine,' I said.

'Give me a little . . .' Marlow called to the man, and the man stroked his member until it stiffened slightly and rose clear of his groin. Even at that distance I could see its full length. His pubic hairs had been shaved around its base. He cupped his balls in his hand.

Marlow watched all this closely.

Neither Pearl nor the woman paid the man any attention.

'Fine,' Marlow called to him.

And the man relaxed his grip and his member immediately lowered.

'I paid for him to come here from Valetta. Him and his two brothers, all of them shaving by thirteen. Guess how old he is.'

'Twenty-five?' I said.

'Sixteen. Speaks about fifty words of English, and most of those you wouldn't utter in decent society.'

It occurred to me only then that I was still sitting with him because he hadn't been satisfied with my answers.

The man who had brought our drinks went to the array of cameras, checked them and slid in their plates. I knew from having watched Marlow work in the past that he personally undertook only a small part of what needed to be done. He called these others his 'technicians'. Often, he said, all that he needed to contribute to the proceedings was his name. I was never certain if this was meant as a joke or a boast, both or neither.

The naked man and woman returned to the sofa beneath the lights. Pearl brought out a diaphanous costume for the woman, and I recognized it immediately – a nereid from *Helen of Troy* – and knew just as immediately that its choice tonight had not been coincidental.

'Imagine Stoker's face if he could see it now,' Marlow said to me.

But my amusement at the suggestion was genuine and I laughed with him.

Pearl helped the woman into the flimsy material.

'A few pictures of her in growing disarray, and then our little Maltese goat appears on the scene,' Marlow said.

I looked and saw that the man was again erect, and that he was grinning broadly as he watched Pearl and the woman together.

'You wonder which excites him the most,' Marlow said, meaning Pearl or the near-naked woman.

Before I could answer him, he said, 'Mind, last week, it was one of his *brothers* Pearl was dressing for him. From goat to lively goatherd. I imagine it gets very lonely up in those Maltese mountains night after night with no women for company.' He turned to me and smiled. '*Are* there mountains in Malta?'

'I imagine so,' I said.

'Me, too. I imagine so, too.'

His technician took the first of the poses, clearing the low stage, moving from camera to camera, checking only briefly before exposing the plates. Another man followed close behind and removed these, inserting new ones.

'Clumsy,' Marlow said, mostly to himself. 'Don't you agree? Photographer to photographer, that is. But the fixed plates still give me the best results.'

'Repeat printing quality,' I said.

'Exactly. That's it, exactly. I imagine you know considerably more about the mechanical side of these things than I do.'

This was hardly likely to be the case – though I might briefly savour something of the *intent* of the remark – and so I denied this.

'Still,' he said, 'I appreciate your understanding. All this. All anyone else ever wants to do is to pore over the finished product.' He called for the boy to position himself with the woman. Pearl applied more colour to the woman's cheeks as he approached them.

The woman leaned forward and took the boy's member in her hand. The boy stood posed with his hands on his buttocks, half turned from the camera.

Marlow called for him to face it.

'I have to tell him every time.' He then motioned with his hands. 'Pearl . . .'

Pearl went to the boy and turned him.

The woman, who was now sitting in front of the boy, drew back his foreskin to reveal the even darker flesh beneath. She held the palm of her hand behind the organ. Leaning further forward, she put the bulbous end to her dark, pursed lips.

'Two external,' Marlow called to the man operating the cameras. 'Sequence,' he said to me. 'The event in all its essentials. Anticipation, titillation, fulfilment. Does that sound tired?'

I shrugged.

'Clichéd, then? I hear myself repeating myself more and more often.' He turned away from the woman and the boy. 'He sends most of what I pay him back home to Valetta, to his good Catholic mother. Every time he arrives he asks me how much I'm giving him, and then he goes through the same tedious pantomime of telling me what a good and dutiful son he is.'

I glanced at the boy, his organ now in the woman's mouth, her hands clasping his buttocks, her lips formed in a perfect circle against the dark skin and stiffening flesh. The boy had moved his hands to his hips. He was grinning – arrogant almost – his eyes wide and watching the top of the woman's head. They were perfectly still, though their motions, the gentle rocking and swaying, drawing and pulling were easy to imagine, and I watched them for a moment before realizing how closely Marlow was now watching me.

'Go closer,' he suggested to me.

I shook my head at the offer.

'How is Mrs Webster, Alice?' he said then. It was another calculated and carefully timed remark, another sudden turn, and this time its intention made me angry. But before I could respond to him, he said, 'My apologies,' leaving me wondering if he had indeed made a mistake, a remark he regretted.

'You talk about "concerns",' I said.

'Oh?'

'Alice. *That*'s what concerns me at present.'

Now it was his turn to be caught off guard and he waited for me to go on.

I fished in my pocket for the cards I still carried. I had no intention of allowing anyone at the Lyceum to see them. I gave him one.

'Alicia? Alice?'

'She considers it more professional, a distinction,' I said.

'And is she truly in possession of these . . . powers?'

'She prefers "gift".'

'Is she in possession of this gift? Truly?'

I had expected mockery bordering on scorn, but instead he seemed genuinely interested, intrigued almost.

'She's been doing it for a long time. She and my daughter are setting up this new enterprise between them.'

He turned the card in his fingers. 'I'm all in favour of enterprise. Will they succeed?'

'My daughter believes so.'

'And Alice, Alicia?'

'I imagine so.'

'May I keep this?'

My instinct was to say no. 'Of course,' I said. 'It's a business card.' I started to explain to him about the *Christian Herald* and their post boxes.

'Oh, Bliss knows all about them,' he said. 'He knows somebody on every paper in the city. Sometimes it's the owner – Lord this or that – and sometimes it's the man standing in the street making farthings selling the things. That's *his* gift, see – Bliss's – knowing exactly *who* to know, and knowing how and when to cultivate all these associations, these connections.'

And when to sever them?

At least I would be able to tell Cora that I'd started handing the cards out to my business associates.

'My mother . . .' Marlow said, and then hesitated.

I expected to hear him say that she attended séances.

'She, too, imagined she possessed such a gift.' He drained his own glass and refilled it. 'She never acted upon it, of course, but to her dying day she was convinced of her own psychic powers.'

Of course.

'And you?' he said.

I didn't understand him.

'Are *you* convinced she possesses such powers, such a gift?' He watched me closely as I considered my answer.

'How can I doubt her?' I said.

'I know exactly what you mean,' he said. 'I loved my mother and so I indulged her. She even visited mediums and came away dismissing them as frauds.'

Alice had done the same.

'Alice?' he said.

'She has conviction,' I said, knowing how inadequate this sounded.

We were both distracted by a call from the man taking the photographs. Pearl again stood beside the woman. The boy waited to one side, his organ flaccid. He repeatedly ran his thumb and forefinger along its hanging length.

Marlow looked to Pearl, who shook her head at him.

'How long?' he called.

Pearl calculated her answer. 'Twenty minutes?'

'He's no better than one of his rampant goats,' Marlow said to me. Perhaps he even believed the fiction of the boy being a goatherd.

Beside Pearl, the woman on the couch wiped her face and breasts with a cloth. The costume was by then around her broad thighs, revealing everything she chose not to hide of herself. She said something to the boy and he laughed at her.

'Are you in any way concerned for your wife?' Marlow said to me, yet another turn, drawing me away from this small missed drama and back to him.

'I'm not sure,' I admitted. 'Concerned, perhaps, that she'll fail, make a fool of herself, lose money.'

'And that people like my mother might turn up?'

'I just don't want her to get hurt. Cora's involvement is different. It's Alice who has the most to lose.'

'Beginning with her own belief in herself?'

'It matters to her,' I said.

'Even though you once imagined – hoped, perhaps – that it would all one day end?'

'I suppose so.'

'Then I understand you perfectly,' he said. 'I suppose you too will have your part to play in the enterprise?'

I told him about the cards, my so-called contacts.

'A week before she died, my mother told me that she knew to the hour when that would be. Did you know that William Blake lived not a hundred feet from where we're sitting now? Lived and died. Our greatest mystic.'

I shook my head.

'He saw the angels that came to gather him up to Heaven.

They stood around his bed, waiting for him, and he held conversations with them. In front of everyone else who was there. Flesh and blood versus angels. Imagine that.'

I wondered if some greater, more pertinent point were being made, but could not discern it.

'I wish her success,' he said. 'Your wife.' And he held my gaze for a moment before turning back to Pearl, who signalled to him that the models were ready.

The boy was close to the woman, his erection again formed and rising to his hairless belly. The woman was on the sofa, lying on her stomach, her legs being positioned by Pearl, one knee on the floor, the other beneath her. Pearl rearranged the costume over her waist, drawing it up her back to fully reveal her buttocks and what lay between. The woman's face was hidden by the cushion she held.

At Marlow's signal, Pearl beckoned the boy forward, and he came.

11

As usual – more to the point, as *intended* – it was possible to hear Irving coming long before he actually appeared. Everything remained a performance, a drama, an arrival, a small explosion and a departure. It was impossible to imagine the man sitting alone, without his body bent to some intense pose, his face down, his forehead resting on his fist, a look of either pained anguish or utter surprise on his face.

'Transpontine tawdriness,' I heard him shout.

The men shifting scenery pushed past me along the narrow corridor.

'South of the river,' Jimmy Allen said to me. '"Transpontine".'

South of the river. Another country entirely, filled with the heathens and clowns of the music halls and palaces of variety, Moorish temples, cheap titillation, laughter at any price and blinding illuminations.

The scenery men complained and swore at the awkwardness of their work, walking sideways and backwards to manoeuvre the flats towards the side exit and the waiting carters.

'When in Rome . . .' I said to Jimmy Allen, who shrugged and returned to the newspaper he was reading.

'Completely unnecessary, not in the slightest necessary,' Irving shouted.

The scene-shifters stopped moving, put down their loads and waited with their backs to the wall. The approach of royalty.

'You may *consider* it necessary, but it isn't. Absolutely not.' Irving's voice echoed in the narrow space, sharpened and focussed against the bare walls and floor.

I braced myself against his appearance, only to be caught off guard by the arrival of Howson ahead of him, performing a kind of shuffling back- and side-step immediately in front of Irving.

'Are you noting all this down, Mr Howson?' Irving said to him.

Howson rapped the notebook he carried.

These rapidly moving delegations were a common occurrence. Irving beating the bounds of his domain, making his presence known in that small, close kingdom over which he exercised complete and irresistible control.

Howson saw me in the corridor and we shared a quick, sympathetic glance. He raised his eyes to the ceiling.

'Ah, Jimmy, Jimmy,' Irving called to Jimmy Allen. 'Please, don't get up. Heart good to see you. I can't remember when last . . .'

'Same time last week,' Jimmy Allen said to him.

Irving reached out his hand, clasping Jimmy Allen's in both his own.

'You're a funny man, Jimmy, a funny man. I swear I'd put you *on* the stage were you ever to consider it.'

'Right,' Jimmy Allen said. It was something Irving always said.

I saw that Howson was again watching me, and seeing that he had my attention, he motioned surreptitiously over his shoulder. And at that same instant, Stoker appeared, accompanied by one of the female dressers. The woman was wide and slow, panting with even that small exertion. I saw that Stoker resented being held up by her, anxious to regain his rightful position by Irving's side.

'If we might pause for a moment,' he called to Irving. 'Mrs Craven.' He motioned to the woman.

Irving stopped and turned.

'My dear lady, of course. Jimmy, another seat?'

Jimmy Allen took the woman a stool.

Irving looked more closely at the dismantled scenery amid which he now stood. 'Is this moving?'

'To Southall,' I told him.

'Not required here?'

'Problems between sets,' Jimmy Allen said, helping Mrs Craven to lower her bulk on to the stool. 'Not enough room. We're clearing backstage. They need room to bring the new flats in and get the side-drops up.'

'Are you sure?' Irving said. 'Absolutely certain? It seems a lot of effort and expense for the few feet gained.'

'Absolutely,' Jimmy Allen told him, as unassailable in his own way as Irving was in his.

'Then let it be done,' Irving announced. 'Let work proceed.' He waved his hand in a flourish.

It was being done, I thought. *Until you arrived.*

'Here in a supervisory capacity, Jimmy?'

'Something of that nature.'

Irving looked at me. 'Mr Webster,' he said. He seemed uncertain of what I might be doing there.

I nodded my acknowledgement.

'Are we delaying you?' Stoker called to me. He seemed somehow unsettled by my unexpected presence there, by my sudden closeness to Irving.

Irving thought for a moment, his hand to his mouth. 'Of course,' he said. 'Webster.' Turning to Stoker, he said, 'Man to whom you were desirous of speaking.'

I almost laughed at the words.

Still in front of Stoker, Howson held my gaze.

'Oh?' I said, looking directly at Stoker.

'Perhaps at a time more convenient,' Stoker said. He came away from Mrs Craven, clearly relieved to have finally detached himself from the woman.

'Nonsense,' Irving told him. 'Here is the man, here you are. Seize the moment.' He went to the edge of the stage and looked out over the dark auditorium, seeing there only the full house of the coming evening.

Stoker came to me, pushing Howson ahead of him. 'I believe there are some irregularities,' he said.

'In the accounts?' *The accounts are your concern, not mine.* I felt inexplicably brave, guessing he would say nothing to alarm Irving.

'In accounting for certain costumes,' he said. The same complaint, the same vague accusation bordering on threat that Jimmy Allen had delivered to me a week earlier.

Conscious that he was watching for my response, I feigned a lack of concern. Only three days had passed since my conversation with Marlow, and I could not ignore the possibility that some connection existed between these two events.

'What have you lost?' I asked him. I wondered what part

the panting Mrs Craven was now playing in all this, what substance she might add to his threats.

'I'd prefer to use the term "misplaced",' he said.

'Nearer the truth, probably,' I said, knowing what a goad this would be to him.

'Quite,' he said. Thrust, parry, thrust. 'Mrs Craven informs me you sent a variety of outfits directly from your . . . your studio – ' he took pleasure in adding a cold edge to the word, 'to Southall. *Midsummer Night*. Likewise the juvenile maid costumes from *Pity*.'

I closed my eyes for a moment. 'The former went down there about two months ago,' I said. 'The latter a week or ten days afterwards. I'm sure if you checked their records . . .' *Stay in that same vague territory*, I told myself. Leeway, slack ropes, endlessly changing configurations and moving shadows around the same few brightly lit spaces.

'Mrs Craven says nearer four months for the *Dream* outfits, and at least a month after that for the others. It seems repairs were undertaken. Here *and* there.'

'I daresay she might be right,' I said, smiling coldly at the woman. I wished Howson would stop looking at me like he did. I sensed Jimmy Allen taking an interest in what was being said.

'I have seven, possibly eight outfits I cannot account for,' Stoker said.

Out of hundreds. I shrugged. 'Ask again at the depot. Once I've photographed them, I have little idea what happens to them.'

Did Stoker smile to himself at the remark? 'But *enough* of an idea to know whether or not they've been put into storage once you've finished with your picture-taking?'

'My photographs.'

Another slight flaring of his nose? 'Of course. Your photographs. So all you can confirm with any certainty is that you had the costumes in your studio and that then you sent them to Southall?'

'As instructed,' I said quickly.

'So if—'

'Someone delivers them to me,' I said. 'And then later, someone else comes and takes them away. I'm given instructions – usually by you or Henry – and I respond to those instructions.' I glanced to where Irving still stood, hoping to draw him into the discussion, knowing that his first instinct would be to run his calming hand over what was happening. 'Someone delivers them, and then someone else arrives to take them away. Sometimes the costumes come straight from the dressing rooms, sometimes on racks, sometimes wrapped in tissue. Costumes, bits and pieces, everything.' Debris cast into the slowly rising wind.

'Bits and pieces?' Stoker said.

'Scarves, shawls, stockings, gloves, the occasional piece of headwear, that kind of thing. I might even still have some of the accompanying invoices and instructions if you want me to look.' I resisted saying 'Again'. 'Some in your hand, some in Henry's.'

'Name in vain?' Irving shouted to us without turning.

'Nothing of consequence,' Stoker immediately called back to him, again giving away a great deal.

Whatever he was now implying, or hoping to accuse me of, he was clearly not yet sure enough of his ground to involve Irving in whatever might ensue.

'So you may still have those lists?' Stoker said, his voice lower.

'Possibly. Mostly they accompany the outfits to Southall so that they can be checked again at that end. I only use them as a guide so that I might properly attend to what's asked of me.' I let my own voice rise by that same clear note.

'But the lists might still, in fact, be there – in Southall?'

'The costumes?'

'The lists.' He said it as though clinching a hard-won victory.

At the edge of the stage, Irving began tapping his foot. He wanted to move on, for Stoker to bring whatever was happening here to an end and to accompany him.

Stoker looked back to Mrs Craven, who was now using her hand as a fan. Her face was slick with sweat.

'You don't think *she's* misplaced them, do you?' I said in a stage whisper loud enough for the woman to hear.

'Here,' she shouted. 'I heard that.'

'Calm yourself, Mrs Craven,' Stoker said to her.

I smiled at Howson and he tried to return the gesture.

Stoker missed this, catching only my concerned look back to him.

'What?' he said.

'No one spoke,' I said.

He tapped Howson on the shoulder and Howson jumped. 'Show Webster your own list.'

Howson took a sheet from his pocket, unfolded it and gave it to me.

I read it, recognizing some of the outfits still at Golden Square. Others I knew for certain had been returned by Marlow to Southall. I pursed my lips and shook my head as I looked slowly from the top to the bottom of the single sheet.

'Like I said, I'd need to see the lists still at Southall,' I said. 'I don't order the stuff to be delivered there myself. I merely follow instructions.'

Stoker tutted audibly at this. If Mrs Craven's dates were correct, then I guessed that some of the unreturned costumes would have been with Marlow for almost two months now. He seldom kept them for more than a week or two, and in the past he had always been quick to return pieces upon my request.

'Do you *need* the lost – misplaced – articles?' I said. 'I'm going down to Southall soon – tomorrow, perhaps, day after at the latest. I could look around for you.' I tried to sound magnanimous; I knew Mrs Craven never ventured that far, that her own small fiefdom of the dressing and sewing rooms was smaller and even more tightly bounded than Irving's own. 'Perhaps Mrs Craven could accompany me. If she has a clear idea of what's supposedly missing . . .'

Stoker saw immediately that he was backed into a corner and he pretended to think about what I'd suggested. There was little chance of him calling my bluff. We both understood this, and in the brief respite between us, we made our calculations accordingly.

'You do accept,' I said to him, my tone now almost conciliatory, 'that there would be considerably less confusion if you didn't insist on such a close and complete record being kept?' It was another of the man's projects to compile a so-called workbook for every production: facts, figures, accounting; actors, sets, costumes, props; past histories, dates, places, further projections and possibilities. One production, one book containing everything that might ever need to be known about it for restaging or taking on tour: pictures, lists, plans, places, people, profits, profits, profits.

Stoker paused to consider what I'd just said. He knew better than any of us how the Lyceum's chain of command worked, how these Chinese whispers filtered down from the light into the dark, from centre-stage back, and from there into the recesses of the dressing rooms and all those other locked, unvisited, lost corners of the place.

I wished Howson would turn back to him and address him directly, instead of keeping his anxious gaze on me.

'Is this by nature of a warning?' I said to Stoker.

'A warning? To whom?'

'To all of us,' I said. 'Yourself included, perhaps. To devise a better, more *efficient* and accountable manner of keeping a proper tally.' I knew the word would pierce him.

'I believe efficiency—' he began.

'Perhaps a way of confirming the handing over of responsibility,' I said. It was the last thing I wanted; without these gaps and missing links in the chain, I would have no arrangement with Marlow. I wondered if I were brave enough to say to Stoker that he shouldn't blame himself for whatever failures or lapses of procedure he was trying to press firmly into my hands.

'Give me back your list,' I said to Howson.

Howson started to do this, but then Stoker put a hand on his arm.

'I don't think that will be necessary,' he said. 'I shall need to keep some record for myself for when the misplaced items finally reappear. You're probably right – someone at the depot has wheeled a rail into the wrong position, pushed a case too far back.' His tone made it clear to me that he did not believe this.

'Perhaps,' I said. 'I've certainly not seen anyone walking the streets of Southall dressed as Bottom or King Lear.'

Howson laughed at this, stopping abruptly.

'*Do* you believe someone might try to steal them?' I said to Stoker. I waited for his answer.

In three years, everything I had loaned to Marlow had been either collected or delivered and then returned without fail. Seldom had outfits been damaged by him, and whenever I had spotted any damage, he had always been quick to apologize and to pay for the necessary repairs. I had occasionally taken the extra money from him and then pocketed it. Making repairs would only attract attention. And besides, the costumes were damaged in the course of their use, and all regular repairs were marked down to wear and tear. And both Stoker and Mrs Craven knew this as well as any of us.

'Were any of the costumes damaged, do you think?' I asked him.

'Damaged in what way?'

I shrugged. 'I mean, has Mrs Craven put them to one side to perform her own small miracles?' Meaning had they been taken from the racks and then forgotten or misplaced upon their return from either her or the countless women she employed on Irving's behalf. So far I had managed to point a wavering finger of blame in every possible direction.

'It's possible,' Howson said unexpectedly, surprising both Stoker and myself.

'Of course it is,' Stoker said absently, meaning *When I want your worthless opinion, then I'll ask for it.*

'Sorry,' Howson said. 'I only meant—' He fell silent, caught between the two of us. I started to wish he'd say more.

'Perhaps a possibility you might consider?' I said to Stoker. His own pointing finger was by then completely withdrawn. The whole encounter had taken less than ten minutes.

I waited for him to speak. If he took a step back now, then I would take a step towards him.

'*Abraham.*' The name sounded like a shot in the silence. Irving turned to look at us. 'Are we finished here?' He held out both his hands to his invisible audience. 'Is our business here concluded, or are we destined to be detained forever afterwards on its small tides and currents?' I wondered if any of us knew the part.

'Coming, Henry,' Stoker called to him. He felt undermined from all sides. 'Mr Webster has been of inestimable help.'

I held a hand to my chest. 'I only wish I could have been,' I said to him.

'Nevertheless, I believe we do understand each other on this matter, you and I, Mr Webster.' The emphasis on 'Mister' was just a little too much – as though he himself were perhaps titled.

'I imagine we do,' I said to him.

'Tedium,' Irving called to him. This time he took a step towards us, but only one. 'Must these backstage matters consume us so entirely or so frequently? Surely, you—'

'As per, Guv'nor,' Stoker called to him. He tried to laugh. We all heard the false note of the word. Then Stoker gave Howson a slight push, and Howson, unprepared for this, stumbled into me. I reached out and held him, pretending to catch him, to prevent him from falling, to steady him. I held him for considerably longer than was necessary, asking him if he was all right, if he had got his feet.

Howson said he had.

'It wasn't my intention—' Stoker began.

'No, of course not,' Howson said.

'A simple accident, that's all,' I added. 'Eager to get on. You're a busy man, entirely understandable.'

He wanted to tell us all to get out of his way, to let him pass, to leave him. He wanted to be beyond all our eyes and ears, to be alone again with Irving.

'Perhaps I need detain you no longer,' he said to Howson. He pushed past him, and then me, straightening his tie and brushing down his jacket to rid himself of our contagion. He walked quickly to the edge of the stage, exchanging no more than a nod with Jimmy Allen as he passed him.

'Ah, good,' Irving said. 'Everything satisfactory?'

'Completely,' Stoker said.

Howson, I saw, appeared to be about to follow Stoker, but I held out my arm to prevent him, lowering it the instant he understood my intention.

'Is that it, then?' Mrs Craven called from her stool.

'She'll need help standing up,' I said to Howson.

He looked at the woman and nodded. 'Coming,' he called to her.

I went to Jimmy Allen and the pair of us watched Stoker and Irving cross the stage to the far side. We both saw Irving pause as he reached centre-stage, watched him turn and bow, twirling his hand in a lesser flourish.

'He can't help himself,' Jimmy Allen said softly.

Stoker, I saw, was careful to continue walking, not to intrude upon Irving's small and silent pleasure.

'And Stoker neither,' Jimmy Allen said.

I didn't understand him. 'Meaning?'

But he refused to answer me, merely looking up at me and shaking his head.

A moment later, as the two men finally disappeared into the opposite shadows, he said, 'You know exactly what I mean. Sharp as a blade, Stoker. Sharp enough to cut you.'

'Then I'll have to watch I don't get too close,' I said. I pretended to watch Howson pull Mrs Craven up from her stool.

'Stoker's as sharp as you *think* you are,' Jimmy Allen said.

'I know,' I told him.

'I know you do.' He turned back to his newspaper, this final warning sounding like a heavy lid closing on a solid box.

12

Alice held her first advertised séance four nights later. To my surprise, both she and Cora insisted on my presence for the occasion. The pair of them then spent the days prior to the gathering almost wholly in preparation for it. By 'presence', Cora informed me, they meant simply that they wanted me to be somewhere in the house in the event of any emergency, or, as she insisted on putting it, any 'unforeseen circumstance'. I was another pair of hands, nothing more. The last thing either of them wanted was for me to be actually present, or even to be seen.

Following my encounter with Stoker, I had decided to stay away from the theatre for a few days. The next time, I knew, he would seek me out when the two of us were alone and frame his accusations more forcibly. He would be angry at having achieved so little in the presence of so many others, and this would only serve to sharpen his resolve.

The front parlour was cleared and the table and chairs set up. New, heavy curtains were hung at the window and door. The room was cleared of some of its clutter. All the pictures and ornaments were removed from the mantel. A damask cover was laid on the table. Cora measured the distance between the chairs. Every crease and fold was smoothed from the cloth. Mirrors and pictures – even our marriage certificate – were turned to the walls. New and good-quality mantles were fitted to the gas jets, and these were tested in the room's near-darkness for Alice to assess the most appropriate levels of light. I was impressed by the lengths the pair of them went to, and again mostly at Cora's urging.

With the new curtains, blocked door and covered fireplace, I told Cora I was concerned about the amount of air in the room. She listened to me and then laughed at my concern. I expressed the same anxiety to Alice, and her response, though muted, was much the same. Cora accused me of being determined to find fault with what the pair of them were doing. She said I was trying to undermine them. Every time she spoke, it now seemed, I heard someone else's words.

On the day before the séance, I encountered Cora coming out of the local newsagent's with a bundle of papers under her arm. As far as I knew, she read nothing except her magazines. I asked her if she was searching for something, and then endured her obvious evasions until I finally realized what the papers were for.

'Does your mother know what you're doing?' I asked her.

'Looking at obituary details? Of course she knows. It's just to give her a helping hand.'

Years ago, I had told Alice that I considered this to be little more than deception, cheating.

'It's what they all do,' Cora said, as though this explained and excused everything.

'Of course,' I said. For days now, my every concern and argument had evaporated in the heat of their shared enthusiasm.

But she still heard my lack of conviction, my disappointment, perhaps.

'What?' she said, instantly indignant. 'You want her to sit there with nothing?'

'She has her gift,' I said. If she heard the irony in my voice, then she ignored it.

'Of course she has, of course. And like every gift, she needs to handle it carefully.'

I wondered what this was meant to explain. My own daughter.

'It's all part of my new role,' she said. She grew calm and smiled as she spoke. 'Part of my professional responsibilities. *I*'ll be the one to find out what I can. All *she* then has to do is to employ her powers.'

'Prompted by you.'

'Precisely.' She looked from my collar to my feet. 'Was there anything else?' she said impatiently.

'Anything else?'

'That you wanted to say to me. I'm busy.' She tapped the papers. 'As you can see.'

Now I was a distant and unwelcome outsider, a threat to their enterprise.

'Of course,' I said, and she took the opportunity to walk quickly away from me.

After a few steps, she paused, turned and called back to me, 'Do *you* know any of the sitters?'

'I don't know. I doubt it.'

Alice had shown me the names of the people who had responded to her advert. Six women and two men, husbands. The names had meant nothing to me. Eight sitters. Usually, there were only two or three, four at the most. I wondered what she hoped to achieve with so many. Surely, most of them would now receive nothing from her. All of them, however, would arrive expecting something. With two or three sitters, then some response might be achieved, but with eight? Or perhaps it was only six. Perhaps the husbands were merely other 'presences'. I considered this likely. But even six was a large number. I'd done my best to suggest all this to Alice, but, as with all my other concerns, she had refused to listen to me. She told me what each of the sitters, including the husbands, was paying her. She now referred to the sittings as 'consultations', something else insisted upon by Cora.

I heard the doubt and suspicion in Cora's voice when she asked me if I knew any of the sitters, and I took advantage of this.

'It's a lot of people,' I said.

She came reluctantly back to me.

'Have you said that to her?'

I admitted that I had.

'Thought so,' she said.

'What do *you* think?'

She shrugged. 'Perhaps not all of them will expect so much. Perhaps some of them will just want to see what she's capable of. Perhaps a single visitation or voice will be enough.'

'Perhaps,' I said. It was possible, but unlikely.

'It's why I'm doing all this,' she said, indicating the papers. 'One of the couples, the wife just lost her mother. Her obituary's in some of these. You can learn a lot from reading those things.'

Surviving family members, ages, occupations, reputations, interests, personal and professional attachments, service histories.

'I know,' I said. It was the sum total of my concessions. And, in truth, I didn't want Alice – either of them – to be shown up or to fail at the outset of this joint venture. I doubted if the sitters would ever accuse them openly of any degree of fraud, but that too was always a possibility. Years ago, I had gone with Alice to watch a medium performing at the Progressive Library on Southampton Row and had almost laughed aloud at the number of professional invalids she had employed, and then again at seeing her bite into a capsule of soda to induce the frothing of her mouth at the height of her trance, her so-called and much advertised 'cold abstraction'.

'So you see . . .' Cora said.

'Of course.'

'"Psychic Consultations".'

'Is that—'

'It's what I want her to start calling the sittings. It sounds more . . . more . . .'

'Businesslike?' I suggested.

'Modern. It makes her sound as though she knows what she's doing.'

It seemed a strange and telling remark to make, but I let it pass without comment.

'I'm sure the evening will go well,' I told her.

'Of course it will. Did she tell you that we've had almost three dozen other responses?'

The news surprised me. 'For sittings?'

'"Consultations", yes. In only six days. Over thirty responses.'

'How will she fit them all in?' Until now, Alice had held her séances no more frequently than once a month, and even then often only at the insistence of her regular and satisfied sitters.

'I'm trying to persuade her to do them on a regular basis,' Cora said, her excitement rising. 'Once a week, perhaps. Even more sitters, clients, depending on what they expect.'

I was alarmed at the prospect of this, but again I said nothing.

'Next thing you know, you'll be hiring halls,' I said, joking, immediately wishing I hadn't.

'I know,' Cora said.

'Seriously?'

She shrugged. Alice would have immediately baulked at the idea. 'I'm still trying to persuade her,' she said. 'Not regularly. In their responses, some of them said they'd be happy to pay more for private consultations.'

'More chance of a visitation, I suppose,' I said.

She looked at me for a moment before going on. 'It's something I'll need to look into.'

'She's not a particularly strong woman,' I said. 'Her constitution. You know what she's like after sittings with even her regulars.'

'That was before she had *me* to help her,' she said firmly.

'Of course.' I told her I was on my way back to the house and offered to carry the papers for her, but she declined, telling me she had other errands to run before returning home. She waited where she stood as I walked away from her.

By the evening in question, the number of responses Alice had received had doubled to over seventy, and none of us could hide our surprise at this – surprise, delight and confirmation of her expectations, in the case of Cora.

An hour before the sitters were due to arrive, Alice came to show me the new dress she'd bought for the occasion. I hadn't seen her dressed like that in ten years, and seeing her thus transformed was another surprise. It was black, and fringed with jet beads at the hem, collar and cuffs. It showed her figure, close at her waist and thighs. I admired it, sensing her own uncertainty.

'Cora chose it,' she told me.

I'd already guessed as much.

She lifted the low hem to reveal the new shoes she was also wearing. These, too, I admired. In addition, she would wear a pair of evening gloves and carry a scented handkerchief.

'She seems to know what she's doing,' I said, meaning Cora.

'It will still be me sitting there,' she said. There was suddenly something of the old intimacy between us, and I put my arm around her shoulders.

'She's "organizing" me,' she said, smiling.

'Something I was never able to do, eh?'

She looked at the clock on the wall. 'We're serving them Madeira wine when we first gather at the table. There'll be a bottle on the cabinet. The husbands and wives sit together. Cora will identify those working hardest against me, any unbelievers. "Sceptics", she calls them.'

'Would they pay good money just to come and denounce you?'

'Cora says we have to be prepared for every eventuality. Every sitting and every sitter is an opportunity. She's going to keep a list of all those sitters we might encourage to return.'

'Spreading the—'

'And those we ought not to encourage to return. She says that word of mouth is everything with these things.'

'And those who get no satisfaction, who talk to no one?'

'From the other side? Cora says that there are people who will always keep trying.'

'Hoping they'll be successful in the future?' Something else for her to list.

'I can't *refuse* them,' Alice said. 'Cora said that on these first few occasions, I might even offer partial refunds to those who make no satisfactory contact.'

'To encourage them to return and pay again?' I said.

'It's good business. And it's what they want. Fishermen don't stop going fishing because they have a few dry days. If anything, it makes them even more determined.'

'Of course it does,' I said. I wondered which of her magazines Cora had gleaned that particular piece of wisdom from.

'Where will *you* be?' Alice said. I felt her hand tighten on my arm.

'Tonight? Upstairs. Unless summoned, you won't even know I'm there.'

We were interrupted then by Isobel, who had been engaged for the evening, and who was also under strict instructions to keep out of the parlour.

She came into the room and looked at us where we stood, our heads close, my arm still around Alice's shoulders.

'Everything ready for the big night?' she said.

'I think so,' Alice said. 'You know what's required of you? Cora has made everything clear?'

'Crystal,' Isobel said, looking at me as she spoke.

'If we need you to assist, you or Mr Webster—'

'I'm sure we'll know about it,' Isobel said.

Alice stepped away from me.

'Until ten, you said,' Isobel said.

This surprised me. 'That late? How long will the sitting last?'

'Cora thought two hours was appropriate.'

Twice as long as usual – perhaps a necessity occasioned by the larger numbers.

'Good value for money,' Isobel said. 'That and the wine. Nothing like a drop of something to make a body more tearful than they already are. You should try gin next time.'

'Strong spirits would be entirely inappropriate,' Alice said.

I wondered if she was about to make a joke.

'Wine is considered more—'

'Appropriate,' Isobel said.

'More commensurate,' Alice said. It was the wrong word, but only I saw that.

'Right,' Isobel said. 'What should I do now, then?'

'See Cora.'

'If you say so.' She left us, and walked along the passageway calling for Cora as she went.

'Are you paying her extra?' I asked Alice.

'Cora suggested time off in lieu.'

I heard Cora approach Isobel and issue instructions. The sitters would be there in less than half an hour.

'We insist on payment in advance,' Alice said absently. 'It's common practice. Additional gratuities are at discretion.' She was starting to distance herself from me. It pained me to hear her parroting Cora like this.

'Of course,' I said.

She went and stood at the door. She held up her hand and rattled the beads at the cuff. 'Is it too much, do you think?'

'You look beautiful,' I told her. The word had come without hesitation or thought and surprised us both. 'Beautiful and perfect for the – ' I almost said 'part' – 'occasion.'

She smoothed her hands over her stomach. I sensed she was warming to the role, the way actresses changed as they began to dress and apply their make-up.

Cora came in to us and immediately asked her mother why she wasn't resting, lying down at least, preparing herself, harnessing her energy, conserving her strength, clearing her mind.

'I'm fine,' Alice told her, and I heard the first true note of quiet confidence in her voice.

'Yes, well . . .' Cora said. 'But you have to start listening to me, to what I tell you. Otherwise, what's the point?'

Alice went to her and the two of them embraced briefly and left the room together. Waiting behind, I had seldom felt so alone.

I went to the kitchen until the first few sitters arrived and were directed into the parlour by Isobel. Cora insisted that it was the only part of the house they would occupy. There was an outhouse beyond the scullery. Two hours and the wine might necessitate the use of this, but that was all.

Alice and Cora prepared themselves. I listened through the door as the further arrivals were greeted, this time by Cora. Isobel stood with me.

'She sounds like a talking machine,' she said.

'It's probably important to establish a routine and then to stick to it,' I said. Like every performance of the same small drama.

Alice herself remained upstairs until all the sitters were in place and waiting for her. It was harder now to hear what

Cora might be saying to them. From the men and women themselves, there was mostly silence.

I heard low voices, nervous laughter, the touch of glasses.

At the appointed time, Cora brought in Alice, and I heard a brief round of soft applause. The closing door was my cue to leave and to go upstairs to my room. In two hours I would listen out for the sitters' departure and then come back down.

I left the kitchen and climbed the stairs.

A few minutes later, as I sat at my desk and considered how I might fill my time, there was a single rap on the door and Isobel came in to me.

'I never heard you,' I said.

She indicated her stockinged feet and held a finger to her lips. 'I thought you might like this.' She put an opened bottle of wine in front of me. 'Your daughter bought four bottles and opened them all. They sip at it like birds.'

'It'll save,' I said.

She looked at my desk. 'What are you doing?'

'Preparing for tomorrow.'

'The theatre?' The place still held its allure for her and I heard this in her voice. 'You don't keep any pictures here?' she said. 'Actors, actresses, that kind of thing.'

'Some,' I said. 'A few.' I took a bundle from a drawer and gave them to her. Copies I'd made for Marlow and which he had returned to me as unwanted or unsuitable.

She looked at them closely and remarked on each one. Then she tapped the neck of the bottle, and said, 'Cora said to bring it up to you.'

'Help yourself,' I said to her, guessing the words were a prompt.

She poured herself a glass, sipped it and pulled a face.

'Too sweet?' I said.

'I prefer gin,' she said, and we both smiled at the remark. Indicating the photographs, she said, 'They're beautiful,' leaving me uncertain whether she meant the costumes or the women modelling them. Most of them would have been no older than she was.

I started to tell her about Stoker and the record he was compiling.

Halfway through the pictures, she lost interest and put them down.

'I'll try and persuade Alice to pay you extra,' I told her, knowing how unfair she would consider the current arrangement.

She shrugged, unconcerned. 'It's probably up to your daughter,' she said.

'Alice employs you,' I said.

'I thought that was you.' She grinned at me as she said it.

'Alice and I together,' I said.

'You wouldn't think it.' Her tired complaints ended there.

Nothing of what might have been happening two floors below was audible to us.

After half an hour, and another glass of the sweet wine, she rose and said she had to leave. She said it as though expecting me to object to her departure, or at least to be disappointed by it.

'I don't hear no screams,' she said, standing in the open doorway and grinning. 'Everything sounds very civilized. Ghosts like that, are they?'

But then, and as though in response to this mockery, we heard a single loud scream, and then the sound either of someone falling or of something heavy being knocked over.

Isobel jumped at the noise. 'Christ,' she said.

There was a second, lesser noise, a shout rather than a scream. A door opened, and was followed by the sound of footsteps and voices. I heard Cora calling for me.

'Wait here,' I told Isobel. 'Come down after me.'

'I hear what you're saying,' she said, smiling again. 'What do you think it is?'

I ran down both flights of stairs, arriving at the open door just as Cora was returning to the parlour with a glass of water. She seemed surprised to see me there.

'It's nothing,' she said. 'One of the sitters.' She was panting, her eyes wide. She seemed more excited than scared by whatever had happened.

'Is Alice—' I began.

'She's fine.' She looked up the stairs at Isobel, who was now descending. 'Where were you?' she said to the girl.

'With him,' Isobel said.

But this was of no consequence to Cora, who ignored the remark and all it might have been intended to imply, and who then went back into the parlour, opening the door only enough to allow her in and then pulling it shut immediately behind her. In that instant, I looked into the darkened room and saw Alice sitting at the head of the table, her hands spread before her, her face down, her eyes closed. One of the two men said something to Cora and then laughed nervously. I heard one of the women sitters half crying, half laughing, both fear and relief in her voice.

Then the door was closed again and I waited where I stood with Isobel.

'She's not giving much away,' she said, considerably less intrigued than I was by whatever might have just happened.

In the closed room, a round of applause started and grew loud before falling off. I heard Alice thanking people.

Isobel put her ear to the door and I pulled her away. I told her to go back to the kitchen, and then waited where I stood for several minutes longer, listening to the murmuring voices within.

Part II

Part II

13

It was by chance that I saw Bliss through the window of the Metropolitan Café three days later. I was on my way back to the Lyceum after an absence of almost a week. Until a few months ago, the Metropolitan had been our usual, though infrequent, meeting place, either at Bliss's own request or under instruction from Marlow. I had never been in a position to insist on the meetings myself. On several occasions, I had been summoned there by Marlow personally, only to be then confronted by Bliss, who either repeated his client's instructions to me, or who simply handed over a sealed envelope, afterwards departing as quickly as possible. Whatever half-promises the man had made to me on our first, secretive encounter in the Lyceum foyer, little had materialized. I might have gained financially from my association with both him and Marlow, but – my rare invitations to Marlow's studio aside – I was mostly kept apart from them, another 'circle' whose bounds had been quickly made clear to me.

He sat where we usually sat, close to the far wall, his back to the high mirror, and with a view of both the café entrance and the street outside through the half-frosted windows.

I went in and he saw me immediately, watching me closely as I crossed the crowded room towards him. A waiter approached me and blocked my way to him – or so I imagined – before stepping aside and holding his tray of glasses above my head. He said something to me in hissed Italian as I passed him.

Bliss smiled at the encounter. His cane lay against his chair, a pair of thin kid gloves and a small case on the seat beside him.

Only as I sat opposite him did I see that there was a second cup and half-filled glass beside his own. He smoked one of his slim cigars, retrieving this from the ashtray at the centre of the table, carefully rolling it to remove the ash. There was always an order to these things where Bliss was concerned, a measured routine and satisfying precision.

'I don't believe we have an appointment,' he said, though seemingly little surprised or discomfited by my unexpected presence. '*Do* we have an appointment? Have I been remiss?' He beckoned to the same waiter, pointed quickly at the table and then flicked up three fingers. The man acknowledged him with a nod and left us.

I'd gone into the café upon seeing him there to ascertain what he might have said to Marlow about my concerns regarding Stoker and his suspicions. In addition, I wanted to impress upon him – upon Bliss personally – the true significance of Stoker's veiled accusations. I'd thought long about this, and had convinced myself that it was a matter of equal consequence to both Marlow and myself. But even as I prepared myself to say all this, I knew that neither Bliss nor Marlow would truly share my concern, and that the only one of us in genuine jeopardy now was myself – a condition that would be little improved by any ill-considered demands on either Bliss or his profitable client.

'What did you say to Marlow to make him aware of my concerns?' I said. It was an abrupt and regrettable opening after all my silent deliberations.

'What did I *say*?' He was amused by my effrontery. 'To my *client*? To the man whose interests I am paid to consider, encourage and protect?' He added a sharp emphasis to the last word.

'You must have said something,' I insisted, but with little true conviction.

'I'm sure I did,' he said. 'But simply because I may have expressed doubts or concerns of my own, it does not necessarily follow that my client has acted directly upon that . . . advice.'

I was used to him talking this way. He sometimes sounded like a man dictating a contract to a secretary or a typewriter; or like an advocate in court, being at once both precise and yet open to every interpretation. He would often phrase the same remark in several slightly varying ways and any argument would fade or retreat ahead of this gentle prodding.

'Doubts and concerns about me?' I said.

Instead of answering me, he rose from where he sat and motioned over my shoulder. At first I thought the waiter had returned, but when I looked I saw Pearl coming towards us.

She sat beside me. She too was little surprised by my sudden appearance at the table.

'What a pleasure,' she said to me. She gave me her hand and then withdrew it at the first touch. 'Are you free to join us? I'm sure our business can wait.' She smiled firmly at Bliss.

It seemed yet again all a succession of coded signals, clarifications and reassurances.

'Mr Webster wants to know why I've been going behind his back to Marlow,' Bliss said.

'Why "behind his back"?'

I wanted to explain myself to her, to insist that I was being misrepresented, but I knew exactly how this would look to her, to them both.

'I thought Mr Webster was the one who took pleasure in spying on people,' Pearl said, smiling as she spoke. She was referring to the occasion on Regent Street.

Bliss laughed at the remark.

Pearl put her hand on my own and squeezed it gently. 'Don't take things so seriously,' she said. 'No one minds.' Withdrawing her hand and turning to Bliss, she said, 'And if something *has* been said that Mr Webster needs or has a perfect right to know about, then it's only fair that you tell him.'

I saw again how quickly and completely my argument would be lost in this easy understanding between them.

The waiter returned and laid out our drinks, and we fell silent as he did this. When he was done, Pearl thanked him. She knew his name and called him by it. He spoke in Italian to her and she responded fluently. I saw by Bliss's eyes that he too understood what was being said.

'You surely understand by now what a hazardous profession Marlow is engaged in, and how easily compromised or jeopardized that might be,' Pearl said to me when the waiter had gone. Her voice was low and she held my eyes as she spoke.

'Of course I do,' I said.

'And you still believe you are being unfairly criticized – accused? – of contributing to that jeopardy?' She waited for my answer, pursing her lips and shrugging. She looked from me to Bliss and back again.

I knew then that it would be unwise to repeat any of my concerns regarding Stoker and thus create an even greater liability of myself.

'Perhaps,' I said. 'No.'

'Please understand me, Mr Webster,' Bliss said. 'If Marlow had any serious concerns about your – shall we call them "arrangements"? – if he had any concerns whatsoever, then he would act upon them.'

I nodded my concurrence at this.

'Good. And has there been any mention of . . . severance, of detachment, of these arrangements being brought to an end?'

I admitted there hadn't.

'Well . . .' He held up his palms.

I could imagine him pacing slowly back and forth in front of a jury.

'In fact, I believe you and Marlow had a conversation of no small consequence when you last met.'

'Oh?' I tried to remember.

'Last Friday,' Pearl said. 'The Maltese floorshow.'

I still didn't know what Bliss was referring to.

'I don't quite . . .' I began to say.

'Oh, nothing specific,' Bliss said. 'Sorry. No – I merely remember Marlow telling me that subsequent to your conversation – that you struck him as an interesting man. Hidden depths, and all that. He told me you had given him ideas.'

'Ideas?' I was more confused and wrong-footed than ever.

'That was the word.' He sipped his coffee.

I faltered for a moment between flattery and mistrust.

Pearl slid my own small cup and saucer towards me.

'I didn't spy on anyone,' I said to her.

'I know you didn't.'

'I saw you, that's all.'

'Of course you did. Me or someone who looked like me.' She ran a finger across her lips.

I wondered why she still insisted on this denial.

'Impossible,' Bliss said, holding up his own glass to her. 'Two Pearls in this tiny city?'

'Why, kind sir,' Pearl said.

Bliss indicated for me to share in the toast.

'And rest assured,' he said to me, 'I shall say nothing of our encounter today. Nor of your possible concerns.'

Because Marlow's own concerns might then multiply? Because something might grow out of nothing? Because I would become more than a risk to the man and no longer worth the effort? Because Bliss knew all this, and even after all that time I myself still had no real idea of how swiftly and completely I and my services might be discarded?

'I appreciate that,' I told Bliss.

After this there was a brief and awkward silence between us, and I felt like the intruder I was.

Pearl looked around the room. Others there knew her and she exchanged nods and waves with several of these.

When she eventually looked back to Bliss, she said, 'Perhaps you might show Mr Webster. It might help.'

'Help in what way?' Bliss said, clearly unwilling to comply with whatever she was suggesting to him.

'To impress upon him the serious nature of these things – these "associations" as you prefer to call them.'

Bliss considered what she'd said for a moment and then reached for the small case beside him. He took out a newspaper, laid it on the table and then turned it to face me. The headlines told of an arrest for murder and I started to read, half expecting to find the same story Jimmy Allen had revealed to me almost a fortnight earlier.

But it was another story, another murder entirely.

'Man called Aston-Fox,' Bliss said. 'Arrested and accused of strangling a twelve-year-old girl in – ' he lowered his voice, '"perverse circumstances". She was found naked and dead, he naked and unconscious. You won't find that in there.'

I finished reading the brief report.

'Did he do it?'

He shrugged. 'It seems likely. It's the kind of . . . the kind of . . .'

'Perversion?' I said.

Bliss sighed. 'He certainly had strange – extreme – tastes. And a predilection for . . .'

'Young girls?'

'Strange and excessive practices.'

Pearl looked around us as we spoke, ensuring we were not overheard.

'He was a customer of Marlow's,' she said, making everything clear to me.

'His family are all baronets and minor lords,' Bliss said disdainfully. 'They have estates in Worcestershire and Hereford. Aston-Fox has lived here, Mayfair, since leaving Oxford with half of the family fortune in his pockets.'

'And you believe the police will trace a line back to Marlow during their investigations?' The report said the police were following several lines of inquiry, but this meant little.

'It's always a possibility,' Bliss said.

And it was his job to sever that line and then to search out any other connections that might also lead to Marlow.

'Marlow undertook commissions for the man,' Pearl said, her own concern rising but controlled.

'Employing twelve-year-old girls?'

Neither of them spoke for a moment. I looked again at the newspaper.

I repeated my question.

'Sometimes,' Pearl said. 'And sometimes we told him they were twelve.'

'When they were what – thirteen, fourteen?' The legal age of consent was still thirteen; it hadn't been twelve for at least fifteen years, and there was always campaigning for it to be raised even higher.

This time Bliss reached out and clasped my wrist. 'I doubt you are in a position to make these judgements, Mr Webster.'

Pearl looked directly at him and he released me.

'My apologies,' he said. It had been a revealing moment.

'So you see,' Pearl said.

I told her I understood.

'What does Aston-Fox say in his defence?' I asked Bliss.

'So far, very little. He's waiting for everything to get taken care of. His father is a High Court judge. He himself has friends in very high places.'

'And low, presumably,' I said, unable to resist.

Bliss smiled coldly at this. 'And low. Of course, nothing is helped by the Whitechapel hysteria that still gets stirred up every time someone – a woman – is murdered.'

'Are the police suggesting . . . ?'

'Of course not. But none of it hurts their case where public opinion is concerned.'

I was again reminded of what Jimmy Allen had shown me, but kept this to myself.

'In addition,' Bliss went on, 'the public and the press are again baying for results.'

'Did Marlow ever photograph the strangled girl?' I asked Pearl.

She hesitated before answering me and I held up my hand to stop her.

'We just need to wait for this to blow over,' Bliss said.

'The investigation and trial will take months, perhaps years,' I said.

'I meant the outcry in the press. Once that's suppressed, the whole thing will be quickly forgotten.'

'Until the next time,' I said.

'And that is likely to be of absolutely no consequence to any of us,' he said angrily.

'Were any of Marlow's pictures found in Aston-Fox's possession?' I asked Pearl.

'There are plenty like Marlow supplying the same market,' she said, another evasion.

'Which is the cause of our second headache on this otherwise beautiful summer's morning,' Bliss said.

I waited for him to explain.

By way of answer, he turned the pages of the paper and pointed out a second article.

'The London Vigilance Committee,' he said. 'The stick stirring in the cesspit has roused them to action. They've already raided Exeter Street and the Islington Passage studios. They know where to look. And the police are more than happy to take instruction from Wheeler if it makes them look to be busy and achieving results.'

'Who's Wheeler?'

'Oliver Wheeler is the chief purging compound and head of the Committee. MP for somewhere in Surrey. He knows Marlow, or at least *of* him. He's even mentioned him by name in Parliamentary speeches and papers. And whatever else happens, he's certainly not going to let this particular bandwagon go trundling past without leaping on board and gaining himself a few extra votes.'

'It sounds as though Marlow's in a vice,' I said.

Bliss laughed again at the remark. 'Perhaps I exaggerate the dangers,' he said.

'Meaning?'

'Meaning Marlow is more than capable of avoiding unwelcome attention when the need arises. You should know that much by now.'

And meaning that Marlow was somehow being kept well-informed of the Vigilance Committee's intentions and the police's interest?

'Let's see what happens with Aston-Fox first, shall we?' Bliss said.

I sensed that Pearl was unhappy with this.

'Did you know the girl?' I asked her.

She hesitated before answering me. 'Not well. Briefly. She arrived about a year ago, didn't stay long, took off after Marlow had employed her for a few weeks.'

'Presumably to pastures more rewarding,' Bliss said.

'But the connection to Marlow might still be made?' I said, and he nodded once. I tried to remember the face of the girl I'd seen with Pearl – she'd been much older, twenty perhaps – but couldn't.

'It says somewhere in the report that Aston-Fox may have

been blackmailed by the victim,' Bliss said. 'The police are already searching out others who share his predilections. Everyone they talk to will throw up their hands in outrage and disgust and back away from the man.'

After this, there was a further brief silence between us.

'So, now you see,' Bliss said, watching me.

'I hope . . .' Pearl started to say, but then fell silent.

'You have my assurance,' I told her.

'Thank you.' She seemed almost relieved that someone else – someone beyond their own close circle – had been brought into their confidence.

'Does Marlow still use the girls?' I asked them, but neither of them answered me.

'You are owed no favours, Mr Webster,' Bliss said eventually, reverting to his old formality. 'The confidence is shared as much for your benefit as our own.'

'I understand that,' I told him. I understood, too, that I now possessed the smallest part of that power which occasionally fell from Marlow and settled upon others.

'According to our sources,' Bliss said, 'Wheeler will go after the Finsbury Park and Somers Town boys next. All a long way from Golden Square.'

I gave nothing away at the mention of Somers Town, but I immediately tried to understand how my dealings with Solomon might, with perseverance or ill-luck, be followed back to Marlow.

'If there is anything you yourself – you personally – might now need to do?' Bliss said cautiously.

'There's nothing,' I assured him.

'Possibly. But you might give some consideration to the matter.'

I conceded this.

'Did Marlow have any hand in the girl's involvement with Aston-Fox?' I asked Pearl.

'Only the photographs, the introduction. It happens often enough. Wealth and poverty, desire and provision – it's a simple enough equation.'

'Of course it is,' Bliss said.

Pearl held my gaze. 'I met her three times, at the most. I cleaned her up and dressed her for him.'

'And made sure she understood what was expected of her?' I said, regretting the remark immediately.

She drew back from me. 'You make it sound as though I coerced her, as though she was an unwilling or unrewarded participant.'

'Webster,' Bliss said, genuinely shocked by my accusation. 'Was there any need for that? Pearl?'

She shook her head at him.

'I'm sorry,' I said to her. It was a sincere apology. It was also another of those ill-defined and shifting lines the three of us seemed to cross back and forth over forever where Marlow was concerned.

'I mean it,' I said. 'Whatever part you played, it had nothing to do with what Aston-Fox stands accused of.'

'Precisely,' Bliss said, still watching Pearl, who remained unconvinced. 'See what you've done?' Bliss said to me.

And hearing the words, hearing his own suppressed and fearful uncertainties, I felt more powerful and equal in his company than I had ever felt before. Less than half an hour had passed since our chance encounter, and yet in those few minutes – in my own imagination at least – a great deal had changed.

'Pearl?' Bliss said again.

'Apology accepted,' she said. She held out her hand to me and I took it.

'Good,' Bliss said. He looked at his watch, signalling his departure, and in that instance I wanted nothing more than for him to go and for him to leave Pearl and myself sitting at the table, her hand still in mine.

But she too rose to leave.

Bliss took out his wallet and laid a note in his saucer. 'Please,' he said. 'Finish your drink. I imagine this has come as a great surprise to you.'

'A little,' I said.

'A little? Then perhaps . . .' He left the rest unspoken.

I rose beside Pearl and she embraced me.

'Will Marlow . . . leave, go away?' I asked her.

'Perhaps. Briefly. We'll have to wait and see what happens.'

'We all have a part to play,' Bliss said, another reminder of my own responsibilities.

'Of course,' I told him.

He shook my hand and then led Pearl through the crowded room to the door.

I moved to where he had been sitting and watched them through the window. He kissed her cheek and they immediately separated, walking in opposite directions into the passing crowd. His cigar still smoked in the glass bowl at the centre of the table. I picked it up and drew on it, tilting back my head to blow the smoke towards the high, ornate ceiling.

14

Unsettled by what I had just learned, and uncertain now of the farthest consequences of Aston-Fox's arrest, I decided not to return to the Lyceum.

I did, however, go to the side entrance on Burleigh Street and asked one of the stage-hands I found there if either Howson or Jimmy Allen were in the building. He went to look, returning a few minutes later with Howson.

I walked with him to Waterloo Bridge.

'Is this about Mother?' he said.

'Has he said anything?'

'No more than usual.' He waited for me to explain further, anxious to return to his work. He knew nothing of my arrangement with Marlow. And in turn, Stoker himself, whatever his suspicions or his own connection to Marlow, would be equally careful not to reveal anything incriminatory. Or at least not until the blame for my own transgressions could be squarely apportioned and then exposed with a full and unavoidable confession.

We crossed the bridge halfway and Howson stopped and looked over the parapet at the water beneath us. Then he turned his face to the sun, by then directly above us in another cloudless sky.

'I know something's wrong,' he said. 'All that business with Stoker on the stage.' He waited for me to answer him, and when I said nothing, he continued walking, pausing for me to catch up with him. 'I won't ask you,' he said.

'It's nothing serious.' I tried to sound convincing. 'In fact, if it weren't for Mother and his endless meddling and insistence on recording everything, it'd be nothing at all.'

'Please, don't lie to me,' he said. 'We've known each other for five years. There's no need.'

'I didn't—'

'Just don't tell me anything simply to assuage your own conscience or to involve me in anything . . . anything . . .'

We continued walking to the far side and then waited briefly before turning back. We both understood that we were in that other country there, on that far shore, beyond all sight and hearing of those others forever watching and listening out for us.

'Have you given Stoker all the accounts?' I asked him.

'Everything I had,' he said. 'He'll be clucking over them now. *Are* you avoiding him?'

'I thought it might be wise.'

'There's no need,' he said. 'They've gone away for a few days.'

'Stoker?'

'And Henry. Paris. Henry has no part for a fortnight. Stoker went with him to make arrangements for a tour. He sends mail and telegrams daily.'

'How long will they be gone?'

'Henry said to expect him when we saw him.' He shook his head at the tired phrase.

'And Stoker?'

171

'He thought a week. They only went yesterday.'

I felt a sudden relief at hearing this.

'Is it to do with the costumes, your photographs?' he said, unable to resist.

'Stoker thinks I'm not keeping a close enough eye on everything coming and going from Southall.' It was a half-truth and he half believed me. It was enough.

We started walking back over the river.

'It's always *something* with him,' he said, meaning Stoker, and knowing that the man was just as likely to point an accusing finger at him one day as he was now pointing it at me. He stopped and looked out over the river again. 'Is there anything I can do?' he said. 'I get invoices from the carters and pantechnicon people most weeks.'

'With specific inventories of everything they've transported?'

He laughed. 'Hardly. Just notes that they've shifted something or other.'

It was the reassuring answer he had intended it to be and I acknowledged this.

'Why does he bother?' he said.

He leaned even further over the stonework. A string of barges sat moored directly beneath us. Men worked on their decks and in their low, cramped cabins. I heard foreign languages, Dutch or German.

'Eel boats,' Howson said. 'My father and his brothers work on the river. Between the Tower and Deptford.' He indicated where barrels of living eels were lined up on the narrow quay. A smell of pitch and turpentine from the nearby naphtha factory filled the warm air. He licked his lips and then spat heavily into the water. 'Taste it?' he said.

'It's in his nature,' I said, meaning Stoker. 'There's always an itch, always something that he thinks he can improve upon. Do you answer his telegrams?'

'From Paris? Some. Most are just distant cracks of the whip.'

'Any reference to me?'

'Nothing so far,' he said. 'He'll more than likely have his hands full with Henry.'

'Wiping dust from his shoulders and brushing dirt from his path.' It was an old joke.

'Something like that. There's always someone strewing palm leaves and blowing trumpets where Henry's concerned.' His own growing disillusionment was evident in everything he said, making me wish I felt able to confide more fully in him.

'And usually it's Stoker conducting the orchestra,' I said. I put my hand on his shoulder and he turned back to the river.

After a minute, we resumed walking. He suggested returning to the theatre with him, but I told him I had business elsewhere. It sounded as though I was avoiding him, a rebuttal almost after everything that had just passed between us.

'Southall?' he said.

'Perhaps.'

'A full inventory would satisfy him,' he said as we reached the far bank. 'Just something down on paper. It won't necessarily have to correspond with the realities of the matter.'

'I know,' I said. But everywhere I looked these 'realities' were refusing to 'correspond', were fracturing and re-forming, moving in and out of focus.

I carried on walking with him to Lancaster Place, where we parted. I promised him that I would return within a day or two. In turn, he promised to contact me if he heard of Stoker's intention to return early.

I caught a bus leaving Maiden Lane to the Euston Road, where I got off at Eversholt Street and made my way to Solomon's. I walked by a circuitous route, arriving at his home and shop via Ossulston Street.

The shop blind was drawn and a Closed sign hung in the door. I walked past on the far side of the road, watching out of the corner of my eye for signs of life inside. In all the years I had known Solomon, the shop had been open twelve hours a day, often including Sundays.

I thought I saw an illuminated inner room – the passageway leading to the living quarters, perhaps – but couldn't be certain. I wondered what signs I might see of any police activity in the street. I looked for other slow walkers or watchers, but there were none. Further along Ossulston Street, at its junction with Aloysius Passage, there was an alleyway leading to the rear of Solomon's, to a gateway giving access to his small back yard. Ensuring I was unobserved, I went in. The gate was unbolted and I opened it.

In the narrow yard I looked up and saw both Solomon and Marta standing at a window looking down at me. I raised my hand, but neither of them responded to this. Marta turned and spoke to Solomon and I saw him cup her face in his hands. The window was bordered with dirt from the nearby railways, and looking at them like that was like looking at a joint portrait framed in an oval mount. Then Solomon left her and Marta remained where she stood, looking down at me. I waved again, and this time she raised her hand in response.

I made my way to the back door just as Solomon unlatched

and unlocked it. I went in, passing through a wash-house into the kitchen as he waited where he stood, carefully watching the yard and alleyway behind me.

'You know?' he said. 'Already?' He finally came in to me, calling up the stairs to his wife.

'That the police were here?'

'She was terrified. They came to both doors at the same time, banging and banging, shouting in at us, commanding me to open the doors before they broke them down, calling to tell us that they knew we were inside.'

'What did you do?'

He looked at me as though I hadn't understood the first thing of what he'd just told me.

And only then did I fully realize what he was saying – all the echoes this violent summons had evoked.

'I let them in, of course. It is what one does. British police-men. They were not strangers. These men were not going to drive me from my home and then burn it and everything it held behind me as I fled. What do you—' He fell silent as Marta appeared, beckoning her in to us.

'Does she understand the cause of all this?'

'She knows they searched everywhere – the shop, our home, my developing room and studio, and that they grew more and more angry at finding nothing.'

'They took nothing away with them?'

'Such as?'

I heard the anger and suspicion beneath the forced calm of his voice.

'Whatever it was they were looking for,' I said.

He looked at his wife. 'At first she thought they were coming to tell us that we had no right to be here. She was relieved when I was able to convince her that this had nothing to do with their search.'

'Did they tell *you* why they were here?'

'I'm not stupid. The day before, they were at Kaplinski's and Abbot's. And today, before they came here, at Morgenthau's at Jacob's Island. If they were searching photographers' studios, then they were looking for pictures. Something, no doubt, in connection with that girl and her murderer.'

'They told you?'

'Oh, happily. Just as they told me that they had cast-iron evidence that *I* had taken some of the photographs they were searching for.' He was shouting now, and Marta spoke to calm him. He fell silent, breathing deeply for a few moments before going on. I knew not to speak. 'I told them to look anywhere they wanted. The man in charge said that whatever they found, they'd find *something* to charge me with. Unfortunately for us, his growing disappointment served only to stoke his frustration and anger.'

Marta spoke to him and he answered her.

'She says I am being negligent in my duties as your host.'

Marta held a chair for me, angling it to the small window and the light.

I thanked her and took it.

She then said something else to Solomon and he shook his head at her. She busied herself making tea for us.

'Have they been to you?' he asked me. 'Is this how you know?'

'Me?' I did my poor best to hide my concern at the speed with which this was all now happening. I had only met Bliss and Pearl two hours earlier, and then only by chance. If I hadn't spoken to them, and notwithstanding everything the newspapers might already be reporting and speculating on, I would have been as blind, as ignorant and as directionless as everyone else at the centre of this gathering storm.

'You think you are somehow beyond their sphere?' Solomon said, already gauging my reluctance to answer him.

'At the Lyceum, you mean?'

'No – at your home, your studio.'

'It's hardly that,' I said. And for the second time that morning I felt that sudden cold hand passing over me.

'Kaplinski's studio is smaller than your attic room,' he said. 'As is Morgenthau's. *They* were not ignored. If I were you, I should prepare myself.'

Marta gave us both a cup, a saucer and a spoon. The three pieces sat uncomfortably in Solomon's large hand.

'We even have silver-plated fish knives,' he said to me, smiling at his wife and at everything these small, reassuring observances and protocols meant to her.

Marta sat beside him, holding her own cup an inch above the saucer, its handle pinched between her thumb and forefinger. I remembered my father always making a point of pouring the tea from the cup into the saucer to cool it before drinking it, but more to make a point about the uselessness of the saucer in the first place. My mother would have understood Marta perfectly.

'Why did they imagine you might be in any way involved in the first place?' I asked Solomon, my voice low and even so that Marta might not understand the nature of my question.

But it was a question that revealed considerably more than it prompted, and he considered his response before answering me in the same calm tone.

'Because someone has been watching the shop and they know that you are a customer?' he said.

I felt the remark like a blow. 'I'd never heard of Aston-Fox or what he's alleged to have done until a few hours ago,' I said. 'It's in all the papers.' Every word was a step away from him and he understood this better than I did.

'Perhaps,' he said. 'But I know people, and you *certainly* know people in that line. And perhaps, in some instances, the people I know are the same people you know.'

I saw immediately what he was telling me, about the connections already made.

'It's a small world,' I said, hoping this would be a sufficient answer.

Marta urged me to drink my tea.

'It certainly is,' he said. 'And sometimes in that small and ever-shrinking world, young girls, children, are desecrated and murdered by wealthy English lords.' He looked at me hard as I kept my silence, then turned to Marta as she resumed speaking to him.

After a few minutes, she left us and went through into the closed shop.

'I've told her to open up, to keep busy.' He watched her go, perhaps contemplating this new small terror he had brought into their lives. Or which, perhaps, he considered *I* had directed towards them.

'A good idea,' I said. I told him I was sorry for not having fully understood what he'd tried to tell me earlier.

'She is convinced they will return.'

'Unlikely,' I said.

'*I* know that,' he said, his voice raised again.

'Why do the police think there are photographs connected

to the killing?' I asked him, hoping to learn more of whatever might have been inadvertently revealed to him.

'Because there *are* photographs?' he said.

It was another sharp jab of an answer.

'Do you think *I* might have taken them?' I asked him. 'Do you honestly believe I might have taken photographs of that nature ever?'

He considered his answer and then slowly shook his head.

'Because I haven't,' I said unnecessarily.

'I believe you.' And next he might say that he knew I knew who had taken the pictures, and this tissue-thin, clean, uncreased and unblemished screen of truth would be punctured, torn apart and discarded. 'They certainly found *something* at Abbot's,' he said. 'And at Morgenthau's. Abbot I knew about, but Morgenthau was a surprise.'

'Pornography?'

'Men and women, women together, yes. And also some old calotypes of hanged men and decapitated Lascars. You know these markets better than me. They even brought some of Abbot's pictures to push in my face. I thought for a moment that the man in charge was going to do the same to Marta, to use her to make me reveal something to him. He certainly seemed desperate and vindictive enough.'

'And did he?'

He shook his head. 'He said she seemed a clean, decent and honest woman. He told me to consider her shame. He told me that the pictures sickened and disgusted everyone who looked at them.'

'Did you see them?'

'I had no choice. I put on a little outrage of my own for

him. I told him I had never taken such a composition in my life. I even threw in a few Polish words for effect.'

'You'll have convinced him,' I said.

'Why? Because, like you, I was telling the truth? Or because I merely *sounded* convincing? Please, don't answer that. Like I say, your concern now should be for yourself. The wave has rolled over us and we are still standing. Abbot and Morgenthau, however, may be made to thrash around in the foam for some time yet.'

'Were they independent operators, do you think?' It was another sly question, but whatever I learned from him I might be able to pass on to Bliss – or, better still, to Pearl – and something of value might yet be salvaged. Again, I was thinking only of myself, but if he saw this then he said nothing. And whatever I learned, it would surely be of *some* value to Marlow, and also of consequence were I soon to be confronted and questioned, which now seemed inevitable. I surprised and disappointed myself by the ease and the speed with which I made all these half-formed and self-serving reckonings.

'"Independent operators"?' he said. 'You even sound like them.' He meant the police.

Before I could respond to this, the shop bell rang and we both fell silent as the customer, a woman, spoke to Marta.

'Mrs Stein,' Solomon said, identifying the voice and language. 'Coming to catch up on the gossip, to see how soon we are to be deported. Or perhaps we're a bomb factory, anarchists. Perhaps we're smuggling in the Jews and the Russians. Perhaps *here* was where the lord committed his murder.' He called his greetings through to the woman, establishing our presence. The bell rang again a minute later upon her departure.

Marta returned to us, speaking first to me. '"By Appointment Only",' she said. '"Exclusive Gatherings and Confidentiality Guaranteed".'

I struggled to understand her.

Solomon tried to silence her, but she was determined to continue.

'Say and see,' she said.

I finally understood what she was saying to me.

'Séance,' Solomon said. 'She saw your wife's advertisement in the *Herald*.'

I looked back at Marta, who smiled hopefully and then nodded vigorously at me.

'Our son,' Solomon said. 'She still . . .'

'She held her first one,' I said. 'Her first since the advert.'

'Marta was very impressed by the thing.'

'I could mention . . .' I said to him. I had so far said nothing to Alice. It seemed the least I might do for him now.

But he shook his head. 'No need. She has already replied to the advert. To a box number. Enclosing this address cut from one of our letterheads and a deposit. She is still waiting to hear. Three days.' He smiled at his wife as he told me all this, but his own feelings on the matter were clear to me. 'If she is successful, I've agreed to accompany her, to translate. Tomasz spoke English better even than me. Will your wife reply?'

'My daughter has taken over that side of things.'

'A proper little business, then,' he said. 'Perhaps there is a discount for a double-booking, or for friends of the family?'

I could imagine Cora's response to this last suggestion.

'I'm sure I could arrange something,' I said.

'I was joking,' he said. 'About the discount.' He spoke to Marta, perhaps telling her what he'd just suggested, and her enthusiasm grew with everything he said. 'She too will countenance no discount,' he said to me. 'But perhaps if your wife is busy, you might push us further along the waiting queue a little?'

I told him I would talk to Alice.

'Alicia,' Marta said. 'Alicia.' She took my hand briefly.

I left them after a second pot of tea, leaving through the shop, which was now brightly lit. There had been no other customers in the time I'd been there.

Solomon came out into the street with me.

'Do you think you're still being watched?' I asked him.

He looked back and forth along the street and shook his head. 'I doubt they have enough men. Besides, why would they return having found nothing? I imagine now that they will search out bigger fish to catch. Men elsewhere who might better serve their inquiry.' He held my gaze as he said this. Another warning, another small shift in the balance of debt and obligation.

'The people responsible,' I said.

'Some associations are always more rewarding than others.'

I agreed with the oblique remark, but only because there was no other course open to me.

I walked home from Somers Town, following the Camden Road to the Seven Sisters junction.

Arriving at Lennox Way, I heard the noise of the building work ahead of me, and approaching Belford Street, I saw the machines and braziers which lined the road leading to the embankment and cutting work. Dozens of heavy horses stood tethered along the side of Saint George's church. Engines and boilers smoked and billowed steam into the already overheated afternoon air. Men dug out and barrowed soil. Bricks and timber were being unloaded from a line of waiting carts. A small crowd watched the work, gathering along Murray Street, where the bars served drink through their windows and permanently open doors.

Passing the Clarendon public house, I heard a familiar voice, and looked in to see Isobel sitting there with two other young women, the three of them surrounded by workmen still in their boots and dirty jerkins. Muddy footprints covered the bar floor.

I was careful not to be seen by her, stepping back into the small tiled porch.

Isobel seemed to me to be the leader of the three girls. She laughed the loudest and seemed determined to encourage the surrounding men. She was drunk, and the small table at which the girls and men sat rattled with its full load of glasses.

A foreman appeared beside me in the doorway and shouted into the bar for the men to return to their work. They complained at this, but then obeyed him. He swore at the more reluctant among them, threatening them with dismissal.

The small bar cleared quickly, leaving Isobel and the girls with only half a dozen other regulars scattered around the room. It reminded me of the emptiness of the theatre following a full-house performance.

I considered going in to her – another chance encounter – but then thought better of this. But something still held me there, and I stood and watched the three of them as they sorted through the remains of the drinks, topping up their own glasses.

One of the girls whispered something to Isobel, and the

pair of them burst into raucous laughter. The third girl made a gesture with her hand and the laughter grew even louder. They started to sing, linking arms and swaying from side to side. The others in the room watched and then applauded them. Isobel rose unsteadily in her seat and took a bow, leaning low over the table of glasses. She fell back into her seat, pulling the others closer to her.

'Going in or coming out?' The voice surprised me and the man behind me waited with his hand on the outer door. I was blocking his way and he pushed past me, opening the inner door fully and revealing me briefly to everyone inside.

I stepped away quickly, uncertain of whether or not Isobel had seen me there, but guessing this was unlikely, especially considering her drunkenness.

I went back into the noisy street and continued home.

15

'Count it, count it.' Cora ran to me the moment I entered the house. She waved a fan of money in my face.

I saw Alice standing further back along the hallway, and I wanted to ignore Cora and go straight to her.

Five days had passed since the séance – five days during which I had hardly spoken to either of them, and certainly not about what had happened there. Each time I'd tried to raise the subject of the séance and the air of alarm it had created, I'd been told not to ask, to wait until Alice was ready to explain. Eventually, Cora had shouted at me and I had known not to persist.

'Count it, count it,' Cora said again, and this time she pushed the money into my chest.

'Just tell me,' I said, instantly deflating her excitement.

She lowered the money and turned to her mother. 'I told you this is what would happen. I told you what he'd say.'

I'd heard her talk like this often enough before, but there was now a note of surly, almost aggressive confidence in her voice.

'Money from the séance?' I said to her.

'Where else would I get *twenty pounds* from?'

It was a small fortune.

'Congratulations,' I said to Alice, who smiled nervously back at me.

'Subtracting four pounds for expenses,' Cora said. 'Wine, services, various commissions.'

'She's making most of it up as she goes along,' Alice said, but affectionately.

'No, I'm not,' Cora insisted. 'It's business,' she said to me. 'Tell her. Tell her it's business. Deductible expenses.' Even she seemed uncertain about this.

'I went to see Solomon,' I said to Alice.

'Who's Solomon?' Cora said.

'He and Marta were searched by the police.'

Alice acknowledged this, telling Cora to let me pass her.

'The girl was supposed to be here,' Alice said to me when I reached her. 'We thought you were her. She hasn't showed up.'

Alice had met Solomon and Marta on only a few occasions following our arrival in the house, and had afterwards only known of them what little I'd recounted to her. Even at that distance, she had shown no interest in the couple or their history.

She yawned and rubbed her eyes, looking to me as though she had only recently woken. She had stayed in bed the whole of the day after the séance, and for much of the ones which followed. I took on trust Cora's assurances that her mother was neither ill nor injured, only exhausted by her exertions during the gathering.

I continued into the back room, waiting for Alice to follow me.

'Solomon thought they might come here,' I said. I tried to sound casual, unconcerned.

'Who?'

'The police.'

She showed little true alarm at the suggestion.

'Apparently, they're searching the premises of all photographers. Something to do with a case they're investigating. It's all just a matter of routine. You know how they are.'

'What crime? Why photographers?'

I pretended to be uncertain, suggesting that everything I knew I had just learned from Solomon. 'They've found some photographs in connection with a case they're working on and now they're trying to establish who might have taken them.'

Cora came into the room behind us. She'd overheard most of what I'd just said, and I knew that, unlike her mother, she did not entirely accept my explanation. I waited for her to say something, my answers already well considered in advance of her questioning.

But instead, she said, 'She's been waiting all day to tell you what happened, and all you can talk about is something that's happened to some so-called friend or other? Solomon who? Grundy?' She laughed at her cleverness.

I wanted to shout at her to shut up and to leave us.

'Sorry,' I said to Alice, and then, further diverting her, 'I also saw Howson. He sends his regards.'

'Howson? Oh, Charles.' She remembered the man, but not well. Her last visit to the Lyceum had been two years ago, one of Irving's Christmas extravaganzas for the staff and their families. She had stayed an hour and had then insisted on being taken home because she was suffering from a headache. Last year, upon receiving the same invitation, she had said nothing.

'Tell him what they said,' Cora urged her, our path away

from Solomon complete. 'Tell him how many further book-ings they wanted to make.'

'It's true,' Alice said to me.

'Five out of the eight. And one of them only refused a further sitting because her husband told her to.'

'Well done,' I said. The repeat business both surprised and disappointed me, but I kept this well hidden. 'Perhaps we'll finally shake off some of our debts.' I tried to sound encouraging.

'Debts?' Cora said.

'They're always there,' I said.

'Of course we can,' Alice told me.

Since arriving in the house, we had invariably been several months late with our rent. Other bills were paid according to need, most of these also in arrears. Usually, after a month's delay, the landlord's agent sent a letter feebly threatening us with court action if we didn't pay something within the next fourteen days, which we invariably did, however little of the outstanding sum this might be.

I'd long since convinced myself that it was why I had allowed myself to be persuaded by Bliss to go and see Marlow in the first place. My income had almost doubled overnight, but regardless of this, the money owed never seemed to be reduced. I'd further persuaded myself that this was one of those unavoidable and widely accepted facts of life for all men in my position.

'Debts?' Cora repeated. She held the notes tighter to her chest, as though I was about to reach out and grab them from her. 'This isn't for day-to-day household expenses. This is . . . this is . . .' She struggled for the word, but it eluded her. 'This is *separate*,' she said eventually, her meaning clear to us all.

'Separate,' Alice said, though whether in agreement with Cora or questioning her, I wasn't certain.

'Of course it is. This is your earnings. *Our* earnings. Everything done properly. Like I explained. We open a separate account. Business. And with everything connected to the business put in and taken out as and when required.' She was pleased with the small speech.

'Perhaps a small part of it could be used,' Alice suggested.

But I saw there was no real argument in her. She remained distracted, unfocussed in her thoughts and what she said.

'I suppose it makes sense,' I conceded to Cora, but only for my wife's sake.

'Of course it makes sense,' Cora said. 'Just think of all the outgoings.'

Including her own wages and expenses? Including everything she spent in exercising her new-found power?

And as though I'd said this out loud, she said, 'We'll be increasing the advertising, for a start. Perhaps we could even increase the number of sittings.'

Alice looked alarmed at the suggestion.

Cora saw this and said quickly, 'Not for them all to be like Tuesday night. Some individual sittings for high-payers. Some for bigger groups that perhaps don't take so much out of you.' She faltered in the face of her mother's growing concern.

I saw my opportunity. 'Is that what happened?' I asked Alice. 'Did last Tuesday tire you more than you anticipated?'

The two of them exchanged a glance.

After a moment, Cora bowed her head and said, 'Tell him.'

'Tell me what?'

'Wait,' Alice told me. She rubbed her face and then sat opposite me. 'Leave us alone,' she said to Cora.

'Leave you? I'm your—'

'Please.'

'I'm supposed to take care of you.'

'Then go and record the money in your ledgers, make sure everything's accounted for and up to date.'

'Ledgers?' I said.

'She's been to a stationer's. Bought all sorts of ledgers and account books.'

'Because we *need* them,' Cora said defiantly.

I could see that the idea of doing as her mother suggested now appealed to her, outweighing her reluctance to leave the room and to be excluded from whatever Alice might finally be about to reveal to me – of which, presumably, she was already well aware.

She rolled the banknotes between her palms. 'I'll need your signature when I've done,' she told her mother.

'What for?' Alice said.

'It's good practice. Business practice. You'll need to sign off each page as it's completed.'

Her work today would involve only a few lines of calculation, and most of that unnecessary and devised solely to satisfy her need to do it. Everywhere I looked, the whole world and its workings was being reduced to its record-keeping guardians and their fastidious compilations.

'Of course,' Alice told her, and Cora finally left us.

'Lock the door,' Alice whispered to me.

I did this, hearing Cora climb the stairs above us.

'*Did* something happen?' I asked her, drawing my chair closer to hers. 'Something you didn't anticipate?'

'Not really. She's right about the money needing to be properly accounted for.'

'I know.'

'And perhaps some of it could be used to pay off our debts.'

'They never seem to grow any smaller.' I'd hoped she might at least smile at the remark, but there was nothing. She was delaying telling me something, and I knew not to insist.

I reached out to hold her and she drew her hand beyond my reach.

'You knew about Cora and the newspapers,' she said. 'Before the sitting.'

I remembered our encounter. 'As an aid to your . . .' I didn't know what to add.

'I knew one of the women had recently lost her mother. The obituaries contained a great many details.' She paused. 'The strange thing is, once the séance started, I started getting much stronger feelings about another of the sitters completely.'

'Another woman?'

She nodded. 'She told me she was there in the hope of contacting her granddaughter, a young girl. She said her own daughter, the girl's mother, was still too grief-stricken to come with her. She'd already been to other mediums. She said she knew that only so much time could be allowed to pass before the lingering spirit was beyond my reach.' She hesitated. 'The girl was eight years old when she died.' She looked up at me as she said this and her hand came back to me and I held it.

'The same age as Caroline,' I said, feeling the dryness in my throat.

She smiled. 'I told her I could well understand how her

daughter must be feeling, how she must be grieving, what she had lost.'

I began to feel even more uncomfortable hearing all this. The photo of our daughter still stood on the mantel above the unlit fire. Alice looked up at it and smiled again.

'She told me she knew I would feel the same,' she went on. 'She said she saw something in me that she had not seen in any of the others she'd visited. She called it a quest. All she wanted was to know that the child was happy and well, and that, being so young, she was being taken care of in the Hereafter, that there was someone looking after her, holding her hand, keeping her safe from harm. She'd died suddenly, see? No one had been expecting her to be taken, no preparations had been made.'

'Like Caroline,' I said, the words little more than a whisper. I felt her grip tighten around my fingers. *What possible preparations are there?* I wanted to add.

'Yes, like Caroline.'

'You were able to empathize,' I said.

'That's exactly what she said.' She was gratified by this endorsement. 'I knew nothing about her except her name – the sitter – and yet there she was, calling on all my attention. I tried to keep my mind open to the others, but all I could see and think of was this woman's granddaughter.'

'Only natural,' I said. I wished I had a drink to sip from, some of the leftover wine perhaps.

'I started crying,' she said. 'Crying and crying. I told the woman to keep whispering the child's name, over and over, beckoning her, telling everyone else round the table to join her if they wanted. Most of the other women did, whispering over and over.'

Tears and communal whispering or gentle chanting had always been part of the performance, anything to heighten the senses, to prime expectation and to raise the heartbeat.

'Except it wasn't really even a whisper, something lower.' She closed her eyes briefly. 'And then I heard the child.'

'Heard?'

'I heard a girl's voice. A small girl. Asking for her mother, "Mama". Not crying, exactly, but panicky, uncertain, lost. "Mama", over and over, and gasping, as though she was crying but not crying, gasping for breath perhaps.'

'And only you heard all this?'

She shook her head. 'The woman, the grandmother – she suddenly shouted out that she could hear it, too. She grabbed my hand, desperate not to lose whatever it was, not to let it slip away from us, me. She was begging me by then, please, please, as desperate in her own way as the child was in hers.' She breathed deeply for a moment. 'I spoke to her. Spoke. The voice of the child spoke, I—'

'To say what?'

'I don't know, don't remember. No, not remember – I don't know. All I know is that I spoke, and that afterwards the woman said she *knew* that she had heard her granddaughter. She'd heard her crying and gasping, then she'd heard her talking, and afterwards she'd heard the girl laughing, happy and relieved. She'd called back to her, she said, but had received no answer. I heard none of it; she told me all this afterwards, when I had regained my composure.'

'And the child was at peace, happy, cared for?' My voice was flat.

'I don't know. I imagine so. The woman was laughing through her own tears, telling everyone else at the table that it had definitely been her granddaughter, that the child had spoken to her, and that she in turn had been able to reassure and settle the girl.'

'And you remember none of it?'

She shook her head. 'Cora told me everything afterwards.'

'She heard the child, too?'

'No, nothing. She said only that she could see the woman was hearing someone she recognized and was able to respond to. Except—' She stopped abruptly.

'Except what?'

'Except – I don't know – what proof was that? Afterwards, two or three of the other women said they'd been aware of something, a presence.'

The word was all-inclusive, both undeniable proof and limitless excuse.

'One of them even said that she too could hear the child.'

'What else?' I said.

'I don't understand.'

She had been about to tell me something else and had changed her story after that single 'Except'.

'There's more,' I said. In truth, I wanted neither to know nor to encourage her to tell me.

She made no denial.

'She was so certain that it was her granddaughter's voice, so certain, so convinced. I couldn't even tell you then the child's name, even though *she* called it out a dozen times. A hundred, perhaps. She said she wished her daughter was with her and then she burst into tears. She said afterwards that she was coming back, as soon as possible, and bringing the mother with her. Cora arranged something with her.'

'And you? Afterwards, when the voice was silenced and the presence no longer—'

'I began to remember. Perhaps not accurately or fully, but something. I began to grasp something of what had happened.'

'Was it anything more than the woman had heard, imagined?'

She nodded quickly, but then said nothing.

'It's happened the same way before,' she said eventually. 'But never so – so – never so intensely, so completely. Afterwards, the woman talked about possession, about the dead child possessing me. I tried to deny it, but she only embraced me and kissed me, thanking me and insisting on coming to see me again. The others seemed no less impressed and affected than she was.'

'Even though no one had spoken to *them*?'

'They understand these things.'

Meaning they all knew the odds and the need to end-lessly recalculate their own expectations, suspicions and beliefs.

'The grandmother went on telling them all how good I was, how impressed she was. She told them she was an expert. You should have heard some of the other names she reeled off. Cora asked her how she'd found me and she said it was Cora's advert in the *Herald*.'

One diversion after another.

'Except?' I said, forcing us back.

She looked at me uncertainly for a moment, letting her gaze wander down to where her hands now lay in her lap. She looked again at the photograph of our daughter.

'Except I was never – the voice – I was never certain, never convinced – she shouted, you see, called out the girl's name, and once she'd done that there was no letting go for her.'

'Or for you?'

'For any of us. Perhaps if I'd known what I was saying, what the child was saying through me, how she had come to me, what she might hope to achieve . . .'

'Why were *you* not convinced?' I said. 'By the child, I mean.'

She smiled again, and a look of calm pleasure filled her face, surprising me after all she'd just revealed.

And in that instant, watching her and seeing this sudden change in her, I knew exactly what she was about to tell me and I willed her not to speak, to remain silent.

I waited, unable to stop her.

'Because in the midst of everything, amid all my uncertainty and my – my unknowing – amid my deafness even, I thought I recognized the voice, I thought I—'

'Don't,' I said finally. 'Don't.'

But she ignored me and went on. 'I can't deny it, I can't turn from the truth of the matter. Don't you see?' She reached out again to hold my hand.

'You heard . . .' I said, already faltering.

'I heard Caroline. It was *her* voice talking to me.'

'No,' I said. 'No. You're mistaken, wrong. A moment ago you said you heard and remembered nothing. It's a coincidence, that's all, the ages of the girls, their sudden loss. You only heard what you—'

'I know,' she said firmly.

'You can't know. How on earth can you *know*?'

'I can't tell you how. All I know is that if it had been something or someone else, if I'd contrived the voice or pretended to hear what I wasn't hearing, then I would certainly have remembered *that*.'

However vague and unconvincing this sounded, it was enough of an explanation for *her*, and her own conviction seemed genuine enough.

I sat upright in my chair, not knowing what more to say to her.

'I never spoke,' she said. 'To her, to Caroline. I never spoke to her.'

'Because you didn't know *who* you were talking to,' I said. 'How could you have done?'

'I should have realized sooner, recognized her.'

It had been four years since Caroline had died. What voice? What language? What would there still have been to recognize? But it was beyond me to suggest any of this.

'I can't accept it,' I said numbly and uselessly.

'I know. I've known for the past five days.' She remained in her reverie, holding herself now, still smiling, unassailable in her belief. 'And I know that you will want to deny me, to make me – what? – see sense?'

'I just don't want you to be hurt, to upset or distress yourself,' I said, and that too seemed both inadequate and dishonest of me.

'I know that, too,' she said. 'But my only distress was caused by not realizing straight away what had happened.'

'But why? And why after all this time?'

She held up her hand to me. 'I know,' she said. 'I've asked myself every question you can think to ask me a thousand times over. I understand as little of this as you do.'

I heard footsteps above us.

'And Cora knows everything?' I said.

'We discussed what we'd both seen and heard afterwards, when the woman had gone. The first thing Cora told me was that I'd been wise to wait until we were alone. Something to consider for future sittings, she said.' She smiled at her living child's cleverness. 'Perhaps you too will come to acceptance.'

Come to acceptance? Perhaps I too *would come to acceptance?*

'Perhaps,' I said. I wanted more than ever to tell her that I was having none of it, that I didn't believe a word of what she'd just said, to tell her that she couldn't even convince *herself* of what had or hadn't happened – not truly – let alone convince anyone else. I wanted to tell her she was a fraud. Otherwise why not tell the bereaved grandmother? Why not tell *her*? But I saw how none of this would help my argument. I *did* want her to see sense, but I also saw how far beyond all this she now was, how far beyond it she had been for the past five days, lying in her bed and thinking only of her dead daughter and all that she might now achieve, all she might retrieve and reclaim of what had for so long been lost to us.

'Cora said it was my reward,' she said absently.

And you believed her.

'She said everything that happened was to our advantage in some way.'

'I don't want to hear about it,' I said.

'No, of course. You need time.'

'Don't,' I said, meaning for her to stop talking.

'I do understand, of course I do.'

I wanted again to shout at her – to tell her that she understood nothing, *nothing*, that time was of no account, no account whatsoever, and that what she had imagined, what she had *done* and what she had confessed to me was destructive and wrong.

I left my seat and went to the door, forgetting that I'd locked it, rattling it in my frustration and urgency to leave her and causing the key to fall to the floor. Alice went on speaking to me, but it was more than I could do now even to look at her, let alone answer her.

16

Irving and Stoker returned, and with them came a week of even greater heat. The warmth built up beneath the roof of the Lyceum, and throughout the building doors and windows were fastened open in an attempt to encourage the cooler air of the auditorium to circulate. It was the same every summer, and every summer Stoker announced plans to do something about the stifling air. But by the time the various schemes had been devised, planned, prepared for and costed, the heat had invariably fallen. The additional cost no longer made sense; the summers were always short; autumn would soon be here; we were troupers; we would endure. Stoker himself seldom appeared dressed in anything except his buttoned-up jackets and stud collar shirts with his tie pulled tight to the top.

I was with Howson when a boy ran to us and said that Irving was calling a meeting with all his senior staff down in the auditorium. And even in that young voice I heard the magic, the privilege and the thrill of conveying the man's summons. I even heard it in the echoes as he ran along the web of corridors and passageways to complete his errand.

Howson patted the papers he had been examining into a neat pile.

'Perhaps Mother's brought us all back a present from gay

Paree.' He took out a handkerchief and wiped the sweat from his brow, cheeks and neck.

I pretended to laugh, too conscious of my last encounter with Stoker to be anything but apprehensive of this one. Since my meeting with Bliss and Pearl, I had tried to contact Marlow via the usual channel, but with no success. There, too, I saw nothing but the darkening skies of conspiracy.

Howson rose and waited for me in the doorway. 'Do you think Stoker will want me to take the accounts to show him?' It seemed almost a pathetic, demeaning gesture to make.

'Not so soon after their return,' I said. But my response clearly concerned him – perhaps because he too wanted something with which to shield himself against the man.

I left my own work and went to him. He locked the door behind us and we joined the slow stream of others making their way down through the building. Even those members of staff not called for by Irving would want to go and see him after even this short an absence.

Irving was pacing the stage when we arrived. Twenty others were already gathered and waiting there. Stoker and Loveday sat together centre-stage. Jimmy Allen stood amid the stage-hands, all of them keen to return to whatever work this impromptu gathering had interrupted.

'Are we all assembled, are we all gathered?' Irving called eventually.

Stoker rose stiffly from his seat and called for silence.

'Thank you, Abraham.' Irving threw wide his arms. 'Gentlemen, your warm greeting humbles me and makes me glad to be back among you, my own dear tribe. My short vacation – that is the word – has been both enlightening and restorative. Sun, rest, cares and concerns blown away.'

He blew along his outstretched arm and palm. Cares and concerns blown away by Stoker, who would have worked twice as hard and twice as long to keep Irving rested amid all that restorative emptiness.

Stoker himself, I noticed, had looked up at my arrival, smiled briefly and then actually nodded to me. He exchanged the same quick greeting with Howson. I won't say there was any true warmth in this, but I would concede to at least the suggestion of warmth. Perhaps he too had had time to think: to allow everything that he suspected of happening in the theatre to right itself of its own accord and for its steady and well-regulated course ahead to be resumed.

Beyond him, Irving was still speaking.

'Mr Loveday informs me of how hard you have all been working during my absence.'

I exchanged a glance with Howson. Loveday had been noticeable largely by his absence during Irving's holiday.

Jimmy Allen came out on to the stage, causing Irving to pause in his speech and for Stoker to call for a chair for the old man. A sheen of sweat covered Jimmy Allen's face and he wiped at it with his fingers.

Seeing this, Irving said, 'Precisely, precisely. And believe me, Jimmy, we are all feeling it. And you the old India hand.' There was laughter at the remark.

Beside me, Howson groaned, and I guessed from the sudden flick of Stoker's eyes that he had heard this, though possibly imagining it to have come from me rather than Howson.

In Stoker's absence, I had done everything in my power to discover the location of all the costumes and props which had passed through my hands during the previous few months.

I had searched the Lyceum and I had searched the South-all depot. I had examined my own copy of Irving's photographic record, and I had checked and then cross-checked the theatre's accounts of removals against my own secret record of everything I had diverted to Marlow. And by the end of that time – I had been completing the work when Irving's summons had come – I believed I had a solid defence against whatever else Stoker might still wish to accuse me of.

Where items remained with Marlow, I was able to place them deep in the Southall inventories; where items were due for return, I was able to make them appear available for immediate collection. And where I could find items in neither the theatre nor the depot, and yet had no record of loaning them to Marlow, I was able to create a dozen good yet unconfirmable reasons why such items might *appear* not to be accounted for. My final argument in all these instances was that simply because an item of clothing might not be inventoried, then that certainly didn't mean that it didn't still exist somewhere, overlooked, forgotten, diverted, unwanted, being repaired or undergoing some other form of restoration. I was word perfect in all of this. It was all a long way from 'stolen'. The wheat and the chaff of all this blew in the same unpredictable winds and into the same hidden, unseen corners.

I believed I had done a good job. I had even practised the indignation and disbelief with which I would frame my rebuttals against further accusations. My only true concern during all this time was that I had been unable to contact Marlow and to have confirmed by him what he still possessed and what, if necessary, he might quickly return.

I smiled firmly and nodded back to Stoker.

'And so to the purpose,' Irving said, clapping his large hands together and then listening to the dying echo of this all around him. Something else he never tired of doing. 'An impromptu performance. Our dear Ellen is free and in full agreement.'

There was a round of applause merely at the mention of Terry's name. Until recently, she had been away on the Northern Circuit and then in the South West, appearing in both *A Winter's Tale* and *The Corsican Brothers*, alternating performances and appearing twice daily at the weekend. Everything, as usual, a sell-out. Following that, she had been briefly in Germany and Belgium. It was likely that Irving and Stoker had met up with her in Paris.

'It was her dearest wish to be here with us – with us all – this very morning. Unfortunately, she is detained by family matters. But be in no doubt – she will be with us once again soon enough.'

I watched Stoker's forefinger stiffen in a signal and then rise and fall in his lap.

Irving saw this, too. 'Mr Stoker urges me to completion,' he said. 'Quite right, quite so. To the point, enough procrastination and meandering.' He paused for an even longer bout of laughter. 'Old man Macbeth,' he shouted. 'The Scottish tragedy. Here, for one week and one week only, during the late-August interval.'

It would be a popular production; everyone would come.

'The Queen's favourite,' Irving said. 'Shakespeare, the Bard himself.'

'Oh, *that* Macbeth,' Howson said, this time unheard above the applause and rising voices. Neither of us avoided the unlucky title.

Demand for seats would be instantaneous the moment the performances were announced. A week would be nowhere near long enough, but the existing theatre schedule – another of Stoker's closely guarded responsibilities – would allow no overrun.

I saw by Stoker's face that he understood this better than any of us, and certainly better than Irving, for whom some degree of flexibility and unconsidered change seemed always to exist. I imagined what might already have been said by Stoker to try and dissuade Irving from the production. But nothing would have counted against the appearance of Ellen, and Irving's chance to appear alongside her in their one true home.

'There'll be riots,' Howson said. 'This is one for the nobs, and the nobs alone.'

'It's for Irving,' I said. 'How long since he and Ellen—'

'Eighteen months, more. The Royal, Bradford. Tennyson's *Becket*.'

'The King and Queen back in their castle.'

Around us, the applause grew louder. Beside Stoker, Loveday sat and grinned.

'Hard work all round, I'm afraid,' Irving said. 'But you are the men and the women of the finest theatre in the city, in the land, and I know that I am asking no more of you than you are capable of delivering. Miracles, perhaps; miracles indeed; but miracles we have all performed before and many times over.'

'The Gospel according to Saint Henry,' Howson said, and then, raising his voice, 'Three cheers for Henry. Hip hip—'

The uproar which ensued was full and lasting.

'See how easy it is?' he said to me behind his hand as others prolonged the noise.

'I don't see Mother cheering too hard,' I told him.

'He's just spent a wasted week trying to talk the old man out of it, that's why.'

And it was another reason why Irving had added Ellen to the plan: no one resisted her, least of all Stoker. He was brother, husband, father and child to her, and she the mirror image to him. He would have walked across the Irish Sea back to Dublin if he'd heard she'd so much as sneezed there. He would shadow her throughout her brief return and performances, and his eyes would not close for an instant while she was onstage.

Irving signalled for silence, and then, cupping a hand to his ear, said, 'What is it that you ask me? What part shall I take for myself?'

Clearly, no one had shouted to ask him this, but now everyone around him wished they had done so, and several started to call out.

I saw Stoker sit forward in his seat, his head resting briefly in his hands.

'Let me guess,' Howson whispered to me.

'Why, the old King himself, of course, and dear Ellen my wife.'

There was further applause.

He had played Romeo to her Juliet, and Abelard to her Heloise, juvenile lovers all, and after both performances there had been some cruel jokes from the critics which he had affected not to hear, then or since.

'And between us we shall give the performance of the season, of *any* season.'

Even the persistent summer heat would not keep people away. Besides, by then it would be the month's end and the thickening air would be moving again.

'So – shall we do battle?' Irving shouted.

Stoker lifted his head from his hands and joined the applause. Beside him, Loveday clapped twice as loudly, twice as rapidly and for twice as long. He was a clapping machine in a competition of applause.

This lasted a full minute, silenced only by Irving again raising his hands and repeating to us all how much he had missed us and how moved he was now by our response. He took out a brilliantly white handkerchief and wiped his face, a careful stroke beneath each eye to add a little pathos. He was our figurehead, our rallying call, our pennant stiffening in a rising breeze. It would be up to Stoker to start working out all the details, the minutiae of this great event. And he in turn would soon impress upon the rest of us the lesser parts we were about to play. He would approach Howson to discuss costings, and he would come to me to arrange for publicity and promotional material. After which, the drama of the drama would begin anew.

Irving went to Jimmy Allen and Jimmy rose to meet him. The stage-hands and others gathered around the two men. They patted Irving on his back and shoulders and he thanked them all. I doubted if he knew the names of two of the two dozen men. He shook Jimmy Allen's hand, waiting for another break in the noise.

'Not much work for you, dear prompt,' he said. 'Not with the old King.'

'Nor Miss Terry, neither, I should imagine,' Jimmy Allen said.

'No. Precisely right. Nor Miss Terry, neither.' He looked around him. 'Is there a man here who can wait to hear her opening speech in Act One, Scene Five?'

There was a moment of uncertain hesitation and then more applause and loud agreement, all of it safer than laughter now.

'I thought not,' Irving said. 'I shall employ again the script I took so wonderfully and successfully to America,' he said, meaning his own not inconsiderable 'improvement' on the original.

Centre-stage, Stoker rose from his seat and indicated for Loveday to do the same. The two of them came to where Howson and I sat together.

'You had a pleasant vacation?' I said to Stoker.

'Holiday, yes. Very pleasant. Naturally, one is never completely detached from one's duties and obligations, but—'

'Naturally,' Howson said, causing me to wonder again at his new-found bravery.

'Was there anything you wanted?' I said to Stoker.

'Wanted?' He pretended to think. 'I don't think so. Mr Loveday here has fully appraised me of everything during my absence.'

Including the fact that I had not turned up at the theatre for over a week?

I glanced at Loveday, who understood me perfectly.

'Is this a good idea?' Howson said unexpectedly, indicating Irving, who was by then lost amid his admirers, or at least amid the men extending their break from work even longer.

'Henry was very insistent,' Stoker said, and I heard his own defeat in the evasion.

'Still,' Howson said, 'with Miss Terry and everything . . .'

'Yes,' Stoker said. 'It will be good to see her perform here again.'

Even he, it struck me, regretted the formality of this response, simultaneously betrayed by and betraying his own true feelings. He put his hand on Loveday's shoulder and the two of them left us. I half expected Howson to whisper, 'Good riddance,' when they were out of hearing, but he said nothing, merely watching them closely as they went.

The crowd around Irving and Jimmy Allen finally dispersed, and Irving detached himself from his prompt and came to us.

'You are wise to sit,' he said. 'Cooler than this in Paris. Did you know there is soon to be an opera house far, far up the Amazon river? In the hope of attracting all the Italians to perform there. Incredible.'

Both Howson and I rose and waited.

'It can be done?' Irving said to us. 'Here? In the time available? As much for Ellen as myself. More, perhaps. Her public is ever eager.'

She was standing beside us, between us, behind us, sitting in both the seats we had just vacated.

'I daresay a longer period between performances might have been handy,' Howson said eventually.

Irving laughed at the word. 'Handy, yes. But that is what we are – handymen.'

'You'll want photographs,' I said.

'Special performance, special photographs. Ellen and myself in particular. Something new. I swear she looks younger and more beautiful with each passing year. Agreed?' He waited for us both to nod our concurrence. 'Do you have something in mind, some new photographic technique you might employ to advantage? Everything nowadays is so modern, up to the minute. The world moves so swiftly. All the time in the world for some things, yet no time whatsoever for others. I was debating the same thing with regard to the new production with Abraham only a few days ago.'

And I heard the argument in its entirety, each small demand and counter-demand batted back and forth like soft balls. I took pleasure in Stoker's defeat – not so much in the fact that it had happened, but that he himself would have been only too acutely aware of its inevitability from the moment the debate started, destined to flow to this unwinnable conclusion.

'I'll see what I can do,' I told Irving. It seemed clear to me by then that whatever doubts Stoker himself might still have harboured, he had communicated nothing of these to Irving.

'Good man, good man.' Irving grasped and held my shoulder for a moment, his mind already elsewhere, further along the course of that swiftly flowing stream.

When he released me he immediately turned and walked back across the stage, his heels a quickening drumbeat into that endlessly beckoning and promising future.

17

I left the theatre early in the afternoon and made my way along Savoy Place towards one of my photographic suppliers on Villiers Street, immediately behind Charing Cross Station.

I had worked all morning in anticipation of a further visit from Stoker, but he hadn't come. For most of that time I was alone in my room and only the hammering and sawing of the carpenters reached up to me. There would be no true preparation for the new play as yet, but the word of it had run like an electrical current through the entire building and then through the veins of everyone in it. I'd already sent a boy to Villiers Street to let the supplier know I was coming.

I was approaching the Players' Theatre when I became aware of someone close behind me, walking in step with me, and I was about to stop and turn to see who this might be – already suspecting Stoker – when I felt a hand at my back.

'Mr Webster. What a pleasant and unexpected surprise.'

Marlow.

I smelled his cologne and the cigar smoke on his breath.

'Not to say fortuitous.'

I turned to face him.

He lowered his hand and then turned to look out over the water. A small steamer cleared her stack beneath us, surrounded by lighters, their hanging sails blackened with smoke. Flotsam gathered around the vessels, and the river itself seemed hardly to be flowing.

'I was hoping to see you,' he said eventually.

Marlow, I knew, did not live in a world of fortuitous surprises and chance encounters. In all the time I had known him, this was perhaps only the third or fourth time I had ever seen him anywhere except Golden Square.

'Are you on an errand?' he asked me. He made me sound like the boy I'd sent out.

'Not particularly. I come and go,' I said.

'Your own master. Of course.' He took several draws on his cigar.

'Yourself?' I said.

He shrugged. 'A constitutional? Some river air?' He did nothing to maintain the pretence of our chance encounter, and I waited for him to say more, to reveal the true purpose of our meeting to me. I wondered how he knew where I'd be, how long he might have been waiting for me to appear.

'Swans are dying at Henley,' he said.

The remark caught me unawares. 'What?'

'Swans. Dying in the heat. This year's hatchlings. It was in all the papers. The Queen is said to be very concerned. Mind, the old girl seems to live her life constantly in thrall to one extreme emotion or other these days.' He laughed at the remark. Then he touched my arm and said, 'Walk with me. Lunch? Lunch. Have you eaten?'

I hadn't, but coming so soon after our contrived encounter, the invitation seemed too much. But before I could respond, he stopped a passing cab, and before I fully understood what was happening, I was sitting in it beside him.

We rode into the slow confusion of the Charing Cross Road and then along Long Acre. The cab stopped and Marlow climbed out. He paid off the driver and then led me towards the Market, turning before we reached this into an alleyway connecting – or so I assumed – Long Acre with Floral Street. There was a gate at the far end, and nothing of the day's heat or light penetrated the narrow space.

We turned out of this into an equally restricted court, and there Marlow rapped at an anonymous-looking door.

'Private dining club,' he said to me, tapping his nose in the exaggerated gesture of a music-hall villain. 'Places for people like us.' He rapped again, nodding at the man who eventually unlocked and opened the door. This man recognized him immediately, came out and shook his hand. Marlow introduced me to him and he held out his hand to me, too.

'A very good friend and close colleague of mine,' Marlow said. 'I'm fortunate enough to have him as my guest today.'

The doorman released my hand and stood aside to let us enter.

'Shall I sign the book?' Marlow asked him, and thus prompted, the man took out a book. Marlow signed and indicated for me to do the same.

The man then led us up a flight of stairs into the dining room, which overlooked the west side of the Market. Shaded sunlight filled the space, and steam rose in wisps from several heated trolleys at its centre. There were a dozen other diners already there and Marlow acknowledged the men he knew as we waited briefly to be shown to our table.

We were seated away from the window, and menus were swiftly brought to us. Marlow left his face-down on the table.

'No one here knows you,' he said.

'I know.'

'No – not you specifically. I mean, no one here knows you. No one here sees you, hears you, speaks to you, remembers you, talks of you afterwards.'

I told him I understood him.

'The world is such a public place these days. The nights are becoming as bright as day, and every Tom, Dick and Harry can have his say in the newspapers.'

He said all this in a manner which reminded me of Irving and I told him this.

He laughed, and then surprised me by saying, '*Macbeth*? Ridiculous. Will he butcher it to suit himself?'

It had been less than three hours since Irving had announced his news.

'How do you know?'

He was unconcerned by all the question might imply. All this time, of course, I was waiting only for our conversation to turn to Aston-Fox and the murdered girl. He clearly knew I had been trying to contact him.

'Am I not *supposed* to know?' he said. 'Is it a secret? Heroic Henry keeping a *secret*? Whatever next?'

'I suppose not,' I said.

'I was talking earlier to one of your seamstresses, a girl with whom I've had some dealings. She was full of it. Perhaps you might know her.' He told me the girl's name, but it meant nothing to me. 'Devon or Somerset accent, something rustic.'

It was still no clue.

'She was certainly very rustic in her ways, as I remember.' He tapped his fingers on the table.

'So you met me by design?' I said.

He laughed again at the phrase, and shrugged. It was only what we both already knew. 'Florrie, I think she called herself. Or Flossie. I remember at the time thinking it made her sound like one of her father's farm dogs.'

It unsettled me to be reminded like this of these connections to the theatre.

'Does it matter?' he said. 'That I knew of Irving's plans?'

'I just—'

'She certainly knows you. Florrie. Flossie. Perhaps I could arrange a meeting.'

He was not being serious, but I was slow to see this.

'To what end?'

He raised his eyebrows at the remark. 'To whatever end you desired, I should imagine.'

No answer was expected of me. The remark had been more of a test than a genuine offer, and by then this careful detour had served its purpose perfectly.

A waiter approached us and Marlow ordered lunch for both of us. Everything was his regular or favourite choice and the waiter already knew this.

'And wine?' the man said.

'Whatever you think,' Marlow told him.

The waiter picked up the menus and slid them beneath his arm, turning up our glasses before leaving us.

'I pay my subscription for the expertise of others,' Marlow said. 'We won't be disappointed. Now.' He laid the sides of his hands on the table and locked his fingers.

I waited for him to say what I was there to hear.

But he remained silent, looking briefly over my shoulder at the others in the room.

After my earlier encounter with Stoker, I felt brave; or if not brave, exactly, then considerably more confident than I had felt since my encounter with Bliss and Pearl.

'Pearl was telling me of your concerns,' he said eventually.

'Not Bliss?'

'Regarding Stoker's suspicions,' he said. 'Why Bliss?'

'He was with her when I last saw her.'

He shrugged. 'Bliss is more than capable of looking after his own interests. I have every faith in him, and so should you. What was it – this ridiculous Aston-Fox business? Stop worrying. The man has friends in high places. Very high places. No one likes a scandal except the press, upsets too many people. What, you believe for one minute that it will go to trial?'

The waiter returned with our wine. I expected Marlow to fall silent, but instead he went on.

'Aston-Fox and his friends are already whispering in all the necessary ears.'

'The police have already—'

'The police have already done what they always do in cases like this – they've run around and made a lot of noise in an effort to make themselves appear to be doing something useful. I don't suppose it occurred to you to ask yourself *where* they're doing all this running around and shouting. I don't see Aston-Fox or any of *his* friends being hauled out of their beds at an ungodly hour.' He broke off to taste the wine the waiter had poured, nodding once.

I wondered if the emphasis on 'his' was in some way intended to suggest Solomon to me, but decided I was probably reading too much into the remark.

The waiter half-filled both our glasses and then left the bottle in a bucket beside our table with a napkin round its neck.

'Have they been to see you?' I asked him.

'Taste it.'

'What?'

'Taste the wine. Of course they've been to see me. Or, rather, I went to them. I told them I'd heard a rumour about supposedly knowing the dead girl and that I insisted on putting the record straight.'

I tasted the wine and told him what he wanted to hear, that it was delicious. But my lazy approval disappointed him and he repeated the word.

'What did they say?'

'What *could* they say? That they were grateful for my help? That they had no idea who I was or where I might fit into their current inquiries?'

'They didn't know you?' It seemed unlikely.

'Of course they *knew* me, or at least *of* me. And they will certainly have their heads filled with a great deal more once others start spreading their poison.' He seemed unconcerned by all the remark suggested. 'I tell you,' he went on, leaning slightly forward as though to share a confidence, 'Aston-Fox is leaving all those little people and their connections behind him like Napoleon left Moscow behind him.' He thought well of the comparison and laughed at it.

Little people like Solomon? Little people like all his photographer friends? Little people like me? I was being ridiculous. I had never even *heard* of Aston-Fox until Bliss had shown me the newspaper report.

'You do see what I'm saying to you?' he said, waiting.

'Besides, I've got enough on my plate with the blessed Wheeler and his equally blessed Vigilance Committee.'

'One of those other people spreading their poison?'

He laughed. 'Oh, commander-in-chief, I should say, of all those righteous do-gooders and poison-spreaders. They raided the London Stereoscopic Company this morning.'

'The police?'

'With prophet Wheeler leading the charge.'

'Is it close to home?'

He was amused by this, too. 'Perhaps not close in the way you mean, but close enough. Do you know what Wheeler calls me?'

I shook my head.

'"The London Satyr". Practically the first thing he said upon picking up his sword and donning his armour. I've been called many things, but never that.'

The title might have been intended as an ineradicable insult, but I could tell that something about it appealed to him.

'A satyr,' he said. 'It makes me sound like one of my very own Mediterranean goat boys, my little fauns. Is there some more classical definition which might cast me in a better light, do you think?'

'It's a mythical creature,' was all I could think to say.

'But still a creature. Still something of malicious intent, *sexual* intent, something to be feared and avoided.'

'I suppose so,' I said.

'Called me it and then printed it in one of his tame newspapers, the *Christian Herald*.'

I thought immediately of Cora and her advertisements.

'I've never even met the man to speak to, and yet this.' He fell silent.

'Do you think Aston-Fox will leave the country?' I asked him eventually.

He emptied his glass. 'He'll weigh up the odds and then do whatever he feels is required of him.'

'Will that include confessing to the murder?'

It wasn't an entirely serious question, but he laughed at my ignorance or my naivety or both.

'Tell me her name,' he said.

I didn't understand him. 'Whose name?' My first thought was that we had returned to the theatre and the girl there.

'The name of the strangled girl.'

I tried to remember, but couldn't.

'Exactly,' he said. 'So stop worrying. No wind ever blows for long. Even friend Wheeler will run out of puff when he sees how far it's getting him.'

Our soup arrived, clear and lukewarm.

'I daresay you've already heard about what the police have been up to,' he said, his spoon touching his lips. It was a searching question.

'I know some of the little people, yes.'

'Ah,' he said. 'Touché. Or should that be "Bravo"? Of *course* you know what the police have been up to, where they've been. Perhaps you even blame *me* for all this – this upset. But I assure you, it is completely beyond my control. They're like hounds after a fox, no matter how many rabbits, hares or cats they put up and then savage and kill in that supposedly single-minded pursuit.'

'Is that what *I*'d be – a stupid, innocent rabbit?' I regretted the word 'innocent' even as I said it.

'You? *Do* you know the girl?' His voice was raised now.

'Did you even know of Aston-Fox before he stuck his prick into the painted little whore's mouth with his hands already around her neck? Well?'

I glanced at the others in the room, the closest of whom cannot have failed to hear him, but who still paid us no attention.

'No, but I know *you*,' I said. It sounded much more of a threat than I'd intended.

'Meaning?' His voice was low and calm again.

'You took photographs of her. Of him and her together. I don't know.'

'This is precisely what Pearl conveyed to me,' he said. 'Guesswork, supposition and confusion. Please, believe me, I took no pictures of the two of them together – not like you're implying – not like Wheeler himself will soon be implying. I might have taken pictures of the child before someone introduced her to Aston-Fox, but, and again I ask you to believe me, there will be no record of the fact, nothing for Wheeler to find and to stuff into my own mouth in the courtroom. Do you really have so little idea of me?'

It seemed a strange remark to make, as uncharacteristic as his earlier outburst. But I could see that he was making a sincere attempt to reassure me – as much perhaps for his sake as my own, but reassurance all the same.

'No,' I said. 'I mean, I understand what you're telling me. I believe you.' It was an uncertain apology at best.

He let out his breath. 'Perhaps it would be easier to convince you if Pearl was here with us. You do at least understand the high regard in which I hold her?'

And he, in turn, must also have understood something of my own regard for the woman. Or perhaps he understood this better than I did and it was his only reason for mention-ing her now.

He refilled my glass, adding more to his own.

'And you have no concerns about what Aston-Fox might disclose, *were* he to be questioned?' I said.

'Oh, he'll be questioned, all right, already has been. In all likelihood, they've done nothing *but* question him since the child's body was washed and dressed up and put back on display to prod the newspaper-buying public's endless reserves of moral outrage. Do you imagine I'd be sitting here with you now, eating this fine food and drinking this delicious wine, if he'd said anything thus far to actually incriminate me? Because if you truly believed he *had* already set those hounds on to me, then you'd be a foolish man to be sitting here with me now. Perhaps all the other diners are policemen in disguise, detectives.'

I resisted the urge to look around me again.

'I suppose so,' I said. 'But what if Wheeler keeps them pointed at you?'

'Let him. Besides . . .' He wiped his mouth with his napkin. 'I daresay even Aston-Fox, increasingly desperate though he soon may become, would be foolish enough *not* to realize one or two very important things.'

'Such as?'

He tapped his temple. 'Things, though, as I say, unfindable and untraceable, I might still perhaps *know*, might still perhaps *possess*.'

'"Perhaps"?' I said.

'How did you find the soup?'

'As delicious as the wine,' I said. It seemed almost an insult, but he showed no response.

'Stop worrying about Aston-Fox,' he said wearily after a short silence. 'Besides, what possible connection could anyone draw between *you* and the wretched man?'

We both know you, I thought, but said nothing.

'So everyone is safeguarded except the girl,' I said eventually, wiping my own mouth.

He held up his palms. 'Who was it said that the poor are always with us?'

'Jesus?' I said, and we both laughed at this.

'I doubt he meant these particular poor people,' he said. He reached across the table and patted my arm. 'I told Pearl I had every confidence in you. How long have we known each other, you and I?'

'Three years,' I said.

He raised his glass for a toast.

Our fish arrived and the same waiter filleted this at the table, re-creating the creature detached from its head, tail and backbone.

'It's a skill,' Marlow said, watching the man closely. 'Dressed, undressed, dressed again.' When the waiter had finished, he applauded and then signalled for the man to leave us. 'I'll be mother,' he said to me, using a broad palette knife to put one of the fillets on my plate.

'I imagine you have a very full record of things,' I said.

He smiled at the obvious remark. 'As full as I need.'

'Men even *I* might know.'

The smile remained. 'Men even *you* might know. You hold an important position. The Lyceum? Of course men you know.' He looked up from the fish and held my gaze for a moment. 'Ask me,' he said. 'One name. I'll tell you. Perhaps it will help to reassure or convince you.'

I shook my head.

'One name. As a personal favour from me to you. Name someone.' The fish lay balanced on the knife and he slid it on to his own plate. 'No?'

'No,' I said.

'Then I shall respect your wishes and can do nothing other than applaud your loyalty, however misplaced.' Again, I was only too aware of what he was truly telling me.

A moment of silence followed as we ate the creamy fish.

'Oh, I almost forgot,' he said. 'I owe you an extra debt of thanks.' He took an envelope from his pocket and dropped it on the table between us, where it landed with a loud slap.

'What is it?'

He motioned to the envelope and went on eating.

I picked it up and slid out the photographs it contained, suddenly alert to what might be about to be revealed to me.

I looked through the dozen or so poses.

'I call them my "Ghostly Beauties". My "Serenisimas of the Séance".' He took several of the pictures from me.

Naked women developed in ghostly double-exposures in conjunction with men sitting fully dressed.

'I call this one "Pallida Mors",' he said.

'Pale Death.'

'And this one "Thanatos – The Whited Sepulchre".' Three naked women draped revealingly over a tomb.

"Pallida Mors" consisted of a corpse on a bed, an old woman, out of whom was rising the figure of a much younger, naked woman, and beside the bed, holding the hand of his recently dead wife, a husband already caressing his obvious erection.

'It beats the usual, "Maiden Tribute of Babylon", wouldn't you say?'

I nodded my agreement. This was what Bliss had meant when he'd said Marlow and I had had a conversation of no small consequence.

'Only so much we can do with your average nereid, dryad or silky-tailed mermaid. Perhaps ghostly apparitions and spirit women might provide me with a little more flexibility, and there is certainly a welcome and profitable degree of novelty involved.'

I went on looking at the pictures.

'I was hoping to create something along the lines of the Cabaret de Néant,' he said. 'Are you familiar?'

I told him I was. The Cabaret de Néant light-shows reduced a man to his skeleton, stripping away the photographically superimposed layers of skin, muscle and organs.

'You see such terrible and unconvincing forgeries,' Marlow said.

Alice possessed her own collection of these. Double exposures, mostly. Luminescent paint on dark backdrops and taken with a long exposure. Ghosts created out of quinine sulphate on background sheets.

'Silk blown out of their mouths,' he said. 'What is it, "Ectoplasm"? Who thought that one up? Ghostly hands and faces. So why not ghostly breasts and everything else? They're going to be good sellers. I'm going to offer some of my more adventurous clients the opportunity to be included in the poses. They can even watch the women being photographed "over" themselves and then, if found out – not that many will care much about that – they can deny all knowledge of it ever having happened. It will all look as though someone has played a cruel, unwitting joke on them.'

The picture I held showed two girls sitting on the thighs

of a heavily built man wearing a bowler hat. The skilful superimposition made his hands appear at once both deep between their legs and also innocently rested on his own fat thighs. One of the girls was cupping her small breasts. The other offered hers to the man's unsuspecting lips.

'It was talking to you about your wife,' Marlow said. 'Her profession. My mother's own interest in the subject.' He handed the remainder of the photographs to me. 'Bliss is collecting more for me so I might know what's already been attempted. Too many old maids and resurrected corpses for my liking. You can see my own particular angle. Lovers from beyond the grave, love so powerful it transcends all earthly boundaries and mortal constraints. Bliss even suggested superimposing the heads of actual people on to the bodies of others. Imagine that – forget the dryads and mermaids or whatever – imagine seeing the head of your own dear wife or sweetheart on another woman's body – a woman, say, considerably less inhibited in making a display of herself than your wife or sweetheart might be.'

My own lack of enthusiasm for the idea – connected so closely as it was to Alice's recent unsettling revelation – disappointed him.

I finished looking at the pictures and slid them back into the envelope.

'No – keep them,' he said. 'Please.'

To have refused him would have been to offend and disappoint him even further, and so I put the envelope in my pocket and thanked him.

'If you don't want them, then sell them,' he said. 'Sell them, give them away, burn them, tear them into tiny pieces and throw them in the river. I even suggested to Bliss that I perhaps owed you some financial recompense for the idea, but you can imagine his response to that.' He raised his hand to a departing diner at the far side of the room. The place had already half-emptied of these other invisible, unheard men. 'In a way . . .' he went on, '. . . all this ghost stuff, in a way, I'm not much different to your own dear Henry in that department. All that dressing up and pretending. All this being visited by the dead and the dying and the supposedly in-between. All those deathly hands on the shoulders of the living. Not much difference at all. I imagine Shakespeare to be full of ghosts and ghostly goings-on.'

'It is,' I said.

'Including Henry's forthcoming surprise?'

'He's talking about it as though it's already a great success,' I said.

'And it will be, it will be. Who on God's earth is going to fight to attend the performance and then say otherwise? He's a lucky man, your Henry – he gets audiences as happy to applaud themselves as much as anything *he* might deign to offer them.'

I conceded this in silence.

He looked up at the returning waiter. 'Ah, the veal,' he said, rubbing his hands in anticipation, a gesture as precise and as practised as every other.

18

'You were watching me.'

Isobel came into the small room and sat at the bottom of the bed.

I was at my desk, and Marlow's photographs were under the newspaper I had hurriedly pulled over them at her single knock. I was expecting Cora, who, upon my return, had shouted to me that she wanted to see me, but that she was presently 'otherwise engaged'; she would call for me later. I almost laughed at the imperiousness of the command. I had shouted down the stairs that I was busy myself, but was answered only by a slammed door. I felt slightly unsteady, still half drunk after my lunch with Marlow, despite a sobering walk home of over an hour.

'In the Clarendon.' She took off one of her shoes and rubbed her foot.

I said nothing in response to her – what? – accusation?

'With the others. It was full of navvies.'

'I was never in there,' I said.

She laughed at my discomfort. 'Never said you were. Said you were *watching* me. From the porch, through the door.'

'I don't remember.'

She tutted loudly and wagged a finger at me. "Course you

don't. Think I was one of them, did you? The two others. Annie and Susan. *That*'s why the labourers were in – sniffing around something they could afford for once. Pay day, see? That's why they were all drinking in the first place.'

'Who were the women?' I said. It seemed pointless to continue with my denial.

'Known both of them since I was at the Unicorn.'

'The Unicorn?'

'Opposite the Bedford in Camden. I worked there, serving. Not really the kind of place you'd know was there unless you were looking for it.' She waited for me to acknowledge that I understood her. She sniffed the air. 'You been out drinking yourself?'

'I had a business appointment. Lunch.'

''Course you did.' She looked directly at me. 'You had any luck getting me that job as Ellen Terry's understudy yet?' She laughed loudly at the suggestion, and my only thought was that Cora would hear her. She stopped abruptly. 'What kind of business appointment?'

'With a photographer colleague.' Anything that led us away from the frosted glass of the Clarendon.

'What kind of photographer?'

It was an undisguised provocation and I wanted to tell her to mind her own business and to leave. But I was still uncertain of her reason for being there, or, in truth, of my own for indulging her. I became even more aware of the pictures beneath the newspaper.

'Hot up here,' she said, tugging at her collar. She wore a blouse buttoned to her high apron. 'I'm not allowed to unfasten even the collar. Orders from the new Lady of the Manor.' She meant Cora. 'Perhaps I should have come to you first.'

'For what?'

'Permission to undo a few buttons.' There was a salacious edge to her words. 'While this heat lasts. It gets unbearable sometimes. Your wife still wants the small fires lit. Can you imagine it? A fire in the back, another in the kitchen. The only room she wants kept cool is the spook room.'

'The spook—'

'Sorry – the *spirit chamber.*'

It was what Cora had started calling the parlour, encouraging Alice to do the same, but so far with little success; it would come.

'Cora is only trying—'

'She was looking for you earlier.'

She would have heard Cora calling to me.

'She still is,' I said. I laid a heavy book over the newspaper over the photographs.

'So, what do you think?'

'About what?'

'Me unbuttoning. You're a reasonable man.' She ran a finger from her throat down to her apron strap.

I said nothing.

'Anything just to cool myself down. I bet the girls in the theatre don't run around stuffed up like this. I bet you get to see some rare sights there.'

'I don't work in the dressing rooms. There are rules.'

'And we all know what rules are for.'

If there *was* a purpose to her visit, then I was having difficulty working it out.

'Where was it, this business appointment? Anywhere nice?'

'A dining club in Covent Garden.'

'Covent Garden. All right for some. So, what sort of business was it?'

'Theatre work. Private business.'

'Which?'

'I meant none of *your* business.'

She pretended to be offended. She patted the bed. 'Soft mattress, this. I prefer something a bit firmer myself. Like what you saw, did you?'

We were back at the Clarendon.

'Saw where?'

'They knew as well as I did that you were watching us. I told them. They wanted to shout you in to join us. Get rid of the Irish. But I told them straight off you wouldn't come. Told them you'd only come if *I* invited you to join us. A proper gent. They wanted to know what kind of pictures you took. Both of them have done some photographic work. They said perhaps they might know people you knew yourself.' She paused. 'Other photographers. I told them what kind of pictures you took – the theatre and everything. I kept your name right out of it.'

Everything she now said seemed a kind of uncertain, testing threat to me.

'If you've got something to say, then say it,' I said firmly. 'If you must know, I was walking home, I stepped into the doorway to let someone pass and I heard you in there.' It sounded like the lie it was. 'I was there purely by chance. And even if I had considered going in and breaking my journey, then seeing you there – seeing you all – would certainly have made me think otherwise. Satisfied?'

She was briefly unsettled by this outburst, and then she seemed genuinely offended by what I'd said.

'I would have left them,' she said. 'Would you have come in to me if I'd been all on my lonesome?'

I shook my head at the phrase. She sounded like the second in a risqué double-act.

'Perhaps,' I said. 'Probably. You were supposed to be here, working.'

'You can imagine me turning up in that state, can you? I bumped into Annie and Susan and that was that.' She retrieved her shoe and put it back on. 'Besides, they wanted me to stay, said they were on to a bit of business, the more the merrier.'

'And that was more important to you – more of a priority – than coming here to do what you were paid to do? Alice would have fired you if she'd known.'

'And how would she have known? Tell her yourself, would you? Perhaps you *did* say something.'

'You know I didn't.'

'Like you haven't said anything yet to anyone at the theatre, I don't suppose.'

'When the opportunity presents—'

She snorted at this. 'The other two said they might know you. Went on and on about it. Said they'd ask around. Told me I ought to look out for myself. All one big joke to them.'

'Look out for what?' It was hard to know what she meant by all these half-remarks, and which, if any, might contain another of her buried threats.

She smiled at the question and stood up from the bed.

Below us, the door slammed again and Cora called for me.

'Sounds like you're in demand,' Isobel said. 'Nice that, being in demand. Better not keep Her Ladyship waiting.'

I remained where I sat and Cora called again.

'She was furious at you earlier. "Wait until he gets home," she was shouting. The fortune-teller told her to calm down.'

'Don't call her that,' I said, suddenly reminded of everything that had just happened with Marlow.

'Told her to calm down, that she'd talk to you herself about whatever it was that had got the stupid girl so agitated.'

'Don't,' I said again, louder this time.

'Don't what? Call her that? It's what she is.'

'She's your age,' I said pointlessly.

Cora called again, closer this time.

'You ought to leave,' I said to Isobel. I saw that her top two buttons were now unfastened, her apron crumpled from where she had been sitting on the bed.

She saw me looking. 'I could be in here doing something you'd told me to do,' she said. 'Making the bed or something.'

Cora arrived on the landing outside and pushed open the door without knocking. She came in and stood looking at Isobel, who then slowly and deliberately refastened her buttons.

'What?' I said to Cora, who took a moment to consider what she was seeing.

Isobel curtsied to her. 'I fetched him his newspaper up,' she said, indicating the paper on my desk. The smallest corner of a solitary photograph protruded from beneath it.

'That's right,' I said.

'Mother wants you downstairs,' Cora said to me, still looking at Isobel.

'Will that be all?' Isobel said to me. She left us, her smiling face passing only inches from Cora's.

'She takes liberties,' Cora said a minute after she'd gone, during which time she had remained silent.

'I know,' I said. 'I imagine they all do these days.'

'It's this neighbourhood,' she said absently, looking around the untidy room. 'You'd get better servants somewhere else.'

I let the remark pass. 'Where's Alice?' I said eventually.

'In the –' she had been about to say 'parlour', 'spirit chamber. It has a nice sound to it, don't you think?'

I gratified her by saying it sounded more professional, more suited to its purpose than 'parlour'.

'Precisely,' she said. 'Anyone can have a parlour. These things matter. You'd be surprised how much of this kind of business is to do with the *appearance* of things.'

'I can imagine,' I said, as though the disappointing notion hadn't already occurred to me a thousand times before.

'Appearance and suggestion.'

And delusion, desperation, self-deception, lack of fulfilment, despair, fear and downright need. None of which would ever be appended to her own clipped list.

She took a folded sheet from her pocket.

'I've received this.' She handed it to me. 'It's not even proper notepaper.'

I turned the letter over and saw that it was the one that Solomon had written on behalf of Marta to Alice.

'Is that your so-called friend?' Cora said.

I read what Solomon had written, wondering how long the pair of them had worked at the simple formality of the note.

'What is that – "Martha"?'

'Marta. It's a hard "t".'

'Why can't she call herself Martha and make life easier for herself? Mother said we ought to oblige because you know him professionally. By rights, they're a long way down the list. If it was up to me—'

'Do whatever you think best,' I told her.

'Mother said something about a dead son. They mention him in the letter. Thomas.'

'Tomasz,' I said. '"Toe-mash".'

'This Solomon wants to come with her because she speaks poor English. It's something else we're going to have to consider in the future.'

I stopped listening to her and read the short request a second and third time. I knew what it was costing Solomon to do this for his wife.

'He drowned,' I said.

Cora came immediately to my desk and picked up a pencil. 'Paper,' she said.

I slid a sheet from a drawer, keeping my hand firmly on the hidden photographs.

'Drowned,' she said and wrote it down. She asked me where and when and I told her all I knew. 'So it would have been in the newspapers?' she said.

'I suppose so.' I wanted nothing to do with what she was suggesting.

'She sounds desperate,' she said. 'Mother said we might offer the husband a discount – on account of him being your friend, associate.'

'He would neither appreciate nor accept it,' I said.

'That's what I told her. They're proud people, these foreigners.'

And Solomon would certainly know that I'd told Alice everything I knew about their drowned son. And if I tried to excuse myself or to apologize to him for my part in the contrivance, then he would assure me that he fully understood what I'd done. He would probably even lie and tell me that he appreciated my efforts in ensuring Marta was satisfied in her need.

'She said she can see them on Friday.' Three days away.

'So soon?'

'She said you might let him know.'

'I won't be seeing him,' I said. 'Besides, it would look better coming from you. You could write to him using your new notepaper.' Two thousand sheets, headed, plus envelopes.

She brightened at this. 'You're right,' she said. 'What else?'

'About what?'

'Solomon and Martha, their son.'

Everything I said was a small and painful betrayal. I even told her about the police raid and that Marta had been under the impression it had been something to do with their status as nationalized residents. And she wrote all this down, too. It was more than enough for the pair of them.

'A period of great anxiety and uncertainty for the future,' she said. '*Will* they be thrown out?'

'Of course not,' I said.

'Then mother can tell her that Thomas – Toe-mash – is reassuring her that everything will be all right.'

I wanted to tell her not to be so blatantly obvious or so calculating. 'I suppose so,' I said, my duplicity complete. 'Perhaps your mother . . .' I was uncertain what I wanted to add.

'Perhaps she what?'

'All this business with Caroline. Perhaps the spirit of Marta's son won't talk to someone so young. Perhaps—'

'And perhaps he *will* talk to her – through her. It's the

chance everyone takes. I'm sure *something* will be achieved.'
Her conviction alarmed me and made me cautious of saying
anything more on the matter – alarmed me not only because
of its seeming impregnability, but also by the suddenness with
which this high, solid wall had been erected.

'Is that what Alice believes will happen?' I asked her. 'That
Caroline will talk to her again?'

'She's a spirit guide. All the true spiritualists have them.'

And before? She remained oblivious to my concerns.

'How old was Toe-mash?' she said. 'Other children?' She
added my answers to her list.

I asked silently for Solomon to forgive me, to protect his
beliefs and memories of his lost child, as I was trying to protect
my own. I suppose I had always felt this connection to the
man. It was certainly nothing more than that, and certainly
never a connection either of us had acted upon – merely a
shared and unshakeable understanding, an acknowledgement,
nothing ever spoken about or otherwise indulged. And now
here were our two wives enjoined on a similar and parallel
course.

'I wonder if a single sitting will suffice,' Cora said, drawing
me back from these circling thoughts.

'I suppose if the spirit guide offers sufficient information
. . .' I said, hoping my meaning was clear to her.

She looked up from her writing. 'The spirit guide is only
an *aide*,' she said angrily. 'It's what the spirits *divulge* that
matters. This kind of knowledge is merely a *conduit* through
which the spirit world functions.' Her new pleasure in these
convoluted and meaningless phrases was obvious.

'Of course,' I said.

'You sound as though you want the woman to go away

disappointed. She's lost her only son. He *drowned*. You ought to show a little more understanding, a little more sympathy. These people are supposed to be your friends.'

'They are,' I said. Whatever direction I now moved in, I was surrounded by these silently turning currents and eddies of contrivance, deception and betrayal.

'And how well does *he* speak the language?'

'Solomon? More or less fluently.'

'I told Mother it would be a feather in our cap to use the word "international" somewhere in our advertising. After all, there are plenty of foreigners here, and they've all got something in their past reaching out to them. Most of them wouldn't be here otherwise.'

'And with lots of dead relatives,' I said.

'I told her that as well. *Also* to consider, is the fact that they'd come with their own paying interpreters.'

I stopped listening to her, my own daughter, my own flesh and blood, so different from the child I had lost. Or perhaps that too was a delusion: perhaps Caroline would have grown from a child to a woman and have been exactly like Cora; perhaps in time I would have relinquished all influence and authority over Caroline, just as I had unwittingly relinquished it over her older sister; perhaps Caroline existed now more in my own mind as someone I had wholly created, someone beyond all my vivid or fading memories of her. And perhaps this was the greatest delusion of all – greater even than Alice's in believing that she now communicated with our lost daughter; and greater by far than Marta's in believing that her own dead son might now suddenly speak to her after being so long lost to her.

'Can I see?' Cora said.

I hadn't been listening to her. 'See what?'

'The paper. I've placed an advert.' She motioned to my hand, the book beneath it, the paper beneath that.

I knew how suspicious she would become if I refused her.

'Of course.' I rose and stood between her and the desk, sliding the paper from beneath the book, and at the same time ensuring that the photographs remained concealed.

'I've told Mother that if they don't print the advert as prominently as I've instructed them to, then we're withholding part of the account.'

'Good business practice,' I said. Safe ground. The path ahead.

She pulled the paper from my hand and searched through it. She found the advert and then read it as though she had never seen it before. It was identical to the one placed in the *Herald*. I watched her lips forming the few words she had laboured so long over. I saw the excitement in her eyes.

I was no longer of any use to her and so she left me, already calling for her mother as she reached the lower landing.

19

The next day I went with Alice to visit Caroline's grave. Our daughter had died at the height of another summer, on the fifth of August, and on that date each month we made the journey together.

In the beginning, it had been a harrowing occasion, and Cora and I had frequently been obliged to support Alice between us and then to lower her to the grave, where she had sometimes stayed on her knees for up to an hour. For six months there was only the mounded earth and a simple wooden cross as a marker, but eventually this was replaced by a granite surround and a marble headstone with a gilt inscription.

For the first year or so after our daughter's death, I had come to dread these occasions. Whatever improvements Alice seemed to have made in the meantime, all was undone by the visits, and her grief remained raw and uncontainable. I felt embarrassed standing beside her while she wept on her knees, her gloved hands patting the soil as though her buried child might somehow acknowledge her anguished summons.

After a year, Alice had grown calmer, and Cora had accompanied us less frequently, supposedly busy with her schooling. I still dreaded the visits, but I quickly came to understand, and then to accept, my own role in the proceedings. I sometimes visited the grave alone, never telling Alice that I'd been, and my feelings on those occasions were completely different.

On this morning, however, I was uncertain again, wary, and alert to whatever new meaning Alice might wish to impose on the visit in the light of all that had recently happened. It had occurred to me that she might now come to regard our visits to the grave as something considerably more than the simple acts of remembrance they were for me. Perhaps we were now people visiting a sacred grove, an oracle. There was little doubt in my mind that Alice too would have considered all of this during her own long night of preparation.

She passed me on the stairs as I descended, and she surprised me by embracing me briefly, telling me she was going up to dress for the visit, and then smiling at me – all as though to reassure me that nothing had changed and that she understood my concerns. I told her I'd wait for her, unable to broach even my smallest doubts. She seemed almost happy, and certainly less upset or confused than I'd seen her on recent occasions.

Cora was already in the kitchen, sitting at the table and opening the morning's mail.

'Are you coming with us?' I asked her.

She looked up at me in my black suit with its stiff collar.

'She told me not to.'

I wondered if Alice had thought to ask the same of me. How would I have answered her?

'That came for you,' she said.

A solitary envelope amid the pile of at least twenty others. Old clients writing to Alice directly.

'Sittings?' I asked her, and she spread the envelopes along the table to make them look even more impressive.

'I'll soon be able to cut the number of adverts. *Reduce* them. Soon everything will be done by word of mouth.'

Another cool and rising well, primed and starting to flow. It could not have been a month since her first advertisements.

I picked up my solitary envelope. It was from Bliss. Another of his summonses on behalf of Marlow. Or perhaps simply a note to let me know how much Marlow had appreciated or enjoyed or benefited from our lunch together.

Cora was too busy with her own work of slitting and unfolding to pay me any real attention. I put the envelope in my pocket unopened.

'Do you miss her?' I said.

'Caroline?' She stared ahead of her for a moment, unable to answer, or unable to tell me what she believed I wanted to hear.

'You could come with us,' I suggested. In the early months, I'd been glad of her tempering presence at the grave.

'Because of what happened?' she said.

'I just think your mother might appreciate you being there.'

She shook her head. 'She told me to stay at home and to see to all this. There'll be other applications in the afternoon post.'

Most days there were three deliveries, each one bringing further requests, another tide to this uncharted shore.

'Of course,' I said.

'You think it's changed things,' she said. 'It hasn't. Visiting the grave and what happens in *there* –' she motioned to the

241

parlour, 'are two separate things completely. *Everything* that happens in there is – separate, not part of anything else.'

'You can't know that,' I said, wishing I'd kept the thought to myself.

She rose to this immediately. '*Why* can't I? Why should *you* know better? You'd be happy if all this ended, or if—' She stopped abruptly as the door opened and Alice came in to us.

She wore a dark-blue skirt and jacket, not her usual black, and this surprised me. She wore no veiled hat, only a small cap pinned more to the side of her head than to the top.

She waited in the doorway for me to remark on this.

'It's been five years,' she said, smiling hesitantly. 'I thought that perhaps it was time for a change. In fact . . .'

'Go on,' Cora said. 'You can say it. Tell him.'

Alice looked at me, still smiling.

'Caroline told her it was time to stop grieving,' Cora said boldly.

None of us spoke for a moment.

'At the séance?' I said eventually.

'She said I should be happy for her,' Alice said, her eyes still on me.

'Happy?'

'That *she* was happy, contented, and that there was no need to go on grieving so sorely for her.' She brushed imaginary dust from her shoulders.

'Is it a new hat?' I asked her.

'Cora said it suited me.'

'It does,' Cora said. 'And Caroline will like it, too.' She looked at me hard, daring me to even speak, let alone question or challenge the remark.

'It's very attractive,' I told Alice, and she nodded once, her acknowledgement of the effort I was making on all our behalves.

The journey to the cemetery required two bus rides. Alice liked to arrive at the grave by eleven, stopping only to buy flowers from the seller at the gates – white carnations usually, because these were the appropriate blooms for an innocent child's grave.

She indicated the envelopes.

'I'll make a selection,' Cora told her.

I could easily guess the criteria by which that would be done.

Alice watched her for a moment before turning back to me and saying, 'I've written to your friend.'

'She *dictated* it,' Cora corrected her. 'Last night. To me.'

'To confirm Friday.'

'Thank you. It will mean a lot to Marta.'

Cora then made a signal to her mother, which Alice didn't understand. 'The girl,' Cora said, exasperated.

'What about her?' I said.

'Something still needs to be done about her,' Cora said.

'Isobel,' Alice said. It still caused her a small effort to say it. 'I've told her she bothers you too much, that she takes advantage of your kindness and good nature.'

Cora nodded at this. Most of this would have been at her urging.

'In what way?' I said.

'In whatever way she sees fit,' Cora said, holding up her palm to her mother to prevent her from speaking. 'She's not suitable. In fact, she's *un*suitable in every way.' She said this as though it explained everything.

'So have you given her her notice?' I asked Alice.

'Not yet,' Alice said, with considerably less conviction. 'I told her it was a warning.'

'*I* told her,' Cora said. 'Mother told me and I told her. Last night, after she'd been bothering you again, keeping you from your work.'

'I see,' I said.

Again she held my gaze, and again she dared me to challenge her.

I looked at my watch. 'We should leave,' I said to Alice, and I left the room and waited for her to join me in the hallway.

We started on our journey, saying little after what had just been said, each of us lost in our own thoughts of the coming day.

Approaching Stroud Green, Alice said, 'I've been thinking about what you said. About my work, about it being a success, about paying off some of our debts.'

The remark caught me unawares. 'It makes sense,' was all I could think to say, but it was enough, it pleased her, and she held my arm even tighter, pressing her cheek briefly to my shoulder.

'Perhaps there might one day even be enough for you to establish your own studio,' she said.

It was all we had talked of in the early years of our marriage.

'Cora imagines you'll both be millionaires before the year's end,' I said, and she laughed.

'You could spend less time at the Lyceum.'

I could leave the Lyceum completely.

Arriving at the cemetery, she bought her flowers, discarding the few faded blooms as we followed the broad gravel path to Caroline's grave.

The last time we had visited, a lilac tree had stood a short distance away, but this had recently been felled, leaving a vivid stem and a pile of trimmings and sawdust close by. It saddened me to see that the tree had gone. Every tree in the city seemed in danger of being felled. The late blooms had always been a welcome sight, and their scent had filled the air. I had even suggested picking a few and adding them to the carnations, but Alice had always rejected this. I had often stood and looked at the tree while she had prostrated herself on the ground at my feet.

We stopped at the bottom of the grave and we both bowed our heads for a moment. I always spoke to Caroline in my head, calling her 'my darling' because that was what I had called her as a baby and as a small girl in my lap, what I had called her when I'd dabbed the sweat from her fevered brow, and what I had called her when she had died in my arms amid that terrible gale of tears and confusion, screaming and denial.

Alice usually went immediately to the withered stems, threw them to one side and replaced them with the fresh flowers, but today she remained beside me, looking down at the grave and taking a succession of deep breaths – almost as though she was inhaling something more than the calm, scented air of the place.

'I didn't know,' she said to me, her eyes closed, her face now lifted to the sun.

'How you'd feel?'

'I wish it was something you could share in.'

'I do,' I said. 'In my own way.'

'No,' she said, but gently, her eyes still closed, still smiling. 'No, you don't.'

There had been no need for her to tell me this. It was

another exclusion, another horizon growing ever more distant to me.

'Forgive me,' she said, finally opening her eyes and looking at me, her reverie broken. 'I don't mean to deny the strength of your feelings, but you must see how everything has changed. For me, that is.'

I conceded this and told her that I understood what she was telling me. Neither of us truly believed this, but it was enough. There, and then, it was enough. And I had conceded in part because I was still surprised and pleased to see her so content.

She eventually put the new flowers in the pot, resting her hand on the small headstone as she did this.

'We should come more often,' she said.

I resisted telling her that I already did. 'You might come alone,' I said. 'Or with Cora.'

'I suppose so,' she said. 'It's not too far.'

Even a year ago, it would have been a journey into the darkest of mapless countries.

In the months after the funeral, I had felt like a man standing alone on a cliff edge each time I'd come to stand at the grave. Now I felt as though I were standing at a great distance from that fatal edge.

'It's a pity about the lilac,' I said, expecting her to agree with me.

She looked to the hewn stump and mound of chippings. I saw that other trees had been felled and heavily pruned. The voices of workmen could be heard. A fire burned beside the far boundary of the place, its pale smoke rising unbroken into the warm air.

'I suppose they need more space,' she said. 'For more graves.' She looked around us. There was land on either side of Caroline's grave, but I saw that she was right, that soon all the nearby spaces would be filled.

A woman passed behind us, and I turned to acknowledge her. She lifted her veil briefly and bowed to us. She was crying, unable to restrain her tears even for these few seconds. She wore black from head to foot and was carrying a small bunch of white roses.

Alice, I noticed, studied the woman closely as she moved slowly away from us. 'Lucky for us that Cora isn't with us,' she said, turning back to me. 'Otherwise she'd be trying to give her one of our cards.'

The remark surprised me – its levity and tone – and I laughed.

She put her arm back into mine.

'Perhaps she could employ a man to walk among the graves wearing a sandwich-board,' I said.

'That's a terrible thing to say,' she said, smiling.

On our journey there, I'd remained uncertain what would happen at the grave, what she might say or insist on doing there. But I saw now that all my concerns had been unfounded, and that she too had finally crossed a terrible divide.

And almost as though reading these exact thoughts, she said to me, 'You imagined it might be different.' It wasn't a question.

'I didn't know,' I admitted.

'You thought I might attempt to talk to her here, to somehow summon her, that *she* might visit *me* again simply because I – because *we* – were at her grave?'

I started to speak, not knowing what I wanted to say to her, and she put a finger to my lips to stop me.

Then she took the finger from my lips and tapped her

247

forehead. 'Here is where she speaks to me,' she said. 'Here. The grave is merely that – a grave.'

'I know,' I said. And again it was an imperfect and unexamined understanding between us that served us better than anything else.

Upon setting out for the cemetery, the day itself had seemed to me like a storm waiting to break. But now, standing beside the grave and listening to Alice talk, it felt as though that oppressive atmosphere had cleared completely and the sky was again blue and filled with gentle, refreshing breezes.

I left her and walked to the lilac stump, smelling the scent of the blooms in the wet wood. I unfastened my collar and pulled down my tie. I unbuttoned my jacket. I took out Bliss's letter and opened it. It contained an invitation, nothing more, to another of Marlow's studio evenings. I looked back to Alice, who now stood with her back to me. Across the bottom of the invitation, Marlow himself had written to tell me how much he hoped I would be able to attend. I heard the birds in the remaining trees. Alice raised her arm to me and then came towards me.

'What is it?'

'An invitation to visit a fellow photographer.'

She showed no interest in the card. 'A competitor?'

'You're beginning to sound like Cora,' I told her. 'A man called Marlow,' I said, wondering why I'd said it. But again she was only half-listening to me and the remark was no revelation, no confession.

'We could reserve the plots,' she said. 'On either side. For ourselves. To be with her, eventually, together.'

I told her it was an excellent idea. 'We'll visit the keeper's lodge on the way out,' I said.

Part III

Part II

20

I arrived at Golden Square shortly before midnight, an hour after the theatre had closed. Howson had tried to persuade me to accompany him for a drink in one of his usual haunts, and Irving had again parted the sea before him and gone out to a late dinner amid his usual surge of public acclaim.

I had told Alice that I would be working late – photographs for the new production – and that, in all likelihood, I would stay in my room at the theatre. It was the night of her sitting with Solomon and Marta, and the last place I wanted to be was in the house while that was taking place. Nor did I want to confront Isobel, who might already have guessed or learned of her impending dismissal, and who might now be plotting measures of her own.

I made my usual circuitous route to Marlow's, this time passing along Drury Lane, St Giles and Oxford Street. It was a busy night, still holding most of the day's warmth, and continuing airless. I went from Broadwick into Marshall Street, and I was approaching Beak Street when I saw Pearl ahead of me. She was waiting for someone, looking back and forth beneath the gas lighting. I stopped walking and watched her, hidden by the window of the pharmacist's which closed Newburgh Passage. As before, I was uncertain why I had taken this action, knowing only that I would have surprised her coming to her so suddenly out of the darkness.

My next thought was that she was perhaps acting as one of Marlow's look-outs, but I dismissed this as unlikely, knowing how much more valuable she would have been to him at the gathering which would already be getting under way.

I was proved right a moment later when she called to someone approaching her. It was another young woman – not the one I had seen her with on Regent Street – and I stood perfectly still as the girl passed me. I need not have worried; she went quickly to Pearl, paying me no attention whatsoever.

I arrived at the entrance to Golden Square, where a man stood at the John Street corner and watched me closely as I approached. He made no attempt to prevent me from entering. As usual, I took a small but undeniable pleasure in this drama of arrival. Perhaps it was something of what Irving felt each time he walked out on to the stage, or even as he entered the empty theatre in broad daylight.

I went into the small courtyard and then through the usual sequence of doors, up and along the same stairways and passages until I arrived at Marlow's studio.

Inside, Marlow himself greeted each new arrival. One of his models stood beside him with a tray of drinks. She was dressed as a nymph, one of her small pointed breasts revealed beside the sash of transparent material draped over her shoulder. Marlow motioned for an older woman to take my hat and jacket. I was reluctant to lose the latter, but Marlow insisted. The room was comfortably cool, its skylights open to the night, and its passing draughts revealed by the flickering of the candles and the regular dimming of the already low mantles.

Despite having seen me only a few days earlier, Marlow shook my hand and greeted me as though we had not met for some considerable time and this was something he regretted.

'A good night at the theatre?' he said, motioning for me to drink from the glass I held.

'The usual heady triumph,' I said.

'What else?' He studied me closely and then looked swiftly away as I caught his gaze. 'Pearl is here somewhere,' he said. 'Busy, perhaps. How would I manage without her?' He looked to the small, low stage, where a backdrop of mountains hung across its full width, and where his array of patient, predatory cameras stood poised and ready.

'Is there to be a show?' I asked him.

'Of course. Nothing so spectacularly melodramatic as one of dear old Henry's tawdry concoctions, but something I'm sure you'll appreciate.'

I wondered if he meant me specifically. Tawdry. It was the same word Irving used when dismissing his music-hall rivals. Earlier in the day, I'd overheard him railing to Stoker about the recent improvements carried out at both the Alexandra and the Metropolitan, insisting that the Lyceum too was due additional renovations. Stoker, I imagined, would have paled at the suggestion, at its cost and the further disruption involved. There was hardly a week now when something wasn't changed or improved or made 'modern' in the place.

'And Bliss?' I said.

'What of him?' Marlow closed his eyes briefly, perhaps to conceal what they could not help but reveal.

'Is he here, too?'

'Later, perhaps. Bliss has a standing invitation to these

things. Or perhaps he's busy somewhere else, another of his clients.' He seemed distracted, uncertain of more than Bliss's whereabouts.

The door opened behind me and another man entered. Marlow looked at him, made his quick assessment, composed himself, made his apologies to me, and then went to him. I heard the same practised greeting, the enquiry after the man's wife and children.

I walked further into the room. Tables, chairs and sofas were set out in the broader space, all centred on the stage and the coming show. Another waitress approached me, this time fully undressed to her slender waist. She offered me a tray of food, small topped biscuits, one of which I took and ate, uncertain of what it contained. The woman who had served me my drink came and whispered to the waitress and the girl left me to attend to a group of men already gathered closer to the stage.

I felt suddenly alone and exposed in the room, realizing that with the exception of Marlow himself, I knew none of the others, nor they me.

'You look lost.' Pearl stood immediately behind me, a glass in her hand.

'I know no one here,' I said.

She smiled at the remark and all it suggested. 'It was how most of them started out.' She touched her glass to my own, drawing glances from the men around us. She acknowledged these and they raised their own glasses to her. 'Besides . . .' she said, and then paused.

'What?' I asked her.

'Knowing and not knowing, being known and being unknown . . .' She sipped her drink.

'Are you Marlow's hostess for the evening?' I asked her.

She considered this for a moment, but said nothing. She motioned to the woman serving food to replenish her tray.

'You were on Beak Street,' she said, her eyes elsewhere. 'First you were hiding on Regent Street watching me, then you were hiding in the shadows on Beak Street watching me. Is there something I should be told? Is there something Marlow should know?' She seemed more amused than concerned by the question.

'By accident,' I said.

'On both occasions?'

I saw how unlikely this must have seemed to her, but it was the truth.

'I came from the Lyceum by way of Oxford Street,' I said, wondering what this explained.

But she seemed to accept this. 'I believe you,' she said.

This gave me confidence. 'Besides,' I went on, 'how would I have known you would be there at that hour?'

'And Regent Street?' she said. 'One moment you were passing on a bus, the next you were moving in the opposite direction on the far side of the street.'

'You saw me?'

'I told you as much in the Metropolitan. Perhaps you forget that I have developed a certain talent for these things.'

'I still wasn't following you,' I insisted, lowering my voice. 'At least not for any untoward purpose.'

She smiled at the ridiculous phrase and repeated it several times. Then she touched my cheek briefly before emptying her glass. 'Please, relax. I believe you.'

'Did the girl tonight know?' I asked her.

The suggestion amused her further. 'Why should she? Besides, I hardly know her.'

It wasn't how it had looked to me on Beak Street and she saw the doubt in my eyes.

'I met her for the first time earlier today,' she said. She glanced to where Marlow was still occupied at the door. 'At Caudwell's Dance Hall. I was bringing her here by arrangement. First I needed to find her something more appropriate to wear. We separated briefly, that's all. The girl you saw me with on Regent Street I'd recruited from Laurent's Academy on Windmill Street. She'd just been turned down for the chorus at Her Majesty's. A month of propositions and promises, she took.' She smiled again. 'His "Everlasting Virgins", Marlow calls them.'

'Supply and demand,' I said.

'Most of those from outside London he calls his "Norfolk Maids". Anywhere outside London is countryside to Marlow. That raging wilderness. They come to him from Manchester, Newcastle, Birmingham, Bristol, everywhere. They arrive thinking they know everything there is to know, and all Marlow truly wants of them is their wide-eyed innocence, their creamy, milk-fed flesh, their willingness and their youth.'

'And their gullibility?'

She laughed. 'If that's what you'd prefer to believe. What an upstanding man you're turning out to be, Mr Webster.'

'Charles,' I said.

'I know. It wasn't meant to be an insult.'

'I'm not upstanding,' I said. 'Not really. I suppose I have much the same mixture of virtues and vices possessed by all men. I am *here*, after all.'

'As am I,' she said, after which neither of us spoke for a moment.

'Is she here?' I said, breaking this silence and releasing the small tension between us. 'The girl you met tonight?'

'She served you your drink.'

'I never really saw her, recognized her.'

'Of course you didn't. And even if you *had* looked long and hard into her face in full daylight, you still wouldn't have truly *seen* her, let alone have recognized her here tonight. That's why and how all this works, why it appeals, why it continues to be in such demand. I can call her back for you to inspect her more closely if you like.'

'No,' I said, but too quickly.

'Perhaps you could talk to her about her family, about her background, her work. She's sixteen. No one forced her to come here – to London or to Marlow.' She took my empty glass from me and replaced it with another.

'Is that how *you* came to meet Marlow?' I said, the words and the realization arriving simultaneously. It seemed an insulting thing to ask her.

But she saw I had intended no insult and so she answered me. 'Did I arrive lost and uncertain, you mean?' She shook her head. 'I knew more than most what I was letting myself in for. I've been here almost twenty years now.'

'Where are you from?'

'From?' She laughed. 'Norwich, of all places. It's why he calls them his "Norfolk Maids".'

'Because you were the original?'

'Nothing is ever that simple or so easily resolved with Marlow.' She looked back to the door, but he was no longer there, and she searched among the growing crowd until she found him again. He was at the centre of a circle of his guests, all of them listening to him. Prodded by Pearl's gaze, he looked to her and raised his glass to her.

'You work well together,' I said.

'I know.' She continued looking around her, watching the drifting girls, ensuring that no one in the room was left unattended.

'So are people here to buy?' I asked her.

'To view, perhaps. Or perhaps simply to be reminded.'

'Of what Marlow provides?'

'Of what they might be missing, of the debts they might owe him.'

I saw what a breadth of meaning and interpretation the simple answer contained.

'But surely, if they—'

'It's an entertainment, that's all,' she said, finally tiring of my questions. 'Another of Marlow's exclusive little clubs. He flatters them, they flatter themselves, everyone enjoys themselves, and everyone – one way or another – benefits. What you don't seem to understand is that nothing separates Marlow from these people. He's one of them. Everyone here has an eye on everyone else's back.'

'Meaning I should be flattered by my inclusion?'

She sighed and fell silent again.

Eventually, she said, 'I was here before going to my rendezvous on Beak Street. You can imagine the only topic of conversation among the early arrivals.'

'Aston-Fox,' I said. 'Has *he* been here?'

'Not tonight.'

'Isn't Marlow concerned that he might soon start confessing things to the police?'

'Not unduly. He and Aston-Fox know each other well enough to avoid all that. As Bliss has already pointed out, you can't begin to imagine the barrage of denials and the ocean of silence with which Aston-Fox has already surrounded himself. Things will have to get considerably worse for the man for Marlow to start worrying. Besides, just because he and Marlow know each other . . .' She tailed off as something occurred to her. 'You might even say that a single flimsy costume connects *you* ten times more forcibly to Marlow, to this place and all that goes on here, than anything Aston-Fox himself might inadvertently have left behind.'

I considered the truth of this.

'I didn't mean—' she began.

'No, of course not,' I said. 'A warning, perhaps. Between friends.' And I had signed my own name alongside Marlow's in the register at his dining club.

'They *will* come,' she said. 'There is no harm in preparing oneself.'

'No.' *Oneself? Me.*

She looked around us again. 'I should go and talk to others,' she said.

'I hope I didn't offend you,' I said. 'Talking about your past.'

She took several paces away from me. 'If I was easily offended, then that past would have been something else completely,' she said.

We were approached by yet another half-dressed girl and Pearl beckoned her to us. She introduced the girl to me, telling her that I was a very good friend of Marlow's. The girl was called Celestia. Pearl looked at me directly as she said this. Not her real name, the girl said seriously. She was nineteen and from a village in Derbyshire. She wore another diaphanous costume, covering her breasts, but through which her large, dark nipples were clearly visible. She smiled at me and held out her hand for me to kiss.

My first thought was that *she* might have been the girl on Regent Street, looking at the shop dummies, Pearl's arm across her back.

Pearl left us and we both watched her go.

'Are you looking for models?' Celestia said.

I told her I wasn't and immediately disappointed her.

'Not at the moment,' I added.

'I've been here for six months. There's plenty of work. Marlow and a few others. He always likes to know who's using me.' She spoke with a flat, drawling accent I hadn't heard before. It made her assumed name seem even more ridiculous. 'I get a lot of personal recommendations. What is it you specialize in? I can turn my hand to most things.' She laughed, as though she'd just told a joke, and I pretended to do the same. 'You got a business card?' she said.

'Not for this line,' I told her.

'Quite right. Same as Mr Marlow. Can't be too careful. You work close by?'

'Off Portland Street,' I said, surprised by how quickly and convincingly the lie had come.

'I know a few girls work in that part of the world. What you think?'

I didn't understand her.

She took a pace away from me, drew back her shoulders and pushed out her breasts, causing her nipples to become even more prominent against the flimsy material.

'Yes,' I said.

'I got all the features. Ask Mr Marlow. He says I'm compliant. Got a good business head. I *adapt*, that's what I do. You want any kind of recommendation, then all you've got to do is to ask Mr Marlow.'

I imagined Aston-Fox in the same situation.

'You looking forward to the show?' she said. 'I bet now you wish *I* was in it, don't you? Don't lie.' She ran a hand along the length of my arm.

'The show?' I said, betraying an ignorance she seemed not to notice.

'You should have been here last time. Me and a negro Marlow brought in special from the docks. At least that's what he told everyone. A proper savage. Black as sin. Didn't speak a word of the language. I made a proper spectacle of myself. Damsel in distress. You got a camera here?' She motioned to the line of cameras along the edge of the stage.

'Not tonight,' I said.

'Just watching, eh?'

I nodded.

'The African was the biggest I ever seen, if you catch my drift. I swear Mr Marlow and Pearl were both plying me with drink for an hour beforehand. Lubricated, that's what I was, lubricated. Not that I'm one to put up much of a struggle in that direction, of course.' She winked at me and ran her tongue around the full circle of her mouth. 'I think tonight they got a couple of girls doing the stuff. A couple of proper dolly-mops fresh from the Elephant flash-houses. All tastes, I suppose, all sorts. You?'

'I—'

'No – don't tell me.' She screwed up her eyes and looked at me.

I could smell the drink on her breath, mixed with the perfume she wore. She rose on to her toes and held her face closer to mine.

'Let me guess,' she said. She almost lost her balance and I held out my hand to steady her. I felt her breast against my palm. She laughed again. 'No clues,' she said.

I looked beyond her and saw both Marlow and Pearl watching me. Marlow raised his glass to me, and Pearl smiled.

'You like a little domestic? Something in an outfit,' Celestia said.

'No,' I said quickly, caught off guard by the remark.

'You're supposed to say "yes",' she said petulantly. 'It's a game. Say "yes".'

'Yes,' I said.

'Thought so. A little domestic. How old? Almost old enough or just tipped over? A little domestic girl at your beck and call, down on her hands and knees in front of the dirty grate. That it, is it? You sitting in a chair and watching her, Lord of the household, and her down on her hands and knees with her backside up in the air and her skirt forever riding up?' She waited, breathless. 'Say "yes".'

'Yes,' I said.

'And then what? She turns round and sees you watching her like that?' She half turned from me and lifted her own backside to me. 'We're getting the picture now, are we?'

But I was conscious only of Marlow and Pearl, and I wondered how much of this encounter with the girl either or both of them had engineered.

I imagined a dozen similar conversations – though they were hardly that – taking place in the room around me.

'You sitting there, and just you and her all alone in your

big, fancy house, all cosy and warm. Where is it, up Mayfair way?' She waited for me to nod. 'Thought so. And I can see all these thoughts taking place in your head, clear as day.'

'It's not—' I began.

'Not what? You saying it's *not* what you were thinking about, looking at that poor little domestic kneeling down in front of that hot fire? I bet you've even seen that look in her eyes, haven't you? Waiting until the missus has gone out, and her, the girl, forever looking at you like that, like butter wouldn't melt.'

I wanted to tell her to shut up, but I saw how practised a routine this was, how little it truly revealed, and so I let her go on.

She held a hand to my waist.

Over her shoulder, I saw Marlow laughing, and wondered if he was laughing at me. Pearl was no longer beside him. I looked around the room, but was unable to find her. Instead, I saw Bliss in the doorway, just then arrived, impatiently holding out his coat for the woman to take from him. He seemed little interested in any of the others in the room. He motioned to Marlow to let him know he'd arrived, but that was all. Taking a proffered drink, he crossed the room without speaking to anyone and made his way to the rear door. He saw me standing with the girl, saw the drink in my hand, saw her hand at my waist, but he scarcely broke his stride to do anything other than acknowledge my presence.

'Well?' Celestia was saying to me. 'Well?'

'Yes,' I said. 'That's it exactly.'

'I knew it was.' She applauded herself. 'I knew exactly what it was. Mr Marlow says I've got a real gift for it, all this imagining stuff.'

She was the only person I'd ever heard call him Mister, and it somehow made him smaller, less of a mystery, less apart from everything.

'You do know, I suppose . . .' she said.

'Know what?'

'All this . . . all that imagining. You do know that you can make things like that happen? Anything, whatever you want – that you can make it happen.'

'Of course I know,' I said.

But now she was offended by my abrupt tone.

'I was only saying,' she said, her voice suddenly childlike and trembling, as though on the verge of tears. I saw what an actress she was.

I apologized to her and took a drink for us both from a nearby tray.

'I'm not really supposed to drink,' she said. 'Not like with the negro.' She looked in the direction of Marlow, who was now standing with his back to us. She emptied the glass in a single swallow.

Around us, the mantles flared and then grew dim.

'It's the show,' Celestia said excitedly. She took my hand and pulled me to a sofa close to the low stage. I allowed myself to be led by her.

All around us, the other guests and girls did the same.

'We've got a good spot,' she said. She grinned and waved at several of the nearby girls, settling herself closer to me. I felt her leg against my own. 'You're in for a real treat,' she said. She patted my leg, then smoothed the thin material of her tunic over her shoulders.

The lights dimmed even further and the stage was illuminated. A short silence was followed by an energetic round of applause and a few calls. A mechanical piano started playing.

Beside me, Celestia clapped a few times and then let her hands fall into her lap.

On the stage, a girl emerged from behind the curtain and wandered searching in front of the mountain backdrop, her shadow cast sharply over the distant peaks and their surrounding sky, all illusion destroyed.

Someone laughed at this and others in the crowd hissed the laughter into silence.

'Guess what she's looking for,' Celestia whispered to me.

The girl came to the front of the stage, still searching, her hand held stiffly to her brow, shielding herself from the bright sun of the lighting, and looking out at us, peering even harder and moving her head from side to side as though there was nothing but an endless and impenetrable darkness all around her.

21

I woke the following morning to the sound of arguing voices, followed by a succession of slammed doors, each one fainter than the last, and this noise dying in a rhythm of overlapping echoes. For a moment I didn't know where I was, and then I remembered. I was fully clothed, and one of my arms was folded painfully beneath me on the couch where I lay. Someone had taken off my shoes and set them on the floor. My jacket had been brought from the cloakroom and now hung over a nearby chair.

I swung my legs to the ground and sat upright, steadying myself. A bottle of spilled brandy lay on the rug beside me, its fumes filling the air. The girl Celestia lay close by, naked to the waist, her arms folded into a pillow beneath her head.

I looked around me. Others lay elsewhere in the room, men and women, dressed and half-dressed, some still asleep, others starting to revive themselves as slowly and as uncertainly as I was now attempting to do.

A final door slammed, barely audible, but a definite marker of the empty silence which followed it.

I nudged the girl with my foot. She moaned incoherently but made no attempt to rouse herself. I struggled to remember what – if anything – had happened between us, but little came. All our clothing – what little she still wore – remained intact. A line of cosmetic crossed her cheek from her eye. Her hair, which had been fastened back to keep her shoulders bare, was now free and dishevelled and spread in a fan across her flesh. I watched her for a moment, but still nothing came to me. I had enjoyed Marlow's show, eaten his food and drunk his drink. And then, in all likelihood, the show finished, the girl still beside me and even drunker than I was, I had fallen asleep. I tried to imagine who might have taken off my shoes and retrieved my jacket.

I searched my pockets, finding everything as I had left it. My movement attracted the attention of a man on the low stage and he called for me to identify myself. But I said nothing and he simply lowered himself back to his own makeshift bed. In places, candles still burned. A fire had been lit in one of the hearths, and the majority of the sleepers lay close to this.

At my feet, the girl stirred, and this time I drew back to avoid touching her. She opened her eyes and looked across the floor, seemingly unconcerned by what she saw, or by whatever she too now remembered of where she was and what had brought her there. She pulled a face at the smell of the brandy.

From somewhere in the room, I heard laughter. I propped myself up and tried to see, but that part of the studio remained in darkness. I saw a woman, naked and pale in the poor light, rise, stretch her arms and then fold herself back down on to the couch where she lay. Someone spoke to her and she laughed again.

I rubbed my face, smelling the alcohol on my stale breath. I flexed the cramp from both my arms. Finally sitting upright,

I waited until a moment of nausea and dizziness flushed through me and passed. I was unable to focus properly, waiting with my eyes tightly closed for everything to settle. My nausea returned, and for a moment I thought I might be sick. But I remained perfectly still, and the feeling passed. A jug of water stood close to the spilled brandy and I carefully reached for this and drank from the jug, spilling as much as I drank over my chest and hand.

I waited, uncertain what to do, uncertain even of the time – not knowing whether it was still night or if the early dawn had already passed in the heavily draped room.

My uncertainty on that point was answered a moment later as one of the curtains was drawn aside, letting a block of blinding sunlight into the room.

I looked to see who had done this and saw Pearl moving among the sleepers by the stage. I called to her, my voice little more than a croak. She looked in my direction, shielding her eyes against the light in which she now stood dissolved and ghostlike. Failing to recognize me, she came closer.

She paused a short distance from me, going first to the girl on the floor, kneeling and holding her face for a moment, drawing a piece of cloth over her chest and pushing a cushion beneath her head. She lifted the girl's skirt and looked at her legs.

Seeing me watching her, she came to me. She showed no surprise at finding me there.

'You should have gone,' she said quietly but firmly. She looked at the others lying around me.

'I fell asleep,' I told her.

She shook her head at the remark. 'I told Marlow not to invite you in the first instance. This wasn't the place for you.'

Everything she said seemed filled with a deeper, hidden, more dangerous meaning.

'You still consider me unworthy of associating with his usual – what? – associates? Clientele?' I sounded ridiculous and self-pitying. I started to cough and immediately felt sick again.

'And you imagine Marlow himself is still here, do you?' she said.

It had not occurred to me that the man might still be somewhere in the room and I began to look around me.

'He isn't,' she said.

I wondered then if it had been *his* voice I'd heard, his hand on the slamming doors.

'Is this how his more exclusive gatherings end?' I asked her.

'Usually.' The word mocked me. She seemed to be making some calculation as she continued looking around her, some assessment – perhaps something to do with the men who remained and those who had gone.

'I knew what I was letting myself in for,' I said, but with little conviction.

'No, you didn't. Besides, you probably don't even remember half of what happened.'

I conceded this in silence.

Then she motioned to the girl. 'You and her?'

I didn't know – not for certain – and so I said nothing. I wanted to tell her a dozen times over that nothing whatsoever had happened between us.

'It may be no consolation, but it's unlikely,' she said. She stood the empty brandy bottle on a table.

The woman who had laughed earlier rose again and

complained at the sunlight now falling on her.

Pearl turned to watch her, identifying the man beside her.

'I honestly can't remember,' I said.

Any further reassurance from her would have been an indulgence, and so she simply sat and looked at me.

'*Did* something happen?' I meant in the studio, the previous night.

She considered her answer before speaking. 'The Lord Chancellor is bringing Aston-Fox to trial,' she said. 'Wheeler and his Committee have been lobbying the Government to act against all this – Marlow, everyone else – for years. They're talking about making an example of Aston-Fox. It seems the friends he has in high places might not be as untouchable or as supportive as he imagines and needs them to be. And there's certainly growing support for Wheeler and whatever it is *he* imagines he's about to achieve.'

'A show trial?'

She smiled at the suggestion. 'It will just be a trial as far as everyone else is concerned. But whatever it is, Wheeler will make sure it attracts enough attention to send a lot of other people running for cover until the dust settles.'

'Including Aston-Fox's so-called friends?'

'*Especially* them.'

'*Will* Marlow be drawn into it?' I felt a sudden chill at the realization. 'He assured me—'

'He assured you what – that he was above it all? That he was clever enough to remain invisible? When the trial starts, no one will be invisible. All that will matter then is who's in and who's out of favour. Some people will disappear completely and others will be sacrificed at the first available opportunity. There'll be blood on this one, count on it.' It seemed an uncharacteristically melodramatic thing for her to say.

'You think Wheeler will do his best to ensure Marlow—'

'To ensure he gets what he deserves? What Wheeler believes he deserves?' She paused. 'Wheeler will enjoy every single minute of this – everything he's ever called for being handed to him on a plate. Apparently, he's already strutting around the Lord Chancellor's office like the little tin-pot king he is. The Chancellor has empowered him to act as a special advisor to the police and all the interested Reform Committees.'

'And the one person he is least likely to allow to escape—'

'Don't,' she said, as though even the mention of Marlow's name would now bring to pass all she had just suggested. She watched me for a moment. 'You're starting to work it all out,' she said.

'I don't imagine I—'

'You? You don't imagine you *what*?' More mockery, closer to condemnation now.

I didn't know what I'd been about to say, what further excuse I'd been about to make for myself. I drank more water, again spilling it down my shirt.

Something occurred to me. 'Did Marlow know all this last night?'

'He knew yesterday morning. An acquaintance in the Chancellor's office. I tried to persuade him to forget about last night, to cancel everything, but he insisted on going ahead.'

'Perhaps he wanted to see people so that he might warn them of what was happening, what was coming.'

She smiled at the naivety of this. 'Or to see who else already knew and then failed to appear.'

'All the same—'

'All the same what? And you're right – Marlow did want to warn some of them. But not like you're suggesting. I'd say his warnings were more of a cold whisper than a warm embrace, more of a sharp little prod in the ribs than a handshake.'

It took me a moment to understand what she was telling me.

'Is that why you were checking who was still here?' I asked her.

'Partly.'

'He said nothing to me,' I said.

She laughed. 'Then perhaps you're already invisible, beyond reproach and beyond all reach.'

I remembered Bliss's brief appearance at the gathering, his furtive arrival and almost immediate departure.

'Does Bliss know?' I said.

'Of course Bliss knows. Bliss knows everything. He was here again earlier. He swore at me and told me to leave. He said he imagined the place might already have been raided by the police with Wheeler on his charger at their head.'

The suggestion alarmed me. 'It's still possible,' I said. 'We ought to leave.'

'Why? There's nothing here to incriminate Marlow, nothing whatsoever.'

I looked around us.

'What are you looking for? There's nothing. Even the lease is in another man's name. And believe me, anyone who's anyone is no longer here. All that whispering and prodding, remember? Do you seriously think Wheeler and his committee are going to waste their time on people like you when he knows Marlow is somewhere ahead of him, just out of reach?'

People like me.

'Besides,' she went on, her voice lower, 'you have no idea of who *is* here. You don't even know what did or didn't happen between you and her – ' she motioned to the sleeping girl, 'last night. You know as much about it as *she* does, but that's all.'

At the far side of the studio, the naked woman stood upright and searched around her for her clothes. Pearl watched her for a moment before calling to her and telling her to leave. The woman recognized the voice and said nothing in reply. She gathered up her scattered clothing and dressed herself after a fashion.

'What will he do?' I asked Pearl, my voice little more than a whisper.

'He's probably already doing it,' she said.

'And you? Bliss?'

But she refused to answer me. More tracks being brushed clean.

'I collected her for him,' she said absently.

My first thought was that she meant Celestia, but then I realized – though God knows how I made the connection in that state – that she was talking about the murdered girl.

'The dead girl,' I said.

'She was twelve, but Marlow was convinced that she'd pass for much younger – eight or nine, say.'

'Another of his—'

'She came from Colchester. She worked the barracks with her mother. I met her at Liverpool Street and brought her here to him.'

'No one will ever be able to prove that,' I said.

The glib remark angered her. 'So? I still did it. Did it with dozens of them, hundreds perhaps.'

'Not against their will,' I said, remembering what she'd told me the previous evening. I wondered at my sudden impulse to defend her, to help her to justify what she'd done. She, too, was surprised by this.

'I don't want your sympathy,' she said.

'It wasn't sympathy. Just . . .'

'I know.' She touched my arm briefly. 'Her parents have been found. By Wheeler. He's brought them to town.'

'To what end?'

'Publicity. Public opinion. To stoke the usual fires. They might not have cared what happened to their innocent little girl, but they'll put on a good enough show at Wheeler's urging. She sent money home to them. Pictures, too, most likely. Marlow said her mother would be getting them reproduced to sell round the barracks. It happens all the time.'

'But still with nothing to connect the girl directly to Marlow.' It was something else he had been at pains to make clear to me at our solitary lunch. I remembered the knife in his hand, the parting flesh of the creamy fish.

She shook her head. 'It's why Wheeler will be looking for other ways of making the connection. There are a hundred other girls, any one of whom . . .' She tailed off.

'Who might see some benefit in testifying against Marlow?'

'People will save their own necks long before they worry about his, and Wheeler knows that.'

'And Aston-Fox himself?'

'What about him? His is the only neck likely to be feeling the noose.'

'Will *no one* protect him?'

'At their own expense as the clamour starts to rise? Not now. Too late. The public has to be satisfied. Justice being seen to be done, and all that. The newspapers are already turning it into a circus. Sometimes these things die quickly and fade away, but not this time. Wheeler has been waiting for this for too long. And now here he is, the man of the moment, and with so many new and powerful friends.' She paused and smiled. 'There will be a lot of anxious people queuing up to pat him on the back and tell him what a good job he's doing over the next few days.'

I considered all she was telling me, trying again to understand my own position amid this confusion of likely outcomes.

'Marlow still has some costumes,' I said. 'They'll be traceable to the theatre.'

But she seemed unconcerned by the remark. 'Only to someone looking for the connection,' she said. 'I doubt it will be high on Wheeler's list of priorities.'

Unless, of course, Wheeler or the police came to me as a result of having searched Solomon's, and then decided to investigate further any possible connection with the Lyceum. But she was right: it seemed an unlikely connection to be either sought or made.

Neither of us spoke for a moment.

'Do what you feel you have to do,' she said eventually. 'But if doing nothing remains one of your options, then it might be preferable to attracting Wheeler's attention while he's still determined to look elsewhere.'

'Will you tell Marlow I want to see him,' I said.

She shook her head in disbelief at the request. 'You don't

think it might be best to leave here, to keep your distance, and then to forget that any of this ever happened? I imagine that in the coming weeks and months there are going to be a great many others who would be grateful to be able to do just that.'

'And if Wheeler or the police *do* come to me?'

'Deny everything. I don't know. It's unlikely to happen – not as a result of anything they discover here. Wheeler isn't going to squander his chances.'

'On people like me, you mean?'

She refused to answer. There was a great deal of truth and sense in what she was suggesting. But I still could not dismiss completely the idea that Wheeler might now be best rewarded by confronting precisely the people like me – those people with the most to lose and the least to gain, those who felt used, abandoned or cheated by Marlow, those who had been paid or shown or promised just enough by him to keep them exactly where he needed them.

'Did Marlow imagine the police might be here now?' I asked her. 'Is that why we – ' I gestured at the sleeping men and women all around us, 'are all still here, a diversion, something to delay proceedings while he himself moves further and further out of reach?'

And again, she refused to answer me.

We both turned at the sound of the closing door as the wandering, half-dressed woman finally left the room.

22

I left Golden Square shortly afterwards, following Pearl beyond Brewer Street to the rear of the Lyric. We made the last part of this short journey underground, along a curved, white-tiled passageway, the original function of which eluded me. The only light in this tunnel came from small grilles set high into the wall at street level. I paused at one of these openings, breathing in the fresher air and watching the feet of the passers-by. I had no idea of the direction we were heading, but I knew without asking that the route was one kept secret by Marlow, and probably known only to him, Pearl and Bliss; an escape route, even – something unknown and unnoticed beneath all those other routes, and one emerging well beyond the ring of any suddenly closing cordon. .

Pearl waited for me at the junction with an even narrower, unlit passageway.

'Where does that one lead?' I asked her.

She shook her head. 'You won't be coming back here.'

'And the less I know . . . ?'

She considered the remark and all it implied about her still working more on Marlow's behalf than my own, and continued walking ahead of me along the broader passage.

I looked down the darkened corridor and saw only the

faintly lit doorway at its end. Another exit into the outside world? Into a public place? Somewhere Marlow might
emerge and become another man completely?

Pearl grew exasperated by my delay and called for me to
join her.

I had followed her out of the studio via a door concealed
behind Marlow's backdrops, and she had cautioned me not to
wake any of the other sleepers as we'd gone.

Once beyond the door, she had locked and then bolted it.
We had descended two flights of stairs, moved beyond the
building itself and then descended even further to the hidden
entrance of the subterranean passage.

Outside – the Lyric stage door immediately ahead of us –
she told me to wait while she looked to see if anyone had seen
us emerge. Satisfied that we were unnoticed, she told me to
wait again while she visited a nearby shop. Whatever her brief
errand – news of Marlow or of any police action, presumably
– she seemed less anxious upon her return to me.

'Another of his look-outs?' I said.

'There's been no one here,' she said matter-of-factly. 'It's
unlikely anyone would even know about the tunnel.'

'So you do believe Wheeler is already on his way here?'

'We're only ahead of him because of the dead hand of
routine and procedure the police will lay on his shoulder.
Once he's free of them, he'll move fast enough.'

And Marlow was in turn ahead of us. And Aston-Fox
falling further and further behind with every step we took.

She held my arm and guided me towards Shaftesbury
Avenue, pausing occasionally to look in shop windows at
nothing in particular, crossing the street for no apparent
reason, and then doubling back on herself for ten or fifteen

yards. I walked with her, feigning interest in everything she pointed out to me, as though we were a pair of tourists.

We turned into Romilly Street and walked to Cambridge Circus. Convinced by then that no one was following us, she told me it was time for us to part.

'Time for us all to start laying our individual trails away from Marlow?' I said, wishing immediately that I'd kept the realization to myself.

She looked up and down at the passing traffic. 'They'll know exactly which trails to follow and which to ignore,' she said.

I saw one of the puzzles in Cora's magazines – a tangled ball of lines unravelling to twenty dead-ends and a single reward.

'I imagine now you'll—' I began.

'Don't imagine anything,' she said firmly. 'Not now. Leave all that kind of imagining behind you.'

I almost laughed at the ponderous remark, at the impossibility of what she was suggesting.

And then I wondered if this was the last time I would ever see her, and the words were something I was intended to take away with me.

'Where will you go?' she asked me. She continued looking around us as she spoke.

'Go?'

'Now, today – where are you going?'

So she might keep track of me? So she might somehow report my movements to Marlow?

'The Lyceum,' I told her.

Alice wouldn't be expecting me home until that evening. Irving was already calling for the photographic work connected to *Macbeth* to be started. I had intended spending the day getting on with this, withdrawing myself as far as possible from Stoker's gaze. A simple plan. Stoker would forever remain the shadow behind Irving's light, and I would keep myself in front of that man and his light and cast my lesser shadow in the glow of his own benevolent and protective gaze.

'Good,' Pearl said. 'Everything as normal as possible.'

It seemed to me that months had passed since I'd last lived that steady, predictable, normal life.

She raised her hand to a passing cab, but the driver didn't stop.

'Go,' she said to me.

'What about you?' I asked her.

She shook her head. 'Save your concern. If Wheeler gets brave enough to put *me* in the dock, I'll feign complete surprise and innocence and then I'll faint when he parades his pictures in front of me.'

It was unconvincing bravado. Pictures Marlow had taken? Or pictures of the strangled girl? My concern for her was genuine, but she had spent too long with both Marlow and Bliss either to recognize or accept this, and I knew better than to repeat the question.

She hailed a second cab and this time the driver drew his horse through the passing traffic towards us. I wanted her to embrace me, to take my hand, to confirm that we shared a terrible and destructive secret that bound us tightly and inseparably together, but all she did was walk away from me and climb into the cab without either speaking or even looking back at me where I stood.

I waited until she was lost in the flow of the traffic and

then continued on my way to the Lyceum. Rather than walk there directly, I made a short detour via Tavistock Street, continuing this unlikely game of follower and followed. I was not entirely serious in my intent, knowing, as ever, that if I *were* being followed, then I would in all likelihood know nothing of it. In truth, I was doing little more than testing Fate, proving something to myself that I neither properly understood nor truly needed to believe in.

Arriving at the front entrance, I saw Jimmy Allen sitting on the steps there, his legs splayed, smoking his pipe. I called to him and he shielded his eyes to search for me. He was in his shirtsleeves, leaning back on his elbows, and seeing me he pushed himself upright and beckoned me to him.

'Just going in?' he asked me. I heard the warning note in his voice.

'It's only nine,' I said.

'Look.' He pointed to one side.

I looked but saw nothing. 'What am I looking at, Jimmy?'

'The news board,' he said.

And I knew immediately and without looking any more closely what he was pointing out to me.

ASTON-FOX TO FACE GIRL MURDER TRIAL.

'So?' I said. And even that small word dried in my throat.

'One of Henry's circle, a regular. They're saying he strangled a girl, a child. Other stuff, too, by all accounts. Henry's convinced the police will want to come here to talk to *him*. All a big distraction from the task at hand. As you can imagine. Him and Stoker have been in for hours. Henry was in tears earlier.'

'For the girl?' Irving was always in tears.

'Who knows? He's in there now, waiting for them to

appear. Called them the Barbarians at the Gate. You'd think it was *him* they were going to prosecute.'

'What does he know?' I said. I sat beside him on the steps, feigning a measure of respectful concern.

'Know about what?'

'The dead girl. About – ' I pretended to read the board again, 'Aston-Fox.'

'It hardly matters *what* he knows. He knows the man, and for Henry that's enough. The place is mostly empty, but he still called a conference to tell us all what to expect. Told us all to cooperate.'

'What does he expect of *us*?' I said, already making my own calculations about the arrival of the police or Wheeler, and perhaps their special interest in me as the theatre's resident photographer.

He shrugged. 'Aston-Fox was tight with the pair of them. There might be something. It's all just another drama for Henry.'

Everything was just one more drama for Irving.

He drew hard on his pipe, blowing sparks from the bowl and then letting the smoke rise from his mouth over his face into his sparse hair. 'Stoker was even talking about interviewing everyone himself to see what they might know. Save time, he said, avoid all that disruption, find out who the police might most profitably talk to rather than distract everybody from their work.'

'Very public-spirited of him,' I said, hoping he would laugh at the remark, which he did.

'Exactly what Henry said.'

'Perhaps I ought to go in and see Stoker, see what he wants from me,' I said.

Jimmy Allen shrugged. 'He'll get to you sooner or later. He gave us all a little speech about the reputation of the theatre, about Henry's reputation, about the company *we* all might be keeping. Dirt might stick, he said. Important to find out *where* it might stick and keep everything washed clean and shining bright.'

Stoker will have known Aston-Fox as well as Irving.

'This Aston character,' I said. 'What exactly is he supposed to have done? And how can it be connected to the Lyceum? Thousands of people come here.'

'Same question I asked Stoker,' he said. 'And then *he* asked *me* if I knew the names of all the casual girls we'd employed over the past twelve months. Told him I knew most of them – by reputation if not name. "Ah, but not *all* of them, Jimmy," he said to me. I knew enough from his tone not to persist.'

I could imagine Stoker pacing back and forth in front of his audience, probing and unsettling them, looking hard at some and affecting to ignore others completely. I knew exactly where I would stand in that particular parade of suspects.

'What happened?' I said. 'What was the outcome of it all?'

'Except to disrupt us all from our work just like the police were likely to do, and just like Henry was desperate to avoid? Nothing much. Just a lot of Stoker's hot air, as far as I could see.'

'Pity I missed it,' I said.

I expected him to laugh again, but this time he merely said, 'You were conspicuous by your absence. Stoker's very words.'

Why would he say it?

'Not at this time in the morning, surely?' I said.

He was about to say more when a man called to him from beneath the entrance pillars. He rose stiffly, pushing a thumb into the bowl of his pipe. 'That'll be me for the witness box,' he said.

I watched him go, waving the man ahead of him, and as the two of them went into the shadow of the foyer, Howson emerged. Jimmy Allen pointed me out to him and he came and sat beside me on the warm steps.

'Stoker accused *you* yet?' I asked him.

'All but.' He took the cigarette I offered him. He looked me up and down. 'A night out?' he said.

I didn't want to answer him, but I saw how this might now offend him following my refusal of his invitation the previous evening.

'You know how it is,' I said.

'I wish I did,' he said. 'I wish I did.'

'Jimmy Allen was telling me about Mother's little speech. Sounds as though he and Irving are covering their own backs.'

'You'd think the girl had been chopped into bloody pieces and then left scattered on the stage.'

'Does anyone know who she is – was?'

He laughed. 'People neither know nor care. All that matters as far as Henry and Stoker are concerned is Aston-high-and-mighty-Fox.'

'Did you know him?'

'Was I ever invited back with him and Henry and Stoker to an exclusive little opening-night dinner somewhere, do you mean?'

Neither of us spoke for a moment. I closed my eyes against the sun and felt its warmth on my face. It seemed a week since I'd climbed the stairs to Marlow's studio.

'Stoker should keep his nose out and leave it all to the police,' I said eventually. 'They aren't going to appreciate having him tell them how to do their job.' Especially if he was as determined as I had convinced myself he would be to point them in my direction. All these accumulated clues, connections and associations settling like leaves in the sudden calm of an autumn day.

'True,' he said. 'But you know Mother.'

'Jimmy said something else was bothering him.' It was as direct as I could bring myself to be.

'There's always something else bothering him.'

'About me. Jimmy said he wanted to see me.'

He shrugged.

'Jimmy said I was conspicuous by my absence, and that Stoker mentioned it.'

He remembered something. 'Stoker said there were likely to be pictures of Aston-Fox and the girl circulating – you know the sort. He was wondering if the girl had ever been employed here, if you might have taken her photograph for the depot records.'

'Not very likely,' I said, wondering at Stoker's reason for making the suggestion. 'Is that what he said – that I might have taken it without realizing who she was? How could *anyone* have known who she was?'

'Something like that. There are definitely supposed to be pictures of the two of them.'

'I haven't read any of the reports,' I said.

'It's probably just gossip. You know how these things are. Ask me, this is precisely the kind of thing dear old Mother likes to get his teeth into and then shake to pieces.'

'Especially if it helps to protect the reputation of God Almighty and His Earthly Throne.'

'Top of the agenda all round, I should imagine,' he said. 'You coming in? Face the music?'

'Might as well,' I said. Not because I wanted to go in and be confronted by Stoker, but because I now had no alternative *but* to go to him and discover his true intent in having suggested to all and sundry that *I* might have unwittingly photographed the dead girl.

I followed Howson into the foyer.

'I'm signing off the Circuit accounts today,' he told me. 'Stoker's pushing for another audit. With all this happening, he'll get his way. Henry will be sitting in a darkened room somewhere with his head in his hands until all this blows over, or at least far enough away from this place and everybody in it for him to get on with bloody *Macbeth*.'

'It makes sense,' I said, meaning the audit.

'*Everything* makes sense to Stoker,' he said. 'That's the point. That's the problem. And when it doesn't make sense – *his* sense – then he rearranges everything until it does.' He patted me on the back and we parted.

I entered the empty auditorium and made my way through the cold bowl of the room towards the stage.

23

Stoker found me less than an hour later, arriving silently and then pausing in the doorway to watch me at work. I stood with my back to him, knowing he was there, watching me, making his silent assessment and judgement of me. I continued laying out my prints for a further minute before finally turning and seeing him there.

'You look like a busy man,' he said. Anyone else might have smiled at the words, a shared understanding. But not Stoker. Not now. Now, he merely remained where he stood, his hand on the door-frame, and continued looking in at me.

I shook the fluid from my fingers. 'Only *look* like one?' I said.

He looked around the small room.

'You were missed,' he said. 'Earlier.'

'I had no idea my presence was required so early,' I said, fully understanding the game I was entering into with the words.

'Circumstances beyond your control?' he said.

'Not really,' I said. 'Howson said you imagined I might have photographed the girl who was murdered.' I dried my hands on a cloth.

'"Imagined"?'

'If she'd worked here, onstage or off, then there might be something of her, somewhere, a chorus, a group shot.' I let him know how unlikely I considered this. 'Do you need it?'

'Anything to help speed the police with their inquiries,' he said.

'Have they been yet?'

'Coming. A communication was received earlier. Apparently, the London Vigilance Committee are now at the reins.'

'Never heard of them,' I said. I began dismantling one of my cameras to clean it.

Stoker smiled and held my gaze. 'Man called Wheeler. I thought everyone in our line would have heard of the Vigilance by now, if not of Wheeler himself.'

'*Our* line of work?'

'I was referring to the theatre, not this.' He gestured at the camera I held. 'Though, of course, Wheeler has a wide range of other interests and concerns upon which to now cast his condemnatory gaze.' He split the word into its five syllables and pronounced each one slowly.

It was his boldest thrust yet, a blade upon which both Marlow and myself might yet find ourselves impaled.

'I take it you know him, this Wheeler,' I said, my slight emphasis pitch-perfect.

'Our paths have crossed on occasion, yes.'

I decided to push harder. 'According to Jimmy Allen, the newspapers are reporting "unsavoury practices".'

'Apparently, the man involved was a somewhat debased creature.'

'And an acquaintance of Henry's?' I said quickly.

'He merely—'

'According to Jimmy Allen.'

He took a deep breath. 'Henry has a great many – ' he paused, '*acquaintances*. Though I fear – as is the case with Aston-Fox – the relationship is all too often one-sided.' He had come too soon on to this dangerous ground and now he wanted to withdraw.

'Men happy to *say* they are his friend, acquaintance, associate, you mean?' I said. It was his safe path back.

'Precisely. Precisely that.'

'And the "unsavoury practices"?'

He coughed to conceal his uncertainty. 'I daresay we shall have to wait for the newspapers to reveal all. I imagine nothing will be left out once the trial is under way.' He finally came into the room and stood closer to me.

'And your fears for the Lyceum?' I said. 'For Henry?'

'Fears? Disruption, persecution, interference? And never forget – reputation is all.' He looked at the pictures I'd just taken from their trays. 'Are these the Scottish costumes?'

'*Macbeth*? Some of them.'

He flinched at the word, but said nothing. 'I saw you sitting with Howson,' he said. 'I imagine he informed you of my desire to start from a clean slate.'

'The audits?' It was clear to me that he meant much more.

'The complete and comprehensive audit. Every backdrop, every side-piece, every flat, every costume, prop and bottle of cosmetic.'

I saw how the costumes were buried deep in this bundle. We were wandering ever further from the photograph of the dead girl that might or might not exist.

'Whatever you need from me,' I said, 'let me know. What

does the girl look like?' If he could tell me, then he knew considerably more than he was letting on. She would have looked like a thousand instantly forgettable others.

'There are pictures of her as a younger child in some of the reports,' he said. 'Drawings, mostly.'

'Jimmy Allen said something about other pictures — pictures the police were interested in.'

'He seems to know a great deal.'

'Just repeating what he'd read in the papers. You know Jimmy and his newspapers.'

'Quite.'

Everything still at one remove, hearsay and common knowledge.

Eventually, he said, 'The papers say there might be photographs of Aston-Fox and the girl together.'

'The "unsavoury practices"?'

'I imagine so. Not proof that he is her murderer, of course.'

'Of course.'

'But all the same . . .' He crossed from one side of the room to the other in three slow, measured paces.

'Do you believe them?' I asked him.

'Them?'

'The papers. About the photographs. You almost sound as though you believe *I* might have taken them.'

'Not you,' he said, tellingly, and then, realizing this small mistake, added quickly, 'Smoke and fire, that's all. *Something* must have condemned the idiot. Wheeler certainly seems convinced they've got their man.' It was another small but telling revelation.

'And you believe Aston-Fox's friendship with Henry—'

'Acquaintanceship.'

'Of course. And you think his acquaintanceship with Henry will bring this Wheeler character here? You believe Henry and the Lyceum might now be somehow tainted by association?'

He stopped his pacing and turned back to me. He stood without speaking for a moment, and then having decided something, he smiled.

'Games,' he said.

I waited.

'Do you understand me, Webster?'

I shrugged, waiting for him to say more.

'Shall I say his name?' he said. His eyes narrowed, but betrayed no doubt.

'Whose name?' I said.

'Last night, I was unable to accept an invitation to a gathering to which I was invited. Not a standing invitation, as these things so often are, something more . . . *ad hoc*. A professional acquaintance of mine.'

'*Another* acquaintance,' I said provocatively. 'Go on.'

'I was unable to attend because I was made aware of certain information that precluded my attendance, presence.'

I felt strangely reassured and emboldened by the predictability of all this deliberately convoluted and evasive language. There were times when Stoker sounded as though he were deliberately mimicking himself.

'What sort of information?' I said. We were like two blind men feeling each other's faces.

Stoker considered his answer. 'I was told – it was inferred – that Aston-Fox himself might be present at this gathering.'

'Was he at liberty to attend?'

'Apparently not, but few then knew that.' Everything he said was now a revelation one way or another.

'And so you and he might then have been considered more than—'

'Precisely.'

'Then you were wise not to attend.'

I wondered if Aston-Fox *had* been invited to Marlow's evening. No one would have felt safe in his presence, however many times they might have encountered him there before. Stoker must have known all along that the man would not have been at liberty to attend.

'I daresay hundreds of men might know him,' I said.

'This particular gathering—'

'You make it sound like some kind of secret society,' I said. I tried to make the remark sound like a joke, something at which we might both laugh. I wondered what else might now be safely revealed by either of us. After all, if Stoker *had* just admitted even his 'acquaintanceship' with Marlow, then what harm was there in me doing the same? But even as this thought occurred to me, I knew precisely where the harm lay, and that I also had to consider the aftermath of all this, and the knowledge each of us might now forever possess of the other.

'I suppose it is, of sorts,' he said. 'The world is full of such societies. Back in my student days, in Dublin—' He stopped abruptly. The memories were precious to him and he would not allow even this distant contamination.

'You've written of them,' I said, guessing. 'In your novels.'

'I have indeed.' As intended, the remark gratified him.

'Do you know if Aston-Fox *did* attend this meeting?' I said.

'Unlikely. A few other associates of mine were present. I imagine I would have heard by now.'

I felt a shock at hearing this, suddenly bound and constrained.

'And you've heard nothing?' I said.

'Not "nothing", exactly.'

I wanted to turn away from him.

Seeing that I was again off-balance, he said, 'I imagine we at least understand each other a little better, Mr Webster.'

I could do nothing except give him a single nod. I cleared my throat, holding a hand to my chest. 'Fumes from the developing chemicals,' I said eventually.

'Of course. Perhaps you might sit down. Insufficient ventilation.'

It would be pointless now not to pursue the matter of Marlow's gathering, to know for certain in what kind of cold, mutual embrace Stoker and I now found ourselves.

'Do you believe some connection might be made – sought – between this society, Aston-Fox and yourself?' I said. I probably felt more unsettled than he did by the remark.

'Possibly. Though my concern is not necessarily for myself. The theatre, you understand. Henry. And before you say anything, I know that that sounds like an excuse – for myself – but, believe me, it isn't. The men about to prosecute Aston-Fox will not rest until all the rotten wood is dug out. And we all know that even *that* will not satisfy some of them, that once the rotten, the corrupt and the weak wood has been removed, then they must, of necessity, continue gouging away until a certain amount of the sound grain has also been sacrificed.'

'Meaning?' I understood him perfectly.

'Meaning simply that these men and their committees are

set upon their course. Meaning that even if no guilt or suspicion is cast or created by *my* association with Aston-Fox, then *other* connections might also be discovered and considered worthy of investigation by these men.'

He was talking about Marlow again, and about me, and about the distant possibility of someone recognizing one of the Lyceum's costumes on one or other of his models. It was something Pearl had earlier dismissed as impossible, but now Stoker made it sound considerably more likely. Or perhaps it was merely another of his gambits to unsettle me and to leave me following unsteadily in his wake.

'What kind of connections?' I said absently.

But he had said all he'd come to say. 'I don't know. I imagine things will become much clearer as the inquiry into the girl's death progresses.'

'And you're convinced – you, personally – that the police already possess whatever they need to secure their conviction?'

He nodded once. 'I know the man. He considers himself untouchable, invincible, above everything, and certainly above the law.'

I saw then that we might both be best served as these uncertain unravellings and accusations continued by holding each other even closer. It would be impossible now to deny our mutual need and understanding, and the dependency this created.

'What do you intend to do?' I asked him. 'About Aston-Fox and the possibility of these other connections?'

'I daresay there is little any of us can do except wait and see what the inquiry throws up. Perhaps the best we can hope for now is some measure of . . . containment.'

'Self-protection, you mean? The Lyceum?'

'Of the facts. Containment of the facts. Contain the facts, contain the accusations and all the connections likely to be made, and contain the guilt. I take it as Gospel that neither you nor I actually knew the murdered girl.'

I shook my head.

'And only I had even a passing acquaintanceship with Aston-Fox.'

'I never even knew he existed until – ' I almost said *Until Bliss pointed everything out to me in the Metropolitan*, 'I saw the newspapers.'

'So, perhaps some degree of containment might not be so difficult to achieve,' he said.

'Of course,' I said. Thus was uncertain hope reborn and allowed to rise.

'Our only true concerns now,' he said, 'are those connections and associations *beyond* our immediate control and containment.'

Marlow again.

For some reason, I remembered the occasion when I'd seen Stoker and the woman arguing at the rear of the theatre. I had little idea of what this sudden memory might truly signify, but I was convinced that it was a kind of premature confirmation of Stoker's involvement in all that was now happening, and I felt momentarily light-headed with the relief of even this imperfect understanding. And I saw equally suddenly and unexpectedly how much he, Stoker, had to lose by the possible outcome of all these events. It was small consolation, but something.

'Evidence,' he said. The word disrupted my wandering thoughts and I waited for him to explain. 'Those other connections.'

'The ones beyond our control?'

'Perhaps even beyond our imagining. Evidence. That's what the police will be searching for. Solid, tangible, irrefutable evidence.'

Marlow's photographs of the girl and Aston-Fox together. And whatever might then be found to trace a connection between Marlow and the Lyceum. Me, in other words. And now Stoker. Our three names strung along that one tight cord. The warning was clear to me.

'Severance,' he said. 'I imagine that, too, is the order of the day. Especially considering how little time might now remain to us in which to act.' He came even closer to me, and for a moment I imagined he was going to hold out his hand to me. But instead, he turned and walked back to the door.

'If I hear anything . . .' I said.

He looked along the empty corridor ahead of him. 'Containment,' he said. 'And when something cannot be contained . . .' He walked quickly away from me, his footsteps loud on the bare boards, leaving the rapidly deepening chasm of that single unfinished sentence quickly behind him.

24

Three days later, my work at the theatre finished, I went again to Somers Town to see Solomon.

Turning the corner of Ossulston Street, I saw Marta sitting at the shop entrance, and the instant she saw me, she rose from her chair and ran towards me, her arms out, calling my name. My first thought was that the police had returned and that this time Solomon had been taken away by them. But as she approached me, I saw that she was excited, smiling broadly and still calling out to me in Polish.

Reaching me, she embraced me. 'Thank you, thank you, thank you,' she said.

'Alice,' I said, my voice unheard above her own muffled clamour. 'Alicia.'

'Alicia, yes, Alicia.' Four days had passed since the pair of them had visited Alice.

I prised myself from her. She was almost a foot shorter than I was and she reached up to hold both my hands. There were tears on her cheeks.

'Is Solomon in?' I asked her.

'Solomon?' She nodded vigorously and then clasped me again.

Looking over her head, I saw Solomon appear briefly in

the open doorway. He signalled to me and then withdrew.

After a further minute of immobility, anchored by Marta, I disengaged myself and started walking away from her. By then, other women on the street were watching us. A small group stood between us and the shop, awaiting our arrival.

Marta spoke to them, pointing me out to them as the husband of Alicia. One of the women held my arm for a moment, her words as unintelligible as Marta's to me. I tried to look around us, to see if anyone else might be watching. There would be no chance now of arriving at Solomon's unnoticed.

Reaching the shop, Marta made a declaration to the following women, and most of them paused and then reluctantly withdrew. Perhaps I was too important now – as the husband of Alicia – to be shared with them, a venerated visitor they did not deserve.

Inside, the shop was cool, its oilcloth blinds drawn against the sunlight. A smell of aniseed and paraffin permeated the place.

Solomon waited for me behind the counter. He called for Marta to close and bolt the door behind us, which she did. I doubted if I had ever seen her this animated or happy in all the years I had known her.

'I take it the séance was a success,' I said to him, hoping he understood me.

He said nothing for a moment, watching as Marta slid the bolts. I saw the women outside gather closer, crouching down to peer beneath the blinds. Marta rapped on the glass to them and they backed off in surprise.

Solomon lifted the counter and motioned for me to join him, quickly lowering the board as Marta came too. He told her to wait where she was, that I would be returned to her soon enough, and even this denial did little to dampen her spirits.

I followed Solomon along the corridor into his studio. It seemed my life had become a succession of these narrow, constricted passages and small, dimly lit secret places.

Once inside, he bolted that door, too.

'She has been like this ever since we saw your wife. The evening, as you can see, was a great success for her. Everything she wanted to hear, she heard. She is already talking of going again.'

'I told Cora all I knew about Tomasz,' I said. 'About his death.'

'I know that. Please, I'm not accusing or blaming you.'

'I wasn't sure what to do for the best.'

'It was all very obvious,' he said. 'To me, at least.'

'But not to Marta?'

'No, not to her.'

'Alice only wanted to ensure—'

'Please, I am not asking for any explanation. Marta believed, and that was enough. Enough for me, and considerably more than enough for her. You saw her. She has spoken to Tomasz, her dear lost son. Your wife is very expert, and your daughter very efficient as her partner. Needless to say, I restrained completely my own scepticism. Mostly for Marta's sake.'

But also because of our friendship?

He motioned to a chair and we both sat down. The same clear spirit was produced and poured. He wiped the sweat from his face on his sleeve. He looked tired, as though his own day had started early and been long.

'I suppose you know how it is that your wife produces – or should I say "heightens" – her effects,' he said hesitantly.

He was talking about Caroline.

'Her spirit guide, you mean?'

He looked at me and I saw the sudden look of pity in his eyes.

'I'm sorry,' he said, 'that you should be made to suffer such pain so that another's might be alleviated. It seems we – others – benefit only at your expense and loss.'

'She genuinely believes that Caroline is talking to her,' I said.

If he was sceptical about this too, then he kept it well hidden.

'Everything Marta asked of her, she answered. I heard the newspaper reports in much of what she said.'

'And my own remembering?'

'That, too.'

'I didn't want Marta to be disappointed.'

'No,' he said. 'And now the two of them, your wife and my own, have entered into this – this contract together, and I doubt if either of *us* – you or I – is brave enough or foolish enough to come between them.'

'Or to challenge their convictions?'

'Or that.' We both knew it was too lofty a notion.

'Are you happy for Marta to delude herself in this way?' I asked him. It seemed a cruel remark to make and I waited for him to say, 'In the way your own wife deludes herself?'

But instead, he said, 'Is it truly delusion?'

'Without what I told Cora, and whatever she read of the shipwreck, then Alice would have had nothing to say to her.'

'I suppose not, but I have felt just as cold and as angry and as cheated coming out of some church services I have attended. Besides . . .' He hesitated. 'Besides, for a few seconds, a moment . . .' He shook his head.

'What? You found yourself convinced by what Alice was saying, by her act? It's all most of her sitters want of her – to be fooled or convinced. There's often nothing to separate the two things in that particular world.'

'I can see that,' he said. 'She even spoke with a voice that Marta readily accepted as Tomasz's own. It was a perfect illusion. Even *I* found myself unwilling to have it broken. Others at the sitting grew frustrated that only Tomasz was talking to your wife. She said it was because of the terrible nature of his passing and the restlessness this had created, forcing him to wander in that other world, ever desperate to return. Violent deaths and suicides, she said, always produced the most unsettled of souls.'

'I see,' I said. And now the deception was his to maintain.

'Did nothing raise Marta's suspicions?' I said.

He smiled. 'She asked your wife if Tomasz still bore his scar, or if the Afterlife had finally erased it.'

I knew nothing of a scar.

'When he was a baby, I held him up to a window and snagged his cheek on a hook. It tore badly, and because there were no doctors, I stitched up his wound myself. Three stitches. It appeared to heal, but then later became infected and left him with a mark.' He drew a finger over his own cheek. 'Marta insisted otherwise, of course, but she always blamed me for that terrible mark on her only child. Tomasz used to tell her that it only added to his attractions. When Marta asked your wife about it, your wife thought she was talking about injuries he might have received during the shipwreck. She started guessing of these until—'

'Until you signalled to her on your own face where the scar was on your son's.'

He laughed at this guess and made the same quick line on his cheek. 'After which, of course, I was as complicit in the deception as any of them.'

'And meanwhile Marta went on hearing only what she wanted to hear?'

'Your wife collapsed exhausted shortly afterwards. Not wanting to risk too much more uncertainty, I imagine. The pair of them were in tears; others, too. Marta spoke to her dear, lost son, and that dear, lost son answered her. Mother and son. What was a small matter of uncertainty against that?' He drained his glass and refilled it.

'I hope everything goes well,' I said. It sounded like a farewell.

'Of course things will "go well",' he said angrily. 'We all know the course on which these things are set.' He signalled his apology for the remark.

'But some see that course more clearly than others?'

'I don't know,' he said. 'Perhaps seeing these things clearly is not the priority, not such an advantage.'

We both fell silent to listen to Marta giving in to the demands of the gathered women and opening the door to let them into the shop.

'They'll drive away any customers,' Solomon said.

'Or perhaps become new ones for Alice,' I said.

'Alicia.'

Again, neither of us spoke for a moment, listening to the excited babble of the women.

'Is that why you came?' he said eventually.

'Partly.'

'Or because you'd heard that the police had been back.'

I couldn't deny that it was what I'd returned to discover.

'You guessed they'd return,' he said. 'The man who came was the same as before. He waved the newspaper headlines at me. This time he asked me about you.'

'I imagine they're asking about all—'

'About you, specifically. About your work at the Lyceum and your friendship with Marlow. He told me things would go badly for me if I didn't tell them what I knew. He seemed very confident this time that his inquiries were leading somewhere more profitable. I knew from the questions he asked, by the way he spoke, that I was only confirming what he already knew or believed he knew.'

Everything he said felt like a sharp push away from him.

'*Did* Marlow take pictures of the murdered girl? Of the girl and her murderer together?' he said.

'It's a possibility. I think so.'

'Then you *know* so.' He held a fist to his heart. 'And does Marlow also still possess this evidence which will convict the murderer?'

'I don't know.'

'More evasion. Do you *believe* so?'

I nodded. 'Marlow's careful, thorough. If there *is* anything to incriminate Aston-Fox, then he'll use it to good advantage.'

'To his *own* advantage, you mean. Not to yours, not to mine, and certainly not to the advantage of all those others of so little consequence to him, like Kaplinski, Abbot or Morgenthau. The policeman spoke as though he had already flown, gone, disappeared.'

'I don't know where he is,' I said. It was only the beginning of the truth.

'The policeman also said that you and I were great friends and business associates. What a pity, then, that *I* did all the hard work while *you* reaped all the rewards and benefits that *our* acquaintanceship with Marlow conferred upon us.' He waited for my response.

'He invited me to his studio,' I said. 'Marlow. The night of the séance.'

'To confer those rewards and benefits? Money? Do you believe that this Aston man *is* a murderer, more?'

'Marlow said he enjoyed certain perversions. I don't even—'

'And have you seen evidence of those perversions?' He mouthed rather than said the word. No one in the shop would have heard us above the noise still being made there. He cocked his ear for a moment. 'They sound like hens in a coop,' he said, and it was true.

'I've seen nothing,' I told him. 'Everything's whispers and suggestion.'

'You truly believe that?'

I shook my head.

'They arrested Morgenthau and Abbot again. And this time all three of the Ludlum brothers.'

But, as before, though the men might have been friends or associates of his, the names meant little to me. Perhaps as little as I might now mean to Marlow. I couldn't even decide for certain what might now be best for me – Marlow's confirmation that he knew me or his complete and unwavering denial of the past three years.

'Morgenthau's studio was ransacked. "Searching", they still

call it. His windows were smashed. The police considered it their duty to announce to the gathering crowd what he was involved in. People put stones through all his panes.'

'And the police threatened you?' I said.

He nodded. 'I take it by all this that they have not yet been to visit you?'

I shook my head. Neither of us spoke for a moment.

'Are they watching your shop?' I asked him.

He shrugged. 'It's what they *told* me they would do. I told them to watch it as much as they liked, that they would only be wasting their valuable time. Then the detective asked me if I had been afforded the same protection and rewards that you had been given by Marlow. He wondered aloud if some of us weren't once again being sacrificed for the good of others, if we weren't once again paying for *their* crimes and sins.'

'Marlow gave me nothing,' I said. 'Payment, that's all. For what I was able to lend to him. I know nothing about Aston-Fox or the girl or what Marlow might or might not still possess that will condemn the man.' But, though honest, it was too emphatic a denial and we both saw this. 'On my daughter's—' I began to say in an effort to convince him.

'Don't,' he said sharply. 'Not that. I believe you. Everything the policeman said to me was at best a half-lie. *Has* Marlow disappeared and left everyone behind?'

'I don't know,' I said. 'It's possible – likely.' Almost a certainty.

'A man could travel a great distance in four days. And especially if no one was yet looking for him or attempting to stop him. So perhaps there was some truth in what the policeman was suggesting about the role and the fate of those of us already being left far behind.'

After that, neither of us spoke for several minutes. I examined the pictures on his desk and those hanging from the lines above his sink. They were mostly portraits, individuals and family groups, photographs anyone might have taken.

He watched me for a moment and saw my interest fade as I began to consider other things.

'Perhaps you want to search the place, too,' he said, and then laughed.

In the shop, Marta was repeating another of her excited stories about the séance to her equally excitable audience.

'Your daughter said we were not able to return for another month,' he said. 'Your wife, apparently, suddenly finds herself in great demand.'

'So Cora keeps telling me.'

He touched his small glass to mine. 'To our children,' he said.

Our *dead* children.

It was as much as I could do to repeat the words, knowing as I spoke that the friendship between us was all but severed by the razor-sharp blade of that one unspoken word.

25

I was again passing the Clarendon, when I heard Isobel call to me. At first, prompted perhaps by the memory of seeing her there before, and of then afterwards being told by her that she'd known all along of my presence in the doorway, I believed I had imagined the voice; or that some other woman had called out my name – perhaps even to another man – and that I had merely made the unthinking connection. But she called again, louder this time, more insistently, and I knew it was her.

I turned, feigned surprise, and saw her coming to me across the near-empty room, already much closer than I had anticipated.

Reaching me, she held my arm and pulled me towards her. Her boldness both alarmed me and made me cautious.

'Come in,' she said.

At first, I imagined she'd been drinking again, but saw that this was not the case.

'I'm on my way home,' I said. 'I'm expected.' I looked at my watch.

'No, you're not. Not by them two. Come in.'

She continued pulling me and we crossed the room together. For me to have struggled or to have pushed her away would only have attracted attention to the pair of us. She motioned to the landlord, who signalled back that he understood her.

The far side of the room was divided into booths, and she led me into one of these, insisting that I enter it before her, and then sitting close beside me to block my departure. An elderly woman sat slumped at the table opposite us. Isobel kicked her and the woman sat upright and swore.

'Get out,' Isobel told her.

'Who are you?' She looked from Isobel to me.

I knew to remain silent.

'You going to let that little tart talk to me like that?'

'Get out,' Isobel repeated. She reached across the narrow table and struck the woman on her arm.

'Oh, you got some money business, have you?' The woman laughed, almost choking, and then made an obscene gesture with her hand. 'In that case . . .' She opened her hand and laid it on the table.

'Give her something,' Isobel said to me.

I gave the woman a shilling and she sat looking at it in her open palm for a moment before closing her fingers around it and shuffling awkwardly away from us.

The landlord arrived as she went, putting two glasses on the table.

'And him,' Isobel said to me.

The man told me how much and I paid him.

Waiting until he'd gone, Isobel took off the embroidered jacket she was wearing and rolled up her sleeves. Her blouse was already open at the top, revealing the rise and divide of her breasts. She picked up her drink and sipped it.

'I can spare a few moments,' I said.

'He can spare a few moments. I'm honoured.'

Everything she continued to do and say kept me on my guard.

'So what shall we talk about?' she said. 'In those few precious moments, that is.'

I slid my own glass across the table, raised it and then put it back down without drinking from it.

'Not thirsty?' she said.

'I don't understand what you want of me,' I said.

'What *I* want? Perhaps it's exactly the same as what *you* want.' If this was intended as cleverness, then its meaning was still lost to me.

'I see Lady Alicia and Dame Cora had another fabulously entertaining and profitable evening the other night. Who would ever have thought that gullibility came with such a high price tag. Gullibility – you like that? I looked it up.' She laughed at my uncertainty.

'You shouldn't talk about your—'

'About my what? Mistress?'

'I was going to say "employer". You shouldn't talk about your employer like that. Or Cora.'

'Calm yourself. It's not as though I'm saying it to her face, is it? Not as though *you* haven't considered saying exactly the same yourself, now is it?'

I couldn't refute this, and she knew that.

'I'm her husband,' I said, as though this might explain everything I wanted to avoid having to explain to her.

'You can say that again. And what about the girl, what are you to her?'

'Her father,' I said. I wished I'd kept silent.

'Not that you'd know that, either, the way she treats you.'

I waited, unwilling to continue being provoked by her.

'Besides, perhaps all that could change – the employer bit, I mean,' she said.

'Are you saying you're leaving her – us?' It seemed like too simple and too convenient a solution to all of this.

'Perhaps. Not necessarily. What I'm saying is that perhaps *you* could be my employer.'

'I don't understand you,' I said. But I was beginning to.

She bowed her head and picked an imaginary thread from her blouse, her forefinger resting briefly on her flesh. And then she looked sharply back up at me.

'I still don't know what you're saying,' I told her.

She slid her hand from her blouse down to her waist and pushed her fingers into the pocket of her skirt. I felt myself tense against what she was about to reveal.

She pulled something out – a piece of paper – and held it under her hand on the table.

'Something I found,' she said. She looked quickly around us and then smiled.

'What is it?' I made my guess.

'You know what it is.'

'Show me.'

'Lady Alice told me to go up and strip the sheets. Said there were some clean pillowcases in some drawer or other. Imagine the shock I had.' She smiled again as she said the word.

The photographs Marlow had given me, and which I'd locked in the drawer of my desk.

'What drawer?' I said.

'That's the point. She never said. Just "drawer". I suppose you could say I used my initiative. Is that what you'd call it – initiative? I hear the girl walking around shouting about it all day long.'

'My desk drawer was locked,' I said.

She behaved as if she was offended by the remark. 'And with good reason. Like I said, you can imagine the shock I had – there's me expecting to find some clean white pillow-cases, and what do I see looking up at me as bold as day?'

The photographs had been inside an envelope, inside a book, beneath a ledger, pushed to the rear.

On impulse, I grabbed her wrist and pulled away her hand. The photograph lay face-down on the table. We both looked at it.

'You're hurting my wrist,' she said. 'The landlord's a good friend of mine.'

I looked to where the man now stood and watched us. I released her and she made a show of rubbing her arm and looking pained.

'That'll bruise,' she said. It wouldn't. 'What'll I tell my *employer* if she asks me about it?'

'Tell her one of your men friends got rougher than usual with you.'

She smiled at the remark. 'That what you think, is it? Men friends? That's your world, not mine. Though . . .' She tapped a finger on the photograph. 'Judging by this, perhaps it's the other way round – perhaps it's *you* who's got all the explaining to do.'

'I didn't take the picture,' I said.

'And it wasn't hidden away like a dirty little secret in your drawer? Lady Alice know all about this particular little sideline, does she?'

I knew that she would have said nothing to Alice, that this was the whole point of everything now, the fuel and spark of her boldness.

'Alice knows nothing about it,' I said.

'"Course she doesn't. *She*'s too busy talking to your dead daughter, who's big friends with all the other yacking ghosts and walking dead.'

I wanted to slap her face and she saw this.

'Go on,' she said. She turned her cheek to me. 'You won't be the first. Even had it happen in here.'

'Put it away,' I said. It was beyond me to touch the photograph, to grab it and put it in my own pocket. There had been a dozen others in the envelope.

'Take it,' she said. 'Go on. Perhaps you've forgotten about the others.'

'You stole them,' I said, causing her to laugh.

'"Stole"? I nearly fainted with shock and disgust when I saw what you'd got hiding in there. I was nearly sick, sick all over your room. Never mind a bruise, how do you think I would have explained *that* to your wife? I thought *I* knew a thing or two, but some of those pictures could teach us all a lesson.'

I knew she was exaggerating.

'Valuable, are they?' she said.

And it occurred to me only then – *only then* – that though the pictures in themselves were in no way identifiable as having been taken by Marlow, there might have been some other connection to him – identical prints, say, which *did* bear his stamp – a connection which might now easily be made by the men starting to investigate all those otherwise hidden associations.

'Valuable?' I said absently.

'Somebody wanting them back? Just like you do now. Somebody I should know about, is it?' She tapped the picture again. 'The girl doesn't look none too happy, but the man looks smart enough and pleased enough with himself. Somebody in the public eye, is it? Somebody with money, and who might part with a bit of it to get them back?'

I had no idea who the men in the photographs were, and I felt strangely reassured by her greedy, wayward guessing. I wanted nothing more now than to turn the picture over and look at it.

'I don't know who any of them are,' I said, and if the revelation deflated her expectations, then she hid this well.

'You're still not getting my point,' she said slowly.

'Blackmail seems a simple enough thing to understand,' I said, hoping her gaze was still fixed on Alice and not now starting to wander elsewhere.

'You still whispered the word,' she said.

'It's where all this is leading,' I said flatly, hoping she might start to worry that I was growing tired of her game.

'You think that's what – all – I want?'

I decided to push my small advantage. 'You want to become part of it?' I said. 'You want *me* to introduce you to someone who might take the same pictures of you, introduce you to all these supposedly influential and wealthy men? Just like you wanted me to ask at the Lyceum for you?'

'Which you never did,' she said.

'Because no one there owes *me* any favours.' Or at least not until a few hours ago.

The confession surprised her and she watched me for a moment. Then she took the glass from my hand and drained it, signalling for the watching landlord to bring us more.

A moment later, as the man approached us, she said, 'You want to hide it?'

I looked down at the back of the photograph, but made no attempt to conceal it from the man. He set the drinks on either side of it. She, I saw, watched the photograph closely as he did this, ready to slap down her hand if he showed any interest.

'That was a stupid thing to do,' she said when he'd gone.

'Why? You think he wouldn't have seen others like it?'

She conceded this and then finally flicked the photograph over to reveal a man lying on a couch with a ghostly nude kneeling at his crotch, his prick in her mouth, the woman's eyes closed, her breasts hanging free of the loose gown she wore. The man was looking down at her with an expression of both pleasure and surprise on his face. A black-bordered portrait of the same woman hung on the wall beside the man's chair.

'*Is* that what you want?' I said. 'An introduction to all this?' I thought of everything that was happening, of all those others now doing their utmost to erase every lingering trace of themselves, and laughed at what she was suggesting.

'What?' she said uncertainly, but with growing anger, knowing I was mocking her in some way. 'You think I'm not good enough? You don't think I've got what these men want?'

'I'm sure you have,' I said. 'It's just that now is not a good time to be making approaches in that particular direction.'

'What particular direction? What are you talking about?'

A pair of women entered the bar and made their way to an adjoining booth. I thought at first that they might be the same two women I'd seen her with previously, but if they were, then they ignored her and called to the landlord. As they came close to us, she finally picked up the photograph and slid it back into her pocket.

'You still stole them,' I said, assuming she also had the others.

'You saying they're yours, then? You've not just borrowed them? Not just keeping them safe for a friend? Bit of a coincidence, don't you think – you doing what you do, and everything?'

'That's all it is,' I said, but unconvincingly.

'And that's what you'd tell the police, is it? That's what you'd tell them if they came to search the house?' She was bold again, and smiling.

'I can see you've given all this some thought,' I said. 'But why would the police come to search the house?'

She repeated the question, mimicking me. 'You think I'm stupid? You think I don't hear about everything that's going on? Other photographers have been searched and arrested. So why not you? Perhaps I left the other pictures in that drawer. Perhaps the police have already been. Perhaps your wife or your daughter – the living one, that is, the one who enjoys issuing her commands and orders to all and sundry – have already let them in.'

'The police are only interested in—'

'I *know* what they're interested in,' she said sharply. 'And don't pretend there's any "only" about it. The police are interested in what the police are always interested in – making themselves look good, and anything that comes their way that they can turn to their advantage without too much effort.'

The women in the next booth burst into laughter, and this lasted for a full minute. They spoke loudly and crudely, encouraging each other with their gossip. The landlord now stood and watched them rather than us.

'Bet you're grateful I'm sober,' Isobel said to me. And she sipped her drink to emphasize the point.

'Tell me what you want,' I said.

But she seemed suddenly uncertain of what that was. We had circled each other and now neither of us knew for certain in which direction we faced.

'You know what I want,' she said eventually.

'*Have* you taken the rest of the pictures?'

'Don't worry.'

'Answer me.'

She nodded.

'And the police?'

'What about them? You know they're coming, eventually.'

'I've nothing to hide,' I said, causing her to laugh again.

'Not now, you've not. You think in a book, in a drawer's *hiding* something? Out of sight, out of mind, is that it?'

'I'll ask around,' I said.

'Like you asked around at the theatre? Forget it.' She sat back in her seat, pushing out her chest and revealing more flesh. She breathed deeply, causing her breasts to slowly rise and then fall.

'See?' she said.

'See what?'

'How easy and straightforward everything can be.'

'In what way?'

'In whatever way you want it to be.' She ran a hand across her stomach, letting it rest on the taut fabric of her skirt. 'Some things are as easy and as straightforward as you make them,' she said.

'And you'd do all that – in the photographs?' I said.

'And more. You think I walked in off the farm yesterday?'

'For those men, the photographers?'

She grinned at me. 'You see, that's how things could be made even *more* simple and straightforward.' She waited for me to understand more clearly what she was suggesting. 'See? Simple and straightforward because that's how things could be done. Fifty-fifty.'

'You want me—' I began to say.

'Why don't you shout it to the world?' she said. 'Not much of a start to a secret partnership, is it?'

'I can't,' I said.

"Course you can. You just haven't thought everything through yet, that's all. Look at your own daughter. You want her to be the only one with any initiative in the house? Look at your wife. Enjoy being wrapped around somebody's – everybody's – little finger, do you?'

'And you'd—'

'And I'd be the other fifty in that fifty-fifty arrangement.' She patted her pocket. 'Next you'll be telling me that there's no money to be made in these things.' She held up her glass to me, waiting for me to do the same. 'Besides,' she said as the glasses touched, 'all this not-mixing-business-and-pleasure stuff. Who knows – your expertise, my connections, the people I might know . . .' She cocked her head to the nearby women. 'Who knows what we might achieve.'

I saw how swiftly and completely I had been outmanoeuvred by her, how she had set her trap and baited it, and how I now sat entirely within it, looking out at her.

'See,' she said. 'Now that you're thinking about it, you're

starting to see what good sense it all makes. Besides . . .' She took her hand from her skirt and laid it over mine on the table. I felt its heat, its moistness. She tapped her nails on the backs of my fingers. 'You *can* smile,' she said.

And so I smiled at her.

26

The police finally came early the following morning. I was downstairs, alone in the kitchen, when I saw a figure approach the back of the house. At first I thought this was Isobel arriving to start work. I had risen early in the hope of seeing her before either Alice or Cora appeared.

The figure approached the door and put its hands to the frosted glass, pressing a large, male face to the panel. I saw the helmet and understood immediately what was finally happening. I had burned the remainder of Marlow's photographs the previous evening, counting them and guessing that Isobel had taken a further five or six from the envelope.

Realizing that the man at the door had not seen me in the kitchen, I went to it, slid its bolt and quickly opened it, catching him off guard. He stepped back from me, struggling to regain his composure. Close to, he seemed little more than an overgrown boy in a badly fitting uniform.

I waited for him to speak.

He took out a whistle, considered this for a moment and then slid it back into his pocket.

'Are you Morgan?' he said.

'Who?'

'Not Morgan, Marlow. Are you Marlow? Are you him?'
He pointed a finger at me.

Seizing this advantage – but already aware that this whole thing could not simply have been a case of mistaken identity – I acted offended.

'Who's Marlow? My name's Webster. Charles Webster. My wife and daughter are sleeping upstairs. I thought you were a trespasser.'

'Not Marlow?' he said. 'We're looking—'

At that moment there was a loud and insistent knocking at the front door and he looked over my shoulder into the house.

I affected yet more surprise.

'That's the others,' he said.

'What others? What are you talking about? Why should there be more than one of you?'

'Because this is a search. We're searching his studio.' He seemed more confident back on this prepared ground.

'Studio?'

'This is a photographic studio. We've already searched plenty of others.'

'This is my home,' I said. 'My home.'

Behind me, the knocking continued, and I left him to pass through the house and open the front door.

'Can I come in?' he shouted after me, and I invited him to follow me, knowing what further small advantage I might gain by having him beside me as I let the others in.

Arriving at the narrow hallway, I heard Cora above me, calling down to ask what was happening. She saw the boy beside me and screamed, recovering quickly and shouting to ask him what he was looking at. She stood in her dressing gown and night clothes. I called up to her to get dressed, that a mistake had been made. I told her to tell her mother. The constable shouted up his apologies to her.

I opened the door to three further men, two more young constables and a man a foot taller than any of them, wearing a dark suit and a bowler and carrying a briefcase. Wheeler.

All three came into the house and Wheeler took a sheet of paper from the case and handed it to me.

'He's not Marlow,' the constable beside me said.

Wheeler looked at me, and from me to the constable. I thought for a moment he was going to put the paper back in the case and turn away from me. But instead, he said to the boy, 'What have you said?'

The constable didn't understand him. 'He's not Marlow,' he repeated. 'His name's . . .' He'd forgotten.

'My name's Charles Webster,' I said to Wheeler.

'I know who you are,' he said firmly. 'And it's you we're here to see.'

'You said—' the constable said, stopping abruptly. 'On the roster. Today's searches. Down under "Marlow". I thought—'

Wheeler held my gaze as he said all this. 'They're all down under "Marlow",' he said. 'And I see from Mr Webster here that he knows very well why that might be.'

I made a quick calculation. It had been a sleepless night of calculation of one sort or another. 'I don't know anyone called Marlow,' I said. 'At least, I don't *think* I do.'

'Oh, really? Perhaps you might like to reconsider that.'

I pretended to think. 'If you tell me who he is, what he's done . . .' I said. 'Is it someone connected to the Lyceum, perhaps? I work there. I'm a photographer.'

Wheeler smiled at all this. 'May we come in properly?' He indicated the sheet of paper I still held. 'That's a warrant.'

'Of course,' I said.

'His wife and daughter are upstairs,' the constable said.

'Anyone else?'

'Just the three of us,' I said.

'And your studio?'

'What studio? I work at the Lyceum. My studio's there – such as it is. More of a simple developing room, really. I work for Henry Irving. It's much easier doing everything there, beck and call and all that.' I had dismantled anything that might constitute studio equipment the previous evening. My cameras and a few supplies were still up there, but nothing out of the ordinary. 'I keep cameras here, a few films,' I said. 'But that's all. Feel free.' I gestured up the stairs.

'I do not need to "feel free" as you put it,' Wheeler said. 'I act under the authority of the law and under the powers invested in me by the London Vigilance Committee, of which I happen to be the head.' The words were intended as a fanfare.

'And you are?' I said.

'My name is Oliver Lord Wheeler.'

'So you're not a policeman?'

'As I've already explained.'

Behind him, the two constables exchanged a glance and grinned.

'Yet you have authority over these three men?'

'By the power—'

'The London Vigilance Committee. Lord? Is that—'

'Merely a name. My mother was a great admirer of Tennyson.'

The two men shared another glance.

'I see,' I said. He had said the name as though it *were* a title, and as though it was something to which he believed himself entitled.

I stood to one side and let them come further into the house. I led them into the front parlour, where the table and chairs were still set out from the séance of several nights previously.

'Have you been entertaining?' Wheeler said suspiciously, looking around him.

'My wife is a professional medium,' I said pompously. 'This is where she holds her gatherings. She's very highly regarded.'

Wheeler walked around the table, lifting its heavy cloth to look beneath it. The three constables simply stood in the doorway and looked in at the closed curtains, at the pictures on the wall. I drew the curtains and let in the rising sun.

'Do you know why we're here, Mr Webster?' Wheeler asked me.

'I've already explained – I'm not—'

'You're not Marlow. I know that. You seem to be going to great lengths to keep repeating the fact. Your friend Solomon . . .' It was a deliberately unfinished remark.

The constables turned to watch me.

'I know Solomon,' I said quickly. 'Solomon and Marta. Somers Town. I visit him frequently. I was there only yesterday. He occasionally undertakes developing and framing work for me. Are you telling me *he's* involved with this Marlow and whatever *he's* done? Solomon is as honest as anyone I know.'

'You went to see him between the hours of ten to four and twenty to five.'

I feigned surprise at this. 'He told you?'

'And prior to that, a week ago, on the tenth.'

'That's right,' I said. 'Or thereabouts.'

Wheeler finally put the warrant back in his case.

There was a commotion in the doorway and Cora pushed her way into the room, demanding to know what was happening.

'This is my daughter,' I said.

The constable who had already seen her took off his helmet.

'My wife is still upstairs.'

'You woke her up,' Cora said. To me, she said angrily, 'What have you done? Mother was asleep.'

'Your father was just explaining,' Wheeler said to her.

'They want to search the house in connection with a man called Marlow,' I told her. 'Have you ever heard of him?'

'It's a place,' she said. 'Marlow's a place.'

'It is,' one of the constables said.

'They think *I* know him,' I said to Cora.

'I should be very surprised if you *didn't* know Mr Marlow,' Wheeler said, refusing to be drawn by all these incidental diversions. 'As you say, perhaps via your connections at the Lyceum.' He was probing and we both knew this. 'Is anyone else employed here? As your assistant, perhaps?'

'His *what*?' Cora said. 'Him? *I* am my mother's assistant and personal secretary, her business manager.' She confused and then gratified herself by this sudden excess.

'There's Isobel,' I said.

'And she is?' Wheeler said.

'She's my wife's—'

'She's a housemaid, a dogsbody,' Cora said, angry that she had not made herself the centre of our attention.

'Will she be coming in today?' Wheeler asked me.

I looked to Cora.

'I suppose so. Even when she does turn up, she's still not very reliable.'

'I don't think Mr Wheeler wants to hear our domestic complaints,' I said, though of course I was happy to allow each of these small loose strings to become further tangled together.

'Do you know approximately what time she'll be here?' he said.

I had watched him closely when Isobel was mentioned to see if her name meant anything to him, but he gave no indication of having heard of her.

'Did you search Solomon's studio?' I asked him.

'Is that the husband mother saw?' Cora said. 'What have *they* got to do with anything?'

'I assure you, Miss,' Wheeler said, 'we have no interest whatsoever in your mother's professional business. All we are after here—'

'Is Alice awake?' I asked Cora.

'Of course she is. You think she could sleep through all this? I wanted her to remain undisturbed. She was exhausted.'

'Her calling,' Wheeler said.

'Yes, her calling,' Cora said defiantly. 'So if you *are* intending searching the whole house, I'd better go and help her to get ready. Unless you make a habit of rushing into professional ladies' chambers?'

I almost laughed at the phrase.

'Of course not,' Wheeler said. 'The London Vigilance Committee prides itself—'

'The what?' Cora said. 'You said you were the police.'

'Mr Wheeler is also here on behalf of the London Vigilance Committee,' I said to her.

'To do what? What is it now – not another crusade?'

She surprised me. I could have applauded her.

'I assure you—' Wheeler said again.

But Cora had had enough and she turned from him and walked noisily from the room, like a poor actress told to act outraged and for this to be clearly understood by the most distant member of the audience.

'She and my wife . . .' I said to Wheeler. 'It's all a matter of routine, of preparation and then gradual recuperation.'

Wheeler, I saw, having regained some of his own composure with Cora's departure, was now keen to reassert his authority.

'I ask you again,' he said to me. 'Do you know Edward Fitzgerald Marlow?'

I tried to remember if I'd ever heard Marlow called by his full name before. Wheeler, of course, took this for a serious effort of remembering on my part.

'And I can only tell you again that I don't.' It was impossible now for me to retreat from this stand. 'Perhaps if we went to the Lyceum together and you asked the same of Irving or Stoker, then we might get somewhere.'

'I shall *not* be doing anything of the kind with Henry Irving,' he said. 'Nor with Mr Stoker.'

'There are others we could ask,' I said helpfully.

'Oh?'

'Howson, Jimmy Allen, Loveday.' I added several others for good measure.

'Charles Howson's name has already appeared,' Wheeler said.

'"Appeared"? What, on a list of suspects? Perhaps if I knew what this Marlow is supposed to have—' I stopped abruptly.

'What?' Wheeler said.

'Is this about the murdered girl? Solomon said something, but I could scarcely credit it.'

Wheeler looked uncomfortable at the remark.

'It is,' I said. 'And you think there may be photographs here? Of her? Of the man accused of killing her? You surely can't be searching every photographer's studio and home in London. How on earth is *that* going to produce any results quickly?'

I knew by the way two of the three constables nodded in agreement with me that I was right to have said it.

'*Are* there pictures?' I said. 'And do you seriously think *I* might have taken them? Solomon?'

'No one is accusing anyone of anything, Mr Webster. I hope I make myself perfectly clear on that point. You may, however, be correct in your surmise concerning the existence of one or more photographs, and that, of course, is not unconnected to our inquiries here today.'

'Search,' one of the constables said.

'What?'

'Search. We're on a search. The roster.'

'Well,' I said to Wheeler, 'you've already looked under the table. You ought at least to go through the rest of the house.'

The constables smiled at the remark and Wheeler immediately shouted at them to remind them who he was. It was the wrong thing to have done, and he alone did not see that.

I heard Cora on the stairs, calling down to us to say that Alice was dressed and respectable. I heard what an invalid the remark made her sound.

Rather than respond to all these other demands – each one taking him further from the centre of his own authority – Wheeler went to the mantel and picked up the picture of Caroline and held it towards me.

'And this is?'

I imagined from his confident tone that he expected me to say that it was a picture of Cora when she was a small girl.

'Our daughter Caroline,' I said. 'She died. She was eight. A brain fever.'

Wheeler stood without speaking for a moment. 'My apologies,' he said. 'I, too, have lost a child. Two, in fact. Both daughters. My own wife . . . Again, my apologies.'

'Of course,' I said. 'Of course.'

'It's a terrible thing, to lose a child.' He put down the picture, careful to position it exactly where it had stood, and then he bowed his head in prayer for a few seconds. When he'd finished, he looked up and said, 'I do, however, feel that a search of the premises, in accordance with the warrant already presented, should now be undertaken.'

'Of course,' I said. 'Perhaps if you could tell me what you were looking for . . .'

'Hardly the spirit of the thing,' he said. He motioned for the constables to start searching.

Two of the men walked around the table, intending to examine the dresser drawers, but Wheeler stopped them and told them to start elsewhere.

'My cameras and equipment are at the top of the house,' I said.

'Can anything be damaged or affected?' he asked me.

'Not really. As I've already explained, I undertake most of my work at the Lyceum. I'm sure Irving and Stoker would be happy for you to look there. Perhaps you already know them – through your work with the Vigilance Committee, perhaps?'

'Oh, myself and your employers are certainly well acquainted,' he said.

'And do you imagine there's some connection between the theatre and this scandal that needs to be examined?' It was another knot in the puzzle.

'I believe I said no such thing,' he said.

'But you must think there's *some* connection to this Marlow.' An answer was too much to ask for.

'I have yet to assess the evidence and to decide,' he said. 'Material may yet come to light – elsewhere, perhaps – that proves some connection or association.' But even that vague remark was too much of an admission from him and he looked away from me.

'But you still harbour a suspicion that I am lying to you now?' I said.

'Once again, I have neither suggested nor inferred any such thing.'

This was clearly a lie, but I let the remark pass. It told me as much about the man as anything else.

'I don't know what I can say to convince you,' I said.

'No,' he said. He went to the window and sat at the chair there, resting both his palms on the table.

'Your wife . . .' he said, waiting.

'She believes she can communicate with our dead child,' I said flatly. I sat beside him, feeling the warmth of the glass at my neck.

'My own wife,' he said. 'Immediately upon . . . I mean . . .'

'I understand,' I told him.

'And you, are *you* able to communicate?'

I shook my head. 'I possess nothing of that kind of power.'

'Or belief?' he said.

I bowed my head.

Above us, the three searching men went from room to room. I heard Cora speaking to them. I wanted them to finish before Isobel arrived. Perhaps she might walk through the door, see what was happening, make wrong assumptions and then either run from the house or stand and proclaim her own innocence. I saw the hammer that would repeatedly fall on her, the shattered pieces Wheeler would afterwards sift for the solitary grain of truth he needed to find.

'Do you wish to speak to my wife?' I asked him. 'I'll wait here. Ask her if she's ever heard me mention this Marlow.' I remembered only as I said it that I *had* mentioned Marlow to her, upon opening his invitation as we walked from Caroline's grave, but she had been lost in her usual reverie in the cemetery and I doubted if she would remember this. '*Did* Solomon know him?' I said.

'I believe the men who went there were forced to defend themselves from his wife's tongue.'

'Marta,' I said. 'She and Solomon lost their only child. She came to see my wife five nights ago. I suppose you'd say it was a small world.'

'Oh, it is,' he said. 'A very small world. A very small world indeed. And especially once you learn where all the connections lie. Start making those vital and telling connections and the world shrinks at an incredible rate. One man knows twenty others, who in turn each know twenty more. And those four hundred know each other and all the empty spaces in between.'

'I suppose so,' I said, knowing precisely where the truth

of this unspoken threat lay. 'And I suppose it will make your work in finding Marlow straightforward.'

He smiled at the word and the criticism it veiled.

'*Are* there photographs?' I asked him.

'You tell me,' he said. It was his final, blocking move: thus far and no further.

One of the constables came back into the room.

'Well?' Wheeler asked him.

'Some cameras and bits and pieces. Lots of pictures of actors and such, bits of scenery.'

'Theatre work,' I said.

'I saw Irving as Mephistopheles,' Wheeler said.

'A great success.'

'So they say.' He again looked away from me as he said it.

Another of the constables appeared and shook his head. 'Your wife was asking for you,' he said to me. 'She seems upset. Your daughter's with her.'

'Please, extend my apologies,' Wheeler said. He rose from where he sat and went out into the hallway, calling the final constable down to him.

I followed the four of them to the front door and held it open.

'We may have reason to return,' Wheeler said, but with little conviction.

'I'll ask Irving and Stoker,' I said. 'Perhaps they may even be acquainted with Aston-Fox.'

'They are,' he said quickly, watching for my reaction.

'I see,' I said.

He held my gaze for a moment longer and then he turned and followed the constables back into the street.

27

I composed myself for a moment and then went up to Alice. What I had spent weeks anticipating as an impending disaster had arrived finally in an hour of near-farce and confusion, leaving me uncertain of what I had gained or lost, and how close or how far Wheeler and the police still were from me.

I tapped on the door before entering and a few seconds passed before Cora said, 'Enter.'

Alice was still in bed, Cora sitting on the mattress by her side.

'A simple mistake,' I said to Alice, knowing that she would not believe me.

'Who's Marlow?' she said. She had forgotten the invitation.

'The man they're looking for, apparently.'

'In connection with the murdered girl,' Cora said firmly. 'And not just murdered.' She had become an avid newspaper reader over the past few weeks.

'It was a mistake,' I said. 'No, not a mistake – they're questioning photographers all over the city.'

'They went to Solomon's,' Cora said indignantly.

Alice waited for me to look at her. 'To what end?'

'None whatsoever. Apparently, the man who is supposed to have killed the girl had some connection to Irving and Stoker at the Lyceum. One of their circle who—'

'And so they came here?' Alice said, her voice raised. '*Here*. To *our* home? Have they been *there* yet? The precious theatre? Have they been to Irving's home, Stoker's?'

'I don't know,' I lied. 'I imagine so. You know how these people work – everything up in the air, everyone kept in the dark.'

She knew I was lying to her, but said nothing in front of Cora.

'We were talking about moving house,' Cora said.

'How are you feeling?' I said to Alice. It seemed to me that everything we'd gained on our journey to the cemetery together only nine days earlier had now been lost to us, and much more besides. A photograph of Caroline stood at her bedside. I'd offered to print and frame others for her, but she'd said she'd prefer someone else to do it. Another door closed gently in my face.

'Did you hear what I said?' Cora asked me.

I looked at her, but said nothing.

'Is Marlow a friend of yours?' Alice asked me.

'I've no idea who the man is.'

Her eyes flicked away from me and then returned.

'That's the story he was telling the police,' Cora said, though whether this was done in support of me, or to challenge the lie, I was uncertain. I knew which was more likely.

'I've heard of him,' I admitted to Alice. 'But that's all.'

'He didn't tell *them* that,' Cora said.

No, but I'd left open the possibility of further vague

remembering if anything more definite was established by Wheeler. I knew by then that my signature alongside Marlow's in the register was far from accidental.

'Who is he?' Alice asked me.

I imagined Cora had already repeated everything she'd overheard in the parlour.

'They think he might have taken photographs of the murdered girl,' I said.

'And of her killer,' Cora said. 'Together.'

'What kind of photographs?' Alice said.

I tried to remember exactly how much I had just revealed to Wheeler that Cora might now know. She leaned forward slightly, into my answer.

'They didn't say,' I said. 'Presumably—'

'Something unnatural and perverse between the man and the child?' Alice clasped a hand to the material at her throat. It was as much as she could bring herself to say. She motioned for Cora to pass her a glass of milk to wash the taste of the words from her mouth.

'I imagine so,' I said. Cora would have known this anyway from all the newspaper speculation.

Alice asked me to swear to her that I had nothing whatsoever to do with any of these others or what had happened among them.

I gave her my word.

None of us spoke for a while. Alice finished the milk and Cora took the empty glass from her and put it back beside the portrait of Caroline.

'Do you have anything else to tell me?' Alice said eventually.

'Such as?'

'They seemed convinced – the police – that he knew this Marlow,' Cora said.

I wanted to shout at her and tell her to get out, to stop treating me like a suspicious and unwanted stranger in my own home. I wondered whose side Alice would take if I did say something. There was a further short silence.

'Will they come back?' Alice said, and I sensed that this second, brief interrogation was coming to a close.

'I doubt it,' I said. I looked at my watch. 'I'm late.'

'Late for what?' Cora said, clearly angry that her mother had neither encouraged nor allowed my further questioning. Everything I now did was subject to this same mixture of scrutiny and contempt.

I moved closer to the bed and kissed Alice on the cheek. She winced as I approached her and then held herself steady at my touch. Cora presented her own cheek, her eyes narrowing as I kissed her, too.

I left the house, glad to be finally beyond its confines and explosive atmosphere. I breathed deeply in the warm air. The workmen in the street were already digging and hammering, but even that cacophony did not disturb me now that I was free and walking away from everything that had just happened. A trap had been sprung and I had not been caught.

Today, in addition to their tearing up of the street and the graveyard, the workmen were also engaged in chopping down the last of the trees which surrounded the church, mostly beech and elm, but with the usual sentinel yews at the gateway. As long as we had lived there, a mixed flock of rooks and crows had occupied the trees, filling them with their cumbersome nests, and now the birds, disturbed and made agitated by the cutting, hung in clamorous, shifting clouds above the street and the invading men.

Turning the corner into the Hornsey Road, I almost laughed at the ease with which I had confronted Wheeler and then turned him back. Recently, I'd felt as though I'd been leaping from one unsteady stepping-stone to another – the torrent of all that was happening around me rushing heedlessly on – and that now, finally, those streaming waters had slowed and were growing calm and shallow again.

It may have been an illusory and fanciful understanding, but it was how I felt. I even imagined that if I were now to encounter Isobel on her way to work, then I might confront and rebut her too, using Wheeler's search and defeat as part of my armoury. In a sense, I also began to convince myself that Isobel and her misguided plans for our own impossible partnership had nothing whatsoever to do with Aston-Fox and his trial. Even the photographs she still possessed were not definite proof of any connection to Marlow. In fact, so forceful were these convictions that I looked out for her in the street ahead of me, keen to act on this rising confidence. I knew her route to work, and so it was entirely possible that I might encounter her. She might threaten me with exposure to Alice, but what, truly, might she reveal that my wife wasn't already beginning to suspect? Or if not 'suspect', exactly – Cora still whispering in her ear – then at least to consider possible.

But Isobel was nowhere to be seen, and I knew that I was fooling myself, too elated by my first small victory over Wheeler, and certain only that he would return. Overoptimistic, too, perhaps, about my chances of extricating myself from everything else that I had allowed to be woven around me over the previous months. From being a man who had conquered a raging torrent, I now felt like a man left cold and wet and exhausted in a line of wrack by a departing tide. All in a matter of minutes.

There was no doubt now in my mind that Marlow was far beyond the reach of men like Wheeler, Aston-Fox, or even the Lord Chancellor. In all likelihood, he might not even exist any longer, might never have existed at all except in the deceits, fabrications and outrages he practised on others.

Beyond Hanley Road I knew I would not encounter Isobel, and regardless of what I had felt only moments earlier, I was now relieved by this. I quickened my stride. I would spend a day at the Lyceum ensuring Stoker was true to his word, and then a few days avoiding Isobel at home. And perhaps after that, then everything might become clear again, clear and straightforward, and at the very least negotiable.

Ahead of me was the shelter where I might catch a bus for the Strand, a queue of people already waiting. I walked to the hut more slowly, looking over my shoulder for the approaching bus. Several horses stood tethered to the rear of the structure, drinking from the granite trough there.

It was only as I reached the hut that I saw the news board beside it and the glaring headline declaring: ASTON-FOX CONFESSES ALL. DEPRAVITY CASE REVEALED. FULL DETAILS.

The words caused me almost to stumble, coming as they did at such a moment. There was a kiosk a short distance beyond the shelter and I went to this and bought the *London Mail*. I crossed the road to a bench and sat there to discover precisely what was being revealed.

In truth, I might have learned and guessed as much as I

needed from the few words on the hoarding. The article – topped by pictures of both Aston-Fox and the murdered girl – said that Aston-Fox had been rearrested and then formally charged with the offences the Lord Chancellor had decided to bring against him. He was currently being held at Bow Street police station, pending a preliminary court appearance. Legal experts had already been appointed by Aston-Fox's family, who were still hopeful of a satisfactory outcome. After this appearance, it was likely that further police bail would be denied and that Aston-Fox would be removed to Holloway prison, denied all further applications for bail, and then held there until his eventual trial.

I read on, tensing against seeing Marlow's name, or even my own, somewhere in the article. I knew how unlikely this was, but after the cold shock of the public headline, I was no longer able to convince myself of anything.

There was no mention of Marlow by name, merely reference to 'certain individuals whose identities were known to the investigating officers', and who were now being sought out and interviewed. *Did* that include me? There were several mentions of Wheeler and the London Vigilance Committee.

Cora would buy the paper and then read all but the most salacious of its details – so far very few, and nothing new or shocking – to her mother. And perhaps they would imagine me to be one of these 'certain individuals'. And whatever else they were now prepared to believe of me, at least they would know for certain that Wheeler had already daubed his broad black cross on our own front door.

I read to the end of the article and learned little more. I knew that Wheeler and the police would keep a great many details to themselves. The phrases 'certain acts' and 'unrepeatable perversions' were used, creating considerably more suspicion than certainty, more outrage than understanding, and certainly more lascivious speculation than legal reasoning in the minds of everyone who read the article – all spaces in which Marlow himself continued to be lost to view.

I wondered what Aston-Fox had already confessed – *if* he had confessed – and what panic and betrayal the police were hoping to both create and then to capitalize on by announcing this.

The article promised a further feature in the afternoon edition, in which the murdered girl's parents would tell their own tragic story to the world. It was an easy enough thing to imagine.

I rolled the paper into a tube and pushed it into my pocket. My first impulse had been to get rid of it, but then I decided to take it with me to the Lyceum. There would be little chance that Stoker wouldn't have already learned of everything that was happening, but it would do no harm to suggest to him that I too was fully apprised, our parallel flights through that same rising wind carefully paced and kept at an exact distance apart.

Across the road, a bus arrived at the shelter. There was a delay as one of the horses was changed, and I walked across and climbed the stairs.

All around me, people were reading the same article, all of them imagining the countless other truths of the one sordid and pathetic story and the two people it destroyed.

My journey to the Strand was slow. There was a delay at Endell Street beyond St Giles, and again at Seven Dials along a diversion. I decided to alight and continue on foot. I was not expected at the Lyceum, and anyway my arrival there would again be earlier than usual.

As I walked, I began to consider what I would tell Stoker about Wheeler's arrival and questioning, aware that here, too, there were aspects of the visit – of my interrogation, as I would put it – that I might use to my advantage. It was unlikely that Wheeler yet felt confident enough to go to the Lyceum, confront Irving and Stoker directly and continue his searching there. Perhaps I might even present myself as a further shield standing in front of Stoker and Irving, someone who might already have delayed or diverted those of Wheeler's inquiries hitherto aimed squarely at the pair of them.

I crossed into Tavistock Street, and ahead of me, almost as unexpected as the news board had been, I saw Stoker himself in conversation with two men, neither of whom I recognized.

I watched him for a moment, careful not to be seen by him. He seemed agitated, his voice raised – though still inaudible to me – and he gestured fiercely with the cane he held. The two men, I saw, were afraid of him and kept their distance, perhaps believing he might strike them. They both tried to speak to him, but he shouted each of them down. After a further minute of this, he dismissed the men and they were only too happy to turn and leave him, quickly lost in the crowd.

I took out the paper and continued towards him, waiting until he could not avoid seeing me before looking up from the paper and joining him.

'Webster,' he said. He looked quickly in the direction the two men had taken. 'You've seen,' he said. He flicked the paper with the head of the cane.

'Not really had a chance to read it,' I said. 'Is it telling us anything new?'

Us.

'Not really. Aston-Fox has apparently been recounting all he knows. God knows why they ever released him in the first place. His standing, I suppose. And it's an even greater mystery as to why he didn't seize the opportunity to get away while it oh so briefly existed.'

'Arrogance,' I said. 'The conviction that he was somehow above it all.' I felt brave in saying this, and Stoker faltered for a moment in what he was explaining to me.

'They're not going to risk another bird flying the coop,' he said.

Marlow.

'You think others involved in the affair have already gone?'

'Undoubtedly.'

Before he could add to this, I said, 'Wheeler and the police came to my home this morning. My *home*.'

'I know,' he said, surprising me.

'How? I only—'

'I have my contacts within the Vigilance Committee. People who perhaps believe that friend Wheeler is exceeding his authority and leading the other Vigilance men into waters considerably deeper than they are accustomed to.'

'You *knew* he was coming?' I tried to sound more outraged than surprised at this.

'I could have done nothing to prevent him,' he said.

'You could have *warned* me.'

'Oh? I imagined you had nothing to hide.'

'Nor did I,' I said, recovering quickly from the thrust.

'But my wife and daughter were in the house, asleep, in their bedclothes.' I wondered how long I was prepared to go on pushing the pair of *them* in front of *me*.

'Then my sincere apologies,' he said. 'I was only told after the event that Wheeler himself had gone along. They found nothing.'

'And if you *had* known in advance of Wheeler's presence?' I said.

'What?' he said, but too quickly. 'You think I would have – what? – sacrificed you? For what? To what end?'

To keep yourself in the clear. To keep yourself and Irving in the clear. To keep Wheeler and the police away from Irving and his friendship with Aston-Fox. To keep your own secret relationship with Marlow unsuspected. To make the police believe they had rounded up enough fearful and desperate men to build their case against Aston-Fox without the need to approach you or *your* precious friends and their hallowed institutions any more closely.

I resisted answering him, letting him absorb all these unspoken thoughts. To have given any one of them voice would have been to have had it denied and then destroyed.

Instead, I said, 'Your contacts must have come to you as soon as they learned Wheeler had found nothing.'

'I suppose so.' He made no comment on the fact that I had used the plural, or that I hadn't suggested they'd merely contacted him without coming to him personally.

'Did they tell you what Wheeler now intends regarding the Lyceum?' I assumed this had been the cause of his earlier agitation.

He shook his head. 'Wheeler believes Aston-Fox will confess all.'

'And implicate everyone else involved?'

'You mean Marlow?' he said. It was the first time he had used the name. It was the last of our convenient screens.

'He's already implicated,' I said, equally boldly. 'Wheeler probably knows everything there is to know about him, about his involvement with Aston-Fox and the girl.'

'I know that,' he said angrily. He raised his cane, and for a moment I thought he was going to rap it against my chest.

And if he did this, I wondered if my boldness would extend to seizing it from him and then striking *him* with it. But instead he merely tapped the paper again.

'This will all die with Aston-Fox and his sorry little confession,' he said. He hissed the man's name. 'He knows better than to implicate others, or at least *some* others.'

'Meaning that some people are more deserving of being sacrificed than others?'

'It was ever thus,' he said, smiling at the hollow indignation of the remark. He said it as though it were the most profound and dependable of revelations, and yet one in which he himself could no longer believe.

He started walking towards the Lyceum, and I followed him.

'Tell me everything Wheeler asked you and perhaps disclosed to you,' he said, and I told him as much as I might reveal to him without any real loss to myself.

28

I spent the following days in a kind of limbo, waiting to see where all these convergent and then divergent pathways might now lead; and waiting, too, finally to understand more precisely my own – hopefully soon forgotten – part in these events. It was not difficult to see the variety of excuses I was becoming adept at making for myself. Marlow had created his vortex of ever-quickening circles, and everyone from Aston-Fox to Stoker and myself, Pearl and Bliss and the entirely unknowing and innocent Solomon had been sucked into it. Perhaps I was making too much of my own part in this emerging pattern, but it was an easy thing to do during those days of emptiness and waiting.

Limbo – just like Alice's desperately hopeful and loitering spirits during their own painful and interrupted journeys into the Afterlife.

At home, I saw little of either Alice or Cora, and on the few brief occasions our paths did cross, talk was all of where we might soon move to. Needless to say, most of this was at Cora's urging, but Alice seemed more than happy to go along with everything our eager daughter was now suggesting. Kensington was mentioned. Putney and Clapham. But above all, Cora announced, Chelsea was the place for us to be. By 'us', of course, she meant herself and her mother. I was included in these plans by being told how much more convenient Chelsea would be for my journeys to and from the Lyceum. We might even rent a house large enough for me to have my own studio there. Chelsea was renowned for its artists' studios. And even photography might one day be considered a kind of art. Of sorts. One day. And I might even like to follow my wife's example and become a true and independent professional, working for myself, establishing a worthwhile – 'proper' was the word Cora used – reputation.

Alice and Cora had made 'names' for themselves. What, with the same application, hard work and expertise – and I looked over Cora's shoulder at this point to see if Alice was prepared to smile or even laugh with me; she wasn't, didn't – was to stop me from achieving the same? We would be a family of professionals, another class of people entirely. In our new Chelsea home, with our new circle of friends, and with our three reputations rising and rising like bright new suns through a murky dawn.

Cora told me how far into this wonderful future her mother's bookings now stretched, and I was surprised to learn that even at the rate of only two gatherings a week – or *per* week – Alice, Alicia, perhaps soon even *Madame* Alicia was now 'fully booked' for fifteen months ahead, and with new requests arriving daily. And with people prepared to wait, to remain in contact in the hope of a cancellation, and even to put money down on deposit to secure their place at the table.

I listened to all this and I agreed to it all. I even started to imagine my own studio in another, larger and better-appointed room at the top of another house. Or perhaps not at the top; perhaps on the ground floor, looking out over a garden somewhere. Somewhere I might work at what I wanted to work at, in privacy, with all the necessary and up-to-date equipment – the sort Stoker always baulked at buying – and earning more than enough money to make that business a success. I began to understand the allure of all these easily paid-for dreams.

I saw nothing of Isobel in that time, and when I finally asked Alice where the girl was, she said she didn't know. Cora was waiting to sack her. After which, there would be some-one new, someone hard-working, trustworthy and reliable. We would need to employ someone new anyway when we moved. And perhaps this time there would be more than one maid. Who knew? If Isobel was happy to stay away and ruin her chances with us in that new life, then let her, it was her loss.

I searched my room in case Isobel had hidden the remainder of Marlow's photographs there, but found nothing. Each time I was alone, I expected her to appear and to repeat her demands to me.

Cora gathered up details from the letting agents, and she and Alice sat together and studied these, their roles of parent and child now almost completely reversed. The first thing *I* did, each time a possible house was mentioned, was to look on a map to see how easily Alice and I might make the journey from our new home to the Stroud Green cemetery. I knew that wherever we went, this would present few problems to us, but I still felt the need to see the two places together, on the same map, and to trace my finger along the route between them in advance of our first actual journey.

At the Lyceum, I saw little of Stoker after our encounter on the morning of Wheeler's search. He had come to me later the same day with instructions from Irving concerning the new production, but had had nothing new to reveal to me. Both he and I knew that he might easily have sent one of the stage-hands up to me, and that by coming himself he was in some uncertain way confirming the unspoken pact between us. Ellen was due to return to the theatre in a few days' time, and the same electricity filled the place which always filled it upon the announcement of her imminent arrival. Five days, Stoker said, a week at the outside.

'Still making her his wife and himself her husband,' Stoker had said to me, and I alone was privy to the first cracked note of envy or contention the remark contained.

'He still loves her,' I said. 'And she him.' But nowhere near as much as Stoker in his own determined and indulgent way still loved her.

'Of course,' he said. He gave me the list of photographs Irving wanted for publicity purposes. The list contained none of himself in the leading role. It had been seven years since his last Macbeth, and there were too many new lines and creases on his face. He joked about this, allowing everyone to deny it in his presence.

'I can't imagine anyone else up there with her in the two roles,' I said. 'Can you? Anyone at all?'

But this had been too much for him. 'No,' he said firmly, unwilling to speculate. 'Irving is Irving.'

It was an answer to, and an explanation of, everything. *Irving is Irving.*

'Is it possible?' He motioned to my instructions concerning the costumes Irving wanted photographed.

'If everything is where it's supposed to be,' I said.

'If it's lost, then we buy or make new. This is too important an occasion to allow ourselves to become bogged down in such incidental details.'

'I agree,' I said.

It was the firm, broad eraser wiped across three years and hundreds of pages of scribbled errors and deceits.

He left me after that, and in the days which followed I saw nothing further of him.

Daily, I bought all three editions of the *Mail* and studied every news hoarding I passed. Little that was new was revealed about Aston-Fox. He had been taken to Holloway. He was back in court. Further charges might be laid. Further evidence was still being sought, further witnesses questioned. The murdered girl's parents had their say. Over and over. I doubt they had ever shed a tear for her before she had run away from them; they were shedding enough now to float her coffin out to sea.

Aston-Fox's 'circle', I imagined, had shattered like a dropped china plate. If he had once been at their centre, then that centre certainly no longer held. Lifelong friendships dissolved overnight; memories ended; all certainty burned; and darkness and cold flooded into those previously privilege-warmed and ambition-lit halls where Aston-Fox and his entire world had once existed.

I knew even then, as I read and re-read this repeated news – anything to keep Wheeler's fires properly stoked and re-plenished – that Aston-Fox's would not be the last of such outrages, and that a thousand more might now follow, each one piling its own sticks of indignation, outrage and disgust on to the same growing blaze. I knew too that these feelings would not become numbed with repetition, but that they would be made to burn afresh with each new revelation.

On the fourth day of this waiting, I left the Lyceum early in the evening and walked through the audience already converging for that night's performance. I was still amid this crowd when I saw Pearl ahead of me, motionless and watching me as I approached her. She was standing at another news board – it seemed they were now every few yards along every street – and she glanced from me to its headline as I reached her. I had thought that I would never see her again. At first I could not look at the words – normally so difficult to avoid – imagining that this was a signal from her, something I needed to know.

When I finally came close to her, she held out her hand to me.

The board announced that an unidentified man's body had been pulled from the river.

'Is it Marlow?' I said. I felt numb, uncaring.

She looked at the words as though they meant nothing to her. Then, realizing my concern and the mistake I had made, she laughed. 'They pull bodies from the river every day,' she said. 'Marlow, throw himself in the river?' This also amused her, and I relaxed. 'Perhaps to wash himself clean, you mean? I hardly think so. The time for that is long past. Though I imagine there might be a few more jumpers in the foreseeable future.' She paused. 'Except it's never that, is it – foreseeable?'

'The trial will be months away,' I said.

'Perhaps. Wheeler is said to have concluded his investigation. All those he wants to bind to Aston-Fox at the trial are supposedly already firmly secured. Some say Wheeler was reined in, others that he wandered too far for comfort.'

I told her of his arrival at my home four days earlier.

The news genuinely surprised her. 'You?' she said.

'Has he been to see you?'

'He came the day after the party, after we two had parted. I told him I was an acquaintance of Marlow's, nothing more.'

'And he believed you?' It seemed unlikely.

'I don't care what he believed. All that matters to Wheeler is evidence.'

'What about Bliss?' I hadn't seen the man since his brief and furtive appearance on the night of the party. I knew now, of course – as everyone who was also present must have known by then – that the gathering had been nothing more than an orchestrated smokescreen, an elaborate scent-laying, within which the host alone would detach himself from us and then disappear completely, leaving behind these countless other trails for the pursuing hounds. Pearl herself would have had no small part in this deception.

I was about to say something about this, when she said, 'Bliss? Gone, too. I haven't seen him.' Meaning she'd been searching for him?

'Do you think he's with Marlow?' I said, meaning that of the three of them, she alone had been left behind.

But she shook her head at the suggestion. 'Marlow is in Marseilles.' She took a telegram from her sleeve and showed it to me. Her mother was enjoying a marvellous holiday. Everything was going to plan. The arranged itinerary was perfect. She would be moving on soon.

'My mother died when I was twelve,' she said.

'And "moving on"?'

'It's Marseilles,' she said. 'He could go anywhere. He sent the telegram upon his departure. I don't know. North Africa, Cairo, the Greek Islands, Istanbul, beyond.'

I saw the vastness into which Marlow had disappeared, unknown, unobserved and untraceable.

'Bliss *could* be with him,' I said.

'Bliss was his agent, that's all. A perfect and perfectly profitable arrangement while it worked and served them both—'

'But nothing more than a threat once that arrangement was over?'

She slid her hand beneath my arm. 'Will you come with me?' she said. 'I was waiting for you.'

'Where?'

'Golden Square.'

Her answer surprised me and I hesitated in my step. I felt her hand tighten on my arm.

'It's the last place any of us should go,' I said.

'It's perfectly safe; I wouldn't be asking you, otherwise.'

'Why?'

She looked ahead of us as we resumed walking.

'A final service to Marlow, an obligation.'

'Obligation? How on—'

She withdrew her hand. 'I'm sorry, I shouldn't have asked,' she said. She turned her back on me and continued walking.

I waited a moment, saw that she was set on her path, and then ran to catch up with her. Once beside her, I raised my arm for her to hold me again.

'What are you doing?' I asked her.

'Something I agreed with Marlow a long time ago. Something I always imagined Bliss and I would undertake together.'

I tried to imagine what this might be.

'Wheeler might have people watching the place,' I said.

'He did. Not any longer. He took them all away earlier today. Do you think he was stupid enough or desperate enough to believe that Marlow himself might ever go back there?'

'No, but perhaps his associates . . .'

'Or his friends merely calling to see where a completely innocent man might now be?'

'And all the time Wheeler's watchers were being watched in turn by Marlow's own men?' I said.

'Wheeler employed constables. Most of them still in their uniforms. Marlow's men saw them a mile away. Wheeler's got everything he needs where Aston-Fox is concerned. No one will see us.'

I knew what a report to Wheeler of me approaching anywhere near Marlow's studio would suggest to him, but I believed her and I continued walking with her.

We approached Golden Square via the passageway opposite the Lyric, following the tunnel beneath the building adjoining Marlow's studio. On Brewer Street, Pearl signalled to a man at a barrow and he gave her an 'all-clear' signal in reply.

At the end of the tiled tunnel we climbed the stairs and followed the passageways in a reverse journey of the one we had made a week previously, passing doors that had been broken from their hinges, and others smashed from their frames.

'I suppose Wheeler feels obliged to leave his mark,' she said dismissively, making him sound like an animal establishing its territory.

We climbed through the building and arrived at the corridor leading to Marlow's studio. Here, too, doors had been forced open and floorboards pulled from their joists. A cabinet that had once stood against the wall now lay in shattered pieces along the full length of the corridor.

The door into the studio itself was ajar, one of its panels missing.

Pearl pushed it fully open and went in ahead of me.

I followed her into the empty space, conscious of the noise we made on the loose, bare boards.

The room had been completely and thoroughly stripped of everything it had once possessed. There was no furniture, no carpets or rugs, no pictures on the walls, no ornaments on the mantels. No photographic equipment, no backdrops, no cameras or tripods; not even the marks on the floor where these had once stood. Nothing. All that remained of anyone or anything were the cold ashes in two grates. There might have been a square or rectangle of unfaded paper on the walls here and there where pictures had hung, perhaps a barely discernible line on the boards where a rug had lain, perhaps a few worn circles where chairs had stood, but other than this, nothing.

We wandered into the cool, deserted space as though it were a tomb.

Pearl looked around her, pleased with what she saw.

'Is this what Wheeler found?' I asked her.

She nodded.

She walked to all parts of the room, sniffing the air as she went. I followed her to where Marlow's cameras had once stood at the low stage.

'Developing fluids,' I said. 'They will have soaked into the woodwork.'

'Again proving nothing,' she said. 'Even if Wheeler identified it, even if he smelled it.'

Another – in this instance, literal – evaporation amid all the other evaporations in Marlow's wake. As dramatic, as telling, and, ultimately, as short-lived as the waters churning in his wake now.

'What does he want you to do?' I asked her.

'Just this. Just to come, to be here,' she said.

'To return after Wheeler?' I said. 'To give Marlow some kind of final word?'

'I suppose so.' She seemed both intrigued and gratified by the remark, and for the first time since encountering her outside the theatre, I relaxed. I was glad to be with her, and I knew as I watched her moving like a ghost around the empty room, absorbing each of its lost resonances and tremors, hearing its clamour of fading echoes, and recalling a thousand memories of her own in the place, that this was definitely the last time I would see her. Whatever I had believed before, I would never see her again after that day. She was a connection to Marlow and now that connection was severed and she would disappear as swiftly and as completely from my life as he himself had already done.

I wondered if she had always intended searching me out instead of Bliss to accompany her here on this sacred errand.

I went to her where she stood at the larger of the cold fires.

'Will Marlow send another telegram when he arrives at his final destination?' I asked her.

'I don't know,' she said. 'Perhaps there is no final destination.' And in that empty room those few words sounded like nothing more and nothing less than the howl of pain and anguish they were – a howl of love and loss and longing that might now never cease.

I put my hand on her arm and neither of us spoke for a moment, our silence a seal on the completed task.

'When Aston-Fox finally feels the noose around his neck . . .' she said eventually.

'You can't seriously believe he'll hang?' I said.

She shrugged. 'I doubt if it even matters. All that matters now is that Wheeler rids this city of all its depravity, filth and corruption, and that its God-fearing citizens are allowed to live out their lives without either the shadow or the stink of all that depravity, filth and corruption coming anywhere near them.'

We both laughed at this – at the great lie it revealed and the even greater truth it buried deep – and our laughter echoed around us in that emptiness like the noise of trapped birds struggling to escape into the sunless places close above us.

29

We left Golden Square shortly afterwards. Outside, beyond all the passages, tunnels and alleyways, there was an unfamiliar draught in the warm stale air.

'It's going to break,' Pearl said.

'Break?'

'The weather, the heat. The newspapers are saying there's a summer storm on its way to us.' She looked up into the pale clear sky as she spoke.

I was waiting only for her to hold out her hand to me and then turn away. I wondered what I might say to her. She'd already told me that she was leaving the city. Marlow had paid her well and Bliss had managed profitable investments on her behalf.

It was beyond me to ask her where she would go, to trace her own unseen path into the world beyond.

She looked back at me. 'What now?' she said. 'For you.'

'The theatre,' I said. 'And then home.' Those same two poles. I might return to the Lyceum, but I had little intention of working there, merely passing the rest of the day before returning to the house to find myself a stranger again.

She finally held out her hand to me. 'Apparently, it's been

coming towards us for the past twelve hours, across the overheated continent. It's already raining heavily in France.'

On Marlow, I almost said.

'Thunder, lightning, downpours, flooding, everything.' She kissed me on both my cheeks. 'You'll forget all this,' she said, her mouth close to my ear. 'Marlow, Bliss, me, all this.'

She was wrong, but I said nothing.

I felt her hand go limp inside my own and so I released her. She took a single step away from me.

We stood on Shaftesbury Avenue and the mid-afternoon shoppers moved around us in what seemed a kind of clumsy but perfectly choreographed dance. Despite the coming storm and the change in the air, it was still warm, and the afternoon sunlight filled the street with its dusty, liquid glow, through which the slow dancers moved almost as though it resisted them, dissolved in both its glare and in its haze. She watched these men and women for a moment, all these anonymous others, and then she took several paces away from me to join them.

I stood motionless and watched her go. She paused, searched, waited, and then she too was lost to me, not even a shape or an outline amid so many other molten, drifting figures.

I waited where I stood for several minutes longer before turning in the opposite direction and walking to the Lyceum.

I went to my room, and during the hours I spent there, I saw no one. Not Stoker, not Howson, not even Jimmy Allen. There was no performance that evening, and so the theatre would remain mostly empty until the following day.

The place felt as much of a tomb to me as Marlow's

ransacked studio had been. More than a tomb – a mausoleum, say, something grand and overpowering and more devoted to the drama and everlasting nature of death than a simple tomb or grave might ever be.

I left at seven and made my way home through the onset of the summer dusk.

30

There was no rain yet, but it was clear by now that the weather was changing. It was much cooler, and the shifting of the litter and already-fallen leaves in the streets was evidence of a steadily rising wind. The usually pale sky had darkened – first to a smoky pink edged with grey as some atmospheric effect or other was made plain with the falling temperature, and then growing much darker, and with layers of slate- and charcoal-coloured cloud moving in a high and rising mass from the south.

I felt a sudden quickening of the wind as I walked the final short distance home.

When Caroline had been alive, she had often waited for me at the corner of the street, a few doors from our own, looking out for me as I climbed the gentle slope. And upon seeing me, seeing me wave to her and then crouch down and hold out my arms to her, she would run towards me at a gathering pace, stopped only by her collision into me, whereupon, having steadied myself, I would rise and lift her into the air and spin her, holding her against my chest and over my shoulder until all of her sudden energy and momentum was lost, absorbed into my body and then passing in a tremor through me into the solid ground beneath us. I would feel this happen, feel her small and fragile body and all its vital forces absorbed into my own.

There were days when I had set off home already looking forward to this meeting, always disappointed when something kept her from the corner. She would hang laughing uncontrollably over my shoulder and then babble her day's news into my ear. News of the things she had done, the people she had seen, what she had eaten, what she had worn, what her mother had said to her, what her sister had said, what she had said to them. A whole day in those few spinning seconds. And all between being lifted and held and then put back down and released again, her small arms loose in their sockets as they bore her weight, and with me still holding on to her as her feet found the ground and she steadied herself. I had shown an exaggerated interest in everything she told me, the same few tales and complaints and pleasures over and over.

And after this, we had walked the short remaining distance together, hand in hand, my daughter reaching up to me, and me reaching down to hold her as she hopped and skipped and ran and slowed beside me. When there was time, I had told her what *I* had done during that long day of separation, of all the scarcely believable things that had passed before me at the theatre. She was going to be an actress herself. An actress, a dancer, a singer, a girl in the chorus, a scenery-painter, a ticket-seller, a cloakroom-attendant, a flower-seller, a playwright, a dresser – every day something different, depending on my tales.

And later, these stories would resume at bedtime, when I would sit with her as she fell asleep. Sometimes, I would go on spinning these tales long after her eyes had closed, lowering my voice to a whisper for the simple pleasure of sitting with my child and watching her sleep, secure in the knowledge that she was happy and well and safe, and secure too in my own fierce conviction of the endless future and what it held for us both.

For a year after her death, I could not turn that corner except with the hopeless expectation of seeing her there again, running towards me with her arms out. And when she did not come, when that one small miracle did not occur, I could not help but also feel the sudden blade of sadness which pierced me again and again, and nor could I stop the tears which filled my eyes as I continued home to that cold and lifeless house.

After a year, I started varying my way home, following it to the Seven Sisters junction and then either diverting from my direct route or walking much further than I needed. I approached the house from every direction possible, but my arrival there was always much the same.

Now, walking in the rising wind and falling heat, I came to the corner, turned it and paused. Sparks from the workmen's braziers flowed up into the air like fireworks. Leaves and other debris from the felled trees gave the whole street the appearance of a stark autumn. Awnings billowed and sagged repeatedly above the shop doorways.

I stopped at the corner and looked around me. The hoarding by the bus stop now said, simply, 'RAIN', as though this were both a great and scarcely believable prediction and a portent of considerably more.

Arriving at the house, I saw that the front door was open and that Isobel was sitting on the doorstep.

I went to her and stood over her. It was the first time I had seen her since our time together in the Clarendon.

'Already raining on the Downs,' she said. 'It's definitely coming.' She seemed unconcerned, listless. She was out of the wind where she sat and she fanned herself with her hand.

I went past her, causing her to rise and then follow me inside.

'Nobody home,' she said.

We went along the darkened hallway together.

'Told me to tell you they were going to stay the night at your wife's sister's. They're looking at new houses.'

Victoria, Alice's sister, lived in Bayswater. Alice visited her every two months, usually staying overnight. Both women still referred to the district as 'Tyburnia'.

'I heard the police finally came,' she said.

I resisted provoking her by asking her if that was why she'd stayed away for so long.

'Bet that shook you up. Bet you thanked your lucky stars for me then.'

'Because you'd destroyed or stolen the photographs?' I said.

'Better than *them* finding them,' she said, but without any anger in her voice, and with only a trace now of her usual gloating. She grabbed my arm and drew me away from the stairs and into the parlour.

A decanter stood on the table, Madeira left over from the last séance.

She poured herself a tumbler of the sweet wine and drank it like cordial. She refilled the glass and gave another one to me.

I asked her what she wanted.

'Don't tell me you've forgotten our little arrangement,' she said.

'Of course not.'

'Perhaps the police will get desperate and offer a reward for information,' she said. 'It's what they usually do.'

'Meaning you'd show them the pictures?' I said.

The directness of the remark and my obvious lack of concern made her wary.

'I might,' she said. 'Why – you think the police *wouldn't* find the pictures interesting, them already having been here and found nothing?' She looked around us at everything the dimly lit room contained. 'I've been talking to a few friends,' she said. 'People you – we – might profit from.'

'I daresay,' I said.

'You daresay what? You aren't even listening to me.'

'I am,' I said, but with no conviction.

'Right, well,' she said. I doubt if even she knew whether the offence she now felt was real or imagined.

'What else did Alice tell you to tell me?' I said.

She considered this. 'Nothing. All she said was that the pair of them were going to look at houses and then on to her sister's.'

'Not even—'

'She told *me* that my services would no longer be required. Said I was to wait until you showed up, tell you where she was, and then go. She said you'd give me what I was owed.' She smiled at this. 'Is that what you're going to do – give me what I'm owed?' She lifted her foot to the edge of the table, barring my way to the door. Her shoe fell to the floor and she prised off the other.

'Where will you go?' I asked her.

'As far as you're concerned, nowhere.'

'I've no idea where we'll be moving to,' I said.

'I daresay she'll tell you. Eventually.'

I went to the window and looked out. The sky was darker still and the tops of the few remaining trees moved back and forth in the wind. I searched the dirty glass for signs of rain, but there was nothing yet.

'You ought to leave,' I told her. 'Before the storm.'

She laughed at the suggestion. 'You think I've never spent the night out in the rain and cold before?' She finished her second drink. 'Besides, it might not even get here. Just because—' She stopped abruptly and then said, '*They* were here. An hour after your wife went.'

'"They"?'

'The Jew and his wife. I just remembered. He stood down at the gate, but she came up to the door and started knocking, bold as brass, jabbering on at me about something or other.'

'She wants to see Alice again,' I said.

'I got that much. Alicia, Alicia, Alicia, all the bloody time. She even tried to push past me into the house. I had to shout her husband up from the street to calm her down. He came up that path to her like he was walking on hot coals.' She laughed at this.

'What did he say?'

'Who cares what he said? He wanted to know if you were in and I told him you weren't. I told him straight that nobody was in. He stood looking up at the roof and the window like he didn't believe me. I only got rid of the pair of them by telling him that the police had already been and that in all likelihood they'd be back again soon enough. He tried to pull her away after that. Screaming, she was, a proper embarrassment. He practically had to drag her away. He said that she thought that if she came personally to see your wife, then *Alicia* might agree to see her. He even showed me the money he'd brought with him.'

'What did you do?'

'Told him that if he got rid of her, then I could show him a far better way of spending it.'

I could imagine Solomon's shame, disgust and embarrassment at the suggestion and all that was otherwise happening.

'He pulled her away fast enough after that. I told him to keep her away. He said she was cursing me, and I told him to tell her to curse me as much as she liked.'

'You should have—'

'Don't tell *me* what I should or shouldn't have done. I didn't even need to be here – I was only waiting for you to get home.'

She fell silent after this, refilling her empty glass and then rubbing her calves.

A sudden chill filled the room, a draught between open doors, blowing into the entire house. She shivered and held her arms across her chest.

And an instant later there was a vivid flash of lightning which filled the window and cast the whole room into stark relief. She screamed at the unexpectedness of this and then clasped a hand to her mouth as the near-darkness returned, followed a few seconds later by a low rumble and then a sudden loud explosion of thunder. Torrential rain started falling almost immediately, and I went to the front and back doors and closed them. The front was sheltered by the small porch, but at the rear of the house the heavy rain was already splashing inside and forming a pool on the linoleum floor.

Isobel followed me through the house and then back into the parlour.

There was more thunder and lightning, the flashes and peals no longer so clearly connected as one explosion followed another and as they grew more frequent. The rain blew in a sheet against the windows and ran in rills from the dry sills and gutters.

I went upstairs to close the windows there, and she followed me again, ignoring me when I told her to stay where she was.

I arrived at my makeshift studio, and she followed me into that, too. I had scarcely been there since Wheeler's search, and the room was in disarray.

Water dripped from the loose frame of the small window, and I put a developing tray beneath this, watching as the drips steadily increased. The whole of the sloping roof seemed to tremble beneath the thunder. A louder peal than usual suggested that the storm was now directly overhead, and that it might soon move away and its excesses slacken.

I stood at the window and looked down. The street beneath me had already turned into a river, and the gaslights were extinguished. In the darkness the rain was near-invisible, but when it was illuminated by the lightning I could see that it was falling as solidly as the water in a waterfall.

Above me, I saw the disturbed birds circling their lost trees, their noise drowned by the falling rain, silhouetted against the lightning, and looking to me more like giant swarming insects than the rooks and crows they were. I wondered how they managed to remain airborne amid the wind, water and electricity of the storm.

Behind me, Isobel went to the bed and sat on it. Only then

did I see that she had brought the decanter with her. She put this on the cabinet and let herself fall backwards on to the dishevelled sheets. I looked around me at the scattered papers and packets and bottles. I was distracted from this by the sound of Isobel's sudden laughter, and I watched her where she lay. The laughter quickly turned into a choking cough, and she pushed herself upright to regain her breath.

'What's so funny?' I asked her.

'Nothing,' she said. She drank more of the wine to clear her throat, then started laughing again. 'Everything. You. This. Everything.' Her hair had come loose when she'd let herself fall, and it lay over her eyes and cheeks in a long, uneven fringe, so that all I could see clearly of her where she lay was her laughing mouth, her full lips, her teeth and her wet and shining tongue moving from side to side, curling and straightening on the flow of her mockery and the warm, stale breath of whatever she was saying to me.

Salvage
Robert Edric

'Black, gripping and superbly told'
THE TIMES

IT IS THE not too distant future. The Gulf Stream has ceased and the climate is plunged into turmoil. England has changed.

Civil Servant Quinn is dispatched to conduct an audit on a remote plot of land up North, designated for a brand new model town. But he swiftly realises how inflammatory his presence is when confronted by those on the sharp end of the new reality: Owen, a suicidal farmer whose livestock has been destroyed after a slew of viruses; Winston, a disillusioned journalist with a gallery of photos that show the truth about the site: and Pollard, the local man of God whose faith is up for sale.

But is is Anna, Quinn's sometime girlfriend, in charge of filling the dead cattle pits, who faces the deepest abyss of all. As the heavens open once again, the mountains of toxic soil that surround the site slowly begin to shift, and Quinn will face the ultimate test of his integrity.

'Grips the reader from the start'
SUNDAY TIMES

'This is his 19th novel and – against some hot competition – one of his very best'
INDEPENDENT

'A carefully thought-out picture of a bleak future that works as a critique of the present'
GUARDIAN

9780552776257